"The Grateful Dead have been the backdrop of many novels, but *Tiger in a Trance* is the first one to portray the lives of the Deadheads themselves. The dialogue is fantastic—sharp, economical, and authentic. . . . Excellent."

—Jim Carroll, author of *The Basketball Diaries*

"[An] entertaining first novel." —*The New York Times*

"[Ludington writes] with deft, economical prose and [has] a wonderful ear for dialogue that would make Hemingway proud."

—*Chico News & Review*

"Echoes of Kesey, Kerouac, and Alex Garland waft like pot smoke through this first novel." —*Men's Journal*

"Max Ludington is an obviously accomplished and promising writer. His style is graceful, his characters are alive, and he can tell a story. As a generational novel, *Tiger in a Trance* reminded me of *The Sun Also Rises.*"

—Philip Caputo, author of *Horn of Africa* and *A Rumor of War*

"[Ludington] manages to capture the darker underbelly of the world of the Deadhead. . . . At first romanticiz[ing] the open road, the thrill turns ugly and the novel starts to read more like William Burroughs than Jack Kerouac. It's a good trip."

—*Hartford Advocate*

Max Ludington

TIGER IN A TRANCE

Max Ludington's fiction has appeared in such publications as *Tin House, Nerve,* and *Meridian.* He received his MFA from Columbia University and now lives in New York. *Tiger in a Trance* is his first novel.

tiger in a trance

tiger in a trance

max ludington

ANCHOR BOOKS

A Division of Random House, Inc.

New York

dedicated to the memories of

tom head and steve hutchings

acknowledgments

First, I need to thank my parents, without whose love, patience, and support (not to mention the care packages of books arriving at all my far-flung locations, which kept me reading) I might never have written a thing; and my brother, Nick, for being a faithful friend. And Shayna, for everything. Thanks also to my loving grandparents and the rest of my excellent family. For invaluable help with this book in all its stages I am indebted to my friends Nelson Eubanks, Gordon Haber, and Natasha Radojčić-Kane. Let me not forget the whole showgoing crew: *EVERYONE!* You know who you are. Thanks to my agent, Peter Steinberg, for believing in me, and for his Midas touch in finding Gerry Howard, the perfect editor for this book. So many others, known and unknown, have helped me along the way, and I thank you all.

I'm still walking, so I'm sure that I can dance,
Just a saint of circumstance,
Like a tiger in a trance.

—JOHN PERRY BARLOW, "SAINT OF CIRCUMSTANCE"

O something unproved! Something in a trance!
To escape utterly from others' anchors and holds!
To drive free! To love free! To dash reckless and dangerous!
To court destruction with taunts, with invitations!
To ascend, to leap to the heavens of the love indicated to me!
To rise thither with my inebriate soul!
To be lost if it must be so!
To feed the remainder of life with one hour of fulness and freedom!
With one brief hour of madness and joy.

—WALT WHITMAN, "LEAVES OF GRASS"

part one

november 1985

BAD SCENE IN THE HALL. A guy was freaking out and the cops showed up. I stuck my head out to see. He was shirtless and slick with sweat, wearing only cutoff green army pants, and the two cops had him against the wall. One of them gripped his throat, and they were screaming questions at him. "What's your name?" "What did you take?" Red knots of anger swelled on the heads of the cops, near their eyes. They wielded their arms like fearsome tools of the trade. They were in plainclothes, the short one obvious with his buzz cut, stonewashed jeans, and tight concert T-shirt, but the tall one scarily close to passing, with a little ponytail and goatee, and a long ratty green trench coat. His finely tooled cowboy boots were a strange touch, though, and gave him away. The prisoner shook his shaggy head and kept squeezing his eyes shut and then pushing them wide, like someone who's lost his glasses. It hurt to look at him. He struggled once against their grip. "Don't you fight us now," said the shorter cop, leaning in and yelling in the guy's ear. "You *trying* to get us to hurt you?" They pinned his straining limbs quickly and smoothly, almost effortlessly, as if born for it, as if thousands of years of natural selection had honed them to hunt confused acidheads.

"Shut the fucking door," Vince hissed from behind me.

I stepped into the hall and shut the door to the room.

They spun him around and began cuffing him. A few other people had filtered into the hall, and some peeked from behind the doors of nearby rooms. I approached the cops, feeling invincible in that way that sometimes translates into reality. I had nothing illegal on me and no outstanding warrants. I shoved aside the vision of them as predators. We were all human beings, and I felt I could get through to them.

"Hey," I said. "This is the last thing he needs. If you leave him we'll take care of him."

"He a friend of yours?"

"Yeah, he is."

"You know what he took?"

"No, but I'd guess a good amount of acid."

"What's his name?"

Here I paused. "I don't know. Listen, we take care of our own."

"Yeah, well back off. He's coming with us."

"Come on." I stepped closer to them, filled with confidence and love. I had to stop myself from putting my hand on the cop's shoulder. "He just needs time to come down. Can't you just leave him here?"

The short cop spun his head violently toward me, driving an elbow into his prisoner's neck. He was too far gone on rage and power to be dealt with, I saw that now. His teeth were clenched, and I could see red streaks under the stubbly hairs behind his ears where the buzzer had scraped the skin. "Back the fuck up! Unless you want to come along, too! We got plenty of room in the car." A light mist of evil sprayed from the pores around his eyes, turning the air between us humid and red. It smelled like burnt hair, and ate right through my confidence.

I stepped back. The prisoner started to struggle, suddenly in full freak-out mode again. His thin white body writhed like a gaffed fish, pouring sweat. His belly button was a sad, lopsided outie. Looking at him, I felt the crushing weight of what he was about to go through. He felt it too, and produced a manic, despairing screech, a sound filled with mortal fear, and tried to spin away from the wall. His hands strained at the metal cuffs. The cops shoved him back into the wall and he kicked at them with one dirty bare foot, hitting the tall one in the knee. They took him down hard to the floor, and his head made that sickening dull thump heads make on carpeted concrete. He kept up the screeching, and as they knelt on top of him and put another set of cuffs on his ankles it turned into crying. "Mommy," he cried, and it was the only word I'd heard him utter. He screamed into the red carpet, bawled crazily. The tall cop, rubbing his knee, laughed.

At this point all of us watching understood there was nothing we could do for him. The cops were flustered and pumped up, ready to include any of us in their brutal tableau. For the benefit of the spectators, the short cop recited the Miranda warnings near the guy's head. Then he said, "Do you understand these rights as I have explained them to you?" Both the cops got a good laugh out of that. The tall one got on the radio as they stood up, telling someone they were bringing one in. "White male," he said. "Late twenties. High on drugs. Incoherent." The short one put his foot on the prisoner's back and pulled a pair of latex gloves from his pocket.

When he had them on, he grabbed the guy's ankle cuffs and dragged him into the elevator by his feet. The guy had shut down now, and was just sobbing softly. He made no effort to twist his head to the side, and his lips scraped against the carpet. I saw him wince as his face bounced over the elevator's metal threshold. Blood bloomed at the tip of his nose, and the elevator doors shut on them.

I walked back to the room and knocked on the door. Silence answered. I knocked again, checking to make sure I had the right number. "It's Jason," I said, and the door opened, still held by the chain. Cole's face appeared in the crack.

"Cops gone?" he whispered.

"Yeah, they're gone."

He unhooked the chain and I walked into the room, where the air was sweating droplets of greasy yellow light. Cole went back to his seat and resumed talking where he had left off at the knock. He was telling his story about the jumper in Rochester. I never knew whether to believe it. I hadn't heard it from anyone but him.

"So the guy was up there on the stadium roof, God knows how he got up there, looking down at the crowd in the parking lot," Cole said. "He started to do a little dance, kind of shuffling back and forth. Then some security guards appeared from inside about thirty yards from him and walked along the edge toward him. People were yelling at him to be careful, to go back, but most of us thought he was just having fun. He had this stovepipe hat on, and he just tipped it to the crowd and stepped off the wall. Must've been a two-hundred-foot drop to the pavement."

Randy, who was kicked back on the far bed, hung his head and shook it. He'd heard the story before, too.

Regina said, "Wow."

I crawled up next to her on the bed, the yellow bedspread

consuming my hands and knees like quicksand. I lay flat before I reached the pillows, to keep from being sucked under, and played with Regina's navel-ring. The small steel horseshoe tipped with tiny jade spheres flipped back and forth under my finger, shining against her olive-brown skin. I rested my head on her ribs. The acid in my own body was still going strong, but it had been downshifting for a half hour or so and seemed headed for a smooth landing.

"Talk about bummers," said Vince, smiling his flagship smile, which cut two sharp dimples in one cheek and one in the other. He put his arm around the local girl he had picked up, a high school beauty in a tie-dyed skirt, leather vest, and beaded headband.

"Yeah," said Cole. "Definitely ruined the vibe for that night's show. Even people I've talked to who were there but didn't see it or hear about it said they felt a weird vibe going around. I think someone must have told the Boys before they played."

Vince's girl was listening silently, wide-eyed and serious. I watched Vince sense that she was uncomfortable with the conversation. "But how about that show tonight?" he said. "Quite a scorcher, huh?"

"Yeah," said Cole. "Jerry shredded on that 'Dew.' But last night was the real shit. I'd lay money that was the only 'Lost Sailor-Drums-Space-Saint' you'll ever see."

"Whoo! Yeah, and that 'Gloria,' too." Vince turned casually to the girl and kissed her lips. Taken by surprise, she kissed back. "What about you?" he asked her. "You have fun tonight?"

"Oh, yeah," she nodded. "I loved it. These were only my second and third shows."

"Well, you caught a good pair."

Through her skin I heard a few gulps of beer making their way into Regina's stomach. Her skin felt buttery under my cheek. Amazing skin. I was the only tripping person in the room, and that

7

made me a little lonely. I was glad Regina was there; she kept coming on to me, but really there wasn't much left between us. We just helped each other out once in a while. Our couplings lately tended to be sullen.

Cole got up and lit a Camel. "Well, I'm heading up to my room."

"Hold on." I pulled Cole into the corner near the door and spoke softly. "Listen, I want to make some money. I've been helping Randy with his shirts for so long, and that's fine, but I want something of my own. Can you hook me up with some cheap acid?"

"You have money? Buyers? When do you want it?"

"Well, I haven't gotten that far yet. But I know plenty of folks, and I've moved pages before."

"Tell you what. The guys I'm staying with are the hookup. Tomorrow morning you can come up and meet them. But it'll just be casual, so don't talk business. Just come up and hang out. Then you'll know them."

"Sounds good," I said. "Thanks, man."

Cole left and the rest of us kicked back in front of the TV. Vince made a bed for himself and the girl on the floor using bedspreads and a blanket. We turned off the lights and watched an old *Mary Tyler Moore Show*. Ted Knight was cracking me up. He seemed to be expanding, stretching to his absolute limit, a universe of benign, self-centered stupidity about to snap back and implode. When the show ended I realized I hadn't actually been laughing out loud, but lying silent and motionless. I was the only one still watching. Randy was crashed out, Regina had undressed and climbed under the covers, and Vince and the girl were whispering to each other on the floor at the foot of the beds.

Regina reached over and rubbed my chest through my T-shirt. She whispered, "You coming in here?"

"I'm still too jacked," I said. "I'm going to be up for a while."

"Okay." She kissed my arm and rolled over. She was drunk, and didn't really care.

A loud ad with race cars came on and Randy woke up. "Turn that down," he said.

I muted the sound and kept watching. In the silence, the TV and my head were connected by a sucking tunnel of light, spinning through blackness broken by flickering shapes that I knew were the corners of the beds and Vince's blanket, but which bore only an intellectual connection with those things. People-shows started freaking me out, humans being laden with all their secret selves. It was too much, imagining what they might be saying about me, the kind of pain or condescension they might be feeling. I found a nature show and watched some bears running and shaking trees and rooting in the ground for food. I thought of the guy the cops had taken away, of his face bouncing into the elevator, and sent out a little prayer for him. The show ended and another began about the Loch Ness monster—lots of shots of the darkly shimmering surface of the lake, men lowering equipment into the water, and the grainy old photos of dinosaur shapes. I heard Vince and the girl having sex, trying to keep it quiet: sharp, stifled exhalations, rustling of the blanket, rhythmic squishing, small moans from her. The TV lit the strangely heaving blanket as if through water. I got a hard-on, but didn't touch it.

WHEN I WOKE, the red LED numbers on the clock between the beds said it was 7:52. Regina's breath puffed irregularly against my neck, carrying the damp memory of beer. The drapes were tightly drawn, the television still on and mute, green light of a rain forest playing from it over the breathing bodies and Holiday Inn bedspreads; as I watched slit-eyed, the camera panned from the jungle to a broad brown gouge in the earth, a strip mine dotted with yellow bulldozers, giant backhoes, and green trucks with tires fifteen feet high. I imagined the authoritative voice-over, which would be extolling the wonders of progress or lamenting the raping of the earth, maybe a little of both.

I slid from under Regina's arm and shuffled past the dead manatee on the floor—Vince and the girl under the nappy ochre blanket—and past the other bed where Randy slept alone, to the shaded window to peek out at the day.

I stood with my face close to the glass, holding the curtain open a crack. It was a white morning over gray Richmond, leftover raindrops still congregating in the lower corners of the window. There was a fuzzy clarity that came in the acid's wake, everything soft and exact and sadly real. I felt diminished, but benignly so. It was one of the things I liked about acid, waking up to a familiar world that had knitted itself back together with imperceptible differences, tiny lost threads of myself woven into it everywhere: I looked for them in the slick glass and black steel of the office building opposite, in the sandpaper texture of the brown plastic drapes, in the beige crosshatched wallpaper and the yellow carpet and the television's pixels and the bedspread and Regina's arm with its misting of black hair, and they were there. I moved back across the room, undressed, and climbed into bed with her.

I had begun to think it was not me she was attracted to, but the drama of being involved with someone whose feelings for her faded easily and had to be fanned to life with constant sex and fights. But now her skin, like everything else, was threaded through with shining shreds of myself, and I found I didn't have to dig too deep for a feeling. When I caressed her, she writhed and moaned tiredly and kissed me, unaware of how she had changed overnight. I took hold of one of her breasts.

Two hours later the phone call came from Cole, inviting me for breakfast on the seventeenth floor. When I hung up, I saw Regina looking at me.

"I'm going up to talk to Cole," I said quietly.

"I'll come with you."

"Well, I have to talk to him about some stuff."

"You can't do that with me there?"

"It's not his room. Listen, maybe this is a mistake."

"A mistake? How?"

Three other people were asleep in the room, and I wondered if any of them were listening. "You know I love having fun with you, but we've talked about this. We split up a while ago and this keeps happening. Maybe it's getting confusing."

"Are you confused?" She was in bite-and-scratch mode now, propped up and drilling me with her sharp dark eyes.

"Yeah, a little," I said.

"Well, I'm not. I said it was just for fun and that's what it was."

"Good," I said. "I'm going upstairs. Do you need a ride to Worcester with us?" This was the wrong way to phrase it.

Regina looked at me stonily for a second, about to answer with some angry question, then seemed to think better of it. "No, I'll go with the Jersey crew."

I took the elevator to seventeen and found the room at the end of the hallway. A very thin guy in a towel and beard answered, fresh from the shower but still battered-looking, his face prematurely creased, his wet brown hair straggling down to the middle of his back. "It's not room service," he called back into the room.

"Is Cole here?" I asked.

"Yeah." The guy motioned with his head for me to enter.

The room was a suite, an expansive sitting room at the end of a hall with a closed door leading to the bedroom. Sitting on the floor in the middle of the room was a wiry, clean-shaven dude surrounded by stacks of money, bills of every denomination laid out like some complex game of solitaire. He didn't even look up at me. *Cole, Cole*, I thought, *hanging out with the high rollers as usual.*

"Cole!" called the guy in the towel, and in a moment Cole came out of the bedroom. He smiled, exposing the off-center gap where he had been missing an upper tooth since before I had known him. The missing tooth somehow added youth and life to his face instead of draining it the way it would have in most people. Nothing could sap Cole's natural charisma; it oozed from the pores of his dark-brown skin, and seemed to have less to do with charm or wit or self-confidence (though he *was* charming and witty and self-confident) than with something biological, some glandular emission he had been born with. Cole was one of the few black guys in the scene and had been on tour for almost a decade. He knew pretty much everyone. When I had first arrived, he had brought me under his wing and made me feel at home, and he was still introducing me to people.

"Hey Jason." He walked over and gave me a hug. "This is Saul," he said, indicating the toweled guy, who was changing into jeans. Saul nodded at me and slowly pulled his pants up. I nodded back, catching a glimpse of his abnormally large penis as he tucked it in with his hand.

"And this is Don," said Cole.

I turned and looked at Don. I hadn't recognized him without his beard, but we had met the previous summer, living on the beach for a month in Santa Cruz with a bunch of other heads. "I know this guy," I said. "Cole, don't you remember that night you came to Santa Cruz for that party in the hills. We were all there together."

"Oh, shit, that's right," said Cole. "You guys were at Greyhound Rock together. I forgot."

Through this, Don concentrated on the money. He finally lifted his head. His brown eyes were a little too close together, and he looked like he was searching for something in my hair. "Don," I said. "How the fuck are you?" I offered my hand and Don grabbed for it, but missed me by an inch. I laughed.

Don's face relaxed and he smiled. I still wasn't sure he had recognized me. "The human character is three small stones in a basket," he said.

"Jesus, shut up with that. Will you please?" said Cole.

"Do you know what the stones are?"

Cole said, "He was dipping sheets yesterday and he's still tripping. Should've used gloves and a mask."

Don's eyes stayed on me. "Do you know what the stones are?"

"What kind of basket?" I asked.

"Ha!" Don looked at Cole. "A man with questions. You brought me a man with questions."

"Oh, yeah," Cole groaned, having turned on the TV, not even looking over.

Don turned back to me. "A thinker, I see." His expression implied we two were unified in that. "A small basket, if you must know. Three small stones in a small basket. Do you know what the stones are?"

"The id, the ego, and the superego."

Don inhaled sharply in astonishment, looking around the room, trying to share it with Saul and Cole, but they were sunk in a cartoon and he came back to me. His eyes slid off mine without completely focusing. The astonishment made him start laughing and shake his head. He said, "No. Not it. But a real answer, a true answer, the best one I've had all night. Very good, but"—he wrinkled his nose disdainfully—"forget Freud, my man. As should we all. Yes, I say that to everyone:" he threw back his head and yelled at the ceiling, "Forget Freud!"

"Do you remember me?" I asked.

He looked at me directly, his gaze focusing for the first time, and then stood up. "Fuck yeah," he said, and embraced me. "Jason. My brother."

"How much money is there, Don?" Cole asked from across the room.

Don let go of me and looked at the stacks of bills on the floor, perplexed. "Oh, fuck!" He went back to counting it. There was a knock on the door and Cole answered it.

A waiter wheeled in a cart filled with silver-domed dishes, a pitcher of orange juice, a silver coffeepot, and a gravy boat filled with maple syrup. The waiter's eyes widened when he saw the piles of money on the floor. "Jesus," he whispered.

"Thanks, man," said Cole.

The waiter wrenched his head away from the money. "Sure. Just charge it to the room?"

"Hell no. Cash up front, always. We live by it."

"Okay." His eyes drifted back to the money, which Don was still trying to count. "Fifty-nine dollars."

Cole reached down in front of Don and slid a hundred-dollar bill off the top of a stack.

"No!" Don said.

"Yes," said Cole. "It's good. For the people, and all that."

Don nodded, still counting under his breath.

"Here you go." Cole handed the bill to the waiter. "Keep it. That's for not seeing anything."

The waiter smiled as if this were something asked of him all the time, and left the room with a glance back over his shoulder at Don.

"Aren't you paranoid about that waiter seeing all that money?" I asked. "What with all the busts the past two nights?"

Saul spread his hands to encompass the room. "We're sold out," he said. "They could raid us right now and they'd find nothing, absolutely nothing." He smiled, then shook his head. "But it has been a nightmare here. The lots were crawling with cops. Over two hundred drug arrests, I heard. One of our buyers even got popped." He lifted the lid on a plate of scrambled eggs and inspected them.

As we were drawing up chairs and setting the table to eat, the bedroom door opened and a very tall thin girl with mounds of dark curly hair came out. She was sleepy-eyed and beautiful, dressed in a long white robe with *Holiday Inn* embroidered ornately on the breast pocket.

"Oh, I can smell that coffee," she said.

Don, who had abandoned his money-counting and was poking curiously at a plate of scrambled eggs, looked up and rushed to her. "Darling," he said, trying to embrace her.

"Yeah, yeah." She pushed him away.

"I was being serious," Don said from behind her as she approached the table. "Why does everyone always think I'm being cynical?"

"Remember the boy who cried wolf?" the girl asked over her shoulder.

Don nodded, coming back to the table, and muttered, "I've made my own bed, yes."

"Jason," said Cole, "this is Jane. Jane, Jason."

"Hi."

"Nice to meet you," said Jane, smiling wearily and taking a seat across the table from me, next to Saul.

"Oh no you don't," Don said. "Don't sit there. I don't trust you next to him."

"What are you talking about?"

"This person," said Don, pointing at Saul. "He goes prancing around, showing off his great big whang to everyone, and I know you women can't resist it. Once you've laid eyes on it, it becomes a presence in your mind, you can't stop thinking about it, you're inexorably drawn to it. Look at him, just sitting there, silent. He knows he doesn't need to say anything. Strong and silent, he just needs to expose himself and let nature do its thing."

Jane began loading her plate with eggs and looked calmly up at Don. "Obviously someone in this room is obsessed with Saul's whang."

"Yeah," said Saul to Don. "If you really want to know how it feels, I could put a bag over your head and fuck you in the ass. Anything for a friend."

Cole and I laughed.

"You were better off strong and silent," Jane said.

I focused on her cheeks as she chewed. They were plump and lightly freckled, and made soft rolling movements.

"Fuck you all," said Don. "I'll be in the bedroom when you decide to stop ganging up on me." He seemed cheerful as he grabbed a pack of cigarettes off the coffee table and left the room. I thought about asking Saul about their prices, but Cole had told me not to talk business on the first meeting. I took two pancakes off the stack and doused them in syrup.

9 5 NORTH from Richmond was drizzly and gray, and I let Randy do most of the driving. I spent the hours reading and watching raindrops shakily climb the curved edge of the Volvo's windshield. We had sold a lot of T-shirts in Richmond and were flush with cash, but we needed to find a shirt wholesaler in Worcester and stock up again.

As we passed through Baltimore, I said, "Remember making this same trip last year?"

"Yeah," said Randy.

"Remember that redneck who fixed Regina's car for a hit of acid?"

"Classic shit," was all Randy said.

That had been the first night I met Randy, in the parking lot of the Richmond Coliseum, and I remembered my first impression: Randy sitting in the passenger seat of his orange '71 Datsun 240Z, kicked back with the doors open and the stereo blasting the theme from *Chariots of Fire* at levels that caused me and Bob to hear it long before we came in sight of the car. Hartford Bob, who the following summer had also lived on the beach in Santa Cruz with Don and me, had been dragging me around, telling me, "You got to meet this guy Randy who picked us up on the road. He makes the coolest T-shirts." Bob was high on some liquid acid he'd shared with Randy before the show and couldn't find where they'd parked. We had been zigzagging crazily through the lot for half an hour when we heard the heady music drifting across the rows of cars and for no particular reason began to move toward it. Out at the end of a row, where the cars tapered off into deserted asphalt, we came upon Randy, and it was a glorious sight, his tall frame reclined in the bright car, eyes closed, a huge smile on his face, the cheap old speakers shuddering with overwork on every crescendo and blurring every roll of the timpani. Bob called his name as we approached. He looked up at us, spread his arms wide, palms up, as if the music were a giant sphere he was trying to present to us, and pronounced Vangelis to be a genius.

Eventually Chris, Bob's traveling partner, found us, and I went and got Regina, who was my ride. This was before she and I hooked up. Unable to afford a room, we had all camped in the Virginia hinterlands after leaving the show, and Regina's Ford Granada wouldn't start in the morning. We pushed it with Randy's car to a 7-Eleven that sat alone on a swampy road. It had gas pumps but no auto shop, and a small group of local men gathered around the open hood to try diagnosing the problem. They leaned over the engine like a herd of buffalo around a watering hole, cocked arms hefting Big Gulps and lit Marlboros, murmuring the names of various engine parts that could have crapped out, recounting times those various parts had crapped out on their vehicles, and telling Regina to hit the ignition now and then. Finally one authoritative voice pronounced, "Looks like y'all need a new coil," and all the others nodded in agreement and wandered away, as if they had only been waiting for his opinion to resolve the dilemma.

"Ah, the mortal coil," I said.

"I know a place where y'all can get one cheap," the man said. He pulled apart the two sides of his jean jacket, revealing a small paunch encased tightly in a green T-shirt. "It's hard to find, but I could drive you there. Even put the fucker in for you if you want."

"That would be great," I said.

"What y'all got for me?"

"Well, we don't have much money. I hope we can even afford the part."

"Y'all's hippies. Got any LSD on you? Stuff like that?"

So we dug up one stale old hit of acid from the glove compartment and laid it on the guy, for which he happily gave us a ride to the salvage yard and replaced the part. Afterward, I rode with Randy to Worcester, and we had been riding together ever since. The Datsun had died the following summer in Ventura, and in the fall I'd wrangled the Volvo for three-fifty from an old hippie.

I WAS BEHIND THE WHEEL when we took 84 East out of Hartford and chugged up into Worcester. For me, Worcester had always consisted only of the Centrum and three or four hotels. It was reddish in the light from the sunset, a confirmation of some old vision to which all my vague passing thoughts of it had pointed: a stand of simple red cubes and rectangles sprouting from the mulch of the withered and overrun Eastern deciduous wilderness, a dead place given life once a year when the Dead passed through.

We swiveled off the highway on a tightly looped exit ramp in the middle of town. The beige concrete wall on our left as we navigated the frontage road was striped along the top with red sunlight. A fat homeless woman waddled beneath the stripe, her head swinging from side to side, and as we approached she stopped and leaned back against the wall. She was stroking her wispy beard like a thoughtful scholar when we stopped behind a line of cars near her. Her gray hair was long and matted and shot tendrils in all directions from under a black wool cap. I stared at her, and she seemed unaware of me. The top of her head didn't quite reach the stripe of dying sunlight, which was climbing higher up the wall away from her. She searched some inner distance with lucid eyes, trying to work something out in her head. Then the light turned, and as the line of cars began to move she nodded resignedly and waddled on.

I pulled into the hotel lot, across from the Centrum. Cole had said he'd go half on a room with us, and to get a nice one. He'd had to stop in New York to do some business and would arrive later that night. The desk clerk's eyes glazed over when Randy and I walked up. He was a tiny, angry young man of a type that I recognized, like a Chihuahua, his dry brown hair cut high above his ears, with big dull eyes and a pinched mouth that protruded from his bony white face.

"We'd like a room please," I said.

"Oh," said the man, as if surprised by this request. "I'm sorry, all we have left are suites."

"Okay, then I guess we'll take a suite."

"Yes, well, our suites are two hundred and thirty dollars a night." This statement was meant to close the negotiations.

"Okay. We'd like to pay for two nights up front. You do accept cash, don't you?"

The man's mouth puckered into a little asshole on his face. "Yes," he said.

"Good. Do you need a deposit for the telephone? Because we'll be making quite a few long-distance calls."

"Yes. A twenty-dollar deposit for long-distance service."

I flipped the cash onto the desk breezily, enjoying pissing the guy off. It was more than half of what we had, a major outlay, and I hoped Cole would come through with his end.

"Are you crazy?" Randy asked in the elevator. "Most of that money's mine."

"I know, don't worry," I said. "Guys like that just get to me. I've got a deal in the works that will make up for it."

We reveled in the room's sumptuousness. We showered and kicked back in brown overstuffed armchairs to watch cable. A hotel room was always a wonderful thing, no matter where it was or what its condition. It became our own—a sanctuary with piped-in TV and air, ice down the hall and clean towels every day, a home of sorts—while our status remained transient and our location unknown to the world. I broke out a joint and convinced Randy to share it with me. Randy didn't smoke much pot, and didn't drink at all, but occasionally dosed up on acid or Ecstasy for shows.

We were on the twenty-third floor, and outside the generous south-facing windows the departed sun had left the sky bluish-black. The lights of the town gave me an insular feeling: American Normalcy embraced us all around, and the local news jabbered on about the lives of the people whose lights glittered below us, what their weather would be like, whose house had burned down, which bus stop shelter had been plowed over by the bus itself, no one injured thank God, what the mayor proposed to do to help the homeless. A little boy had written to the president and received a personal invitation to the White House. Sucking softly on the resin-damp joint, I felt an affinity for all of it, the whole big dumb American movie. I loved it as the small-town son gone to the city loves the prairie home he can never really return to. And like that son I knew something the people back home seemed ignorant of: that the place I had moved to was as much a part of America as their little hamlet. Maybe, in its greatness, more so.

There was no show that night, and we had nothing to do but hunt down a T-shirt wholesaler for the morning. Thinking of the money I had promised to make up, I decided to wander around the hotel a bit, see if anyone I knew needed anything.

I chose floors at random and walked the halls. The hotel seemed weirdly quiet and was peopled with strange characters. The first person I saw was a pudgy man on fourteen in a short-sleeved business shirt, black slacks, and stocking feet, puffing through his nose and sweating in a red-faced and vaguely degenerate way as he stalked effortfully back to his room from somewhere. He was taking pains to smooth out his walk and keep his gut from bouncing. Then an older woman asked for help with her bag from the elevator to her room, and when I obliged, she tipped me a quarter and said, "Get a haircut," cackling evilly. On four I passed a girl of about sixteen sitting on the floor outside a room talking on the phone, its cord stretched tightly from the closed door; her clothes and hair were clean and conservative, but messed rebelliously around the edges—sweater untucked, socks dropping low on her shoeless feet, chestnut hair tousled, beige skirt riding high and unladylike on her spraddled legs, showing the crotch of her white tights—and her mouth was set in a stubborn frown. She held the phone to her ear and mostly just nodded, and as I neared her I came to realize she had only one arm. I tried to reconstruct my view of her body to account for the possibility she might have her right arm hidden behind her or tucked into her sweater, but the white sleeve neatly turned in left little doubt. She looked up at me with a hazy and forlorn expression, seeming not to notice that I had been staring rudely. "I *know*," she said impatiently into the phone just after I passed her. I wondered if she might be there for the shows, but her clothes and expression spoke clearly of unwanted parental custody. On my way back to the elevator I passed her again and she made eye contact and rolled her eyes dramatically, pulling the phone away from her ear for a moment. I smiled and nodded in commiseration. Someone on the other end was telling her how to live.

The eighth floor was deserted. At the end of the hall I turned around. Gold and blue faux-Persian designs stretched out endlessly in front of me toward the elevators, where two chrome cylindrical ashtrays stood like sentries. While I walked I spaced out on the linear silence of the hallway. I was about to pick another number and try a final floor when up ahead the elevator spat out a guy in jeans and a red polo shirt who tripped over the lip somehow and fell forward into the wall in front of him, as if he had been pushed. It took the sound of his voice to jar my recognition. Vince, laughing, turned and yelled into the elevator as the doors closed, "Fuck you!" He laughed some more and the elevator left, its occupants remaining out of sight.

"Well fuck you, too," I said.

Vince looked at me. "Heeeey, Jason. What. It. Be?" He slapped my outstretched palm drunkenly.

"Lovin' life," I said. It was Vince's usual expression, and I had taken to using it around him. The word on Vince was that he had dropped out of Berkeley. He was some kind of math genius on a scholarship, a prodigy who had come up with some new theorem or proof while he was still in high school. Now he used his brain to figure out new ways to scam into shows and snake on girls. He was a master at both.

"Yeah, yeah," he said. "Same here, bud. Come on down to my room. Chris and Nick are with me. Regina, too."

"Regina, huh? I thought she rode up with the Jersey crew."

"We saw them at HoJo's and she came with us. I think she's after Chris's dick."

"Good. Mine can get a rest."

Vince laughed again. "Yeah, yeah. Come on."

In the room, smoke slid in layers near the ceiling, and emerald cities of Beck's bottles stood on the round table near the window and on most of the other flat surfaces. Nick was reclined on one bed, bottle in hand, and Chris and Regina were on the other, her head on his chest. The furniture was of a lower order than in our suite, two cheap wooden straight-backs by the table and a small hard cuplike armchair in the corner.

When she heard my voice, Regina's head popped halfway up and then almost as quickly back down to Chris's flannel shirt. "Hey, man," she said.

"Hey," I said.

Chris and Nick were brothers, California boys from Chico who shared the same dark brown hair, blue eyes, and elfin features.

"When did you guys check in?" I asked.

"Couple hours ago," said Nick.

"Huh. The little fuck at the front desk told us all he had left were suites."

"Well, a woman checked us in."

"Interesting." I grabbed a dripping Beck's Vince had pulled from the cooler of ice for me and popped the cap off with my lighter. "So you guys need any pages?"

Chris reached for a pack of Camels on the bedside table and lit one. Nick said, "Nah. We're hooked up for pages, 'less you can do better than forty-five."

"If I could do forty, tonight or tomorrow, how many would you guys want?"

Nick thought for a second. "We might take twenty or thirty off you. Since when are you the hookup for pages?"

"I'm not. I just met somebody, and I need a little extra cake."

Regina took the cigarette from between Chris's fingers and dragged on it. She hadn't looked at me since I walked in, but now she did and her look was loose-lipped and blankly satiated, a look she usually got after hard sex, a look that in the past had made me feel a little proud at having fucked so well but now created a stab of jealousy in me.

"I'll call you guys when I hook up with my guy and let you know if I can do it."

"Cool, bro," said Nick.

"Have a seat and down a few with us," Vince said. He had dropped into the small armchair and was trying unsuccessfully to turn on the television using the remote. "Motherfucker," he muttered, pounding the buttons.

"No, I've got to take off, but thanks for the beer." I carried the half-finished bottle out of the room and down the hall.

Back upstairs, I found the suite empty and figured Randy had gone out for a bite to eat. I sat down and tried to watch television, but soon turned it off. I walked to the window and looked out at the clear night sky. I thought of the one-armed girl's forlorn face. It came back to me with such clarity, as if I knew her well. When I drew my eyes back from the city—its vague cubist forms lit from within, the stippled darkness beyond—the window showed me my own reflection.

2

THAT SAME WINDOW the next morning was a big Polaroid of brilliant blue as I woke on the sofa, bringing to mind a set of old snapshots from my mother's albums: sand dunes a mile high outside Sharjah. Climbing to the top with Dad and James and looking out over the polished golden desert, the endlessly shifting landscape that always looked the same, its migrating dunes forever moving, but in relation to nothing. Taking running starts and launching from the tops of the dunes out into the wind, flying, landing on the steep slope halfway down in an avalanche of fine sand that ran downward and flattened like sluicing water. My mother had taken pictures of me and my father and older brother leaping through the air, framed against the faces of the dunes, the color of which the old film had captured surprisingly well, or backdropped by the sky above—which was the same Kodachrome blue as all old picture skies—if she caught us at just the right moment. She had one of me and James with our fingers dipped in the shallow surf of the Gulf of Oman, which was as far as we would go into the water, our father having regaled us with stories of sharks along the whole drive there, how these were the most heavily shark infested waters in the world, how even fishermen here lived in deadly fear of attack. When we had arrived at the shore, no amount of backtracking, recanting, or cajoling could get me and James into that water. Our father swam out and we stood rooted on the beach. I peeled my eyes against the glare to keep my father's tiny bobbing head in sight. I stood on my toes, my chest gripped tight whenever a wave rose and obscured my view, fearing he might not reappear.

We had been living in Beirut, and the trip around the Persian Gulf was vacation. Sharjah was the city of cranes in my mind, a place where every direction you looked buildings were going up in a constant struggle to spend all the oil money. The cranes nodded all along the skyline, stiffly mobile counterparts to the oil derricks throughout the desert and out on the water, making the place incredible, like the site of some old-time-movie Martian invasion. It was a country where there were road signs prohibiting car dumping, and indeed occasionally the desert roadsides were littered with abandoned Renaults and Mercedes, the general attitude being when a car broke down you bought a new one. The four of us had shopped at an outdoor market in Dubai, and I was proud of my father's haggling skills—we were ten yards from one stall, walking away, when the owner hailed us back and met my father's price. We ate in a Chinese restaurant near the port where huge metal crates the size of train cars were being unloaded by the thousands onto the cobbled piersides. Nothing seemed to be going out, only coming in.

At the Holiday Inn in Sharjah, our basic rooms had cost over three hundred dollars a night. The beach had been so close to flat that at low tide it was eighty yards wide, and at high tide we could walk out fifty yards and still be only chest deep. There had been a young African bellman named Tomas at the hotel who could do five hundred push-ups at a time and break a cinder block with his bare hands. James and I, at twelve and ten years old, were in awe of him, following him everywhere and begging him to break something or show his karate prowess some other way. We exchanged postcards with him for about a year afterward, mostly grilling him on his daily push-up count and anything he may have smashed recently with his hands. We became obsessed with doing push-ups, with building up our numbers, and we had contests to see how many pencils we could break at a time until our father discovered his raided supply drawer and made us switch to twigs. That had all been shortly before the Lebanese civil war forced us to move to Cyprus, the last move we would make as a complete family. By the time the replies from Tomas stopped coming, James and I had begun to lose interest anyway, and our father was soon to leave for Syria, where he would die.

Pushing my father's face from my mind, I swung my feet to the carpet and sat up. In the mirror over the low chest of drawers opposite me, I saw myself. My long blond hair was kinked into acute angles on one side from the pillow. Dun bags stretched under eyes that were exact duplicates of my father's. Really my face was less a blend of my parents' features than a computer mock-up made using distinct features from both—my father's eyes and hair, my mother's upturned nose and full lips, my father's small trapezoidal chin. The only things there that were mine alone were the bags under my eyes, a couple of small pimples, and a front tooth with one corner chipped off where I had cracked it against the side mirror of a car in Syracuse the year before, when I passed out sucking nitrous in the lot. My brother had gotten his own face, the source of his hazel eyes and wide cheekbones lost in the swamp of the family gene pool. He had always held his face calmly, as an expression of who he was, but mine needed breaking in, molding to my own shape.

I tied my hair back, put on a loose black cotton sweater and jeans, and rousted Randy. We went down to the hotel dining room and just made the eleven o'clock breakfast deadline. Two tables away, the one-armed girl sat eating with a woman whose false-blond coif rose in brittle wings from her forehead and cupped down her neck like the shell of a horseshoe crab. Surely, I thought, they were eating late because of the time required to produce such ugliness. I could see the older woman only in partial profile, an occasional glimpse of a sharp flat mouth-corner expertly augmented with red lipstick, carefully taking in bites small enough not to endanger the makeup. Her tailored skirt suit was red to match the lipstick, and a black Chanel purse hung from the back of her chair. The girl was facing me and was an intense counterpoint to her mother (for that was doubtless their relationship). Her left arm held the fork in an improper fist and she shoveled heaps of eggs and potatoes into her long full mouth whose shape skewed perversely as she chewed. In the morning light, her lank hair was a shade off chestnut to the mousy side. She raised her somber brown eyes and caught me staring, and again, there was no discomfort in her reaction. She frowned slyly through a huge mouthful of hash browns, as if to say, *I don't know what you could find so interesting.* I smiled and looked away.

"We've got to find that wholesaler, get the shirts, and get on top of screening them," Randy was saying.

"Yeah," I said. I sliced off half my cake of hash browns and shoved it into my mouth. I looked back over, chewing grandly, but the girl was lost in her empty plate, trying to tune out whatever her mother was saying.

When we had the boxes of plain white and black T-shirts,

Randy and I set about silkscreening them. The designs on the screens were all Randy's, and they were good. Randy was serious about his artwork. When he was sketching designs for screens or cutting them into sheets of acetate with a razor blade he could sit silent for hours, light brown bangs obscuring his eyes, hands moving with slow fluid precision over the work. The main design we were selling on this tour was of a lone skeleton dancing in a desert landscape under a starlit sky. This was not a typical, mindlessly happy skeleton of the kind seen everywhere on Dead tour, but a long, elegantly misshapen specimen, contorted in a troubling way, its arms crossed in front to form an X, one foot lifted high, head thrown back, its face expressive of complex inner schisms—some unnamed turmoil shot through with epiphany. They were selling so well it was hard to make them fast enough.

First we made a batch in white ink on black shirts, which we both agreed was the best look for this design, though it wasn't what sold best. The framed, tightly stretched screen was attached to a flat Masonite board by hinges at the base, and one by one we pulled the shirts over the board, which served as backing for the screening process and kept the ink from bleeding through onto the backs of the shirts. Randy poured the ink across the top of the screen, took the long rubber squeegee and dragged it down slowly, pressing hard, and then slowly back up, forcing the ink through the unsealed portions of the screen that composed the design. Then he lifted the screen, and with my clean hands I pulled the shirt off and set it aside to dry. When Randy got tired of screening we switched places. Then we washed the screen and switched to white shirts. First Randy turned on his minicompressor and airbrushed bright red, yellow, and blue quadrants onto the shirts, and when the paint dried we screened them in black ink. These were the ones that flew out of our hands in the parking lots, and we charged more for them, but I reserved a certain respect for the buyers who chose the black shirts.

By the time we finished screening it was early evening and the crowds had started to gather outside. Time to sell. We already had tickets to both Worcester nights, so we could concern ourselves purely with making money and having fun. We each took a small knapsack filled with shirts outside.

Being right downtown and unconnected to any park, the scene at the Worcester Centrum was packed into the sidewalks and small outdoor lots flanking it, and overflowed onto some of the side streets. I turned right out of the hotel and right again, walking along the side of the venue. I draped a black shirt over one arm and a white one over the other and turned into the first small parking lot I came to. This lot had filled up quickly with early arrivals, many of them tourheads. Some stood by open coolers hawking beer and sodas. Some labored over grills or gas stoves, making stir-fried vegetables or burritos. The rear and side doors of vans and buses stood open and music played from stereos, mostly live Dead, the songs overlapping one into another as I walked. Tarps and tie-dyed bedsheets were used as awnings and decoration on many of the vans. From somewhere I heard the hiss of balloons being filled from a tank of nitrous oxide, and every so often the cautious sotto voce of a lot dealer murmuring "Doses" or "Buds." I nodded here and there to people I knew or had seen around, and sold three white shirts at once to a group of wandering locals, then a black one to a heavy, arrogant old-time head, who found it necessary to list for me the years in the mid and late seventies when he had been on tour. He got huffy when I didn't have XXL, but finally bought an XL.

I saw a couple I knew from Virginia at the back of a brown, wood-paneled station wagon selling stir-fry. They were both chubby and always smiled as though I were an old friend, so I'd come to feel like one. I had traded tickets to them for food the previous spring in Hampton, where tickets had been scarce, and had seen them around ever since. I'd forgotten their names and they'd forgotten mine, but they always fed me when I came across them. Those two tickets had continued to feed me off and on for eight months. I wolfed the spicy vegetables and rice and we rapped for a while about the Richmond shows.

Halfway down an aisle of cars I saw Jane coming toward me. She held a piece of cardboard covered in black velvet draped with beaded necklaces and earrings. Seeing her gave me an unexpected start.

"Hey Jane, how are you?" I said.

She looked at me blithely and smiled. "Just fine, thank you."

"I'm Jason, remember? From yesterday, in the room with Cole and Don?"

"Oh, I remember. You'll have to forgive Don. He was kind of out of it."

"I didn't think so. Most people aren't as interesting as him when they're tripping. Unless you're tripping with them." I folded the shirt I was holding away under my arm.

"Yeah, well, it got old for me after the first twenty-four hours. He didn't come down until last night." She made brief eye contact with me, then cast her gaze down. She had learned what a torment her big, round, speckled green eyes were to boys, and kept them in reserve.

"Wow." I looked more closely at the necklaces on her board. "That's some nice work. You make it?"

"Yes I did. Thank you."

"Didn't figure you for needing to sell things in the lot, being hooked up with Don and all." I immediately regretted saying it, and saw her face close down, but not completely.

"This way I never have to ask him for cash," she said. It was a personal admission I could tell she was uncomfortable making, and I was thankful to her for bailing me out.

"Speaking of which, do you know where he is? I may have some business for him."

"He's got his scene pretty well set up. He doesn't take on a lot of new business. But he might make an exception for you."

"Why for me?"

"He kept telling Cole how you and him had this amazing time last summer in Santa Cruz. He likes you."

"Well, good for me."

She laughed, and the muscles in her thin neck tightened into bowed vertical lines; the sound was deep and had the effect of making her seem older and wiser. The top button of her loose blouse was open to a triangle of freckled breastbone, behind which was the place the laugh had come from. "Where can I tell him to find you?" she asked.

"Room twenty-three-seventeen at the Sheraton." I pointed over her shoulder at the hotel. I thought my voice might have wavered, but I wasn't sure.

"Oh wow, we're on that floor. I'll tell him. Maybe he'll come by your room before the show."

"Cool," I said.

She smiled at me and walked on. Her smile: just slightly wider at one end, a soft scimitar, pouching her freckled cheeks and topped with big playful green eyes. Behind it hovered a hint of worldly melancholy. A smile that made my stomach flip with need. I walked and tried to think myself back from the brink, but my head felt stuffed with crumpled newspaper. My stomach continued to throb and float. This was no fooling around.

I WAITED IN THE ROOM from six to seven and was about to leave when a knock came. It was Don.

"Hey man," I said.

"S'up?"

We arranged ourselves across from each other in the sitting area. Don's demeanor was dimmer, faded like an oil lamp run low, since I had last seen him. Stubble now darkened his face.

"So Jane said you might want something."

"Yeah. What could you do sheets for?"

"That depends on how many you want."

"Twenty. Maybe thirty."

"Tell you what. I'll give you my good customer price 'cause you're a friend. But I hope you understand, I don't do referrals. Cole was a little out of line yesterday. So word-of-mouth stops with you."

"No problem."

"Okay then. Thirty apiece, if you take thirty."

It was better than I had hoped for. "You got it. I can have the money together tonight, I think."

"You think?"

"Well, you know how it is. But don't worry, these are good people, old-time folks."

"No sweat, man. It happens, doesn't happen, whatever. You in tonight?"

I slapped my pocket. "I've got my ticket, yeah."

"Cool. Me too."

Business dealt with, I leaned back and packed a bowl. I lit it and passed it to Don.

"Thanks," he said, cupping the ceramic pipe in his smooth brown fingers.

I watched him take his hit. "So, how long have you and Jane been together?"

He lifted his head, holding in the hit, his eyes bulging a little. He held up one finger for me to wait, then blew the smoke out in a long stream. "Not so long," he said. "About three months. But it seems like longer. We're way tight. She is the bomb, isn't she?"

"Yeah, she's great."

"She's the first girl I've been with where I'm not even looking at anything else."

I took the pipe from him and put it on the table. "That's a good thing," I said. "I'm not sure I've ever had that."

We both relaxed and waited for the pot's muggy high to descend on us.

Don said, "Want to sample the product?" For the first time a smile broke onto his thin face, like a diver surfacing in murky water.

"No thanks. I dosed for the last show down in Richmond. I don't really do it too often."

"Hey, you should know what you're selling, I always say. How about we split one? Just a half to get you going for the show. That's all you'll need."

"What the hell," I said.

Don reached into his pocket, nodding. "Yeah," he said, drawing the word out into an expression of pure satisfaction. He pulled about a quarter sheet of blotter acid from his pocket and tore one hit off the corner.

I opened Randy's art box and took an Exacto blade from an upper tray. Don used it carefully to split the hit of blotter in half. I took my piece and put it on my tongue, and Don did the same. *Here we go again,* I thought.

"Here," he dropped the rest of the hits onto the table. "In case you need samples." Don was really smiling now, anticipation having animated him. "You going to trust me?" he asked.

"Yeah, of course I am."

"Good. I'm going to trust you, too. You need those pages fronted for a couple hours, you got it. Whatever." He reached out his hand and we clasped in a soul handshake. "No more business," said Don. "Now let's just go to the show. I have a very good feeling about tonight." We headed for the door together, instant showmates.

INSIDE: no more selling, moneymaking, lie-telling, the crowd just sweeping in interlocking rings around the outer-circumference hallway, each person describing a personal circle, arc, or parabola before descending into the stomach of the stadium through one of the short feeder halls; all scattered energy unified now by collective anticipation. The way people moved, the character exuded by their bodies, was languid and assured. There was a smoothness of gesture in the tourheads, a lazy knowingness in their outlook, which infected the rest of the crowd and mingled with the excitement. The stiffness of the outside world seemed foreign here when seen in an usher or security guard. Some of them looked almost arthritic. We walked through the bleacher seats in the rear looking for Jane. We didn't find her, but stopped for a joint with three dreadheads I knew who were just sparking one up.

"Guys, this is my good friend Don," I said as we sat down with them. "Don, this is Anthony, Clay, and Pete."

"Yeah," said Anthony, shaking Don's hand. "I've seen you around, brother. Alpine last summer, remember? At the Americana."

"Oh yeah. That was a sick evening."

The joint came my way and I slowly inhaled a huge hit, taking the ripe smoke in tiny gulps one after another, then passed the joint to Anthony, whose long dreads were thick as my wrist and swept back into a bunch behind his neck. He tilted his head back a few degrees and raised the joint to his mouth, staring right through the arena's ceiling and the cloud cover and the atmosphere and the imaginary edge of the universe. His blue eyes were large slanted ovals with small tucks of skin at the outside corners, and this gesture was the one: a gesture so luxuriant and unstudied, so meditative and supremely self-confident, that it included both the saint and the hedonist.

He opened his mouth and smoke emanated from him. " 'China Cat' tonight," he said.

"Sounds good," I said. Don was standing and ready to keep moving. "Thanks, guys." They nodded at us, one small dip of the chin, which was their sign of respect, and we moved on.

"Jesus," Don said as we walked. "That night at Alpine was crazy. A whole floor of the hotel was tripping, everyone. All the doors to the rooms were open all night. Total insanity. The hotel didn't stop it, but they kicked us all out the next day."

"Wow," I said. "I was at those shows, but we camped out. That's where you met Anthony?"

"We didn't exactly meet. But I remember seeing him. He was with this incredible-looking dreadhead girl."

"Yeah, that's Jenna. She hasn't been around this fall."

"She was something, boy. Sweet God. That's really why I remember him."

"She is beautiful."

Don smiled, and I could almost see Jenna's diamond-shaped face and almond eyes floating in his mind. He shook his head. "What am I talking about? I've got Jane now. I hope I never see that girl again." He said this almost as an incantation, to strike her from his mind like an invading spirit.

We found a feeder hall with a clear but distant view of the stage and room to dance. Some other tourheads had already gathered there and started a coat pile, to which we added ours. I emptied my coat pockets into my pants before laying it down, a precaution I took though I had never had anything stolen at a show and expected I never would. I stepped up to the front of the opening, where the walls on either side of the hall blew outward and the ceiling disappeared, giving the impression of being in the bell of a great concrete horn. The stage was set as usual: twin drumkits on a raised platform behind the three mikes, the keyboard station set up on the right side, Persian carpet gracing the center and giving it the look of a living room, which in some sense it was for the band.

The acid hadn't kicked in yet, but my adrenal gland was working with a little anticipatory gusto. I dug my Camels from my pocket and lit one, savoring the moment. The stellar pot, along with the imminence of the acid and the show, was as fine a feeling as any. There was no place on earth I'd rather have been than there, with my own people. On their good nights the Boys tapped into a continuum that stretched back to whatever it was they had discovered at the Acid Tests. It was a torch they carried forward; sometimes it faltered, and sometimes it blazed like a sun. You never knew. I took a deep breath of stadium air as I surveyed the crowd, and thought I caught the first inner whiff of the drug as the visual panorama of people and colors seemed melded with the air itself for a second, entering my mind through my olfactory nerves. Cigarettes, pot, cloves, bright cotton, sweat, adrenaline, skin, concrete, dirt, serious elation, patchouli. It smelled like home.

The lights fell. The crowd noise surged in response. I turned and looked out into the hallway, at people rushing for the interior like smoke for an open car window. The stage became merely groupings of red green and white lights from the stacks of equipment. A mist of white light, so weak it barely existed, had its source somewhere behind the stage, and I saw the drummers' silhouettes as they took their places on the raised drum platform. Garcia's guitar came out first, just a few single-chord pumps to test the sound and tuning, then Brent pushed a run out of his organ and Billy began hitting his bass drum three beats at a time—*thump-thump-thump, thump-thump-thump*. The tuning went on for a minute or so and the crowd quieted. Garcia hit some bluesy riffs and at first I thought it would be "Hell in a Bucket," but they broke into "Alabama Getaway" and the dancers all around me exploded into movement. I would have preferred "Hell in a Bucket" as an opener, with its meaner guitar lines, but when I was dosed I tried to avoid being a critic. It was about motion, and milking the show for its great moments, using the music and movement as a meditation, trying to dance completely spontaneously, without thinking beats and bars ahead, becoming an extension of the sound. I let myself be mildly taken in by the straight-ahead rock 'n roll of "Alabama Getaway," but it wasn't until the central jam of "Promised Land," another rocker, that the acid began to seep in full force and I abandoned reservation and joined the fray.

Whipping hair all around. Black, blond, brown, bleached, greasy, clean, dreadlocks. Loose natural-fiber clothing everywhere covering bony limbs flying double-jointedly around twisting trunks as I danced into the middle of the small crowd in the hallway opening. Hands fluttered in front of faces like mating birds and bodies spun, jumped, swayed, and convulsed. The set list stopped mattering so much. Whatever the Boys chose was okay, right for the moment because it was what was happening. I caught sight of Don in the middle of "Dupree's Diamond Blues," his eyes clamped shut, his high not for sharing. He was doing a strange, stilted, high-stepping boogie with great seriousness, and suddenly he was the skeleton from Randy's shirts, had become in my mind the fleshed embodiment of that conflicted figure.

At intermission I wandered the hallway alone and saw no one I knew, which in itself seemed significant. The high from the half-hit was clean and mild, making a soup of the light and air and sound buzzing on all sides, and sending colorful molecular impulses through my veins and arteries when I swept my eyes quickly across the flowing people.

I came upon Don and had to gather in wild tentacles of nervousness when I saw Jane was with him. The sight of her amplified everything.

"You found her," I said.

"She found me," said Don. His face was flushed and his eyes excited, but otherwise he didn't seem heavily affected by the acid. Only then did I look around and see that I had come full circle to where we had been dancing for the first set. "What do you think of the acid?" Don asked.

"Nice. Very clean and smooth."

"Yeah, freshness guaranteed."

"You up, too?" I asked Jane.

"No," she said. "Just a joint of kind bud. I like Ex if I'm going to trip, anyway."

"You guys seen Cole around tonight?" I asked.

"No," said Jane. "Maybe he's still in New York."

"Well if you see him, remind him he's supposed to stay with me and Randy."

"Will do," said Don.

"You going to be in your room after the show?"

"Yeah, probably."

"Cool."

I saw the house lights drop behind Don and Jane, and people began finding their spots for the second set. The quirky, upbeat opening riff of "China Cat Sunflower" came through to us and I smiled. "Anthony called it. Nothing like a nice 'China-Rider' to start off," I said.

"Yes yes yes," said Don.

I moved to the front of the opening to get the stage in view, roiling dancers packed in all around me, moving cheerfully against each other. A row of girls in flowing Indian skirts swayed and spread their thin undulating arms like slack ropes being shaken underwater. When the transition jam at the end of the song came, we all got down to serious business, physically yanked about by Garcia's howling bent notes, faces strained or smiling or introverted, moving toward the next song like possessors of some arcane knowledge bound by oath not to squander it. Glancing up amid this frenzy, I saw Jane standing at the front, where the tier overhung the floor of the stadium. Her hands were on the railing, her eyes closed, her face inclined to receive the music at an oblique angle. We all knew what the next song would be, and that gave the vibe and the dancing a feel of group momentum, but sliding into "I Know You Rider," the tempo seemed too fast and I couldn't hook into it. I sidled to the edge of the knot of dancers and stood where I could see Jane, and beyond her the stage.

41

FOUR HOURS LATER, nothing to do with the acid deal was working out smoothly. I hadn't been able to find Nick and Chris to get the money, and hadn't seen Don since the show. Our room was a little crowded, and I was sitting against the wall in the corner with a guy possibly named Roger who was reciting a litany he had been laying on anyone who would listen.

"First I was drinking brewskis and smoking fatties in the lot," the guy was saying, "then I ate four green gels before the show, and a bunch of Ex, and then I was on the sixteenth floor drinking vodka and snorting lines of coke. A guy sold me some opium for the comedown, but I think I lost it somewhere, then I ate some more Ex and acid. Want to spark a joint?"

"Yeah," I said. "I could go for that."

"Cool. You got any buds?"

"Me? I thought you did."

"Nah." Possibly-Roger got up and felt his way along the wall to the door. He stood staring at the doorknob for two or three minutes before opening it and sliding out around the frame.

Watching him disappear into the hallway, I was hit with the change-of-atmosphere bug, a mild case of it since the acid had mostly worn off, but there it was. Fresh air, new places. I pushed myself into a standing position against the wall and felt for the room key in my pocket. I pulled it out and looked at the blue plastic Sheraton diamond. I would need it to get past security in the lobby. I found Randy on the sofa deep in verbal communion with a beautiful dark-haired girl. I said, "I'll be back in a little while." Randy just flicked his eyes my way and nodded, trying not to lose the moment.

I took the stairs, concrete and white-lit, twenty-two flights down. At the bottom, mesmerized by the long spiraling descent and the gray stairs scrolling by beneath my feet, I stopped before pushing the crash-bar on the exit door. I listened to the hum of the building: furnace, heating ducts, elevator motors, fluorescent bulbs—and above, within, through it all, a needle-sharp whine that might have been electricity itself shooting through the wiring like firing synapses through a brain. I was inside this thing, this building, and about to be outside. Through the door and the wind changed everything, flinging tiny raindrops at my face, blowing clean through my skull and cleaning out my mind. I walked down the sloping empty side street the fire exit let out onto. As the street descended, there began to be long triangular holes in the side of the building near my feet, then higher, moving up to chest level, where I saw they opened into the basement parking ramp. My Volvo was in there.

When I got to my car I stopped to look at it. The white paint was dull and streaked with gray-brown road silt. The rounded trunk with its soft subtle fins faced me. 1967. The car and I were both eighteen. I unlocked it and sat in the passenger seat, leaving the door open and one foot on the ground. Both front seats were covered in sheepskin, which the previous owner had for some reason sewn on. I activated the car's only luxury feature, a cigarette lighter that worked even without the key turned, grabbed the pack of Camels from the dashboard and lit one. The acid was mustering a resurgence, and the concrete beam in front of me sagged a little under the weight of a triangular shadow thrown by the one dim bulb along the row of cars. I felt my own cheek with one hand, the bones under the skin, this strange old fleshbox I lived in. Dropping the lighter still warm into the ashtray, I plugged the small boom box wedged between the seats into the socket and turned on the radio. I spun the dial slowly, searching for something to listen to, and stopped when I came to a melancholy trumpet solo. I smoked and the trumpet's glowing sound sluiced along the surface of my tongue, its texture moving from smooth to breathy, with moments of roughness, the inner voice of some ragged soul. It told a story of yearning and heartbreak, of pain pressed into diamond-hard beauty, and each note was filled with fugitive hope. When the solo was done there was a brief piano interlude and Chet Baker's simple, wounded voice eased into the last verse of "I'm a Fool To Want You." I reached forward and rubbed the dashboard. It was the first car I had ever owned. "How you doing?" I asked. The car didn't answer me. The song ended and another began, with no DJ in between, and this time I recognized Oscar Peterson's piano. I tilted my seat back as far as it would go and put one foot up on the dash.

There followed an indeterminate period of time during which the DJ's gravelly-smooth, ultrahip voice blended in and out of one mellow jazz tune after another and all was weightless memory. I felt again a time during the show, in the final far-reaching jam of "Playing in the Band," when I'd dropped deep into Jerry's groove, my body tied to his notes—not through any personal symbiosis, but because everything, including me, was happening at once. That was the groove you strove for, the oneness trip that dancing could take you on. I breathed, feeling the cold air dispersing inside me, thinking that even remembering it was dwelling in the past. Finally I sat up and brought the seat back upright. I unplugged the radio. The change-of-atmosphere bug had run its course and I wasn't dressed warmly enough to stay outside. I found myself shivering. I gave the dash one last pat before closing the door. "See you tomorrow," I said.

As I turned away from the car, someone across the aisle said, "Talking to your car?"

I spun toward the female voice, startled. I saw the orange ember of a cigarette hovering at the silhouette's side. I could make out one side of a smooth white face. A curving shade of cheekbone, pursed lips, an ear.

"Yeah, I guess so," I said.

"You just looked so peaceful, and the music was so nice, I couldn't help stopping and spying on you."

"That's okay. Do I know you?"

"No," came the answer, and she stood away from the car she was leaning on and walked toward me. Something in her gait was strange, just a hair off-kilter, and then I knew just before she became visible. She was wearing a thick down jacket and the right sleeve was tucked into the pocket. She took another drag as she neared me, and leaving the cigarette in her mouth offered me her left, her only, hand. "I'm Melanie."

I took her hand in my right and gave it a brief squeeze. "Jason," I said. A silent moment passed after we dropped hands, and she took the cigarette from her lips again.

"How'd you lose your arm?" I asked. The words formed themselves suddenly, and I felt only distantly mortified by them.

"Car accident," she said. "My dad was driving."

"When?"

"Seven years ago."

"That's rough."

"Yeah," she said, and flicked the butt hard, end-over-end across the row of cars, leaving a faint trail on my eyes, "that's rough." The cigarette splashed brightly orange off the roof of a car in the corner of my vision, like far-off warfare.

She looked at me. "You on tour with the Dead?" she asked.

"Yeah. Doing that thing. You ever see any shows?"

"No. I tried to get my mom to let me go to one of these ones, but she said no. I'm supposed to be in trouble."

"For what?"

"I got kicked out of school. Boarding school near here. My mom's trying to get them to give me another chance." She dug a pack of Marlboros from her jacket and pulled one from the pack with her lips. My hand in my own pocket was already on my lighter, and I took it out and lit her cigarette.

"What did they kick you out for?" I asked.

"Oh," she made a dismissive gesture with her hand, smoke trailing it, "I was in a boy's room after lights-out."

"Wow. Strict, huh?"

"Well, we were naked and drunk and in bed together."

I laughed. "I see. He get kicked out, too?"

"No, it was his first offense. Those things usually get blamed on the boy, but in my case they probably figured I came in there to prey on him like some kind of succubus with a bottle of Popov and my tits hanging out."

"But that's not how it went," I said.

She looked thoughtful for a moment, dragging on her cigarette. "No, that's pretty much how it went."

We laughed together, and in the laughter's aftermath I lit a cigarette of my own, smiling and shaking my head.

"You have a room where we can get drunk and naked together?" she asked.

This brought me up short. I inhaled some smoke and nodded. "Yeah, sure."

Up in the room the crowd had evaporated, and I saw with relief that Randy was alone on the sofa and hadn't gotten into the bedroom with the dark-haired girl. I introduced Melanie and got a funny look from Randy but nothing more. She went into the bathroom.

The suite we had taken had only one king-size bed, and though Randy and I could easily have shared it, the sofa was spacious and comfortable and we had decided to take turns on it. There was even a half-bathroom in the sitting room, for cocktail parties. Melanie came out and I pulled two of the last three beers from the minifridge near the bar and took her into the bedroom.

I held the bottles up. "Not enough to get us drunk, but it'll have to do."

"Perfect," she said, kicked off her shoes, and fell onto the bed. She picked up the remote, punched the television on, and accepted the opened beer from me.

She had taken the left side of the bed, which left her missing right arm facing toward me as she lay on her back, and made me feel awkward when I stretched out beside her. It seemed to me a strange or thoughtless choice for her to have made, until she rolled to me and we began kissing, and I realized that her left arm was free to embrace me instead of being trapped under her.

When her shirt came off, the place where her arm had been was only a small round bump off her shoulder, the skin on its outer surface smooth and white and veinless, the front of its inner edge ringed with pinkish scar tissue that shot back toward her body in points, like a quadrant of star drawn roughly. She threw herself around in feverish but natural-seeming motions, sometimes lacking the balance another arm would bring, but never shielding me from it or self-consciously ignoring it or keeping it from touching me. When I reached for the scar and touched it at first, thinking to alleviate tension, she reacted as she might have had I touched her knee, smiling and pressing it toward me but not lingering on it significantly. This quality itself—fearlessness, insouciance, strength, resignation, whatever it was—would have been slightly eerie in a girl her age even had she not been missing an arm, and it moved me to look deeper for its source. In her dark eyes and in the tilt of her features I thought I could infer something of what I expected from an amputee, a fissure, a dichotomy of expression as I looked from one of her eyes to the other, but if it seeped into her actions and words it was only as sexual ferocity.

It took a few minutes for me to come around to knowing I was excited by her missing limb. Partially it had to do with her imbalance, my body becoming the stabilizing element. But also, it occurred to me that her whole person was packed into a smaller space than had been intended for her, and it seemed to fuel her ferocity, as if her body were having trouble containing her.

"I don't have any condoms," I said, when we were naked and she lay on top of me.

"I'm on the pill," she said.

"Don't you worry about other things?"

She rolled off me but stayed close, her arm across my chest. "I've been with three boys. I know for a fact one of them was a virgin, and the other two were not far from it. And since you seem to be cautious, I'm willing to trust you."

She smiled at me and I smiled back, and we shared a conspiratorial moment across the vast gaps in her reasoning. Then she rolled back on top, put her hand in the middle of my chest for balance, and wiggled her ass. "Help me out here," she said, and I reached down to guide myself.

IN THE MORNING she was sleeping on her side facing me, but far away across the wide bed, and a thought occurred to me. I slid over to her and shook her lightly.

She opened her eyes and I said, "Hi there."

She tried to smile, her thick lips not quite remembering yet how to form one and ending in a squinting half-frown. "What the fuck do you want?" She ran fingers along my ribs.

"Won't your mom be wondering about you?"

Her face squinched in distaste. "Wondering? Sure, she'll be freaking out. Let her. She's used to me taking off overnight."

"She won't have them searching the hotel or anything, will she?"

"No." She looked at me and raised her eyebrows. "Worried about getting into trouble, huh? Don't. She hates scenes more than anything. When I was little once I got lost in a department store and after a while I got scared and started to cry and a salesgirl found me and paged my mom. Her reaction when we got to the car was to yell at me for embarrassing her."

"Ouch."

Melanie stretched and yawned and rolled over so her back was to me. The sheet pulled away, exposing her stump. In a moment of tenderness I cupped it in my palm and squeezed softly, finding it a little fatty, but with a core of bone and gristle slightly off center underneath.

"Can you feel that?" I asked.

"It's my fucking shoulder," she snapped. "Of course I can feel it."

"Sorry." I pulled my hand away. Later, I would learn to treat her stump the way she had trained herself to: as just another part of her—different, contributing to her uniqueness, but not extraordinary.

We lay apart and silent for a while. Then she spoke, her back still to me, and her voice was different, a sad musical sound like a trumpet. "Sometimes I imagine it's out there somewhere, even though I know it burned up in some hospital incinerator or something. Three times I've dreamed myself having it back, being whole, only three times. Other times I dream I see it through a crowd and everyone's stepping on it, or I find it somewhere, under a pile of laundry or in my bookbag, and I don't know what to do with it but I run around trying to find a doctor to sew it back on. Sometimes it comes to me, moving like a person on its own, and maybe it's too small for me because it's still a nine-year-old arm, or maybe it's grown along with me. It speaks to me, we sit down and have coffee and catch up, and it tells me what it's been up to and where it's been living and how it misses me, but I never remember exactly what it said in the morning. It always seems like if I could remember I could maybe go find it. One time it gave me its phone number and I repeated it to myself over and over in the dream so I wouldn't forget, but the numbers disintegrated as I woke up. I couldn't keep my mind around even a single digit of it."

I didn't know what to say. I was struck. I moved closer to her and kissed the back of her neck.

"Do you want to hear how maybe we're alike?" I asked.

"Yeah," she said. "I do."

I told her about my father, how he had gone to Syria to cover a story and had been arrested, accused of spying. How the American consulate had tried for four days to get him out before the news came he was dead. Other inmates had attacked him, the Syrians said, misguided patriots all of whom would be put to death, have no fear. But they maintained his guilt on the espionage charges. I told her about my dreams of my father: never ghostly apparitions, but glimpses across crowded streets and in airports, frantic dashes through mobs of people to find him, but always the one glimpse was all, and always, in that split-second glimpse, we would catch each other's eye and a moment of connection, recognition, understanding would swell between us and then disappear before becoming whole. It was that moment I was chasing in the dreams, not some idea that my father might still be living. Usually I was aware that I was dreaming, and that my father was dead, but I needed the moment to last longer, to reach fruition so I could hold on to it, carry the feeling of it with me into waking.

Melanie rolled to face me and just looked at me for a minute, searching, trying to see if I was for real, and for the first time I saw fear flash through her eyes.

"I know it's not the same thing," I said.

"I guess not," she said. "But I know why you told me."

Silence became uncomfortable. She got up and began to dress. I was surprised at the ease with which she did it. It didn't look smooth, but it got done fairly quickly. She saw me staring and said, "You believe I was right-handed? Pretty fucking impressive, huh?"

"Jesus yes," I said. "You going?"

"Yeah, I better. She'll be ripshit by now. Yes indeed," she was slipping her sneakers back on without untying them, "hell to pay."

"I hope it was worth it."

She knelt across the bed on one knee and grabbed the back of my neck, pulling me toward her. "Oh, fuck yeah." She smiled and kissed me. "Sweet boy."

Her profanity aroused me, the word *fuck* adding smut to her smile, and I wrapped her in both arms and squeezed her ass. "Sure you can't stay for a few more minutes?"

"I better not. It might turn into longer. I'm going to write down my parents' phone number in New York and you call if you want to. Tell them you're a friend from the chess club at Weatherbee and they'll put you in touch with me if I'm not there. That's the only thing I did at that school that everyone thought was good for me."

"Chess club?"

"I was captain. Not even the teachers could beat me." She went over to the desk and scribbled on a piece of hotel stationery, pulled

51

her coat from a chair nearby, said, "Bye, now," and swept out the door. I was just starting to feel a pang of hurt at the abruptness of her exit when she stuck her head back in. Her voice softened as it had earlier. "I mean it, Jason. Call me."

"Okay."

"Are you going to?"

"Yes, I'm going to. I'll be there next week for the Meadowlands shows, and I'll call then. Okay?"

"Yes yes yes," she shook her head side to side on each repetition and squinted happily. "Okay. Ciao, baby." And she left. Somehow that *Ciao, baby* made her suddenly seem a little childish—her own age, really—and it was like a chink in the armor of her false maturity, an expression thrown around by high school girls to make them feel worldly. I liked her maturity, how good she was at it, how it was beginning to solidify into the real thing. But I also liked seeing its flaws, which made her real.

3

MY MOTHER'S APARTMENT hadn't changed in the eight months since I had seen it. In fact it hadn't changed much since she'd moved into it six years earlier. The dark hardwood floors were strewn with earth-toned Turkish kilims and carpets containing the deep beautiful reds and greens of old vegetable dyes; bright finely detailed landscapes hung on the living room walls alongside family portraits and antique Ottoman tiles—all things, with the exception of the portraits, that my father had collected in our time abroad. He had also collected books, and the library was lined with them— many rare first editions, many not-so-rare, and a wall of paperbacks. He had been a true lover of books, never collecting purely for speculation or prestige. Being in the apartment had always felt both soothing and disturbing. Although James and I had gone away to boarding school shortly after our return to the States, spending little time actually living in the apartment, it was as close to a home as I had. But something about it had always symbolized the absence of my father to me. It was the place of my mother's aloneness, where she gathered around her her husband's things and the memorabilia of their life together, always ready with a sentimental or humorous story about the past, about him, the way a retired diplomat keeps souvenirs and stories of a long career.

I knew that to most her attitude meant she had assimilated the loss with grace and open eyes, refusing to be broken by it or shut it away, and to some extent this was true, but she had needed to be alone in order to accomplish it. She had moved to New York, where her marriage had its earliest courtship, where she had attended drama school, rather than back to Philadelphia where she could have rested in the bosom of her family. She could never have gotten through those first few years with the same apparent grace if she had had to live day in and day out with two speaking, breathing reminders of her husband. It was the inanimate mementos that helped her survive, the rugs and antiques and photo albums, while James and I were sent, for our own edification and character building, to boarding schools and summer camps. Grief had made her tired and was itself tireless, and she had needed space around her to manage it. But now that her life was in a groove that she found acceptable—with a manageable number of friends and social engagements, the occasional half-year romance with men she never introduced to us—she missed her sons and acted as if it were we who had left her, not she who had sent us away. James lived in Boston and was a jazz guitarist, and I had dropped out of high school and was "traipsing all over the country" as she put it.

She welcomed me and Randy in as she always did. I had called from Rochester to let her know we would be in town for a few days.

"You'll be in your room, of course," she said to me, sitting with us in the living room when we arrived. "And Randy, you can stay in James's room." She had met Randy twice before and was fond of him.

"That sounds fine, thank you, Mrs. Burke," Randy said.

Her light brown hair had been recently highlighted, and it had a hint of a wave to it, styled without giving in to the current trend toward volume. "You're quite welcome. And please, you must call me Elizabeth." She turned on me. "So, how's tricks, Jason?" she asked. She had a flair for combining high and low modes of speech, which came from her drama schooling. There was a challenge, maybe a resentment, in her tone.

"Great," I said. "Everything's cool."

"Well, that's what's important, I guess. Got to be cool these days."

"I'm going to put my stuff away." I got up and walked to the hall for my duffel bag.

"Did I say something wrong?" she asked.

"You're being uncool," I said over my shoulder.

I went into the library and unloaded a few books from my duffel. Whenever I was home I traded in the ones I had taken before and took some new ones. Without me they would have been nothing but shelf-dressing. I found spots for *The Rosy Crucifixion* (which I hadn't finished); *Rabbit, Run; The Comedians;* and *A Farewell to Arms.* I walked slowly along the shelves looking for interesting titles or writers I had read and liked. I picked out *The Green Ripper* by John D. McDonald. My father hadn't been a fan of the beats or any of the druggie writers, and I had had to find Burroughs, Kerouac, Hunter Thompson, and Kesey on my own. I pulled down a first edition of Walker Percy's *The Moviegoer* and put the two books into my bag. I'd come back for more before I left.

IN MY BEDROOM, Randy and I sat smoking cigarettes.

"I can't decide whether to call her."

"Why not?"

"Well, it was a strange night."

"Strange how? She's weird or something? Or is it the arm?" Randy reclined against the wall across the narrow bed and ashed in an empty Coke can in his hand.

"Neither. Just intense. In a way I'm not familiar with. Plus, she's a sophomore in high school, which makes her sixteen."

"So what? If you hadn't dropped out you'd be a senior now. What's the big deal?"

"I guess there isn't one."

So I called.

"Hello," a woman's voice drew the word out expectantly, and I found myself irritated at the sound of it.

"Hello, is Melanie there?"

"Who's calling please?"

"My name is Jason, ma'am. I'm a friend of hers from Weatherbee. We were in the chess club together."

"Oh, are you calling from school?"

"No ma'am. My father's ill and I came home early for the holidays. I'm in New York."

"Well, I am sorry to hear that. Nothing serious I hope."

"We hope not." I left a pause hanging.

"Well, I'll go get Melanie."

I heard hard shoes clacking across what sounded like marble, and then the woman calling, "Melanie! Someone on the phone for you. A friend from school."

Another extension was picked up and Melanie screamed, "I've got it, Mom!" and shortly the first one was hung up. Only then did Melanie speak to me. "Jason?"

"Yeah. How are you?"

"Oh, Jesus, not so good. It's been pretty hellish here. Weatherbee wouldn't take me back, and my parents are keeping me locked up."

"Think you can get out and meet sometime in the next couple of days?"

"I don't know," she said. "It's going to be tough."

"I told your mom my father was sick and I was home from school because of that. Maybe you could say I need a shoulder to cry on or something." I cringed at my choice of words.

"It might work. But I don't think so. Give me your number."

I gave it to her and hung up. I looked over at Randy, but he was staring at a book of Magritte paintings and knocking the head of his cigarette into the can.

COLE CALLED THAT NIGHT. He had been in New York the whole time, having decided to stay and party and let the tour catch up with him. Randy and I took the subway downtown that night to the Residence Inn where Cole was staying with a couple of guys from New Paltz. The room was like a small condo. It had a kitchenette, a refrigerator, and a suite of plush off-white furniture that made a strange background for the scraggly individuals sprawled out on it. The aura of a massive binge hung in the clammy air. Cole was expressionless in a pair of Guatemalan shorts and no shirt, sitting forward on the edge of the sofa. The television was turned off, its dull-black screen stretched wide like a big blind eye.

I had met Riff and Luke, the New Paltz guys, before. I introduced Randy. Riff, with his dark curly hair bordering on an afro, began to put a huge chunk of freebase into the glass pipe with an air of routine that spoke of how long they had been at it. There was no ceremony left in the act. Luke leaned forward and took the pipe gently, and as he lit it with a mini butane torch I could see the smoke billowing into the spherical chamber in its stem as if in slow motion. Luke was a very tall, gauntly handsome guy, straight-haired and a little sunken around his eye sockets. He lifted his head and passed the pipe to me.

It had been some time since I had done cocaine, and I'd only tried freebase once before. Traveling with Randy, I had gotten used to using only hallucinogens, and the occasional beer or booze. Randy disliked powdered drugs, with the exception of Ecstasy, and held coke fiends and junkies in low esteem. I sucked on the pipe as Luke lit it for me, and as a formality offered it to Randy. I was surprised when he accepted it and took a small hit, saying, "That's enough for me," and passed it along to Cole.

It wasn't long before the initial rush began to wear off and the familiar jones unsheathed its claws, attaching itself to my rib cage on the inside and licking at my spine with its rough, catlike tongue. It always managed to take me by surprise. *Oh yeah*, I thought, *I remember now. This is why I avoid this stuff.*

We freebased most of the night, and I battled guilt for not staying in and having dinner with my mother. She had tried to talk me into it, and then to guilt me into it. I hadn't stayed, but the guilt had moved in and the cocaine washed it to a squeaky sheen and nourished it and sicced it on me. It took shape in my mind as a fierce, grotesquely hairless dog. She was alone. She had lost her husband. She never saw her sons, and then when I did come I just dumped my luggage there and cruised downtown to party. But my mind countered defensively: I had suffered the loss, too. Was the loss of a father any easier than that of a husband? And besides, if it were up to her, I wouldn't be in New York now at all, I'd be up in Vermont at that boarding school, the one from which I had found it impossible to get expelled.

The guilt chewed through my defenses. I tried not to imagine her sad; the thought of her crying over me or things I'd done was something I could not handle—a thought that by turns pulled me toward her, making me want to embrace her and soothe her and convince her I was all right, and then just as strongly repulsed me toward resentment.

Around five in the morning I decided to quiet my mind by forcing it into sleep. I lay down on the carpet with a blanket and a pillow. Keeping my eyes closed was like clenching my fist around the wrist of a weak but struggling person and trying to hold them in check. Eventually my will solidified around that effort and I stopped having to concentrate on it, and my ears stopped converting the voices of the others into language, and the shaven dog and other apparitions lost their sharpness in my mind, and the carpet's scratchy fibers became part of the skin of my feet, and, for a split-split-second, nothingness.

A JOLT OF TERROR woke me and I was cringing and gasping and the agent of my doom crouched dimly above me shaking me and slurring my name for effect.

"Jesus, chill out, man. It's okay. We have to leave. They're throwing us out. Okay? Time to get up."

It was Cole. I dragged myself up and looked around. Randy was near the door holding Cole's bag. Luke and Riff were no longer there.

"What's up?"

"They're kicking us out. We didn't pay for yesterday. So it's time to go now."

"Where are Luke and Riff?"

"They left. They went back to New Paltz. They'll be back tomorrow. Come on."

"What time is it?"

"It's eight o'clock."

The three of us walked two blocks through the strange sunny New York morning. At the subway entrance I gave a dollar to a homeless man. We took the six train uptown, and I felt a certain communion with the grimy and graffitied windows, as if they were the filter through which I looked out at the world and the world a maze of dank tunnels. I felt at one with the yellowish train-car floors, marbled with filth, and the steel-on-steel clatter of the wheels on the track kindly battered my mind into silence.

My mother was awake when we arrived and I tried to brush past her, Cole and Randy in tow.

"Hi, boys," she said. And then to Cole, "I don't believe we've met."

"Mom, this is Cole."

"Hello, Cole. You guys want some breakfast?"

"No thanks, Mom. We need to go to bed."

"Burning the midnight oil, huh?"

She was trying to be hip, and it always seemed to work on my friends. They all loved her.

"Yeah, just a little," Cole said, immediately dropping into her mode and smiling at her, his charm made uncanny by the crash he was certainly going through. "I'm very sorry for showing up uninvited. You don't mind if I take advantage of your hospitality for the day?"

"Why no. Of course not. Jason's friends are welcome. Especially if he keeps bringing home such polite young men."

The harmony I had felt with my surroundings on the subway turned to dissonance in my own room: the soft clean bed, the lightly starched sheets, the down pillow, the silence; my mind was greasy and my body unruly, out of keeping with the memories the bed brought up of my younger selves home from school on vacations. I felt undeserving of such pristine comfort. But pristine comfort has a way of wooing, and I was soon asleep.

THE LAST PICTURE taken of my father shows him standing in front of an overturned jeep with two Syrian soldiers. They have their arms around each other. The black-and-white photograph was taken months before his final trip to Syria, by an Associated Press photographer who accompanied him to cover the Syrian army's entrance into Beirut. My father and the two soldiers are smiling broadly and dripping blood from various wounds, which their expressions say are too inconsequential even to consider. His head is laid open at the temple, blood runneling down the back of his cheek and along under his jawbone. He is cradling his right arm to his stomach, his left draped across the soldier in the middle, the driver, a short pear-shaped young man with a dark mustache thick as sawgrass. The other soldier is mustached and short also, but thinner, his fatigues better fitting, with the slightly mussed look of an officer in the field—two buttons undone on his shirt and stubble coming in on the rest of his face. They were thrown clear when the jeep slid off the dirt road and rolled down a stony embankment and are filled with the euphoria of survival, bursting with their luck. There is the flash of immortality in their eyes—all three.

How many times have I looked at that picture? Gone searching through the stacks of albums under my mother's piano for the scarlet one with the faded gold arabesque border and the leather peeled back at one corner of the spine exposing frayed cardboard underneath? I always start at the first page and work my way to it, past pictures of my mother's Cyprus church group—mostly English and Greek-Cypriot ladies with a few diplomats' wives thrown in, an Irishwoman, a Lebanese, a beautiful Dane I fantasized about—the only one missing being my mother, the presence behind the camera. I turn past pictures of my grandfather's sixty-fifth birthday party, for which my mother flew from Cyprus to Philadelphia—I remember that week as a time of rugged freedom, the three males left to shamble around the little house leaving glasses and plates around and board games scattered on the living room floor overnight, eating hamburgers and fried eggs and bowls of cereal anytime we wanted. Past my brother winning the fifty-yard-dash at the British school, and my father, in flat loafers, winning the fathers' race, and me placing ninth out of twenty-five for my age group in the three-mile run. The penultimate picture being the group photo of all the competing athletes at that Track and Field Day, James and I just two pale disks among over a hundred, blurred and serious-looking. Flipping that stiff page (taking care not to catch two under my fingernail and be faced with the series of empty pages that follow), and struck by the black and white after all that color—how real it seems, like the world after two hours in a movie theater—black and white taking up half the page. The smiling, bleeding faces. The bright sun and dusty arms across shoulders. The gazes meeting the camera in perfect, adrenalized unison: three men who are alive.

As I closed the album I heard my mother in the kitchen. A pot lid clinking. Something being banged off a spoon. Randy and Cole were still asleep in my brother's room. She put something heavy (a cutting board?) down on the counter, and a minute later a sizzling sound. I thought of going in and helping her, but the bumps and clinks and occasional footsteps were like a code and I just sat listening to them. There was a time, in other houses, when that code had been an invitation; hearing it from another room I would be slowly magnetized by it and would find my legs carrying me into the kitchen to see what was for dinner, taste it, pretend to be annoyed when asked to help. The sounds that made up the code were the same now, but it was as if the code had a different solution key, each individual sound a slightly altered meaning. What it meant to me now was this: Love me from out there. Love the idea of me, which can be real as long as you don't test it.

I WAS DEVELOPING AN OBSESSION with Tall Jane, as everyone called her. *Developing* is maybe the wrong word, because it seemed to appear fully formed. More like I discovered it. Nick found me at the first Meadowlands show and asked if I could still get that price on sheets of acid, and I swung a deal with Don that night.

In his hotel room by the Meadowlands, Don was cheerful and voluble. It came out that I was a reader, and he regaled me with his theories on society.

"I subscribe to the idea that all property is theft," he said. "I say this not as an indictment of property, but as an argument for the inevitability of theft." His eyes had the look of a philosopher who's been marooned on a desert island and is finally, after many grueling solitary years, getting to speak of his ideas. "Property among men is a given. It can't be avoided. As long as we've stood on two legs we've owned things. This is my club, my woman, my cave. Try and take one of them away and you've got yourself a fight. Even animals are territorial, for God's sake. But we don't *actually* own these things anyplace but in our own minds."

Jane came in and I began tuning him out. Any proximity I had with her was uneasy for me. Small things stuck with me: the slender sway of her hips walking through the door of their hotel room, the arch of her pinkie when she smoked, the way she folded herself up when she sat on the floor, legs tucked under a long yellow cotton skirt, toes poking out under the hem. I had to physically restrain myself to keep my eyes off her.

Don fronted me sixty sheets of acid, saying I could pay him the next day, and I headed out. The lobby of the hotel was covered in dull pink carpet patterned with crisscrossed gold rods, and as I walked through it I got a rush. I wasn't high except for a joint much earlier, before the show. This was the quickening of thought and perception that comes with breaking the law. I felt myself becoming larger, sharper, more vital. It wasn't a matter of good or bad, positive or negative, it was a matter of the size and extremity of my actions. What I was doing put me at odds with the organized forces of society. I was a public enemy, and I enjoyed it, not because I hated society—I didn't, really—but because I found romance in the idea. And because it bound me a little tighter to the people I had aligned myself with. In that big lobby, with its uniformed employees, its security guards near the front door trying to keep the heads at bay, I saw the Dead scene as distinct, like a bead of quicksilver rolling around in a tub of water.

There were two security guards by the door and another near the elevator, checking people for hotel keys as they entered. Two people per key was the rule. They had no idea what a feeble defense this was against the scamming hordes. Heads were wandering the lobby between the checkpoints, waiting to see someone they knew who had a key. I could see the multiple-key ferrying operations in full swing, people bringing their friends up one at a time until the rooms were full. Outside, no doubt, keys were being dropped out the lower-floor windows to packs of waiting partyers. I saw Hartford Bob ruffling his greasy curls and shuffling aimlessly across the lobby, trying to avoid the guards. I had seen him inside the show and knew he was Ex-ing heavily. He saw me coming from the elevators and headed for me.

"Hey, Jason." He gave me a brief hug. "You got a key, man?"

"No, I was just visiting. I'm going into the city if you want a ride."

"I need to get upstairs, man. There's this chick, Shelly, who wants to fuck me. I've just got to find her room. I forgot the number."

I laughed. "I hope you find it."

"Yeah, god, me too." He raised his head and looked over my shoulder, and from the clear attraction in his eye I thought he had seen her. "Look at that."

I looked around and saw the object of his interest: a black grand piano in the corner, surrounded by potted trees. Bob walked toward it. I stood and watched him. When he reached the piano, he smirked over his shoulder at me. Then he twisted the ends of an imaginary handlebar mustache, flipped back an imaginary set of tails with his hands, and sat on the bench. Just as he raised the lid on the keys, the guard by the elevator, a black guy built like a defensive end, saw him and made a beeline for him, not hurrying, but serious. The guard was halfway there when Bob spread his hands out formally, freezing half an inch above the keys for a second, then slid into the opening bars of "Someday My Prince Will Come." He knew he had to prove himself, and he began improvising lightly, beautifully, back and forth across the melody. The guard slowed, then stopped, staring at Bob's back. The soft jazz filled the room unobtrusively, adding a touch of peace to the embattled atmosphere. After a few seconds the guard nodded his head, smiling, and went back to his post. I left Bob there playing and walked out.

At a hotel in the city I sold forty sheets to Nick and Chris and the other twenty to Vince. I made six hundred dollars in three hours, counting the time it took to drive over to Don's hotel the next morning and pay him.

The second night at the Meadowlands, I searched for Jane in the parking lot before the show. I wandered around selling T-shirts and keeping an eye out for her. When someone stopped me to buy a shirt, I'd look constantly over their shoulder, annoyed that the transaction might make me miss her. When I did see her walking with her velvet board of jewelry, I stopped to talk to her, and I knew it was becoming clear to her that I was smitten. But she didn't seem to mind. The more tongue-tied and wide-eyed I became, the more her smiles warmed to me. When she smiled I had to look away because I was afraid something inside me might pop if I let myself drink it in for too long. That night, inside the show, it was hard to get into a groove dancing, and I found myself offering wordless prayers to the universe to bring her to me.

4

THE CROSS-COUNTRY DRIVE. I've always loved it.

The auras, for instance. The familiar sharpness, the history-paved-over aura of the East Coast that peters out little by little through the purplish-brown leafless November hills of western Pennsylvania, its edges still lingering like frayed gauze into Ohio where the Midwest begins its soporific expanse. After Ohio it's all farms and small convenience stores, sagging strip malls, John Cougar Mellencamp on the radio. The small cities are like chance conglomerations, people and buildings swept together at low points as if by draining water. There's a beauty to riding through southern Indiana's oceans of brown cornfields awaiting spring planting, stately run-down farmhouses and box trailers and mobile homes floating like white barges and dinghies on the placid land, listening to "Ain't That America?" and smoking and bobbing your head, singing along with the chorus.

In Indiana, we stopped at a big mall to shop for sneakers. It was five-thirty and people were streaming in from the stacked parking lots, having all just gotten off work, determined to dump their paychecks back into the economy before they even received them. The structure sat surrounded by flat asphalt and parking ramps, farting steam from its back end where the heating system struggled to keep the shoppers comfortable.

At Sears we found what we were looking for, the mainstay of Dead-tour footwear: Converse Chuck Taylor high-tops at fourteen dollars a pair. They were comfortable, cheap, and, being made only of canvas and rubber, relatively karma-free. Also, there was the brand name. Converse: opposite, contrary. If Nikes were about winning, Converse were about opposing, or, more beautifully, transposing certain elements of a thing to turn it into its own opposite—conversion. The word contained both rebellion and alchemy. Randy bought blue, and I bought black. Then we strolled through the mall's wide, vaulted walkways, under skylights, past fountains and lush trees and the food court where we ate warmed-over bean tacos and drank Cokes.

Small children everywhere tried to yank their parents around, pulling their arms and straining in the direction of arcades and toy stores, but the parents would not yield. I didn't see a single parent giving in, except to buy their children soft-serve ice cream at the mouth of the food court to shut them up. Otherwise, they stayed their own courses. The first Santa of the year sat gloomily in an atrium, but his only customers were a few slouching junior high kids who would probably tell him they wanted kegs of beer or hookers or submachine guns. Adults walked dazed through the place, as through a palace filled with treasure. Their heads swung wildly from side to side afraid they might miss what they were looking for, which was not a specified item but some vague dreamed-of thing that would complete some circuit of happiness in them. In a store filled with beautiful useless gadgets, we bought a set of walkie-talkies guaranteed to have a range of one mile. They made us happy. We walked separately around the mall, informing each other of our actions in cop-speak:

"I'm standing in front of the Gap, over."

"Anything happening there?"

"Observing a female individual who is of the extremely attractive type, and there is activity in my crotch. Over."

"Don't let her out of your sight until I get there. I'm on my way."

"Subject is bending over to look through a stack of shirts. Observing rounded buttocks. Extreme crotch activity. I repeat: extreme crotch activity. Loss of control imminent."

We took Route 70, which would carry us all the way to southern Utah and become 15 down through Vegas into LA for the Long Beach shows. We crossed Illinois, Missouri, Kansas. In Kansas the Great Plains become endless, taking up the entire state, and when you enter Colorado it seems wrong that there's nothing to mark the border but a sign, no change in the landscape, just more flat brown. Coming up on Denver, the Rockies rear up stunningly, like a miracle out of the low foothills, telling you nothing is endless; an end is always a beginning.

I preferred driving through the long nights, when we had the planet to ourselves. Nighttime trucks were ghostly behemoths, huge unmanned beasts of burden, and cars were dimly glowing worlds just for their inhabitants. The names of places meant more at night, shining on their signs in the headlights: Bethune, Golden, Arriba, Silver Plume, Rifle, Parachute. I remembered them, tried to understand the cryptic sentences they formed. And of course the white lines, bordered at the periphery of the headlights by dead grass, encroaching sand, earth, snow, dynamited rock faces, culverts, scrub brush, forest: the edges of things, hints of hidden vistas. While Randy slept I smoked and guzzled twenty-ounce coffees and put on the headphones with Fela or Lou Reed or Coleman Hawkins, or I listened to the rushing air and the engine, or crazy preachers and cheesy DJs on the radio. Delirium sometimes brought strange fears and visions in the predawn hours; cars coming the other way were suddenly on the wrong side of the road, the white line at the shoulder seemed to be leading me into a tree or signpost, indistinct lights flicked across the sky like UFOs. I felt the demons and angels that inhabited truck stops and side roads and overpasses and places where people had died, felt them as ominous propulsions causing me to jam the gas pedal to the floor, or as auras of protection and well-being that made me slow down and bask in them before they were left behind. When morning finally caught up with us—reaching brightly out across the starry sky or materializing slowly from inside white clouds—it always felt like the end of a lifetime, and for a few moments as the day broke, I looked back on the night with a nostalgia I imagined was like that of an old man for his youth.

Near dawn the third night we slashed through a desert rainstorm that didn't wake Randy. The old wipers struggled vainly to throw the deluge aside, and I slowed to forty, unable to see much. Then suddenly we were out of it into green starlight. To the southeast, stark black shapes of flattop mountains—ominous as the bodies of sleeping dinosaurs—were crowned by dimly glowing haze, backlit by the very first infiltration of sun, and all else was still night. An orange point of light pulsed near the top of the closest mountain. After staring at it for a minute, it came to me that it was a campfire. I wondered about the men sitting around it. Were they hunters? Fugitives? Drifters? Maybe just kids partying. I settled on fugitives. Prison escapees roasting a prairie dog killed with a rock. They were bad men, but they had made a daring escape and I was rooting for them. I lost sight of the fire as the sun rose behind the mountain, sharpening its silhouette for a few minutes and turning the eastern sky into a gold-platinum alloy.

We stopped at a roadside store called Pay 'n Take in southeastern Nevada to buy snacks and cigarettes. Some high school kids hanging out by the slots and video machines snickered at our hair. There were a couple of low whistles, but when we looked over they shut up. After we bought our stuff, Randy dropped a quarter in one of the slot machines and immediately won twenty-five dollars. The store owner, a gaunt man of about fifty with a smoker's voice, came over as we were sweeping the coins out of the trough.

"You boys twenty-one?"

"Yeah," said Randy.

I was afraid he might take the money back.

"Got ID?" he asked.

"No, we lost it," Randy said.

The man nodded his head and seemed to think this over. "Take what you've got there and get on out," he said. His tone was not quite unfriendly.

The high school kids followed us into the lot and one of them hissed at us. I wasn't sure what this meant, and I guess Randy wasn't either, so we ignored it.

"Hey you guys," the kid said.

We were at the car and we turned toward them. The lead kid approached us furtively and the other two hung back a few yards.

"You guys got any weed?" the kid asked. He had buzz-cut brown hair and was a little fat, but he carried it with an air of confidence. He was next to Randy, and I was on the far side of the car by the passenger door.

"No," Randy said. "Sorry."

"Come on," the kid said. "I know you guys got some. We got

money if you could sell us maybe just a joint." He looked over at me.

"Sorry," I said. "We're dry as a bone. I wish we did have some." I thought of the bag of great *indica* bud in my knapsack, pot like these kids had never dreamed of, and wondered how they might handle it.

The kid shrugged and turned away, walking back toward the store. "Hold on," I said. "Come here."

I opened the car door and sat down on the seat. I unzipped the front pocket of my pack, worked the baggie open without pulling it out, and extracted a small heart-shaped green bud. The kid was standing next to me. "Here, take that."

"How much?" he asked.

"Don't worry about it. Enjoy."

His squinting kid-toughness evaporated for a second and his eyes widened. "Wow. Thanks, dude."

"De nada."

Back on the highway, Randy shook his head. "That was about the stupidest thing I've seen."

"Yeah, but think of the fun those kids'll have. That'll ruin them for the shwag Mexican they're probably used to."

"Think of the time you'd do, no, make that *we'd* do, in some godforsaken Nevada jail for selling to a minor."

"I didn't sell it."

He gave me a look.

"Okay, it was stupid. But maybe that kid will learn something about generosity, too, while he's tripping out on that *indica* and thinking how he got it for free."

"Judge," Randy whined, "I was only trying to teach the kid some *values*. You understand Judge, don't you?" Then suddenly he wasn't smiling. "Oh fuck." He was looking in the rearview, and I looked back and saw the state trooper. A white Caprice, wide and low across its lane a hundred yards back and closing like death. The black rack of lights on top wasn't flashing, but watched us with dark menace. The whole thing flew vividly through my head: the arrest, the seedy holding cell, the harsh Nevada sentence, the prison time, and of course the anal rape.

"Don't worry, man," I said. "I'll take responsibility for everything."

Randy was silent, chewing on the inside of his cheek. I faced forward, and I could see the cop car in the side mirror. It came up onto our tail and rode us. I watched the corner of the roof rack, waiting for them to light us up. Our speedometer pointed exactly at the speed limit, and I suddenly felt that was suspicious and wished Randy would speed up just a hair, to show them we had nothing to hide. I was about to tell him to do that when the cruiser washed over into the other lane and slid smoothly past us, accelerating and quickly becoming a small white bead on the road ahead.

We both breathed for a minute, then Randy said, "No more stupid fucking around. Okay?"

EVEN ON THE WAY into the LA basin, as the low hillsides began to sprout condos like patches of white lichen, I felt good things in store. In California anything was possible.

Another beautiful thing about the tour was that we were always headed home. Out on the road we'd pass other carloads of heads and smirk and flash peace signs at each other or rap at gas stations. The legendary travelers on the American frontier—pioneers, mountain men, rail-riders, Jack Kerouac—had all followed their own evanescent ideas of a destination, and some had found them or built them, but we were true nomads: our home traveled with us. There was no need for us to be the lonely, peregrine souls our predecessors had been. If we had an elusive goal, a Shangri-la we pursued, it was one of the mind, maybe of the soul—those final frontiers—but we tried not to take it too seriously. At the end of every long drive there would be a stadium, a parking lot where Grateful Dead Land was beginning to sprout up: a van here, a school bus there, longhaired kids wandering the sidewalks and motel lobbies, all the harbingers of heavy, primordial rock 'n roll gathering in the air.

Randy and I got a room in a little twin-level motel near the Long Beach Arena, and we ended up right next door to the hard-partying Jersey crew. Frankie had come up with a vial of Ketamine. At the time I hadn't heard of it. The name Special K hadn't been invented yet. Frankie got it off a veterinarian in Berkeley. He and Evans and Earl and Vince spent most of their time holed up in their room whacked on this stuff. Frankie claimed he left his body and traveled to Pluto. The first night they tried to get me to take some, but I looked at the vial and saw the warning label, which read, *For use in cats and subhuman primates only*, and I declined.

The second night, after the show, Randy transferred his stuff into a black '71 BMW 2002 he had just bought with all his T-shirt money. Lauren, his old girlfriend, had come down from Seattle, and they were going to head back north together the next morning. I got the urge to strike out alone and decided I'd head up the coast that night, find a secluded beach to sleep on, maybe strum a few tunes under the stars. I went next door to see if Earl could sell me some buds, and Jane was there. Just her and the four Ketamine tripsters. She was sitting in a straight chair near the flimsy desk and holding the remote, smoking a cigarette. A small black puppy slept in her lap.

"It's good to see you." I walked over and gave her a hug.

It took me a while to get through to Earl about what I wanted. He kept trying to translate what I was saying into some language of groans he was inventing. Once he understood, he didn't want to be bothered with weighing it, so he let me eye out an eighth-ounce for myself from his big bag. I was a little generous.

"Well," I said. "I'm heading up the coast tonight. Find a beach and sleep under the stars. Guess I'll see you guys at the Kaiser shows."

"You want company?" Jane asked. She smiled. Her round cheeks were a deadly complement to her tall thin frame.

"Sure." Then I said, "Where's Don?"

"Don won't be joining us," she said.

She had very little with her. All of it fit in one black cotton Mexican bag that had a shoulder strap running from its drawstring mouth to its base. She slung it over her shoulder and tucked the tiny sleeping puppy under her arm, waved to the guys in the room, and we walked straight out into the parking lot. Getting into the car with her, winding slowly out to the freeway, I felt a childish nervousness. Not teenage jitters—that would have been only natural—but something from farther back, nervousness steeped in wonder, fear combined with the feeling that nothing could possibly go wrong. It made me remember when I was nine, driving down a Swiss mountain with my family at night. We had been skiing and needed to get to a hotel near the airport for a morning flight. There was snow coming down, and my parents had disagreed about whether we should leave. My father prevailed, as usual, and we piled into the rented car. My mother buckled herself in and every so often muttered things under her breath like, "*Insanity*," or "Sheer *madness*." Around the turns I could hear her sharp intakes of breath as the car drifted in its lane. I shared her fear, but my father's face was so slow and serene as it took in the road ahead, his movements so sure and solid as he rotated the wheel and worked the pedals, that I couldn't help being infused with his confidence as well, and fear and confidence formed a delicious soup in my chest. It was the first time I experienced something like being high. The feeling turned to pure excitement, charged that night with wonder, and every glowing snowflake and quiet shush of tires moving sideways on snow exploded minutely into my memory. As we headed north on the 405 through all of LA, I felt the same way about the lights winking conspiratorially at me from the buildings and hillsides, and I felt kinship with the people inside those apartments and houses, families with little boys sleeping in back bedrooms while the parents watched the late show and drank gin or beer, drunks fighting sleep to postpone the terrible morning, coke-addled struggling actors chewing each other's ears off about all the work they'd almost gotten, maybe even a few real movie stars on benders in hotels; so many unknowable lives. They were still awake with us, had stayed up late so their lights would be on when Jane and I passed.

It was a different world when we hooked back up with the Pacific Coast Highway. We cranked the windows all the way down and let the sea air whip through the car. The beach houses of Malibu slid by, most of them long and low, giving a slow motion feel to the drive. The smell of the sea, the palms and small beaches and waves like easy breaths, made the garish city behind us seem like overkill. Jane kicked off her black canvas slip-ons and propped one long foot on the dashboard while she smoked. She was so tall that this brought her knee very close to her face, her wide white Indian-print skirt becoming a tent.

Don had dumped her, she told me. He flew into an irrational rage during an argument, threw three hundred dollars at her and told her to go get her own room, and while she was at it she could look for another ride up to the Bay. She had taken the money, but had walked down to the smaller motel and hooked up with the Jersey crew instead of spending it on a room. "He can go fuck himself," she said. "That's it."

I didn't answer this, but nodded my head. I didn't think it would be wise to agree that he could fuck himself, but I wanted her to know I sympathized. She was staring out the window. I wondered about my friendship with Don. It was hard to know how far into the wrong I was, and whether he and I would get beyond this. The morality of the situation was hazy. It was possible that what was happening was only natural, and nothing would come of it, but I had to admit that wasn't the likeliest possibility. I wanted to ask Jane how she thought Don would take it, but bringing him up seemed a bad move; also, it would be assuming that something was actually happening between us, which hadn't been established.

We stopped at a convenience mart for some water and puppy food. Wandering around in the little store together was exhilarating—Jane called questions to me across the aisles as if we were used to shopping together: "How about some peanuts?" "Sure, sounds good." The bleary-eyed Mexican clerk must have taken us for a couple, and I hoped he was right.

We drove out past Ventura along the coast and found a state beach that had a small parking lot. I pulled my sleeping bag from the trunk and stuffed a pillowcase with sweaters. Wooden steps led down to the beach, and we walked north about two hundred yards, carrying our shoes, and tucked ourselves up near some scrub and low sandy pines. The puppy was awake now. It strained against the long piece of clothesline Jane had fashioned as a leash and ran yipping around us, biting at our ankles. We laid out the bag and sat down on it. It was a calm low tide, and the water was some distance away, its whispers blowing airily across the sand and over us.

I had thought we might smoke a joint, but the feel of the place needed no enhancement. The puppy was getting hysterical, pulling on any loose piece of cloth and shaking its head viciously. Jane gave it the toe of her shoe to latch onto and it began a tug-of-war with her, its growl a high-pitched parody of fierceness. We shared a cigarette and waited for him to calm down, but he didn't.

"He's got some pit bull in him, I think," Jane said. She decided to walk him and try to tire him out. She took him down to the water and he barked at the small waves, attacking them. I could hear her laughing softly and talking to the puppy, but I couldn't hear what she was saying. She ran northward along the beach, and the dog followed. Her upper body became invisible against the ocean as she receded, but the white cloth of her skirt still floated and shape-shifted spectrally, and the pale flashes underneath were the soles of her feet. She kept going until she disappeared completely. I stared hard into the night, waiting for some sign of her to reappear, and my chest clenched just slightly, the way it had eight years earlier by the Gulf of Oman, watching my father swim.

She didn't come back for a long time, and I climbed into the sleeping bag and lay on my back awake, trying to make my mind blank. A high black pine branch swayed overhead against the almost-black sky, hypnotizing me.

"You up?" she whispered when she got back.

"Yeah."

"He's still pretty hyper, but he sure tired me out."

She tied the leash to her wrist and crawled in with me. The dog began chewing on my hair and pulling it, his lungs sounding like a tiny steam engine running full-tilt.

"This isn't going to work," I said. "Here . . ." I untied the lash from her wrist and stood and walked the puppy to a nearby tree, tying him so the cord would bring him up just short of us. I gave him my sweatshirt to bed down on. He barked for a few minutes, but then quieted down. Jane was breathing heavily, either from strain or emotion, and I wrapped her in my arms. I kissed her cheek (it was firm and round, better even than I had imagined it), and ventured another farther in, catching the hiplike swell at the base of her nose. She kissed me once, on the side of my mouth, and we fell asleep that way.

"AAAAHHH!" I woke to my own voice screaming. Pain in the side of my head. I put my hand there and grazed the tail end of the puppy retreating from its guerrilla attack. It had slipped its leash and scampered over and bitten right through my ear.

"What is it?" Jane lifted her head from the makeshift pillow and struggled to open her eyes. It was bright out, but we were still in the shadow of the trees, which stretched far out onto the beach before the new sun.

"Look at this." I showed her the blood on my fingers. "That thing just mauled me."

"Wow, bad dog." It was almost as if she were talking to me.

"Jesus, no kidding."

She looked at my ear. "He got right through there. I know what you need."

"What's that?"

"A swim, to clean it off." She was up and shucking her skirt and T-shirt before this could even register. She was wearing panties but no bra. Her tall thin body was round in all the right places, her breasts a little bigger than I had thought. "Come on," she said, skipping toward the water, the puppy leaping along behind in a frenzy of glee, "get moving, slowpoke."

I stripped to my boxers and ran after her. She didn't slow at the light cold surf, but bounded through it and dove in, driven either by fortitude or her own nakedness. I did the same, driven by pride. We swam for a few minutes while the puppy barked shrilly from shore and attacked the waves. We spoke in breathless generalities: "Whooh! This is cold!" "Yeah. Feels great!" We swam close to each other, me following her, then her following me, but didn't touch. When we waded out I shook the sand from my sweatshirt and gave it to her, and she put it over her wet body. She dried her legs with her own long-sleeved shirt and slipped into her skirt. I shed my boxers, put on my shorts, and paced to let the air dry me. There had never been a finer morning.

Back at the car, Jane took a pint of vodka from her bag and swabbed my ear with it. "Hey, I've got an idea." She pulled a velvet pouch out and rummaged in it until she came up with a small gold hoop earring. She flicked a lighter underneath it to sterilize it, then blew on it to cool it, and put it through the hole in my ear. "It's really quite a clean little hole. It's going to look pretty hip."

She pulled back to take in the effect.

"How do I look?" I asked.

"Fabulous," she said, and leaned in and kissed me.

Ten minutes we kissed, there in the front seat of the car. Then we ducked back from each other and smiled, that gauging look after the first kiss. Just having the freedom to stare into her lush eyes, her soft green world, not to have to look away, was powerful. One simple fact subsumed all others: she was the most beautiful girl I had ever been with. Looking at her was deep pleasure. I reached and tucked her wet curly hair behind her ear.

"Where's the puppy?" she asked.

"I don't know."

"Puppy!" she called, getting out of the car.

I got out, too, and whistled.

"Here, puppy!"

We walked around the lot, then back down to the beach. Jane went north and I went south along the water, calling out. Back up to the lot, across the road to the wooded hillside, back down to the beach. No puppy.

After two hours of looking, we started to talk about moving on. Since Jane had had him for only a couple of days, she was willing to consider this.

"I'm sure he'll be fine," I said. "He probably just took off down the beach and kept going. Somebody will find him and take care of him."

"You're probably right."

We made another pass over the area. I shook the bushes around where we had camped, whistling, fearing when I bent down that I'd see him crouched in among some half-buried Pabst cans, wagging his vicious little tail. But he didn't turn up. Back by the car, Jane stood looking toward the beach.

"Poor little guy. He didn't even have a name yet."

"Maybe someone else will name him."

She tilted her head back to inhale the breeze off the sea, accentuating the smooth turn at the base of her jawbone, usually hidden by the padding of her rounded cheeks. I thought she might cry, but she smiled instead. "I'll name him right now." She closed her eyes and spread her arms. Her left hand came very close to my face and I tried to take it in mine, but she pulled it back and took a step away from me, her eyes still closed. "The puppy's name is . . ." she made small circles with her hands, ". . . Sign."

"That's the name? Sign?"

"Don't you like it?"

"Sure, I like it. Better than Fido." Right then I became afraid that whatever I thought was happening between us wouldn't happen.

I had my car door open, and she opened the passenger side.

WE HAD THREE DAYS before the Kaiser shows in Oakland, and we traveled slowly up the coast. We got a motel room near Morro Bay, too far from the beach to see the ocean but close enough to feel it, and made love for the first time. We stayed up most of the night, unable to get enough of each other. The next morning, I woke up before Jane and went out on the room's tiny concrete terrace for a cigarette, and to do some thinking. I slid the glass door shut behind me. I was in my boxers and one of Randy's black skeleton T-shirts, and I sat in the metal chair with dirty white rubber webbing across the seat and backrest. The terrace faced east, and below it was a vacant sandy lot grown over with sawgrass, baby palms, rusted iron barrels, and piles of colorful garbage.

"Mornin'."

I looked to my right and saw an old man on the next terrace, only about ten feet away, sitting in his chair and smoking. His skin was brown and sun-ravaged, slipping off his puffy face and pointy shoulders in pastry-thin droops. All he wore was a pair of new jeans, and his tan gut hung out over his beltline as if he'd swallowed a watermelon, accentuated by the skinny arm resting across it.

"Morning," I said.

"Looks like a fine one."

"Yeah." I took a drag and nodded. "It does indeed."

"Feelin' good, are you?"

"Yeah, I'm feeling just fine. How about yourself?"

He uttered a strangled little laugh. "Well . . ." He made a small sweeping gesture with his cigarette that, along with the laugh, somehow explained his entire condition. I nodded and looked down at the vacant lot below.

"I bet you're feelin' good."

I nodded but didn't answer.

"Heard you last night. Fun. Heard your girl." He laughed in the same way. "Wooh! Fun. Bet you're feelin' good." He was drunk.

I nodded and lifted the corner of my mouth to show him I understood, all in good fun, but didn't look at him and hoped he would take the hint. I was thinking about how there was something physical about Jane that tugged at me whenever I looked at her, a gentle pull on some fishing line threaded through my stomach, how her toes and the tendons behind her knees and her collarbone drew my hands to them. But our conversations held no electricity. When we spoke we both projected a false warmth to mask blank distance. We smiled a lot. I told myself I was too young to worry about good conversation; I told myself just to go with it.

"I'd sure be feelin' good. Old man like me could use some of that. Yes, yes. She suck it for you?"

"Take it easy," I said, getting up and opening the door into the room.

"C'mon. Little girl suck it for you?"

"Bye bye." I shut the door behind me.

Jane woke as I was putting my jeans on. She rolled and breathed and told me to come over there. I went to the bed and sat next to her and we kissed and she said, "Get those clothes off and get back in here."

"I kind of want to get going."

"We'll get going after. Come on." She was pulling at me.

"Let's do it later," I said. "In the car maybe."

"Then too." She kissed me and gave me her whole tongue and

that was it: I started scrabbling at my boxers. But much as I wanted to I couldn't lose myself in it. Whenever she got close she started moaning and I backed off my rhythm. "Come on!" she said, so finally I clamped a hand over her mouth and went ahead, and we came at once and she and I both screamed.

I slid off her. "Oh, shit," I said, shaking my head, smiling.

"What?"

I laughed. "Nothing. That was great." The old man must have thought I was putting on a show just for him. I didn't care.

5

JANE AND I stopped in Carmel to spend a night with Harry, who had moved there from New York a few years earlier after his mother died and left him her millions. Harry Waldron was my father's oldest friend and the most consummate cynic I have known. His cynicism stemmed not from insecurity or nihilism or depravity, though he possessed dashes of each, but from a fine distillation of bitterness and intelligence and a strong measure of basic decency which, because he couldn't account for it intellectually (he was too proud of his cynicism) or live up to it, caused him mostly pain. That decency also had the side effect of making him lovable. Cynicism was an art form to Harry, and he wielded it with such grace and acumen that even those who were the brunt of it were usually charmed. Every so often, though, his bitterness would poke through, like a broken bone through the skin.

When we came to New York after my father's death, Harry used to take James and me to ball games, movies, art galleries, concerts. We'd spend weekends at his loft on Bond Street in the

Village, where he had a photography studio and a mammoth record collection. The loft was large, with thirty-foot ceilings and two raised sleeping platforms, one for his bed and a bigger one that held another bed and his stereo equipment. Running between the platforms was a hallway connecting the studio in back with the living room and kitchen in front. Under one platform was the bathroom and under the other his darkroom. There were ashtrays on almost every flat surface, to accommodate Harry's endless production of spent Marlboro 100s. On a Sunday morning I would watch from the guest bed as he would wake and shuffle down the steps from his platform into the kitchen in his white boxers. He would turn on the hot water tap, pull a mug from the cabinet over the sink, dump two teaspoons of Maxwell House instant coffee into it and wait until he was sure the tap water was at its hottest before putting the mug under the stream. In the living room he'd sit—his shirtless chest thin and pale, one bare foot propped on the coffee table displaying a fungal big-toenail, green and opaque as a rotten potato chip—and smoke his first cigarette. There was no music during this time, and talking was discouraged.

Cigarette and coffee finished, he'd slide a pair of pants onto his bony frame and a polo shirt over his head and we'd go out for breakfast. The winos who slept in Harry's doorway and those adjacent knew him by name. Sometimes we'd open the door and find one of them still asleep in our path. "Morning, Tom," Harry would say, and the man would look up heavy-lidded, sniffling. "Mornin', Harry." And Harry would give him a dollar or two for breakfast. It has occurred to me since then that Harry felt a kinship with these men because on some level he knew how fine a line separated them from him. During most of that time following my father's death Harry was sober—his longest period on the wagon—but he was a mean drunk, impossible to be with when he was on a tear, one of those drunks whose self-loathing while drinking gets puked out onto all those who love them most.

He and my father were best friends in high school and had both been admitted to Harvard, but Harry was asked by the university to take a leave of absence after his first year and come back when he was ready to get down to business. That day never came. When the late sixties rolled around, Harry, a little older than your average hippie, got deep into the drug and art culture. His wealthy mother bought him the loft and then cut him off, and he eked out a living as a photographer, doing portraits, weddings, and eventually pulling in decent money making slides of paintings for museums. He was good at this, and when he was on a job, being in the loft could be tedious as he developed and redeveloped rolls of film of a single painting, trying to get the colors absolutely right. "How does that look?" he would ask, holding the slide viewer next to a print of a Monet. "Wow, looks great," I'd answer, and it was true; I couldn't see any difference. "No," Harry would say. "See how the reds are a little too pink?" "No." "Well, they are." And he'd start over.

Inside the front door of his loft were two framed posters on the wall side by side, one of Mozart and one of David Bowie. He had every recording of David Bowie ever made. He had albums, bootlegs, German pressings, picture discs, some of them valuable collector's items. He loved to boast that he had once had dinner with Iggy Pop. He turned me on to rock music and taught me what was good and what sucked. He didn't understand my love of the Dead when I took it up, though he chaperoned me at my first show when I was thirteen. He respected the band, their authenticity, but the music bored him.

I started smoking pot with Harry when I was sixteen (though I had started on my own three years earlier). We were sitting around his living room listening to a very sinister, vaguely necrophiliac neopunk band called Magazine *(I want to drug you / And fuck you / On the permafrost),* and I made an excuse to go to the corner store so I could smoke a bowl. "Listen," said Harry, "if you're going to get high, don't you think it's a little rude not to share?"

So I packed the bowl and we smoked together, no fanfare. Harry didn't get high often, but from then on when I was with him I didn't hide it.

After a simple breakfast in a local diner, we'd usually just wander the Village, browsing at Bleecker Bob's, where the guys all knew Harry and hailed him. Harry would sweep through the store's aisles like an emperor in his own treasure vault, ignoring the "No Smoking" signs on all the walls and never being called on it. Sometimes they'd bring him an ashtray. Lunch at Phebe's, freak-watching in Washington Square, midnight showings of *Rocky Horror:* through Harry I was indoctrinated into Village life.

Harry had an Italian wife who lived in Italy. They had been separated since long before I knew him, had maintained a civil relationship, and never did get divorced. But before that, before my father, Harry had dated my mother. He liked to say that in hindsight, she was the love of his life. He had left the country when their relationship was at a low point and returned to find his best friend engaged to her. It took years for the bad blood to clear. "You ever want to give yourself a scare," he said to me once, smoke leaking from his smirking mouth, passing the joint my way, "think about how close you came to being my son." At the time it didn't sound so bad.

THE LITTLE BLACK ASPHALT ROAD to Harry's house wound very steeply into the foggy Carmel hills, straining the old Volvo's motor, then leveled off and gave way to dirt for the last quarter mile. These were real lush California hills, grown over with ferns and cypresses and pines, and the still fog infused the greenery with California's organic gnosis—that feeling that things are known here if only one would seek them.

Harry's house was sided with natural wood, built into the hill, and his silver Mercedes crouched sleekly in the drive. He greeted us at the door.

"Hey Harry," I said. "How are you?"

"I had an abscess on my ass the size of a softball yesterday." He was gaunt as always in a beige cashmere V-neck, his fingers dangling their standard Carlton 100 (he had switched from Marlboros for tar reduction). A few dubious eels of dark hair still striped the top of his bald head, and his face was a map of wry etched vertical lines that gathered themselves perfectly around the ironic grimace that passed for his smile.

He was in good spirits. Not drunk. I was glad. I gave him a hug.

"Harry, this is Jane."

Harry showed her his best serious face. "Jane. Hi there." They shook hands.

"Jason's been telling me all about you," she said.

Harry looked at me. "And I trusted you."

We sailed down into the village of Carmel in Harry's Mercedes for dinner, cranking the Dixie Dregs at volumes that shook the car to its frame. I drove and Harry sat on a thick foam pillow shaped like a toilet seat. We ate in a restaurant owned by Clint Eastwood, and Harry drank Coca-Cola and shifted uncomfortably in his seat and was on his best behavior.

Harry and I talked about music, about how he hated AA meetings, about the 49ers having lost him a hundred dollars the previous weekend, about how much he loved doing Ecstasy, which I had turned him on to almost a year earlier. He asked Jane polite questions and I listened carefully to the answers: she was from New

Haven, had finished high school there and done a summer Dead tour as her graduation celebration, then deferred her entrance to University of Connecticut and just kept touring. She was a year older than me.

When we got back to the house, there was a small thin man about Harry's age, with shoulder-length gray hair, sitting on the couch. He looked up at us but didn't offer a greeting.

"Kids," said Harry, "this is Liam, my gardener. Liam, this is Jason and Jane."

"Jason, Jane. I'm very pleased to meet you." Liam smiled as he spoke, and his voice was so soft it was barely audible. He had the vestiges of an Irish brogue.

"Come over to trim the hedges, you lazy bastard?" Harry asked him.

Liam laughed. He pulled a bag of pot from his jacket and asked if we smoked. I looked at Jane and she nodded yes. So we sat around listening to Elvis Costello and Al Green on Harry's incredible system and got high with him and the gardener.

THE FOG HAD ROLLED BACK down off the hill and dissipated in the night air. The Carmel Valley stretched below us under a three-quarter moon that silvered the tops of trees, bushes, and houses, here and there a road marked by darting headlights. Jane and I stood on the deck outside the living room. I felt the rough wood of the rail on the skin of my hands. Harry had put on "Exile on Main Street" and the music drifted thinly out onto the deck, making me brim with stoned nostalgia. I passed an arm around Jane's waist. We began softly to kiss, she with her eyes closed. I could see her eyes sliding back and forth under their lids, feel the press of her hip into my hand. I took her earlobe between my fingers. It was a big kiss. There was so much in there and she was far too beautiful for me, I knew that. I tried to take it in stride, not to seem overwhelmed by it. I stood in the face of it as strongly as I could, leaned into it straight-backed, like a sailor taking a swell, and was surprised to find myself able to withstand it, even to control it a little and use it.

When our mouths slid apart we embraced and by my ear I heard her sigh almost in exasperation. "Jesus," she whispered.

I decided not to speak.

"Oh, Jason," she said, still whispering. I loosened my grip and we pulled halfway back, but she took one look at me and dove into my neck again. "Oh, fuck." She pounded on my back with her fist three times, hard: "Fuck, fuck, fuck."

Inside, Harry and Liam sat on opposite ends of the long sofa soaking in the music, Harry with a cigarette and Liam with a smile. We came in through the sliding door and fell together into a wide leather armchair. All four of us were silent until Liam sang softly along with Jagger, "Got to scrape the shit right off your shoes."

Harry put out his cigarette, and when the song ended he tapped another from the pack, reaching for his lighter.

"Shouldn't you be cutting that shit out?" Liam said to him.

Harry inhaled the first drag and said, "Fuck you."

"I'm serious, Harry. It's no fucking joke."

"Don't get serious on me. I'm in no mood. And you're no good at it." Harry forced a laugh and it brought on a cough, which turned into another and then he was hacking and wheezing for a full minute. It was painful to watch and listen to.

"Jesus, Harry," I said. "Are you all right?"

"Fine," he wheezed, leaving the lit cigarette in the ashtray and leaning back. He was panting like a small dog.

"Bullshit you're fine," Liam said. "Don't lie to the boy."

Harry sat still for a minute, quiet except for his whining inhalations, his narrow chest rising and falling steadily slower until his breathing was back to normal. Then he reached forward and took another drag from the cigarette. "Emphysema," he said. "I've got fucking emphysema. So what. I'm an old man. Old men get sick."

"You've got to give up the squares," said Liam. "I shouldn't have let you smoke that joint."

"Let me?" Harry's voice turned dark and firm and he cocked his chin to the side to stare at Liam, a stare that carried the full weight of his condescension. "What are you, my fucking Irish nanny?"

Liam shook his head and looked down.

I said, "Harry, have you tried to quit, or cut down at all?"

"Sure I've tried. I'm smoking these fucking ultra-lights anyway."

"Well, is it bad? What does it mean?"

Harry kept smoking. "Who fucking knows what it means. It's a crapshoot anyway. If I'd been a coal miner I'd be dead already."

The album ended. Harry hit a button on his remote and the Velvet Underground came on. "I am going to quit, though," he said, putting out his smoke and resting his chin on the back of his hand. "I just have to find the right time, the right way. Maybe I'll get hypnotized." His lower lip was shaking minutely from the effort of holding back a cough. Liam picked up a lighter and hit on the roach.

Harry said, "So where's next for you two?"

"We're going up to Oakland for some shows, and we'll probably hang there for a while," I said.

"Far out," said Harry, an expression that coming from him had always resonated with libertine undertones: he was too old for it to be just a phase, and he could never seem airheaded. "I can't understand why you're hooked on that lame fucking music, but I kind of envy you. I can see the draw—no responsibility, just fun and freedom, right? Just travel and raw experience."

"Yeah, that's part of it, I guess."

"Everyone's got to have that sometime in their life. My time was in Rome with your mother in sixty. Freest time I can think of. We stayed in a little pensione, got drunk in jazz clubs every night, slept off hangovers till one or two every day. Saw the sights, but not so many of them that we felt like tourists."

"I'm not sure I want to hear about this," I said. I smiled and leveled a finger at Harry. "Don't you burst my bubble. As far as I'm concerned my mother never got drunk in a jazz club with the likes of you."

Harry got his malicious little grimace in place. His look said, *Oh, the things I could tell you, little boy.* "She drank, all right, kept right up with me. Americans weren't hated over there yet. We danced with everyone in those places—all the locals wanted a shot at your mother, she was a real standout girl. Beautiful. People loved her, and I just rode her coattails to instant popularity. The old lady at the pensione hated us, though, charged us double. We'd come in late and make all kinds of noise."

"Enough with the kinds of noise," I said. But I didn't really want him to stop altogether. "So she was a little wild in her youth, huh?"

"A little? When it was time to fly home, she didn't want to leave. Well, I didn't either, but she was serious. She tried so hard to talk me into staying there. She imagined getting work in restaurants and living in a squalid little flat where I would write depressing cynical poetry and get famous eventually. She had even talked the owner of this little place where we ate every day into offering her a waitress job. She didn't speak much Italian, but she charmed him into it. If I'd agreed, we might still be there. Who knows, maybe I'd be a famous poet by now."

"Wow," said Jane. "That's so cool. What great memories. Why didn't you stay?"

"I wonder that sometimes," Harry said. "But really I didn't want to live in some coldwater tenement in Rome and sling pasta at tourists. I knew I was no poet, and my mother was about to cut me off from funds if I didn't 'settle down.' She did that anyway a few years later." He paused, regaining his train of thought. "It would have been a fucking disaster. Neither of us was cut out for that kind of living, though Beth didn't know it yet. It's much nicer not having done it, to have it to think about. If you do it, then it's harder to idealize it later. This is all probably the reason I went back and married an Italian, after Beth ran off with my best friend. God knows that didn't work out—my marriage, that is."

Jane leaned forward, toward Harry. "She ran off with your best friend?"

"My father," I said.

"Oh, right."

Harry hit the remote control again, and J. J. Cale came on, singing "Call Me the Breeze."

The vision of my mother as wild and popular was hard to digest. I couldn't picture her drinking and laughing and dancing with a stream of desirous Italians. But I believed Harry. I wondered whether my mother ever idealized that time. Whether she ever imagined her life having stayed in Rome with Harry, imagined James and me with darker hair and bleaker outlooks, our unshattered little family spouting fluent Italian over a big lasagna at Christmas. Though of course Harry's drinking would have shattered everything if nothing else did. Harry started coughing again, a deep coarse sound. He doubled over in his seat, buried his face in the crook of his elbow. I wanted to smoke, so I got up and went back out onto the deck and around the corner of the house where he couldn't see me.

6

EARL HAD FOUND a fallen palm branch whose thick end was cocked back like a wrist and formed a big cup of wood, and he was wearing it as a sort of headdress. The branch stuck straight up from his head about seven feet, and he had to hold it there with one hand.

"What are you doing with that thing?" I asked him.

"I don't know. It just looked like some kind of fuckin' hat, so I decided to wear it."

We were in the small park across from the Henry J. Kaiser Convention Center in Oakland. The sky was overcast, and the hundreds of milling heads looked sort of drab in the clean gray light after a hard rain. The place was suffused and mellow, and the people walking around had a cool assurance about them: the Dead always played well at the Kaiser; everyone knew it, and it was no big thing.

"You in tonight?" Earl asked.

"No, you?"

"Yeah, we got a backstage pass gig going, a few of us. Meet us over in that corner at seven and we'll get you in."

"What about Jane?"

"Yeah sure, Jane, too. But don't bring anyone else. It's not really my deal."

"Thanks, man."

"Hey, you know anyone might need some weight of Ex?"

"Not offhand, but I'll keep my ears open."

"I'll give it to you cheap for a half or an ounce. You could make some serious cake." He realized he was still holding the long palm branch on his head. "Fuckin' thing," he said, and tossed it to the ground. A few chips of the rotten wood clung to his dirty-blond hair.

Waiting for Jane back at the car, I sat on the trunk drinking a beer and smoking and listening to the car next to me cranking "The Harder They Come" off a Garcia Band tape—Jerry sounding coked-up and antsy and playing it too fast.

"Hey, what's up, Doctor Jay?" It was Alan. I had met him the previous summer at the Greek Theater shows. He was a stocky, curly-haired ex-carpenter from Rockland County, New York, and he had shared a room with Randy and me for the Greeks. He talked nonstop, I remembered, but had the charisma to carry it off.

"Nothing much. How've you been?"

"Great! Was living up in Chico for a while. Almost got married."

"I'm sorry to hear that."

"What do you mean?"

I paused. "Sorry it didn't work out."

"Yeah, it's just as well. I loved the shit out of her, but she could kick my ass, and often did. I think it was a good thing for both of us."

"Good."

He seemed to have lost his motormouth.

Alan came around the side of the trunk and stood by my head. "You know where I might score a bunch of pages?" he asked.

"A few days ago I could have. But my guy isn't around, and besides, I'm with his girlfriend now and I don't know how he feels about that."

Alan laughed. It came out smooth and wooden, like a bad actor on a soap opera. "You don't know anyone else?"

"No. But I'll keep my ears open for you."

"All right. Thanks." He turned and started walking away.

"Hey," I called. I got up and went over to him. "What about some Ex. I can get some weight at a decent price."

"Yeah, sure. When can you get it?"

"I'll have to see. Tonight later, I think. Where can I find you?"

"I'm at the Hyatt, room eight-oh-three. Call me there after the show. Later, Doc." He ambled squat and bowlegged away into the lot.

Earl and Evans knew three girls with backstage passes, and they got us all in. One person would ferry out the extra two passes and get two people in, then someone else would do it again. I told Earl I might want some weight, and he said he'd front me what I wanted. He gave me the name of the little Berkeley motel where they were staying.

Jane and I danced together for the show, but when I tried to hug her between songs in the first set, she was stiff with me. I thought maybe she was afraid of Don seeing us, so I gave her some space. She was wearing a green cotton dress that flowed around her loosely and was cut deep up the left side so extravagant flashes of leg showed when she swung her hips to the right. I danced behind and slightly to the left of her.

I was on my way to the bathroom at intermission when I saw Don. He waved and stopped me.

"Hey, Jason," he said. "What's up?"

"Not much."

"I heard Jane got a ride up with you."

"Yeah. She asked me for a ride down in Long Beach."

"That's cool. How is she?"

"She's fine, I guess."

He nodded, lighting a cigarette. "I kind of blew my stack."

"That's what she said."

"You know where she is?"

"Near the back, on Phil's side, with a bunch of other folks."

"Thanks, man."

I was about to walk away when he stopped me again. "Listen," he said. "Can I ask you? I'll understand and all, but . . . Are you fucking her?"

I took an involuntary step back. "I wouldn't put it that way."

His face darkened instantly. He pointed his cigarette at me. "Fuck, man. Oh, this is—" He squeezed his eyes shut. "Why'd you do this?"

"I'm sorry," I said.

Don looked at me for a second, then said, "I should hit you, or write you off, but for some reason I'm not going to do either. You let her go, okay? That's it," he made a slicing motion with the ember of his cigarette. "Break it off." He turned and walked away from me.

I stayed near Jane for the second set, waiting for Don to show up, but he never did. The set opened with "Iko Iko," which created a party atmosphere that clashed heavily with my burdened thoughts. Everyone was smiling and bopping around, and I just put my back against the wall and crossed my arms. After the show I took Jane to the apartment of a friend of hers in north Oakland, where we were staying. Her friend Sasha was an art student and lived with her boyfriend, Jim, her cat Bootsie, and Jim's reticulated python, also named Jim. I called Alan's room at the Hyatt, and he said he'd take an ounce of Ecstasy.

In the Volvo I followed Telegraph Avenue up into Berkeley, made a left toward the Marina, and pulled into the motel where the Jersey crew was staying. Earl fronted me the Ecstasy and I put the plastic baggie in my knapsack and headed out for Oakland again.

Streetlights threw their dim orange-tinted urban glare on everything, and as I steered the old car through the avenues I felt again the excitement of outlaw behavior. The world held danger in all its tiny crevices, which sharpened my experience of it. Each set of headlights behind me represented potential catastrophe. I was doing what was forbidden; even the woman I was with was forbidden to me. My guilty thoughts disappeared, and I remembered Don's speech in New Jersey about there being no right or wrong, no real ownership. I thought of Jane's legs wrapped around me, the feel of her heels digging into my thighs: she was with me now, and I would keep her. The decision felt good. I lit a cigarette and let it dangle from the corner of my mouth as I drove, my eyes sliding back and forth watchfully. Through central Oakland, I felt I understood the figures who slouched aimlessly down deserted streets: they weren't actually aimless, but their purposes were in shadow, unclear to the outside world and therefore suspect.

I parked on an empty side street two blocks away and walked through the pink and gray lobby of the Hyatt with my head held high, boarded an elevator, and rode up to the eighth floor. As I stepped off the elevator I remembered the fear I had felt with the state trooper behind us in Nevada, the scenarios that had gone through my head. The excitement I was feeling underwent a chain reaction, a reverse alchemy, becoming simple fear. I turned and reboarded the elevator without thinking and went back down. I walked the two blocks to my car, looking over my shoulder the whole way. I drove to a huge all-night Rite-Aid and bought two large jars of vitamin B tablets. In the car I found another plastic baggie and spent twenty minutes crushing the tablets into powder and pouring it in until it looked about the same as the baggie of Ex. I stashed the real bag under my seat and drove back and parked near the hotel. I took only the vitamin B with me inside. If it wasn't a setup, then I'd bring them the real stuff.

In the room, Alan was with another guy he introduced as Will, who had semi-long black hair and a wide lower jaw. With his thick forearms and shoulders stretching his tie-dye, I figured he was someone Alan had met working construction.

"How's the stuff?" asked Will.

"Always good from this source," I told him, though I didn't really know.

"Can we see it?"

"Yeah, sure." I pulled out the bag. I had made it look like a generous ounce.

"You guys want to do some?" I asked.

"Hell no," said Alan. "Not now."

"You want to weigh it?"

"I trust you, brother." Alan pulled the money from a purple Guatemalan fanny-pack on the table and handed it to me.

Things slowed down. As I took the money, I started to feel a little sick, light-headed. I tucked the stack of bills into my jeans and got up.

"You want to hang for a while, you can," said Alan.

"No thanks. I've got to go." My spider-sense was tingling.

"Where can I reach you if we want more?"

"Just look for me at the shows. I can't really get phone calls where I'm at."

I left the room with the feeling of two fists inside me, pummeling my lungs from behind. I was sure the bust would come now, cops pouring from the room next door and mashing my face into the carpet. But the hallway was completely quiet all the way to the elevators. I rode down alone, the Muzak plinking out a Moody Blues song I couldn't quite place. Then through the lobby and out the door and left around the corner and right onto the side street, and no trouble. Then as I approached my car, slapping footsteps behind me. It was Alan, and I pulled out my car key and started fumbling with the door lock of the car two spots away from mine.

"Hey," called Alan. "Hey, man."

He waited until he got close and then spoke in his surly north Jersey accent. "You fucked us, man."

"What?" I was still calculating my risks.

"Don't fuck with me. I've cut enough blow in my life to know vitamin B when I taste it. It sure as shit ain't Ex."

I looked around, saw no one else. "Come here," I said, walking for my car.

"Where the fuck are you going? Give me back that fucking money."

"Just get in the car with me for a second." I stepped into my car and unlocked the passenger side for him, and he got in. I reached under the seat and pulled out the bag of Ex. "This is the real thing. I got a little paranoid and I was going to come back up once I was sure you guys were legit. I know you, but I haven't seen you in a while. I was just being careful. You know me, man. This is the truth."

He unrolled the baggie and dipped his pinkie in and tasted it. He grimaced from the sour chemical flavor and nodded. "This is more like it."

"You want, you can stay with me until you start to get off."

"No. But you shouldn't fuck with people like that. You're lucky I didn't stove your fucking head in, no questions asked."

"Yeah, well, sorry."

"If this shit is as good as you say, we'll want more tomorrow or the next day, so call the room." He started climbing out.

"Okay," I said.

Driving away I felt a surge of relief, and knew I wouldn't call them back. In the past I had sold drugs to people I knew well, to make extra money here and there. This was different. I drove back to Berkeley, breathing heavily and smoking, paid Earl, and went to join Jane at Sasha's apartment. When I arrived, Jim pulled me into the bathroom, where the three of them were gathered to watch the python feed on a small rat. Jim insisted that everyone in the house witness this event. I had seen it before, but I agreed to watch again—out of respect for the rat, I told myself, whose terrible fate would not go unremembered.

Jim put the brown-and-white speckled rat in the bathtub with the snake, and it snuffled and crawled innocently around the python's coils, oblivious to any danger. The snake, for its part, didn't move a muscle. It waited patiently for the rat to try to tunnel down into one of its loops, and then, when the rat had put itself in exactly the right spot, the snake merely tightened up. It involved only a small amount of movement, and the rat's hind legs began to struggle, its tiny claws scraping against the snake's skin. Once the rat's exertions softened to slow, mechanical kicks spaced far apart, the snake brought its head around and neatly swallowed it, one inch at a time. I expected Jane to flee the room in disgust early in the process, but she stayed riveted on it the whole time.

"Wow," she said when the snake stretched its mouth wide and began to take the rat in headfirst.

"Good boy, Jim," Jim said.

7

AFTER THE KAISER SHOWS, Jane and I took a trip north up to Mendocino and stayed in little seaside motels, walked on cold windy beaches by ourselves, holding hands and trying to find things to talk about. We connected utterly in small silent ways, in skin and traded looks and bodily configurations, in the linkage of fingers and her tongue in my ear, but when we spoke there was instant blockage. Or more precisely it was turning out that we inhabited different worlds and came together in a kind of portal that allowed us access only to each other's bodies and emotions, admitting no intellect. The things that I talked about intensely—jazz, Zen, books—brought on a blankness of eye and hurriedness of speech in her, a lot of Yeahs and Uh-huhs, and when she droned about astrology or beadwork I found myself doing the same. So we fucked a lot, made a fantastic game, a language, out of it. For the first time I became uninhibited in desire, letting things run their course from tenderness into urgency into tender agression; I assailed her body, knowing I didn't need to ask before doing anything, that in fact asking might ruin it. And I sought every way to pleasure her. I worked hard at it, leaving myself spent and raw. I pulled a muscle at the base of my tongue and had trouble with my diphthongs for a couple of days. We got as far as Noyo, where the Volvo threw a rod, before the game started to lose its luster.

We were cruising north, passing a big skunky joint back and forth, windows closed, trails of thick smoke streaking the air between us. As I took a hit, Jane said, "I wonder where Don went. I didn't see him at the Kaiser."

I had the joint to cover my pause and kept hitting on it, hoping she'd move on before I finished. But she stayed silent, looking out the window. When I blew out my hit, she turned to me.

"You think he's okay?"

I nodded, concentrating on the road. "I saw him. The first night. But not after that."

"You saw him? Did you talk to him?"

"Yeah."

She looked straight ahead and exhaled through her nose, her lips tight. "What did you say?"

"I said everything. He asked. So I told him."

She was quiet for a while, then said, "Jesus. Why didn't you fucking tell me this?"

"I don't know," I said. I cracked my window, and the smoky air in the car began slowly to clear. "I didn't want to freak you out."

"Bullshit. Thanks a lot."

"Look, he was bound to find out. It's not like it was a secret or anything."

"No, it wasn't. But you kept this secret from me. What else? You didn't see him any other night? Where is he?"

There was something in her voice that sounded like desperation, a shrill note of maternal hysteria, and dark jealousy oozed into me from behind. I could taste it, like vinegar in my lungs, pushing upward. I spoke through it, in spite of it.

"I heard he went up to Washington with Saul. Some hippie farm up there."

"Tom and Sarah's place. I've been there with him."

Sometimes things really do happen in a certain sequence. Sometimes you realize that the world is all wrapped up inside your chest and will always act accordingly. The engine seized with a minor explosion and a sharp clang.

"Uh-oh," I said.

"That didn't sound good," said Jane.

I dropped the joint in the ashtray, guided the poor bucking car to the shoulder, and stopped. I knew it was bad. The sound had a finality about it. I didn't even bother opening the hood. "I'll walk into town for help," I said, and started out. Stoned: for half a mile on the dusty shoulder I watched the grass to the east roll in pockets of wind that crossed it slowly like the brush of giant invisible hands, and listened to the heels of my Chuck Taylors scraping pebbles and seedpods in the dirt. Before long I didn't feel like walking anymore. I kept going, though, focusing on the positive; I had everything except a running car, all the things that bring satiation: money, high grade marijuana, a woman whose body continually revealed new territory, whose firm softness and blazing green eyes netted me way down low. But I felt the mood I was trying to create stretched thin across the overcast world, just barely greening the grass and tanning the dust, lending a false hint of freshness to the breeze, like a diaphanous membrane under which pale, insipid substance was stirring. A mottled gray seagull, seeming to struggle to stay just above the whispering blades, flapped its way over the field silently, crossed the road, and dropped tiredly past a sandy rise toward the ocean. A blue pickup truck passed going south with a middle-aged woman at the wheel. She didn't look at me. No one came in my direction.

The service station was small, with one indoor bay and four old American cars parked outside, one a Chevy Impala gutted for parts. There was a blue tow truck parked around the side. I bought a Coke at the counter from a kid of about fifteen.

"Anyone here might be able to give me a tow?" I asked him.

"Yeah sure, where you at?"

"Half a mile south."

He walked from the counter back into the garage and I heard him speaking to someone. Then a skinny mechanic in jeans and a Redlands sweatshirt came out. "Got some trouble?" he asked. He was blackened with grease around the hands and neck and his receding shock of blond hair showed black evidence of being smoothed while working.

"Yeah. I need a tow."

"You got it," he said.

His name was Carl, and he towed the Volvo in with Jane sitting on my lap in the front of the cluttered truck. "Where you kids headed?" Carl asked.

"Nowhere special," I said.

"I hope it's *somewhere* special."

"We've been there and gone," said Jane.

"And it wasn't so special." I laughed, but wished I hadn't said it. I snaked my arm around Jane's waist and gripped her thigh on the side near the door, where Carl couldn't see. I kissed her spine through her cotton blouse.

The car wasn't worth the price of fixing it, and I sold it to Carl for forty dollars plus the cost of the tow. We got our stuff out of the car and prepared to leave.

"What about this?" Carl asked, pulling the bag of puppy food out of the trunk and holding it up.

"Know anyone who's got a puppy?" I asked.

"Yeah," he looked at his son. "We got one last week."

"It's all yours then."

When Jane and I walked away toward the center of town with our bags and my guitar slung over our shoulders, Carl and his son stood by the station's door and watched us go, as if we were departing family, and because I didn't know what was next I imagined we were: that these low-slung houses, sagging where the ground had buckled under them, were the ones I had grown up running among, that the smell of fog and gas and rotting shingles and grass I inhaled would always bring on the flood of childhood memory when I encountered it in other places—a small-town kid with dreams of the city now off to live them for better or worse, looking back only once at his father and little brother as he hit the road. The ease with which I placed myself in alternate lives sometimes alarmed me. I did look back once, and Carl raised his right hand halfway for a second, still holding the key to the Volvo in it. The strap of my duffel was already cutting into my shoulder and I realized I should have negotiated a ride with him.

When I suggested a bus back to the Bay, Jane asked if I'd buy her a ticket to Olympia, Washington. We hitched to a bigger small town nearby, and I bought her the bus ticket, and mine back to Berkeley. I never questioned her decision to go north. She said it was just for a visit, and she'd come back and meet me at least for the New Year's shows.

"So, I'll see you soon," I said.

"Yeah, see you soon."

I kissed her, and couldn't keep my hand from moving down

across her hip and into her crotch. I squeezed the warmth there. "You asshole," she breathed into my neck. She dragged me into the small ladies' room and locked it. I pushed her up onto the counter by the sink and she pulled her skirt up to her waist. We were there again, in our zone, following a single set of dictates, but when I tried to go down on her she grabbed my hair and pulled me up, saying, "Come on. Let's not drag this out."

We didn't draw out our good-byes when her bus left, either, but smiled a lot. We overdid the kiss, tongues and all, in the bus's doorway, and I felt stupid as she turned away. I could sense the other passengers watching neutrally from behind the parallelogram windows, but looking up saw only reflected white sky.

I WAS SURPRISED by how much I missed her, and how quickly. Her power in absence only grew. I sat in the little station waiting for the southbound bus and my hands started aching. I rubbed my own cheeks and felt how drawn and bony they were compared to Jane's. I felt physical hunger for her, and it bled through its border into emotion until I couldn't tell the two apart. I started reinterpreting looks she had given me, things she had said, reimagining the bright future I had first conceived for us. I went into the bathroom again and masturbated thinking of her.

It was a long wait, and I bought a three-dollar paperback off the gift shop rack and read the whole thing. It was about a guy named Chopper, the leader of a motorcycle gang, who falls in love with a woman he and his cohorts abduct from a bar and gang-rape. She becomes his girlfriend, and he kills his second-in-command for disparaging her honor. They deal drugs and commit robberies and have lots of great sex, and in the end he agrees on a dare to jump his bike over a local highway where it cuts through a hill, forming a man-made canyon, a stunt his predecessor, the former leader, is said to have performed to win control of the gang. But Chopper's rival—a ruthless newcomer to the gang—has halfway clipped his fuel line and he loses power at the critical moment, sailing down and down into the path of an oncoming eighteen-wheeler, and is crushed. In the epilogue the girlfriend manages to escape the rival's clutches and goes on to a mundane life as a waitress-with-a-past, raising Chopper's son as a normal kid, haunted by the thought that if only she had told Chopper she was pregnant, he may not have tried the jump. The book wasn't as good as it sounds, but not bad for reading in a bus station.

The bus ride down was a cloudy few hours. The inland route offered no sea. The noise of the bus's engine became a new, denser kind of silence that stifled thought as well as sound, and I rode along deafened by it. I gave the book about the motorcycle gang to an older woman across the aisle who asked if I had any magazines, and she was quickly buried in it. I just lost myself in the plush brown-and-black pattern on the seat in front of me, and in the hazy, bleak roadside sameness beyond the window. I may have slept.

Back in the Bay I called Sasha and Jim, and they put me up for a while, but it didn't take long for them to get sick of me moping around. I would lie in the little cot they kept in Jim's office, which became my room, and pierce myself again and again with thoughts of Jane. I glazed my way through a battered paperback of *Notes from Underground* mainly as an exercise in escape, forming the words in my mind one after the other as I read, but they might as well have been in Russian. I drank beer out of the fridge without asking. I refused to watch Jim feed the snake. I rolled back and forth on the yellow wool blanket, the cot's springs creaking, and memorized the texture and smudges of the old white paint on the wall by my pillow. Sometimes I climbed to the roof of the building and smoked cigarettes in the wind, imagining I was the star of a movie looking out over the cold city in the aftermath of a devastating love, the sound track playing "Many Rivers to Cross" or "Landslide" and the camera whirling above my head. I really couldn't stand myself when these thoughts came on.

I ran out of money and starting trekking up Telegraph to Berkeley and playing my guitar on the sidewalk for change. I developed a pretty clean repertoire of Dead and Dylan and old blues tunes and made enough to eat. When Sasha and Jim gave me the hint, I moved into Randy and Lauren's one-bedroom, sleeping on the floor of their walk-in closet.

Cole was in Berkeley, too, turning over large amounts of Ecstasy, and he took me on as a side project, trying to bring me back to life. Sometimes he cut me in on his deals. More often he just took me along so as not to be working alone, and in exchange I stayed in his hotel rooms and did whatever drugs he had. He would pull up outside Randy's window in his little red Mazda RX-7, which he had bought for five thousand cash a few weeks earlier, and sound his horn. The car was quick and fun to ride in, but it was too small to be a good tour car.

"Hop in," he said one morning when I met him outside. We got in and he started driving. As usual I didn't know where we were headed, and didn't ask. It would either be a restaurant in Berkeley for breakfast, to the downtown Hyatt to meet a connection, or on some pointless expedition of mischief. Cole pulled a battery-powered Uzi watergun from behind the seat. "Drive-by time," he said. I found the other gun behind my seat, already loaded. They could fire thirty or forty feet, and sometimes we spent afternoons just riding around soaking people from the car windows and out the sunroof. Businessmen were a favorite target, second only to other hippies.

We crossed the Bay Bridge into San Francisco, and through the flashing dark struts of the bridge thin remnants of morning fog were just visible in the mouth of the Bay, smoky wisps lying close to the water like neglected ghosts. The day was warm for winter, and a dim white flashlight sun hung in the waning haze. We drove downtown first, among the big office buildings, and cruised for targets. It was late morning and the offices held most of their prisoners cooped up, but here and there we found suits standing close to the curb and sprayed them. I always aimed for the head, because the slow realization dawning on them from a body shot, as they looked down at their streaked front, was nowhere near as fun as the sheer astonishment, panicked flailing, and congealing rage produced by a direct facial hit. Headed down Pine Street, we stopped at a light, cranking *Houses of the Holy* on the tape deck. A young guy in a suit was waiting to cross. I gave him a chance: with the gun hidden near the door, bobbing my head to the music, I looked at him and smiled. Anything would have gotten him off the hook, a smile, a nod, whatever, but he just turned his level gaze away without acknowledging me, so I blasted him in the face and Cole soaked his suit from the sunroof. He jumped back and screamed, "What the fuck!" Our light was still red, so Cole yanked a right turn, and as we rounded the corner the guy started laughing, holding his arms out to his sides and surveying the damage to his suit. It was good to know there were people whose bubbles hadn't hardened past bursting.

When we got tired of businessmen, and afraid we might re-encounter some of our victims, we headed for the Haight to hunt for hippies. Across from Buena Vista Park we saw a tall punk rocker long-striding down the sidewalk in massive black boots. His black jeans were tattered, held together in fifty places by giant safety pins, and his T-shirt announced in hand-painted scrawl: "Dick Head."

"All right, slow down," I said as we neared him.

"Fuck that," said Cole, and stepped on the gas. "I saw that guy clock the bouncer at the Blue Moon last week. He's crazy."

"No fun."

Farther down the Haight we saw a bread line, homeless men lined up behind a truck where a table was piled with day-old loaves of bread. We were in a frenzy of troublemaking, laughing hysterically, and as we slowly passed I strafed the entire line with a stream of water. Some of them yelled and the line broke as they came at the car. I saw violence in at least one pair of eyes.

"Hit it!" I said, and Cole popped the clutch and left the running, wild-bearded men behind. Looking back, I saw shaking fists and heard angry cries, and a tall, ragged figure calmly stepped away from the table with a loaf of bread cradled in one big hand. He cocked his arm back smoothly. There was no rush, and no wasted motion. In that moment I saw how down the winding path from star high school quarterback to Haight Street bum this beautiful athletic movement had survived in him, waiting for its chance to surface once again, in front of a crowd, and make a hero of him. He launched the big loaf in a tight spiral, leading us perfectly like a wide receiver on a fly pattern, and it dropped cleanly through the sunroof and exploded on the dashboard, showering our laughter in day-old bread. The knot of men around him burst into jubilation, cheering triumphantly, and he just stood with one fist raised, Terry Bradshaw–style. I wanted to drive back by and congratulate him.

A little later, after vacuuming out the car, we went to meet Dawn, Cole's main Ecstasy connection. We met her in different hotels around the city a couple of times a week. She was a singularly ugly woman, not only obese, but with a wide slurpy mouth that cut her head so deeply in half when she smiled her jack-o'-lantern smile that I pictured the top half peeling back and dropping to the ground like some gruesome geode, exposing the convolutions of her brain. Her teeth looked as if they had been hammered one by one into her gums by someone unconcerned with symmetry, and her heavy cheeks had begun the long surrender to gravity, sliding down below her jawline. But she carried her ugliness with fierce good humor, completely unsheepish, letting it stay right out in the foreground of her interactions. She looked you right in the eye when she spoke to you and never suppressed her smile. In this way she managed to usurp her looks. Her skin was a deep, even olive; had she been pale and blotchy, the effect, the totality, would have been staggering. But everyone has to have at least one positive attribute, and nice skin was hers. I got the sense that her ugliness was somehow the secret to her success as a business-woman, or at least was a motivating factor, the way a tree growing on rocks, though stunted in its upper body, will develop a superb root structure with which to cling. Cole had informed me solemnly one day, as we drove away from her hotel, that she liked me.

"What's that supposed to mean?" I asked, hearing the suggestive tone in his voice.

"Nothing. She thinks you're cute is all."

"Look, Dawn is cool, but what am I supposed to do with this information? Use it to get in her pants?"

"No, I guess not, though if you wanted you'd be in like Flynn. But you could play on it. She'd be in a position to throw some nice business your way."

"No thanks."

Cole didn't know how badly I was still gone on Jane. In fact, the longer she was away the easier it was to imagine she and I had shared the seed of a perfect relationship, one that might have flourished into something sublime and powerful. I pictured us touring together, desert sunsets stretching red and magnificent around us, her feet up on the dash, wind tossing and knotting our hair. Jason and Jane. It had a ring to it. I imagined different people saying it. I thought of us growing old together, though I couldn't really picture it other than knowing she'd still be beautiful. And beauty's what it came down to, what in the end I couldn't fantasize my way around: ultimately it wasn't conversations or real personal connection I envisioned with Jane, but something else more centered on the shape of her hands, the full softness of her cheeks, freckles, the way her small ass rode so high and arrogant above her long legs when she walked naked across a room, her devastating green-eyed smile, the simple, unbelievable fact that she had wanted me. Okay, so I was gone on her mainly as a physical object, but there is a depth of goneness from which that feels like more than enough.

We parked near the Continental downtown and locked the car. Cole swung his empty blue gym bag over his shoulder and we strolled to the hotel. From a pay phone in the lobby Cole called Dawn's room.

The door was propped open on its own dead bolt, and we stepped in. I spun the lock and let the door close, then double-locked it. Ever since Cole had filled me in on Dawn's crush, I had felt a little awkward around her. She was in her perennial position on the bed (aways the right bed if there were two), flipping channels. Lunch lay demolished on a cart near the window, and a bony guy of about seventeen in a long purple skirt and muddy tie-dye was smoking freebase from a glass pipe in the corner. The bittersweet scent of it darkened the room, fought with the clear sunlight spilling through the windows. Dawn accumulated tour rats like an old lady feeding pigeons, probably for most of the same reasons. She had a regular little crew of hangers-on, but this kid was new. His eyes, all milky black pupil, came up and met mine over the pipe for a second and then dropped back to focus on the lighter flame. He moved it sloppily under the pipe and I stifled an impulse to school him, help him get a better hit.

"Boys, boys," said Dawn. "Howdy doo." She smiled, and I could see she was showered and well rested, not high. I wondered how she could tolerate the little sucking troll in the corner, who obviously hadn't slept in days.

"Hidey ho," said Cole.

"Have a seat. Meet little Weasel. Weasel, these are two people whose names you don't need to know."

The kid let out his hit. "My name's Griffin."

"You don't like Weasel? You don't like the name I give you?"

He shrugged, a movement he had perfected. "Whatever."

"You guys want coffee? A joint? Base hit?"

"Dawn's diner," said Cole. "Always full-service."

"I'm cool," I said.

Cole took the open chair near Dawn's bed, and I sat on the other bed and lit a cigarette.

"Can I try one of your Camels?" Dawn asked me. She had Marlboro Lights sitting by the bed. "These things don't have any kick sometimes."

"Sure," I said, getting up and handing her a Camel. I struck my lighter for her, and she cupped my hand as she leaned into it. Her fingers were hot and spongy and left the back of my hand cool with moisture.

Dawn fronted Cole an ounce of Ecstasy, for which he would pay her the next day. She had come to trust him, and it set his buyers more at ease not to have to lay out the money ahead of time.

"What about you, Jason?"

"Me?"

"Yeah. You just going to follow your little friend around all the time?" Still reclined on the bed, Dawn delicately put my Camel out in a glass ashtray she held in her hand, rotating the butt slowly without crushing it. "Don't you know anyone who might want some cheap Ex?"

"Well, maybe. But they're all back east."

"So fly back. This is serious money we're talking about. You're in on the lower floors. You should take advantage. It beats doses or weed by a mile. Profit margin's better than blow even."

"Yeah, well, I'll think about it. Thanks."

"Don't thank me. I'm asking for help, not offering it. I can't move enough to please my guy down south." She lifted the front of her skirt and spread her legs, flapping the material to get air underneath, and exposing the smooth, shaven expanse of her vast thighs. "Weasel! Turn up the AC."

The kid reached for the climate control unit without interrupting his deep study of the base pipe and it kicked on, whirring and drizzling softly.

8

THE FLIGHT EAST was so bumpy they cut the second round of beverage service short. The flight attendant was a small pretty redhead, and looking at her I was reminded of a time when I was eleven, on a flight out of Detroit after an uncle's wedding. My father, drunk beyond the capacity for complete sentences, had taken a shine to a redheaded stewardess and offered me fifty dollars to walk up to her, kiss her on the lips, and tell her I loved her. I did it, and my father, slipping me the cash, slurred something about having a new respect for me. He was so impressed with the power of money over children that when we landed in Philadelphia he paid my ten-year-old cousin to stand on the rotating baggage carousel and scream to the gathered travelers that he was the Shah of Iran and wanted all their money to pay off the Mayo Clinic. It was a kind of absurd spontaneity I hadn't seen before, and I began to associate inebriation with playfulness.

On this trip I had no checked baggage and sailed straight through the terminal at La Guardia with only my knapsack, which contained one sweater, three T-shirts, two pairs of underwear, jeans, a toothbrush, *The Sun Also Rises*, and an ounce of pure MDMA. I had sunglasses on, to mask the black eye I was still sporting. It was fading so slowly I'd started to think it might always be with me.

Jane and Don had shown up for New Year's together, and neither of them would speak to me. Their eyes had glazed over and become blind whenever we walked near one another. Even when I saw Jane by herself in the parking lot, she had cut between cars to the next aisle to avoid me. I followed her, caught up with her. I grabbed her arm and tried talking to her, not realizing we were fifteen feet from Don's car. He walked up to us, out of nowhere, with a fast but normal gait, and his arm slid from his side into a punch with no backswing, like a snake striking, his hand becoming a fist sometime during the motion. He led Jane away, and I sat on the pavement, collecting nose blood in my hands. Neither of them had said a word to me.

I'd decided to take Dawn up on her repeated offer to set me up with a front of Ex. She had even bought my plane ticket. I would pay her back out of the profit, which, at suburban preppy prices, would be considerable.

I turned a corner and was borne down upon by a large phalanx of old couples. Some kind of tour group or charter flight. They walked determinedly, meditatively, and with a hint of desperation, like a flock of badly evolved migratory birds winter had caught napping. Some had walkers or canes, and all swayed grimly as they moved. Locked shoulder to shoulder, they were blind to anyone in their path, focused on some unseen destination, probably Miami or Las Vegas. It occurred to me that I could learn something from them. In their reduced capacity, they had streamlined their minds and movements for maximum efficiency, and there was nothing else for them at that moment but simply *Get to the plane.* I was unable to step out of the way, so I turned sideways to present the least physical resistance. None of them lifted their taut gazes as they shuffled past, skirting me as smooth and closely as smoke in a wind tunnel.

Benton, the one true friend I had made at boarding school (the second school I went to, the all-male ultrapreppy one) was waiting at the curb in his new forest green Volkswagen Jetta. He lived at his father's house in Greenwich, Connecticut, and since his father had retired early to travel the globe, he usually had the place to himself. Benton had become the hub of a circle of rich partyers and drug users who, he assured me, would snap up my ounce in no time. A party was scheduled for that night, and I was the guest of honor.

The house was built into a hillside, some architect's flight of fancy since the three-acre property included plenty of flat ground. On the main level were the kitchen, dining room, living room, and master bedroom. Above it were three more bedrooms, and below were a large den and two-car garage. The short driveway was lined with hedges, and wide flagstone steps bordered with myrtle and sconced ground lights led upward to the front door. Benton parked his car in the driveway and we walked in through the garage, where in the cool smell of concrete and motor oil his father's Mercedes darkly sat.

Benton and I had been thrown out of school together after being caught in the woods on a weeknight waiting for a day student to drop off some booze. A car had pulled up on the dirt road, and we had waved and approached it, only to find inside it the assistant headmaster. Both of us were on thin ice already. The Faculty Disciplinary Committee browbeat both of us for the name of the person we had been waiting for, offering leniency in exchange for the name, but we stuck to our story: we had been out for a stroll. Eventually they threw up their hands and expelled us both.

"Mi casa," Benton said with a sweep of his hand as we entered the den, "es fully su casa, my friend. So do whatever you want. Just don't fuck with any of my dad's shit or go into his bedroom."

"Yeah sure," I said.

Benton crossed the room, his slightly shaggy head of curly brown hair bouncing behind him. "Care to observe the cocktail hour with me?" He slid the doors open on a prodigious liquor cabinet.

"Why not?"

I had also brought some fine California bud, and once we settled back with vodka tonics I pulled it from my jacket and twisted a joint. We sat in the den on two chairs shaped like flattened human bodies and smoked while watching a rerun of *Quincy*.

"How do you like the people-chairs?" Benton asked.

"They're cool," I said. "Comfy." And they were. Reclined there, I turned and stared out the window, which looked down on a large grass yard where two whippets streaked after each other, their sleek bodies set against the earth, mining speed from it with the points of their tiny paws. Fabled Greenwich didn't reek of money as I had somehow expected it to, but only of pure stone and earth, and clean carpets and varnished hardwood and mixed drinks. The people there had tacitly established long ago that the highest commodities were not money and luxury, or even power, but cleanliness and purity, money only a means to those ends. As I relit the roach and sucked another hit out of it, I wondered whether the whippets were a special breed whose shit didn't stink. I imagined them squatting to produce odorless dollops of white putty that would eventually crumble and blow away on their own.

At the party everyone knew I was the man to see. I took customers in ones twos and threes into Benton's bedroom and sold them hits, or sometimes grams. Some of these lapsed and not-so-lapsed preppies were almost as serious about their drugs as any Deadhead, and many were heads in the making. Money erupted from their wallets and Vuitton purses; nobody blinked an eye at my prices or tried to bargain with me, and I gave only the smallest discounts for large purchases.

The Ex high manifested differently here than at shows. There was not the explosion of openness and smiling and unabashed love I was used to in large groups on Ex, but a more staid version of it. There weren't a lot of hugs going around, except between couples mauling each other on the sofas or smirkingly retreating to bedrooms. What they did mostly was talk—about how the high felt, about the futility of the lives their parents wanted for them, about how much they cared for each other—and some strummed guitars badly or drank beer alone in corners. The one platonic hug I saw was between two guys: one walked up to the other and put his hand on his shoulder and looked into his face. "Dude," he said, "don't worry about wrecking my Scirocco." Then they hugged. I didn't take any myself because I knew it would be bad for business. I didn't want to start loving all of them and giving hits away. In a week I'd be back at the Kaiser for the Dead's five-night Mardi Gras run, and then I'd dose up heavily and let the love flow. For now it was better to stay objective.

COLE WAS supposed to meet me at the airport when I got back, but he didn't show up. I waited half an hour, and then took a cab to Randy's place in Oakland. Randy hadn't seen Cole, and the Continental said Dawn had checked out. I waited for one of them to call me, or come by Randy's. A week went by, and the Mardi Gras shows at the Kaiser started. I saw Earl inside the first night and asked him if he'd seen Cole or Dawn.

"Dawn? Big Dawn?"

"Yeah."

"You didn't hear?"

"No, hear what?"

"She went down. Big-time. Word is someone turned state's on her."

"Jesus," I said. "I have a bunch of her money."

"Well, she won't be needing it for a while, I guess."

"When did this happen?"

"Couple weeks ago."

"Wow. I was back east. What about Cole?"

"Haven't seen him around. Maybe he skipped town for a while to cool off."

I kept asking around that week and found out Dawn had hired a high-end lawyer. She had been busted with a pound of Ecstasy. I resolved to keep her money for her and spend only the profit. Her trial wasn't anything like the high profile trials you hear about that drag on for months; three weeks later I heard she had been sentenced to seventeen years in prison.

TWO GIRLFRIENDS of Dawn's were planning to visit her, and instead of heading out for the beginning of spring tour in Hampton, I asked if I could tag along. Scar and Ginny were their names. I didn't know them very well, but they seemed cut from the same general substance as Dawn: funny, cynical, a little bossy, a little ugly.

"How'd you get a name like Scar?" I asked on the drive to the jail. She was a large loose-hipped blonde whose big upright breasts under a tight T-shirt made up for the extra weight.

"I don't know," she said. "It just happened. I used to call myself Star, but then I realized that was stupid and one night we just changed it to Scar." She didn't seem happy with my question, and the rest of the drive went by in silence.

Dawn was surprised to see me there with them. She smiled her gruesome smile at the three of us as she was led to the small table where we sat. Identical tables were spaced throughout the room, and a few of them were occupied by other prisoners talking with visitors. One bone-skinny woman in the blue prison jumpsuit was sitting astride her man and grinding her hips, stretching her mouth wide and practically eating his face as she kissed him. She looked like a snake struggling with too-large prey.

"How are you?" Scar asked as Dawn sat down.

Dawn's smile disappeared. "Hanging in," she said.

The three women talked for a few minutes, and Ginny pulled out a plastic bag full of cigarette packs. It had been three cartons, but the guard had opened each one and inspected the packs to make sure they were sealed. They also gave her a box of candy bars.

"Any idea who turned on you?" Scar asked.

"Yeah, I've got an idea. The person who introduced me to that fucking undercover. I was under so much pressure to move the weight and I got sloppy."

"Who was it?"

Dawn looked right at me. Her voice dropped to a whisper. "It was fucking Cole, that's who. At least he's the one who hooked me up with the undercover cop, so that pretty much puts him at the top of the list."

I was stunned. "Cole?" I said. "I don't think he'd do that."

"You'd be surprised what people will do when they're looking at time."

I really couldn't imagine it. I just shook my head.

"Give me a few minutes with Jason, will you, guys," Dawn said.

Scar and Ginny each gave Dawn a long hug, then walked for the door.

Dawn watched them go. When she turned back to me she gave me the softest look I had ever seen from her. "It was sweet of you to come here, Jason."

"I wanted to see you. I still have your money."

"You keep it." She reached across the table and held my hand. "But can I ask you for something?"

"Sure. Of course."

"Just write me a letter now and then, okay? Scar has the address."

"Yeah, of course I will."

She squeezed my hand tighter. Both of us were sweating. "You're like magic to me. You know that? You're a magical person." She let out a quick breath, a little laugh at herself. "I don't know if you want to hear this, but fuck it." She traced my cheekbone with her moist finger. "I love you. Like you'll never know."

I thought of her spending the next decade in that place. I felt myself about to cry, so I smiled. "Thanks," I said.

"Get out of here, now. And don't let this shit happen to you." She was crying.

I got up and so did she, and we hugged. The gravity of her situation allowed us to dispense with the plodding process of intimacy—both of us slung forward past all that. It was the most spontaneous thing in the world when I pulled my face back and kissed her full on the mouth. Her breath smelled of toothpaste, and we kissed long and softly and I stroked her greasy hair as I stepped away. She looked down, embarrassed, like someone who's been given more than they can repay, but I didn't see it that way.

That night I slept with Scar in her room in Berkeley. We both needed the sex badly, and it kept us up most of the night. She fucked me angrily, knowing I wasn't really attracted to her, mashed her hands into my face so I couldn't look at her, and smacked my ass to coax a little brutality into my thrusts. I tried to think of Dawn while we were fucking, and felt guilty when I found I couldn't bring myself to do it. Shallow, shallow man. I needed to block her out. But still, as I sent my hands all over Scar's wide body, her melon breasts, dug deep down into her, I felt that I was doing the best I could.

The next morning we naturally started to talk about Dawn.

"The scary thing is," said Scar, "I was in the room when that guy came around one time."

"What guy?"

"That undercover cop. Called himself Will. Should have known right off, had to be a cop with arms like that."

I rolled to face her. "Did he have black hair and a Dudley Do-Right chin?"

"Yeah. You know him?"

"Did he have a guy named Alan with him?"

"No, he was alone."

I got up and slid into my jeans, found my socks rolled in the corner.

"Hey, what's up? Where you going?" She was up on one elbow, her breasts pushing aside the sheet, and I almost went back for more.

"Got a plane to catch," I said. "Going back east."

part two

BEFORE MY FATHER DIED my mother used to talk to James and me about him when she tucked us in at night. He was away on trips covering stories much of the time. She would pull the covers to my chin and sit on the bed's edge, her weight tilting the mattress and creating a slight pull toward her, as if my body, having emerged from hers, was still magnetized to it. Sometimes, as a younger child, I pouted and raged when my father went away, and with age this gave way to sullenness.

"Your father wishes he could be here," she would say. "You know that, don't you?"

"Yes," I would say.

"Your father is a wonderful man," my mother would say. "He's so good. And we're all lucky to have him. He loves you and your brother more than anything in the world. When you get older, you'll be able to see what a great man he is, what everyone who knows him thinks of him."

She would reach out sometimes and touch me after saying

these things. She was always touching back then, her lips on my cheek, her cool hand on my face, rubbing Vicks on my chest when I was congested, cool damp washcloths smoothed onto my forehead when I was feverish.

"I know, Mom," I would say. I forgot my anger toward my father for being away in those moments. Her love for him and her faith in him were too powerful to move against on any front; I could only be subsumed by them; I could only feel the same way.

Then came the last trip to Syria. I was starting to get used to it by then. I could see the end of the trip—him walking in the door rumpled and world-traveled, smelling of airplanes and bearing gifts for James and me—as if it were only a day away, and the thought of that happy moment even made me relish his going away. This time he was covering an execution and would be gone only a few days. There was a cheerful round of good-byes as James and I left for school in the morning. I remember hugging him, and the feel of his freshly shaven face on mine, and of his soft crosshatched brown tweed traveling jacket under my hands. That moment blooms for me, becomes a world, and I'm never sure whether I felt it then or manufactured it in hindsight.

The next day was a Saturday, and James and I went on one of our expeditions. We put on our army fatigue pants and our sneakers and went out into the bright, watery island sunlight. We were in Nicosia, in the center of Cyprus, nowhere near the coast, but the sea's influence could still be felt in the gusty winds, in the sharp air, in the odd seagull looping overhead among the hawks and crows.

A few weeks earlier we had found a maze of underground drainage tunnels at the edge of town, and we were in the process of mapping it. The entrance was a massive concrete pipe, six feet high, in the side of a cracked old aqueduct. The farther in we went, the smaller the pipes became, and we had so far balked at anything so small we couldn't turn around in it. We had found three ways out—ladders up through tubes leading to grates in the street. The grates were impossible to lift, but we reasoned that if we got lost, or if there was a flash flood and we had to use them, we could climb up to the grate and yell until someone heard us. One of the ladders—which we designated "Ladder A" on our map, scratching an "A" into the wall at the bottom—came up below a busy shopping street, and we could climb one at a time to the top and look out through the thick grate at people walking by. Sometimes there would be a car parked halfway over the grate, leaving us only a sliver of light between it and the curb, and sometimes—the ultimate prize, more wishful conjecture than occurrence—we would catch a split-second glimpse up a woman's skirt. Mostly we strained to see the heads of the window-shoppers as they paused along the sidewalk. It was exciting, spying on them from our secret chamber.

At the entrance pipe James pulled out the map, which had started as a single sheet of notebook paper and was now four taped together. I carried two flashlights and two sandwiches in a knapsack, along with other tools we thought we might need: a knife, some clothesline, matches.

James scuffled up to the raised lip of the massive pipe, pushing up on his hands until he could get one knee over, then crawling forward and standing. When he stood and turned toward me he was framed in the huge circle of concrete, the background all darkness against which his sun-gilded skin glowed. He was taller than me back then, and in the set of his jaw and his level eyes was already a man. He gave me a tough half-smile and crouched, extending his arm to help me up.

"I've got it," I said, tossing up the knapsack. I tackled the climb with a little more effort than him. When I stood up next to him,

131

my knee hurt from dragging it too quickly over the lip, but I didn't mention it or allow myself to limp.

There was only one large pipe we hadn't explored and mapped, and that was our goal. To get to it we had to pass Ladder A, so we each took a turn climbing up and spying on the shoppers. Again, James went first, and I waited at the bottom for him to come down. The rungs of the ladder were flat rusted iron, and a fine reddish mist sifted down through the shifting slivers of sunlight that worked their way past James's moving body. I turned away into the tunnel to avoid getting it in my eyes. When my turn came, my hands became covered in gritty chips of rust as I climbed. Tilting my head upward, I saw the circular piece of sky at the end of the long tube, sectioned into blue rectangles by the bars of the grate. I felt as if I was making my way through an eye socket toward the back of a big blue eye.

It could have been my father's eye behind bars, I think now, because, as near as I can piece it together, at about that time he was sitting in a cell having been picked up by the Syrian police in the street outside his Damascus hotel. There was a letter he wrote the first night after the arrest, delivered to us only after his death. It was brief and upbeat, referring to the whole thing as a minor mistake; the American embassy was on the case and he'd be home soon. Not to worry. He joked that the food was better than in the hotel. I sometimes wonder if there was a window in his cell, and if his view through the bars showed him a piece of sky—if at the moment I tilted my head back inside that concrete tube he was craning his neck inside a concrete box to see roughly the same sight.

At the top I saw only a few heads passing the shop windows. It was too early for the crowds that came in the cooling of the late afternoon, after siesta. I strained my head around, searching for the opening that had the best angle. Then there was a flash of white cloth, containing an even briefer flash of flesh, and clicking of a woman's shoes moving away. It was as close as I had come to seeing up a woman's skirt, and I decided immediately to lie to James.

"I saw up a lady's skirt," I said as I reached the bottom of the ladder.

"You did not," James said.

"Yes I did! She walked right over the grate."

"What color was her underwear?"

"White."

"Was she good-looking?" The skepticism started to drain from his tone.

"I don't know. But she had nice legs, though." I wasn't even completely sure what constituted nice legs.

"Lucky shit," James said, and not questioning me further was a like a gift to his little brother, allowing me to feel the elevated status of one who has seen a woman's underwear. It was the type of offering I never would have gotten if any of his older friends had been around.

We turned the flashlights back on and moved deeper in. I imagine now that as we made our way through dim filthy tunnels, so did our father, the difference being that our tunnels were round and open-ended; and we were together while he was alone. When we got home later that afternoon, our mother would be sitting silent in the living room alone with the mute telephone, keeping the news of Dad's imprisonment warm inside, a grim lunch for us. But in that tunnel, to which we would never go back, we were still oblivious. There would follow a brief period—a little more than a year—during which there was no exploring of any kind. The mentality was gone. Prosaic reality sat in me imperturbable as a public building, a post office or Pentagon; and stupefied, I took up residence in it, preparing unwittingly for adulthood. I got good grades, played hard on my team sports, did all my homework. But something happened when I discovered drugs, the first of course being cannabis: that old sense of endless findings—adventures, inner landscapes, a world personal to me, the capacity for practical oblivion these things created—opened up for me again, and I clung to it like a lover. I guess James found his equivalent in jazz improvisation. That day, though, before we got the news, we were adventurers together for the last time. We followed our map to its shredded end where the paper had been torn from the notebook. Our feet scraped dried silt and grit, and our lights slid in stretching ovals around the walls in front of us, banking off the curved gray surfaces, as we came to the edge of unexplored territory.

"Sure, Mom." I poured myself a cup of coffee.

I felt like a too-large presence in the apartment. My mother had spent years miniaturizing her emotions—making them perfect and beautiful and manageable, tending them like bonsai trees. My presence, coming from wild experience, chaos, and mind-numbing drug use, felt unwieldy here, out of place, as if I had stepped into a sunny flower garden wearing a thick parka and snowshoes.

But I did my best to acclimate. While hitchhiking across the country this time I had read Suzuki's *Zen Mind, Beginner's Mind*, and I took walks every day, trying to be brand new in the world, the city, my body, in the present moment. I needed to clear my mind of all the coke binges and THC. My long walks were also a way to get me out of the apartment. My mother was putting out the get-a-job vibe, and I knew sooner or later it would come to that. I'd been home three months. My last stint in the city had been a year earlier, after my frenzied flight from what I was sure would turn into a bust by the same undercover cop who had taken Dawn down. It had ended with me leaving the job I'd found as a set builder at a theater, once I realized that luck had spared me the bust, and heading back out on tour with Randy. But now, in debt to all my Berkeley contacts and coming off a two-week freebase bender, I thought I'd try the straight life for real. Maybe get my G.E.D. and apply for college. Things were moving slowly.

Lexington Avenue on a February morning wasn't too interesting, so I took the train downtown and strolled around Union Square. I practiced my Zen thinking, looking on the homeless man and the businessman with equanimity, seeing all with the same transcendental eyes, the eyes of the soul; but really I didn't know what the fuck I was doing. Mainly I watched the women—was there ever a place with more beautiful women?—and lamented the fact that it was February and they all wore winter coats, stockings, long pants. In the Union Square subway station, a steel-drum band had collected a crowd. The bright, ringing notes exploded through the underground cavern like island sunshine, and the layered rhythms—twelve running beats inside four loping ones—induced some motion among the bodies. Here and there people swayed from foot to foot, nodded their heads, briefcases and purses dangling forgotten at their sides. There were even a few smiles scattered around. Up front, two girls began to dance with each other. I could see their undulating heads over the rest, their arms thrown high. One was blond, the other brown-haired, and I heard them laughing when they spun or kicked up their feet, giddy with the crowd's attention.

I found a spot on the side, closer to the front, where I could see them a little better. They both had long hair. The blonde was dressed in hippie fashion, a thick old corduroy coat lined with fake sheepskin, blue jeans, and red Converse Chuck Taylors. I waited, with my Zen mind, for a glimpse of their faces, to see if they were beautiful. I admired the way their jeans bunched slightly at the tops of their thighs when they lifted their legs. A young man in front of me turned around and walked on toward the rest of his day. I watched his pallid face, briefly made wide-eyed and receptive by the music, rebuild itself into the blank mask that protected him. I looked after him as he went, the back of his black suitpants brushing the hem of his charcoal overcoat, a blue nylon knapsack slung student-style from one shoulder. He wasn't much older than me, but already he had learned to walk as if he knew where he was going.

I turned back to the band and stepped into the spot he had vacated, where my view of the dancing girls was unobstructed. They had begun to move more wildly now and were holding hands. The first thing I noticed was that two hands held each other, another swung around the blonde's side, and that was it. Three arms. The brunette was missing an arm; the right sleeve of her down jacket was pinned into the pocket. I stood there for a few more minutes watching Melanie and her friend dance, until the song ended. I imagined suavely approaching and saying something like, "You guys put on quite a show," but when the song was over they applauded with the crowd for a second and then bolted for a staircase where the downtown N train was pulling up. I ran to catch up and slid through the closing train door right behind them.

"Excuse me, miss." I tapped Melanie's shoulder.

She turned around, a look of annoyance primed and ready. Then she saw me. "Wow. Holy shit, speak of the devil."

"And the devil appears." I smiled.

"Courtney, this is Jason. The guy I told you about." She looked back at me. "We were just talking about you this morning."

"Good. I hope."

"Of course good. Look at you." She smiled and looked me up and down, then threw her arm around my neck and kissed me. "Wow. It's great to see you."

They were playing hooky. We got off at Prince Street and headed for a café they knew of. The little buildings along the SoHo streets leaned solicitously toward one another against the bright winter sky, and no wind found its way down to the sidewalks. The air was still and cold and we moved through it smiling and bobbing, speeding up and slowing down, swinging around tiny withered New York trees, smoking, kicking the wire garbage cans just to hear the noise. In my solo walks I had started to think maybe there wasn't much to differentiate me from regular people after all. Sure, I kept my eyes open, unlike them, but no one noticed that: it was New York, and my long hair was not enough even to draw sideways looks. But now we were yelling to each other, hurrying for no reason, for sheer exuberance, dodging the trudging masses. Melanie cursed cheerfully at people who got in her way. "Watch it," she told them. "Dickhead!" she shouted over her shoulder at a guy who said something to her. It felt good to be moving and acting against the grain.

I didn't tell Melanie I'd lived in town for five months the previous year, because I didn't want to have to explain why I hadn't called her. In fact it hadn't even occurred to me. Back then I had been too busy reinventing my time with Jane, mourning the loss of the fantasy I had conceived with her.

"We should hit the Hampton shows next month," Melanie said over coffee. She had become quite the fledgling Deadhead over the past year, gravitating immediately to Courtney, who had seen a few shows and was already hooked, when she got to her new school in town. But she hadn't softened her attitude or caved in to the bright side of hippie fashion. She wore a black T-shirt with a simple picture of a rat on it.

"I can't skip school," Courtney said.

"See," said Melanie, "I've been trying to convince her we should buy a car and go. I can get access to this bank account my grandmother left me. My parents want me to think it's off limits, but I read some of the paperwork, and I can get the money. It's like eight grand."

"Well, I'm supposed to be hanging around for a little while, maybe getting a job," I said.

"Oh fuck that. Come on. We could hit tour in style."

"Why don't we wait until they get to Hartford?" I offered. "There are a couple of Meadowlands shows, too."

"No half-assed shit. I'm going on tour. You two can mope around with your mommies if you want. Fuck school. Fuck my parents. I'm done with all that bullshit. This is it."

The fact that I did not believe in coincidence didn't help me to stay stoic. It was too easy for me to think this chance meeting had happened for a reason; and the pull I felt in my gut, the swelling in my chest at the thought of tour, was real. I had been off tour for half a year, just living in Berkeley and then hitching back east, thinking I was growing out of it. Garcia had been recovering from a coma most of that time anyway, so there weren't a lot of shows happening. But there was that old fishing line, threaded through all my vital organs, being tugged on again; it was powerful, and whatever was at the other end of the line shone brightly, like a clean sheet of rain at the front edge of a far-off squall. By then I'd learned enough to be a little afraid of it, but I also knew that a little fear can fuel excitement.

"Well," I said, still backing away from the idea.

"Yeehah," Melanie said. "You're in. One down. Come on Courtney."

"You don't need me now. I'll catch those Meadowlands shows. Maybe Hartford."

"Suit yourself, sad sack." She threw down the last shot of her coffee and lit one of my Camels off the table. Her skin had a smooth magnetic pallor, and her delicate features were made hard by darting, sullen eyes. She noticed me staring at her, something I couldn't seem to help. Leaning forward, she tossed her head softly to the side and made slits out of her eyes, pulling on the cigarette. Her hair had grown much longer and she shook her head so it fell straight over her lowered left shoulder into her lap, creating an earth-toned backdrop for her pale face. "See something you like?" she asked.

THE SOARING CEILING of the bank's main branch gave the room an ecclesiastical quality. Fluted stone buttresses arched at intervals where the ceiling met the tops of the walls, and molded themselves into tall semicolumns—sunk halfway into the walls—that extended to the floor. Melanie led the way, looking every bit the sad princess come into her inheritance. She wore a navy blue dress with square shoulders, the right one tailored shut smoothly with no sleeve. She wore navy stockings and black shoes with brass buckles. A black leather purse swung at her side. In it were her birth certificate, passport, bankbook for the account, and a letter of permission from her father, whose signature we had spent half a day forging. In the end we had settled for a good but shaky facsimile of it, figuring that would jibe with the story of him being on his deathbed. I was playing the older brother, Steven, who was away at college. My hair was in an immaculate ponytail, and I had on a tweed jacket I hadn't worn since being kicked out of my second prep school.

The representative we spoke to was a sleek young man whose name, Searle Montague, was engraved on a small brass plaque on his desk. His black hair was slicked straight back, and his accent was English.

"Well, of course we must ask for the paperwork and identification. It is a rather large, unscheduled withdrawal." He pronounced it *unshejooled*.

"Of course," said Melanie. She played it perfectly, handing him the bankbook, driver's license, and passport along with the typed letter of permission. "I think it's all there. Although I might have forgotten something. We've all been so scattered, with this awful chemotherapy going on."

"I understand," Montague said, nodding and looking over the documents, then looking slowly through another small sheaf of papers in front of him. "No it's all here. But . . ."

"Yes?" Melanie said.

I shifted in my seat and leaned forward, causing the leather to give a fartlike croak.

"You said you wanted to withdraw the entire amount in cash? Are you sure that's necessary? We can transfer it into a checking account for you and issue you a checkbook. Might that not make more sense?"

I could see Melanie freeze for a second, her brain probably working on the same problem mine was: What would we need eight thousand dollars in cash for?

"That would make a lot more sense," I said. "Wouldn't it, Sis?"

"Would it?" she turned to me.

"Yes, it's only really one thousand of it that we need in cash today, for that thing. Right?"

"Yeah," she said. "I guess you're right. Why don't we do that."

"Fine." Montague stood up with all the papers, pleased we had seen the sense in his idea. "You can both just wait here, and I'll get all this set up and bring back some forms for you along with some starter checks."

"Thank you," I said.

Waiting for him to come back, Melanie cast me a nervous glance. I reached over and ran my palm up and down her back, the gesture of a brother comforting a distraught sister. "Don't worry," I said.

Montague came back a few minutes later with some forms that he himself had filled out from the information on Melanie's identification. All that remained was for her to sign them and take possession of the checks and the ten hundred-dollar bills he laid in front of her.

"Thank you, sir," I said. "You've been very helpful."

"A pleasure," he said. He stood with us, shook our hands, and in parting gave us his best sympathetic smile, skillfully combining goodwill, condolence, and solicitude into one sincere expression. I hoped Melanie's parents wouldn't make trouble for him.

We arrived at a smaller branch of the bank the following morning and closed the account, taking it all in cash. We had lined up a meeting with a guy in Jersey to look at a little Toyota hatchback he was selling, and we bought it on the spot for fifteen hundred, driving with him down to the DMV and putting the car in my name since Melanie didn't have a driver's license.

I DIDN'T TELL MY MOTHER until the day before we left. We were having dinner at the dining room table, just the two of us, a rare occurrence.

"I thought there must be some reason you agreed so easily to have dinner with me," she said. "What happened to staying around and getting a job? What happened to school?"

"My plans changed."

She put her fork down on her plate slowly, and it made two dull clicks before she let it go. "Are you coming back?"

"I don't know."

"Okay, great." She rose and picked up her still-full plate and carried it into the kitchen.

I shoved in another forkful of spaghetti and chewed it. I was preparing the next one, twirling my fork over the mound of pasta, when I heard her plate crash into the sink, clanging against the empty pots.

Then she was in the doorway, and I had to look over my shoulder to meet her glare. She walked over and sat across from me. She had poured herself a fresh glass of wine, and she sipped from it.

"What'll you do for money?"

"Same as I always do. Sell T-shirts."

She nodded. "Who's going to make them? You're not with Randy this time, are you?"

"Let me worry about it, Mom."

"This girl you met, I suppose she has money. And it's her car, too?"

"Yes."

"Women don't like men living off them. You'll learn that."

"Then you'll be relieved to have me off your hands, I guess."

She smiled, unexpectedly, and for a second the tension evaporated. "Mothers are different," she said.

"Not that different."

She remembered why she was angry and her smile disappeared. "Your father worked hard to give you and your brother the best. You think this is what he had in mind?" This was her trump card. She had sprung it on me early. Too early, in fact. It was a weak play, and I was relieved.

"Dad doesn't have anything in mind, Mom. He's dead."

"Don't you talk about him that way."

I laughed. "What way? It's just the truth."

"The truth is you're an ungrateful brat," she said, speaking under her breath as she got up and walked toward the kitchen. Then she grabbed a fistful of her own hair and turned back toward me. "Jason." Her voice was deeper, suddenly devoid of anger. "Don't go. Please. It's enough. You've done this enough. Just stay, please."

I stared at her. She had never pleaded with me before. She didn't move or speak. Finally I said, "I'm sorry. I'm going."

She was in the kitchen doorway, and the bright light behind her made it hard to see her expression. Wisps of her hair where she had grabbed it were bunched up and glowed in the light like sunspots during an eclipse.

"And what can I do about it?" she asked. The deepness of

her voice was becoming unstable. "What am I allowed to feel about it?"

"I'm sorry, Mom."

"No! What am I allowed to do? Explain to me how I should feel." There was a childish quality in her demands that scared me a little. I didn't understand what she was saying.

"Think of it like when you and Harry went to Italy," I said. "You wanted to stay and live there and be free and write poetry or whatever. Well this is me wanting that same kind of freedom."

"I was young and foolish."

I almost laughed, almost said, "Why is it wrong to be young and foolish?" because "Young and Foolish" was a song she performed on her piano so often that it had become a joke between James and me. She seemed unaware of the connection.

Suddenly she was screaming. "This is not about me! Following some fat guitar-playing guru around is not the same as living in Rome and working for a living. It's just not!"

I couldn't seem to shake the sense of comedy. I remembered a friend's father, an older southern gentleman, saying to him, "I understand it's your favorite group, but I don't have to go see the Glenn Miller Orchestra five times a week!" I suppressed laughter. "Hey," I said, smiling, "watch what you say about Jerry."

"I will not! Fat, drug addict, stinking old hippie! It's meaningless. That's what it is! You think what you're doing is romantic or important, that all these kids are your friends, but it's nothing! It goes nowhere!"

My smile became bigger, though I knew it wasn't helping me. I saw how angry she was, and felt the power that comes with being the only calm person in a fight. I couldn't help but use it. I shrugged grandly and looked away from her. "Whatever," I said.

She took a pause, staring me down, trembling. She was beginning to lose control. "If your father was alive to see you," she said, "he'd roll over in his grave."

I had been on the verge of laughter anyway when I heard her start the sentence, but the end of it threw me into hysterics. She started toward me. I couldn't stop laughing, even when I saw her hand go up. I raised my arms to protect my face, and felt the blow land on my elbow. It must have hurt her hand. "How dare you," came as a low growl up from her gut as she struck a second time, hitting the top of my head.

"No, Mom, please." She kept flailing at me with both hands, and I was still laughing, though beneath it I felt now the child's fear of an angry parent—what she had been trying to get me to feel all along. I tried to explain: "I just meant that if he was alive he wouldn't be in his grave. It's just funny." A closed fist landed on my mouth and I shut up. I tasted blood.

She stopped hitting me, moved two steps backward. Her arms fell to her sides. "Oh," she said, looking at the floor, as if she had dropped something valuable there in front of her. Then she fell to one knee, and I thought she really had dropped something. "Oh," she said again, "God," and began crying in thick, low sobs. She curled up on the hardwood floor and held her head in both hands. The sobs came from her in groups, with the rhythm of an engine failing to start in cold weather.

The dregs of laughter were curdled in my throat. "Mom . . ." I knelt by her and put my hand on her shoulder. "Mom?" But she only continued to cry, and I sat down and started rubbing her back. I pressed my mouth against the sleeve of my shirt, leaving a small bloodstain. "It's okay, Mom." She was in another world, her eyes blank as the small painted onions we'd used for a Halloween scarecrow once, except they were leaking tears. I didn't know how to retrieve her. I didn't know if I should try. "I'm here," I said. "I'm sorry."

Slowly she quieted. A long time later, when I looked down at her, she had drifted back in, her eyes still dazed but once again conducting thoughts. She staggered to her feet and whispered "Thanks" and walked off into her bedroom. I cleared the table and did the dishes. Then I packed the things I would need.

2

THE CAR WASN'T TOO CLEAN; it had spots of rust blooming around the edges of the body, dirt and brown stains hardened into the carpets and backseat, but it also had a tape deck and an electric sunroof, and the automatic transmission that Melanie needed. It ran smooth and quiet as we made our escape the following night down the New Jersey Turnpike. We listened to a Dead bootleg from two years earlier in Maryland, a show I had been at, and Melanie drove.

The intricate steaming hulks of refineries floated by on both sides, with million-gallon white tanks grouped at their edges like mammoth aspirins, and I thought of the leviathan hangovers they would be needed for. I smoked Camels and drank syrupy rest-stop Coke from a big paper cup, and every breath of air was a drug whose euphoria was familiar and carried no fear of hangover or crash: to be back in the magnetic slipstream of the Dead's caravan, to be headed for shows. And there was another feeling, from farther back. The plain pleasure of leaving. I had always felt it, and it was a kind of communion with my father. I knew that secretly, underneath the genuine sorrow of parting from his family, he must have felt it too, each time he walked out the door with a bag over his shoulder—that sudden lightness, that sense of rising trajectory.

Only on leaving my mother's apartment, each time, did I become fully aware of the subtle claustrophobia that overtook me while I was there, that inhabited the place like an insinuation of carbon monoxide, and slowly dulled my senses. To be in motion, even through the industrial stink of New Jersey, felt glorious and natural, and I popped out the Dead bootleg and put on some Rickie Lee Jones. I couldn't help thinking about the night before, the way my mother had cried, the featureless distance in her eyes when she lay on the floor. In the morning there had been no outward acknowledgment of it, only a certain caution in her manner as she made me breakfast, and a kindness, an attempt at understanding, in her voice as we spoke. Strangely, I had felt more comfortable, more connected to her. We talked innocuously of other people in the family and what they were up to, of James and gigs he had gotten recently, but I felt as if we were sharing something. I remembered a year earlier, when she had come with me to a Dead show in Philadelphia, where she was visiting my grandparents. She had insisted; she wanted to try to understand what I was into. I resolved to spend the evening with her, but the show was a good one and I couldn't resist going off to dance. "You go on," she said. "I'm really better off just observing it all by myself." So we made a place to meet and I went and found a spot to dance in one of the feeder halls. Two songs into the second set I turned around and saw her in the hallway, watching me. She waved and smiled and I said "Hi, Mom," and went over to her and hugged her. I was grateful not to see fear or confusion on her face as she watched me, and she was grateful that I wasn't embarrassed by her presence. It was a rare

hand on the wheel; her arm looked lonelier than ever for being occupied in such an essential activity. Her brow wrinkled and she smiled at me. "Quit worrying and break out that last bowl, will you?"

We talked about poetry. I read to her from *Leaves of Grass*, which she didn't like much—said it was too ecstatic, too straightforward for her. She had me dig into her bag for her copy of *Ariel*. I had never read any Sylvia Plath. She guided me to a stanza she loved:

And seen my strangeness evaporate,
Blue dew from dangerous skin.
Will they hate me,
These women who only scurry,
Whose news is the open cherry, the open clover?

We drove all night, straight down 95. After a couple of hours Melanie gave the wheel over to me and dozed off, and I took us the rest of the way. We arrived in Hampton Roads, Virginia, at 6 AM on the morning of the first show. We pulled in under the steep blue roof of an International House of Pancakes. I was bleary with road fatigue, and the building looked like a Fisher Price toy. I tottered straight-legged around the lot for a few seconds, yawning and swinging my arms at the silty-white sky, getting the blood moving. Inside, the sparse crowd was all prework locals, none of the heads having risen yet. I watched the hostess's face morph from wary appraisal to dewy-eyed pity when she noticed Melanie's missing arm. We sat in the smoking section and I doused my tall-stack with boysenberry syrup, the violet color of which shone in the white light from the window towering over our booth.

"How long do you think that money will last us?" Melanie asked.

"We could probably string it out through the summer without doing anything else. But I can use it to swing some deals here and there, and there's no telling how long it could last."

"Good."

Melanie was taking it all in stride. She hadn't been on tour before, but somehow she had already divined and adopted the air of a longtime tourhead, enthusiastic but unflappable, one seasoned eye always on the road ahead. She ate ravenously, as always, and I loved watching it. She chopped hunks four-thick off her stack of blueberry cakes and dragged them through the puddle of syrup she kept replenishing. She had to throw her mouth wide to get the bites in, and sometimes they would graze her lips and leave amber drips of syrup at the corners, which she would wipe away with her thumb and suck up. With her mouth packed, her long bulging lips slid from side to side and moved in unpredictable shapes, describing latent question marks and esses, salamanders, the front edge of a bird's wing. She saw me staring and smiled sheepishly, laughing through her nose as she chewed.

Around eight we left the wreckage of our breakfast and drove across the street to the Comfort Inn. We talked the clerk into giving us a room before check-in, then went up and showered together, slipped tired and naked into the bed. She kissed me.

"Use your mouth on me," I said. Lying back, I was so tired I could barely keep my eyes open.

Melanie went down on me and I stared out the window, where in the flat white sky the only motion was an occasional seagull flying past, always in the same direction, so it may have been one bird flying in big circles. With sleep sucking at my mind and Melanie sucking on my body, I gave in to utter delirium; I closed my eyes and pictured anything: trees dripping yellow leaves into pools of warm clear sweet syrup, my breath stirring the surface because it was all in my body, stirring up growing riffles. I wanted to say something, but the short unuttered sentence got itself confused between words and became a hovering bell I couldn't get to ring, and I tried to picture the sound it would make. I felt two fistfuls of linen and didn't remember gathering them.

WITH THE CITY OF VEHICLES laid out around it, the Hampton Coliseum became the spot, the place where it was happening. The country was full of these hollow cathedrals, kept useful by hockey and basketball games, Promise Keeper rallies, golf equipment expositions. Then we came and filled them up for a night or three, made them shine. I was reading Whitman, and thinking of the whole country as holy: every unfurled prairie and oil-stained filling station and filthy city, every mountain range and strip-malled nowhere had its eidolon; but when we gathered for shows it seemed to focus this quality, and the stadiums shimmered like mirages in the rising excitement. Any show might be one of those nights when the crowd and the band got together and hammered out something powerful, joyous, and deeply, if fleetingly, important. The parking lots teemed with old-timers, fledglings, saints, schoolkids, crazies, metalheads, jagged-eyed prophets, punks, junkies, ascetics. Why did so many people congregate around a rock band? Put their lives on hold, or make their lives on tour? To have fun, yes. To party and get high and associate with all manner of freaks, sure. But that couldn't be the crux of the biscuit, as Zappa put it. There was something the music drew from us, and from the ether, and on those nights we became distilled, purified, drunk on it. The drugs and love and sex and craziness were crucial, but it was this lenslike quality of the music that gathered and focused the inner numen of the land, drew us back again and again, and created among us a vortex of expectancy, obsession, and ritual.

In the late afternoon, Melanie and I wandered around the lot looking for tickets. There hadn't been a fall tour because of Jerry's diabetic coma, and the Dead hadn't played the East Coast for eight months, so the crowds were big and starved and tickets were scarce. Though among the faces many were familiar, I didn't see anyone I knew well. Melanie rode on my back for a while, biting my ears and laughing when I screamed, and I liked the feel of her thighs in my hands. Near the stadium we eventually came across a scalper. I hated buying from them, and avoided it on general principle, but we were flush with cash and I didn't want to worry about tickets the whole time. I talked him down to forty apiece, which still seemed high, and got tickets for all three nights.

We bought two plates of spicy vegetable stir-fry from a couple with a camp stove behind their van. The guy, a disheveled kid from North Carolina with a sneaky smile that came and went like a lightning strike on his face, asked me if I needed any buds, and I climbed into the van with him to check them out.

The kid pulled out a preweighed quarter-ounce and held it out to me. "Here it is, dude." His wrist was so pale and thin that the round bone on top protruded like a tumor.

I took the bag and unrolled it. I pulled a long bud out and smelled it. It was good *sativa*, with very few seeds, but I knew I could do better. "Yeah," I said, not wanting to hurt his feelings. "This is nice, but I'm looking for some *indica*. Thanks, though, man."

"What do you mean? This is some good smoke."

"I know," I said. "But it's not what I'm looking for." I got out of the van, thanked him and his girlfriend for the stir-fry, and we moved on.

We met Judah, a tall, gaunt West Coast sadhu with masses of bushy brown hair who wore the shell of a giant sea turtle strapped to his back with his belongings inside and carried a six-foot didjeri-doo as a staff. He played it beautifully too, and I remembered hearing its deep eerie throat-song throbbing and echoing through the streets of Berkeley at night. The sound snaked over the buildings and through the alleys, and you could hear it blocks away. Judah came and went in Berkeley like the weather, his travels mysterious, always solitary.

"Hey there, Judah," I said.

His smile arrived slowly on his sun-browned face, and ruled it completely. "Brother," he said. "How are you?"

"I'm well. How are you?"

"Good. Some fine traveling the past few months. Powerful places. Now I'm trying to be serene on the East Coast."

"That can be tough." I returned his smile. "This is Melanie."

Judah looked at her and gave her a deep bow.

"Nice to meet you," Melanie said.

"Likewise." He nodded slowly, keeping eye contact with her. "Your missing arm gives you power, but you need to be careful. The power comes from pain, and has to be converted."

Melanie's face became serious. "Okay."

"Go well," said Judah, and his long legs carried him past us in great strides. The pale green shell bobbed behind him on its leather straps.

"Wow," said Melanie. "Where do you know him from?"

"The West Coast. From hanging around Berkeley. He's more of a wanderer than a Deadhead, but he goes to a lot of shows out west. I've never seen him on the East Coast before."

"Wow," she said again, shaking her head. "We should get some acid for the show tonight."

"We don't need to trip tonight. Let's just find some buds."

"No. I want to take acid."

"You sure you want to? It's your first show."

"That's exactly why I need to. To get the full experience."

"Tripping at a show is one experience," I said. "Not necessarily *the* experience."

But she wanted to trip and there was no talking her out of it. Over the past couple of years I had wearied of acid. My mind had gotten tired of the work it took to get through a trip, and the places the drug took me became less unpredictable. But I couldn't let her go it alone. So I bought two hits off a guy in the lot whose face I recognized from past tours. Acid was so plentiful and cheap, and so many people I knew trafficked in it, that a couple of hits was something I could usually get for free. I hadn't bought single hits in the parking lot for years, and it made me feel taken down a notch, socially. The guy recognized me, though, and charged me only two bucks. That made me feel a little better. He swore it was fresh and clean.

"No shit, man," he said. "The real deal here. Old school stuff. You could go with half apiece if you wanted to."

Inside, we went to a spot at the back of the floor where I had danced in years past and where we'd likely meet with friends. I gave her one of the hits, and put the other on my tongue. She did the same with hers. We stood watching the people file in and mill around, smoking joints and bowls and cloves and cigarettes, finding places to stack up their jackets and bags.

"How long till it starts to work?" Melanie asked.

"About half an hour, maybe forty-five minutes," I said. Then something hit me: "Is this your first trip?"

"Yeah. I thought you knew that." Her face contracted; she had heard the surprise in my voice.

"No," I laughed, taken aback, but I quickly paved over my apprehension. I smiled broadly at her. "Oh, boy, are you in for some fun." I hugged her and kissed her neck. She pulled me in tighter and buried her face in my chest.

The show opened with "Hell in a Bucket," Garcia shredding beautifully on the bluesy intro, and we started to dance. Melanie had been to enough hippie-band shows at clubs like the Wetlands in New York and heard enough Dead bootlegs to have the dancing down. The acid kicked in around the middle of the set, during "West L.A. Fadeaway." The initial rush was clean and muscular and fast. I could tell right away this wouldn't be an average one-hit trip: it came up behind me like a comet, and I began dancing more fiercely to keep up with it, to maintain a groove and stay on top of the high. If you let the first rush overtake you, it could leave you blinking and confused in its wake and then drag you around hooked to its thrashing tail for the next six or eight hours. You had to climb on top of it from the start, sink your fists in and ride it unafraid—if not in control of it, then at least grafted to it.

By the time the first set ended with "Deal," I was riding it like a pro, bouncing around the room's rafters, conceiving concentric alternate bodies for myself one after the other and letting them burn off in the fireball of the song's final jam, throwing myself heedlessly forward and around, the music becoming both fuel and vehicle. When the set was over, I looked around for Melanie and saw her swaying toward me in her white T-shirt and jeans. She smiled back at me. When I looked into her eyes I saw that she was tangled in the comet's tail.

"You okay, baby?" I asked. My voice felt velvety, liquescent and cool in my chest. It made me want to keep speaking. "This is some way-out stuff," I said, just to feel the sound spreading through me again.

"Yeah." She nodded uncertainly. "I think I'm okay."

"Good," I said. "How about a soda and a smoke."

"Sure."

We went off into the hallway crawling with humanity, where the bright yellowish light dripping from above was like a haze, obscuring rather than illuminating the colorful crowd, the rows of salmon-colored metal doors to the outside, the sour-faced beer-and-pretzel wallahs, the cement columns—all of whose real illumination came from within. Standing in line for concessions, a girl behind us lit a clove cigarette. I smelled it and had to have one.

"Oh, god," I said to her. "We would be very thankful if you could spare one of those cloves."

"Yeah, sure," she said. I watched the straight blond hair that curtained her face pendulum as she nodded, like a rack of gold chains in a light breeze. She popped open the red Djarum tin and handed one to me.

I lit it, hearing it crackle softly, and hung the smoke in my mouth for a moment before inhaling it. "Here," I offered it to Melanie.

"No thanks," she said. "I'll have a regular cigarette."

"No, no." I shook my head and pushed it closer. "Trust me on this one."

She took the clove and pulled on it. As she exhaled she moaned, "Oh, yeah. How right you are."

We passed it back and forth. There's something about the sharp flavor of a clove that cuts right through you on acid, clearing away the sensational cobwebs and melting the gelid saliva in your mouth and throat. It's the only time I ever smoked them.

We bought a large Coke and sat against the wall in the arena drinking it and smoking the clove. Melanie wasn't saying much, but I could tell she was on edge. My own visuals were beginning to go beyond the typical—nothing scary, but rampant melting of colors into each other and trails streaking from anything moving. And red smelled like woodsmoke in my brain.

"Mel, you okay?"

"Yeah," she nodded. Then she said, "This stuff will wear off, right? I mean, you hear about people never coming down."

This is one of the bad thoughts. It can quickly become a bottomless well of fear. "No no no." I took her face in my hands. "That never happens. You hear me? Never. Just enjoy the high. Five or six hours from now you'll be the same as ever. Okay?"

"Okay."

But I could see it wasn't just that. The drug was taking her places.

"It feels weird," she said, "not to have an arm. When I was dancing, I kept throwing my right arm this way or that and then being freaked out when it wasn't there. Back in line I even reached for the clove with my right hand. It's like it's really there until I look at it or try to use it, and then it disappears. I feel off balance. . . . No. What I really feel is what I am: deformed. I gloss over it every day, and now I really feel it. Malformed. Incomplete. Hideous. Oh, fuck. Am I hideous?"

"What? Hideous? Jesus no. You are so beautiful."

"Thanks for saying that."

I palmed her neck. "I am not just saying that."

Her eyes were confused prisms, refracting her mind in slanted, broken beams. I could see her trying, and failing, to reconstruct her cynical veneer.

"Can I tell you something else?" I said. "Without you thinking I'm some kind of weirdo?"

"Too late for that."

"True." I was glad she still had her sense of humor.

"Go ahead."

"I'm not sure I should be telling you this."

"Just spit it out."

"Okay." I put my arm around her, and held the small mound below her right shoulder in my hand. "Your arm kind of turns me on sometimes. Like when we're making love. Is that too strange?"

"Too strange?" Her eyes widened. She smiled. "No, baby. That's about the nicest thing you've ever said to me." She pulled me in and we kissed.

"Hey," came a voice from above. "This is a public place, you know."

I looked up and saw Cole coming toward us in a white tank top.

"Where the hell have you been?" he asked.

"New York for a while," I said. I stood up and hugged him. Somehow his thin body stayed muscular and well toned, though I was sure he got almost no exercise.

"Man, so you missed the San Fran Civic shows, and the Kaiser shows, huh?"

"Yeah. What about you? You were incognito for a while."

"I was living down in Tucson with this woman Nora, getting quiet and domestic. I hit tour again last month."

I reached down and took Melanie's hand and pulled her upright. "Cole, this is Melanie. It's her first show."

"Hey Melanie. Lucky you. Welcome." He stepped in and gave her a slow hug, the same hug he had given me when he first met me. Then he looked back at me. "Oh wow," he noticed my eyes and looked from me to Melanie. "You guys are way up there. Acid or Ex?"

"Acid," I said.

He laughed. "Yeah, school days again. Where are you dancing?"

"Right here."

Cole was reaching into his small black knapsack. "You should come around to Phil's side. A bunch of folks are up there."

"Where are you staying?"

He pulled out a pack of Camel straights and tapped two free. "Comfort Inn." He gave one to me and lipped the other. "Got a light?"

"Yeah. Us, too." I lit his cigarette, the scrape and puff of the lighter vivid in my ears, then brought the flame to mine. The past felt glossed over. I knew I'd have to ask him about Dawn eventually, but I couldn't help being glad to see him. Cole was an institution on tour, and I had spent so long being proud to count him as a friend that it was hard to think of him any other way. I told him we'd see him up on Phil's side, and he took off.

Before the second set started, Melanie got restless. "Come on," I said. "I'll show you around." We took a stroll in the hallway. Near the back of the stage we ran into an Om circle—thirty or so people locked together with arms over shoulders or around waists, swaying and chanting long Oms toward some focal point, their eyes closed. The sound made waves in the ether that brushed against my face. Melanie didn't say anything. We just stood watching. Now and then someone would tap a couple of people on the shoulder, and the circle would part to allow them to join. Billy and Lamar, two West Coasters I knew, were walking past the circle in front of us, and stopped to check out a girl's ass-crack, an inch or so of which was visible above the top of her sagging drawstring skirt. They were smiling; Billy had a nose like a pickax and a sharp hooked smile to match it. He reached forward and tugged on the girl's skirt. Another two inches of crack came into view. He and Lamar reared back and laughed silently. The girl was immersed in the chant and didn't notice. After a second, Billy stepped up and slowly tugged the skirt down again, this time exposing most of the girl's ass. It took her a second to register the breeze and reach behind her. She pulled the skirt up and looked back over her shoulder. When she saw Billy standing there, he laughed aloud, a little sheepishly, and held out his hands in a gesture of helplessness that blamed the whole thing on the beauty of her ass. The girl smiled at him and shook her head.

"Nice move, Billy," I called to him as he and Lamar walked past.

Both of them laughed and waved at me, but didn't stop.

"You know those guys?" Melanie asked.

"Yeah. They're friends from out west."

"They better not try that shit on me."

I laughed. "Don't worry. Billy's cool. His name's not even really Billy."

"What is it?"

"I'm not sure. I just know he's got old warrants or something. He calls himself Billy Genovese, like the mob family. But that's not his real name."

In fact I did know Billy's name. It was George Mandanopoulos, but I was sworn to secrecy. There were a lot of these marginal fugitives on tour, who changed their names or used more than one. Like Riff, whose ID gave his name as Henry Winkler; or Daniel, who went by Chuck—his mother had played the mother of a boy named Chuck in an old TV sitcom. If you could get enough people to start calling you something, that's who you were. And the Dead's arcana offered a deep well of fake names, too. People were always registering at hotels under names like Jack Straw, Billy De-Lyon, August West, and Delilah Jones.

As we were watching the Om circle, the lights fell and the band went into "Sugar Magnolia." The circle disintegrated, the chanters drifting off like sky divers breaking formation to pull their chutes.

The hallway began to clear out, and I headed for one of the openings. Melanie pulled me back.

"It's nicer out here," she said. "Let's stay out here for a minute. More to look at."

"Fine." I didn't mind at all. "Sugar Mag" didn't excite me much. I preferred edgier or more free-form second-set tunes. We started walking again, holding hands. I could feel the erratic pulse of Melanie's mind through her sweaty hand. I looked at her now and then, but she was spacing out on the crowd, trying to be free of herself. The hallway was where a lot of the wilder dancers plied their trades, and we saw them running, swirling, arched over backward, as we moved.

"What are they doing?" Melanie asked, pointing at a loose cluster of people all spinning in place like dervishes, skirts and shirts and robes billowing around them, eyes closed.

"Those are the spinners," I said. "They always do that."

"Why?"

"I don't know. Some kind of trance thing. They have a meditative experience or something. They never seem to get dizzy."

We watched the spinners for a while. Their movements made them blurs, and they infused the light around them with the bleeding colors of their clothing. Some held their arms flung outward, and some clasped them to their chests or pulled them through intricate contortions in front of closed eyes. All maintained worshipful silence during the pauses between songs.

The Boys went into "Scarlet Begonias," and I dragged Melanie through the opening nearest us. We were up on Phil's side, the left side of the stage, right where Cole and the others were dancing. Phil's side was usually the spot, since Jerry's side tended to get more crowded with locals. Saul was there, and Carolina Liz, and Dread Jim, who had cut off his dreads a year earlier. The only dreads in sight were Anthony's, which draped to his beltline; he tossed them around like some medieval weapon when he danced, and had to be given wide berth. Nothing worse than closing your eyes, leaning in to commune with one of the band's crescendos, and catching a faceful of prickly dreadlocks.

I hadn't seen Saul since the summer. I'd heard he and Don had been living together on the East Coast. Jane and Don had broken up for good a year earlier, but I hadn't spoken to either of them.

"Hey Jason," Saul said, when he noticed me dancing near him. "Don would love to see you."

"Really? Why? To bust me in the nose again?"

"Nah. All that shit's in the past. I mean it wasn't just you. Jane was fucking everyone for a while. Hell, I fucked her. Don's beyond that now."

I screwed my eyes in tight, closing them and nodding, to cover the sting that whipped through me. "Is he around?" The sentence leapfrogged over its unuttered counterpart: *Is she around?*

"No, he's meeting us in Hartford. Maybe Philly. He went to New York." Saul looked tired, and he went back to dancing in his languid way, just bobbing his head and occasionally shuffling his feet an inch or two to either side. At high points he would close his eyes and bow deeply from the waist, arms bent, big hands open and hovering like flippers near his thighs.

THE CLOUD COVER had been blown into streaks of gray across the black, with a few stars showing through. The night was cool. The lot after a show didn't have the air of expectancy it did beforehand; the atmosphere was festive but satiated, like people kicking back and belching after a huge meal. We had been gliding aimlessly for an hour or two, not wanting to go back to the hotel room. A breeze from the east, carrying a tinge of the sea, flapped our clothing and pulled lightly at our hair. Melanie's head space hadn't improved, and she was straggling along on my right, clinging to my hand. I would ask her every so often if she wanted something, a cigarette, some food or drink, or to go to the room, and she would just shake her head and force a weak smile.

At the back of a brown school bus I bought us two cups of mint tea, which the proprietor sweetened with honey he said came from his own hives. It felt so good going down our throats that both of us held the cups near our faces and groaned between sips. The steam coated my face, writhing with ghosts as it rose past my eyes. Whiffs of brightness stung my nostrils as a pair of headlights swept across us—it smelled like electricity and lemons, but at its core had the same original musk as all light, carried endlessly forward from the big bang: the residuum of creation. There was the feeling that these hours were timeless, not because they would always go on, but because they had always *been* going on, stretching back into prehistory, slipping silently, unbelievably along beneath the surface of time.

We saw a woman down on one knee in front of a small bed of wildflowers that had sprouted in the dirt at the base of a huge light pole. I thought she was going to pick some, but she clasped both hands over her chest and began, in a beautifully trained voice, to sing an Italian aria to them. She did it softly, but with power and perfection, and the bright tiny pink and purple flowers nodded in appreciation, their colors flaring and rippling like embers under a long breath.

"Okay," said Melanie after we finished the tea. "Let's go back to the room and just watch TV or something. Maybe that'll calm me down."

So we crossed the lot, where few people showed signs of preparing to leave, and walked down the block toward the Comfort Inn. Out on the four-lane county road, which was lined with small strip malls and convenience stores and fast-food joints, there was the surreal sense that we owned this place: heads were the only people moving in that suburban night. Another couple—a lanky boy whose jeans dragged the ground behind his heels, and his moccasined Indian-skirted waif—trudged back toward the venue on the other side of the road carrying bedrolls and Guatemalan satchels, looking for somewhere to crash. A Jetta bearing four smiling scruffy college freshmen skipping their midterms to see shows stopped in a KFC driveway just in front of us, "Touch of Grey" blasting tinnily from the stereo, before chirping off toward the hotels. Up ahead a gas station boomed with late-night business: a green VW microbus, a blue early-eighties Ford Granada, and an old brown Celica were parked by the pumps. A burly guy in a red "The Fat Man Rocks" T-shirt emerged from the store with a bag of groceries in each hand. He stopped in front of the Granada and exchanged a look with someone inside, then he held the bags up like trophies and whooped at the sky before getting in.

We stopped at the convenience store and bought orange juice and a jug of water. The kid behind the counter smiled so widely at me I thought his lavish pimples might explode and I turned away, flinching. After that, as he bagged our beverages and made change, his looks became flickering sidelong glances that sliced at me and made me paranoid. Melanie's bad trip was starting to bleed into me.

At the Comfort Inn the night manager had abandoned the front desk for the back office, and there were four heads—three guys and a big woman who seemed to be in charge—manning the lobby's small sitting area, selling single beers out of a cooler.

"Beer might do us some good," I said. "How much?"

"Miller a buck, Becks two bucks," the woman said. The guy next to her was skinny, his sharp chin tufted with pale hair, and he passed his arm over her mountainous shoulders, let his hand slide down around her bulging hip. He saw me following his hand and grabbed a pound or so of hip flesh and shook it, smiling. She laughed and elbowed him in the chest, knocking him against the back of the small sofa. "Enough of that," she said. With a stab I thought of Dawn. I had never written to her. The crumpled address was still tucked away in my wallet.

"We'll take four Millers," I said.

One of the other guys leaned forward and fished the cans from the icy water while I paid the woman. "You be cool," the guy said, passing them to me. "The manager asked us to tell people have fun but please don't mess up the rooms or the hallways or anything. He said long as things stay cool there won't be any cops or hassles. He's a cool guy, but he'll get in trouble if things get out of hand."

"Don't worry about us," I said. I put the beers in the plastic bag with the orange juice. Melanie had my hand and was pulling me toward the lone elevator. "We're just as peaceful as can be."

TV didn't help. Melanie couldn't stop staring at herself in the mirror, and I kept having to force her to come out of the bathroom. I hung a bedspread over the mirror above the bureau and harried her into drinking three of the beers. It could have been water for all the effect it had.

"You're going to be okay," I told her.

She nodded and said, "I know," not believing it. Then she looked at me and said, "Please stop saying that, will you. How is it that I'm going to be okay? Tell me that."

"This'll be over in the morning."

She hung her head. Her face was the deep color of a radish and radiated heat I could see, waves of red light. Neither of us had started to come down yet. "You don't know what you're talking about," she said.

"Tell me, then. What is it? Tell me what's happening."

"You don't want to know."

She was right. "Yes I do."

She looked at me, black-eyed, only the thinnest ring of brown iris showing at the edges of her yawning pupils. The look shot right through to the back of my skull. I tried to hold it, to be willing to understand where it came from, but I lasted only a second before turning away.

"I'll go find something to help out, some booze or something," I said. "I'll be right back."

She didn't answer me.

Cole had given me his room number, and I went upstairs to see him and Saul.

When I knocked on the door, there was only silence on the other side. I waited a minute, almost walked away, then knocked again, harder. I heard a muffled syllable from the room and someone moving. The person stopped just across the door from me and stood there a few seconds before saying, "Who is it?"

"It's Jason."

Another pause. "You alone?"

"Yes. Just me."

The door opened and Saul beckoned me in. He and Cole were there along with my old friend Hartford Bob. The TV was on but barely audible, showing an old Steve McQueen movie. The one lamp that was on was draped in a blanket, so it gave off only a weak reddish-green glow. Cole and Bob were lying on one of the beds, facing the TV, and Saul went back to his place on the other bed.

"Hey guys," I said. "How are you, Bob?"

Bob didn't answer me, and in a brighter flash from the TV I saw past the shadow of his curly brown hair: his eyes were closed.

"He's out," Cole said. He seemed to have just woken up himself. He picked up the remote from next to his thigh and turned the volume up a little. Steve McQueen was pointing a gun at a big black man and speaking calmly.

"Listen," I said, "I can't stay away too long. Melanie's kind of freaking out. She's on a bad trip. I need something to bring her down, some booze or Valium or whatever. Wouldn't mind coming down myself at this point. You guys have anything?"

Saul laughed, a slow reverberation through the room. "Do we have anything?" He laughed again. "Oh boy."

"Yes," said Cole. "We have anything."

Saul pushed himself into a sitting position on the bed, his feet on the floor, and began rummaging in a black nylon duffel. He came up with something in his hand. "Snort one of these each, and if that doesn't do the trick, which it probably will, then do another."

He handed me four small white rectangular packets, made of the wax paper used for keeping stamps in. I could see there was white powder in them.

"I can't give those away. You can have them for twenty apiece."

"What is it?" I asked.

"What is it?" Saul zipped the duffel shut and looked at me. "It's heroin."

"Jesus. I guess this will do the trick."

"You guess right."

"I don't actually have eighty on me. You want me to get it from my room?"

"Jason's good for it," Cole said from the other bed.

"Yeah," said Saul, "that's cool. Just pay me tomorrow."

"Okay, thanks. Tell Bob I said hello."

Cole reached across the bed and poked Bob in the shoulder, then in the ribs. "Wake up, Bobby. Look who's here."

Bob's eyelids lifted sluggishly, making it halfway open. He couldn't have seen more than my legs. "Hey there," he mumbled, and closed his eyes again.

BACK IN THE ROOM, Melanie was watching a cartoon on PBS with the volume turned way up. She motioned for me to be quiet as I entered, so I sat on the edge of the bed and watched with her. The animation was deliberately primitive, colored in pastel pinks, greens, and blues. The characters waddled stiltedly through motionless outdoor landscapes and spoke in cloying falsettos. As near as I could figure, a young armadillo had been bumped on her head and was suffering amnesia. A mean little girl was trying to convince the armadillo she was a cat, and a nice girl was telling her the truth. The problem was that the armadillo found the idea of being a cat more desirable and persisted in attempting dangerous catlike activities, with no success.

"I brought us something."

"Wait." Melanie's rapt face didn't even flit from the screen. Her focus on the cartoon was manic, unsound. I wondered what it meant to her. I waited, and in the end the armadillo of course realized all the beauty of being an armadillo and waddled into the sunset with her friend, the nice girl. In the last moment, before blackness closed them into a disappearing pinprick, the armadillo tried once more to leap over a fence instead of going under it, banged into the top rail and fell back into the grass, but this time she and the girl just laughed happily.

"Wow," Melanie said, the word hanging out in front of her all alone. She looked at me for some sign that I understood, that I had seen what she had.

"You feeling any better?" I asked.

"Better?" She squinted. Fear welled behind her eyes, as if the word "better" carried with it the possibility of its opposite. Her hand crept unconsciously across her chest and gripped her barren right shoulder.

"Talk to me," I said.

Her fear became stronger, and I could see it, an orange aurora radiating from her. She shook her head, no.

"I think you need this." I took one of the tiny bags, slit the tape sealing it with the room key, unfolded it, and dumped the powder onto the night table. I used my driver's license to push it into a line and rolled a dollar into a tube. "You want to come down?"

She nodded.

"Here." I held the dollar out for her. "Snort this, it'll bring you down."

She rolled across the bed, took the dollar from me, leaned over, and pulled the small white line up her nostril in one sure motion. Then she kicked back on the bed and focused again on the TV.

"My turn," I said.

It was about ten minutes later, as we sat silently glued to the dancing bright screen, that Melanie said out of the blue, quietly, "Oh, thank God."

I looked over at her, and her eyes were closed, her face tilted toward the ceiling. She took a deep breath, and as she exhaled, she moaned: "Mmmmmm . . ."

LYING ON THE BED, as the TV became babble in the middle distance and my charged thoughts were being drowned in warm molasses, I remembered something from years earlier. It was on one of my weekends with Harry Waldron, the second year after my father died. Waiting for the F train, he pointed to one of the iron support posts on the platform. I followed his finger to a tiny word scratched into the brown paint of the post: "Pray."

"See that?" Harry said.

"Yeah, so."

"You'll find it on every post on every platform in the city."

I didn't believe him, and went up and down the platform searching the posts. If I looked hard enough, it was always there. It switched sides and levels—sometimes I found it down near the floor—but it was there. For the rest of that Christmas vacation, whenever I was waiting for a train, I looked for "Pray" on the platform posts, finding it everywhere I went. It was always in the same tiny runic print, pointed in all the places it should have been curved, and from this I inferred it was one man—homeless, I imagined, overtaken by obsessive faith—charged with a mission by his God. I thought it was the craziest, most beautiful thing I had ever encountered. It never actually prompted me to pray, but it comforted me somehow, gave me a warm feeling on cold days, knowing this crazy saint was out there trying to do his bit to improve the world, knowing the subways below those streets all carried that divine admonition. It was beautiful: a monumental undertaking performed with no grandiosity; he didn't scrawl it in spray paint, but scratched it almost illegibly, so small most people wouldn't notice it even if they looked right at it. Once I found a station with its posts just repainted, clean of all markings, and was disappointed. But when I visited there again, just before I went back to boarding school in Connecticut, the fresh green paint on all the posts had been tagged "Pray" again, the scrawled word standing out on the virgin surfaces. This is what I remembered as I lay there having my first heroin rush, which on top of the LSD was more a soothing of the trip than anything else, a warm calm moving through me. My eyes drifted to a triangle of cardboard standing on top of the television that read, "Welcome to Comfort Inn."

WOKE THE NEXT MORNING to a blade of sunlight from between the curtains, cutting the bed in half across our midsections. Stumbled to the bathroom and peed, drew a glass of water. Pushed the curtains partway open and looked out onto the parking lot. The sky was spotless blue, midmorning sun lighting everything with nostalgic vividness. The day betrayed no memory of the night before. A girl in jeans and a brown leather coat sat on the hood of a green Dodge Dart, smoking a cigarette. It was as if time wasn't going by, but just ebbing and flowing and washing everything clean, and I was transported to the blissful summer tours of my early days. I thought about my first summer tour in eighty-five, those venues I still remember as so pristine: The Greek Theater, Alpine Valley, Riverbend, Blossom, Saratoga, Merriweather. I saw how hipness had covered me—many of us—over since then, like a heavy flame-retardant blanket, barely allowing us to smolder. We made the band work hard to cut through our cool, throwing it off only when everything came together, instead of every night. How much rarer now were the truly ecstatic shows? How often these days did I close my eyes and puff out my chest and smile from deep inside as Jerry sang "He's Gone" or looped through his solo on "Tennessee Jed"? How many times in the past year had I become a deep pool reflecting pure joy back at the band?

In a way, the change was natural. Those high points were still there, but innocence had been steeped in experience and I wasn't so easily awed. When I looked over at Melanie, though, her face blank with sleep, her breath entering and leaving her body evenly, I wondered if she would ever experience days like those.

She rolled over, waking up, smacking her lips with dehydration. I brought her the half-full glass of water and held it to her lips as she propped herself up on her arm. She drank it down.

"Thanks," she said, and flopped back onto the pillow.

"How are you feeling?" I asked.

"Oh, fine as wine," she croaked sickly. She smiled and closed her eyes. "Mmm, wine might be nice right about now."

I jiggled a can of Miller on the bedside table that wasn't quite empty. "The champagne of beers," I said.

She laughed and shook her head. "Get that away from me. Jesus, last night was intense. I was a fucking wreck, wasn't I?"

"I've seen much worse."

She lit one of her Marlboros and sat up against the headboard. "For some reason I keep thinking about that guy Judah, what he said to me."

"What about it?"

"Well, I've always thought that having one arm gave me some kind of power. Part of me is proud of it. You know, it can fuck me up like it did last night, but ultimately I feel like I know some things that most people don't. Maybe that's what he was talking about."

"Yeah," I said. "You just have to learn to convert it into something positive."

She looked at me as if I'd challenged her. "I know what he said. You don't have to tell me."

"We're just talking here. If there's a problem, name it."

Her mouth twisted into a crooked frown, as if she couldn't decide whether to laugh or spit, and she sucked on the cigarette. She looked away from me. "Right," she said, a little bitterly, "like a well-done sum."

"What's that supposed to mean?"

She looked at me again and shook her head. "Nothing."

"Look, whatever's wrong, it's a misunderstanding. Let's start over."

She touched my face. "A clean slate," she said. She smiled, but inwardly, not at me. I felt left out of a moment she was having with herself. Then, like the tumbler of a lock falling into place, her expression turned over and fastened on me. She said, "All right. Come here, Boy Wonder," and kissed me.

More and more our lovemaking became the kind that wipes everything else, the world, away, so that afterward you feel alien and the other person is the only thing left to cling to. It's a strange, beautiful, guilty kind of love. When you go out into the world, you carry it like a secret, you hold it over others like power, exchange it through eyes when others speak: *we don't need them, any of them.* You feel superior. You devour it hungrily when alone together. And you anger easily when it seems to falter, in yourself or the other. It becomes as fulfilling and exasperating as caring for a child.

At the other two Hampton shows I sought out dancing spots among the more ecstatic tourheads, to give her that feeling and to try recovering some of it myself. My first spring tour had started right there in Hampton, two years earlier, and I let myself rediscover that wide-eyed kid in moccasins and faded tie-dye: I actually danced to "Touch of Grey" and "Little Red Rooster," songs during which normally I would do no more than bob my head and yawn, and I didn't sneak out to be first in line for concessions when "Don't Ease Me In" closed the first set. High on nothing but air the second night, I stayed on the floor with Melanie, moving all the way through the drum solo, letting the rhythms pound my bones and bring me beyond my modern consciousness into the primal passageways within the beat. I still had access to all those places, the music still opened those doors. I closed my eyes and tranced out through "Space," and was rewarded when Phil dropped the bomb and the Boys charged into "The Other One."

All that didn't last long, though. I couldn't keep it up. A guy I knew came up to me at intermission the first night in Hartford and said, "How'd you like that 'C.C. Rider'?" "I don't know," I said. "I was taking a piss." Taking a piss during "C.C. Rider" had become almost automatic for me over the past year, the slow blues bass line triggering a Pavlovian reaction in my bladder, and I would usually be standing at a urinal when Bobby's lugubrious, off-key attempt at a slide solo reached me muffled by a cinder-block wall. It had actually been a great first set that night, and I couldn't see why anyone would focus on that song.

The third night in Philadelphia, before the show started, Melanie and I climbed the long column of concrete steps on the upper deck to the highest bleacher seats. We sat with our backs against the wall, the crowd throbbing, growing below us, and snorted the other two bags of heroin. Everyone around us was getting stoned. We lit cigarettes and waited for the high. Just as I was feeling the first softening of vision, the gentle plummeting in my chest, a voice was nearby, saying my name. I looked up, but there were a few people on the staircase near our seats. Which one?

"Hey, Jason. Right here."

It was Don. He stepped across Melanie's legs and grabbed my shoulder. I stood up to hug him, the pale rush inside me streaked now with green tension. "How are you, motherfucker?" he said. His embrace was hearty at first, then it hurt a little.

"I'm fine," I said. "It's good to see you."

He let me go. "Saul said you were back on tour." He grabbed my nose between two fingers, smiling. "How's your nose doing?"

I pulled my head back. "It's all better." He was looking right at me. I pointed to Melanie, "This is Melanie. Melanie, Don."

"Nice to meet you, Melanie." They shook hands.

"Likewise," Melanie said.

Don's face and neck looked wirier than before, even through the short beard he had grown back. "You guys doing the whole tour?"

"Yeah," I said. "In for the duration, looks like."

"Killer. Look me up in Worcester. I'll be at the Sheraton under Tom Banjo."

"Nice. We'll see you there."

Don strode back to the aisle, then looked over his shoulder and pointed a finger at me, saying, "Watch out for this guy, Melanie," and glided down the stairs.

The set opened strongly, and we went down to the lower hallway on Phil's side to dance. But near the end of the set, during the good but overlong "Desolation Row," I said, "Let's go back up to the bleachers."

"Yeah, okay," said Melanie. We were dancing sluggishly anyway, and it felt better to sit and soak the music in. The second set was pretty standard fare, though it closed with a good "Lovelight" that got us to our feet. We headed out just as the "Brokedown Palace" encore was starting. Normally I liked the sweetness of the tune, but beating the crowd seemed like a good idea. As we banged through a fire exit behind the stage, I could hear Jerry singing Hunter's lyric, "Make myself a bed, by the waterside."

We turned in the direction we thought our car was in and began walking around the stadium. We passed the statue of Rocky, his arms raised in triumph, cigarette hanging from his lips. "That makes me want to smoke," said Melanie.

"We're out of cigarettes," I said. "But not to worry." I climbed onto the statue's pedestal and put my arm around Rocky's waist for support, then reached up and plucked from his mouth the cigarette someone had wedged there. It felt good being up there with him, so I didn't climb down right away but pulled my lighter out and lit the Marlboro.

"You guys look so cozy up there," Melanie said. "Bosom buddies."

I sniffed Rocky's underarm. "Oh, yeah."

Melanie laughed.

I put my head on his chest and tongued one of his bronze nipples. I began doing my best Burgess Meredith, "Forget Adrian, Rock. What's she got dat I don't? C'mon, Rock. You know I make you hot!"

Melanie cracked up. A few others passing were getting a laugh out of it too, but then I saw a pair of cops coming toward us, staring at me. When they saw me look at them they stopped and shook their heads like they were disappointed in me, which is the cop way of saying, We're trying to be nice guys here, but don't push it. One of them made a downward motion with his finger.

"I should get down?" I tried to look surprised.

He nodded, stone-faced.

I jumped to the ground, and as the cops turned and walked away, I could see them laughing and shaking their heads.

3

MY FATHER NEVER SLEPT WELL. I remember that. His nightly rambling about the various places we lived—the little house in Ankara; the sprawling, vault-ceilinged apartment in Bucharest; the small boxy flat in Beirut, eleven stories up with narrow terraces; the stucco-and-concrete house in Cyprus—always left what seemed mysterious signs of his activity: ashtrays full of Salem butts outside sliding porch doors, stacks of thick hardcover books on the kitchen counter, half a chocolate cake reduced to crumbs, empty bourbon bottles standing on the television as if on display. These things were part of a nocturnal world I couldn't fathom, a world belonging only to my father. I could look through the titles of the books he read, study the shapes of the crushed cigarettes in the ashtray, smell the bourbon in the neck of the bottle, or on his breath when he kissed me good night if he started early, but those clues were thin, insignificant, like laying tracings one atop the other and trying to form a three-dimensional picture; the more layers you pile on, the more indecipherable the whole becomes.

I woke late one night in Cyprus to the sound of a crowd of people laughing downstairs. I got up and walked past my brother's bed and out into the dark hallway. Dim light misted the bottom end of the staircase. A man was speaking, then the crowd laughed again. The door to my parents' bedroom was shut. I walked groggily down the stairs, bending over when I reached the landing to see through the thin iron banister posts into the living room. It looked empty. I got closer to the banister and saw my father's feet, in his brown leather slippers, resting on the coffee table, his hand flicking a cigarette into an ashtray on his lap. Putting my face right up to the posts, I could see his face. He was mostly impassive, but occasionally he laughed silently along with the crowd. The man on the stereo said the word "fuck" very loudly and the crowd roared. My father giggled, lowering his head and nodding.

I went down into the room.

"Dad?"

"Hey, what are you doing down here, Jason?"

"I couldn't sleep." I considered this a very grown-up answer. It made me proud to think it might be true.

"Go back up and lie down. You'll fall asleep."

"I tried. I really can't go to sleep. Can I stay down here for a while?"

He gave me a long look, then glanced at the tape deck. "I guess so. Your mind won't be warped by a few swear words, will it?"

"Hell no." I sat down on the couch with him. The man on the stereo told another joke, and I remember laughing because I thought the word Quaalude was funny. Then he spoke in an exaggerated low voice.

"Who is this?"

"His name's George Carlin." My father sucked on an ice cube from his glass. George Carlin swore and swore and whenever he did I laughed, till I was laughing hysterically, and so was my father. At first I forced it, trying to find the right times and put a knowing tone in it, but then the laughter spread out and took control of my body, and it began to be the laughter itself that was funny. I thought I might never be able to stop.

"What are you smiling at?" Melanie asked.

Our room in Chicago was small but well appointed, with a king-size bed and thirty-six-inch TV. The window faced east onto a sunny afternoon, greenish old buildings snaking along the river, farther off a curved sliver of lakeshore and then the water married to the sky by blue haze.

I tilted my head forward to look at her. "Was I smiling?"

"Yeah, looked like you were remembering something."

I let my head fall back, expecting a pillow and getting instead the Formica headboard. I barely felt it. "Just a time when I had a good laugh with my Dad."

"That's nice. What were you laughing about?"

"We were listening to George Carlin," I said. I wished she'd shut up. For all its ability to relax and anesthetize, I found that heroin also made me cranky and impatient.

"When was this?"

"Look," I said, "answering all these questions is ruining my experience of just remembering it. Okay?"

"Sor-*ree*." She went back to watching *Oprah* in her underwear.

Melanie didn't know I was high on more than a joint. I had walked two blocks to Saul and Don's hotel to invest in some sheets, and Saul had asked me if I had any interest in "the other thing." I said no thanks, but when he broke some out I bought a bag from him and snorted it. "Just always leave at least two or three days between highs, and you won't get strung out," Saul had said. That sounded reasonable enough. Anything that took me further was part of the trip, part of the general sense of positive motion that pervaded the tour—we were all moving, and it wasn't about direction: *away* was direction enough. Away from normalcy, conformity, conscription, away from the mundane joys, sadnesses, and security life in the herd had to offer us. Of course, being human, we couldn't shake the belief that moving away from all that was taking us toward something, but we believed it quietly, each sheepishly harboring our own loose vision of a destination, only the wackiest or most intoxicated ever talking about it openly, Utopianly. I read in Whitman:

> *Desperate, proud, fond, sick, accepted by men, rejected by men,*
> *They go! they go! I know that they go, but I know not where*
> *   they go,*
> *But I know that they go toward the best—toward something*
> *   great.*

My tattered copy of *Leaves of Grass*, taken from my father's library, was getting a workout. I saw that whatever it was we were following, or that was propelling us, hadn't begun with the Dead and the vein they tapped into back in the sixties, because here was Whitman writing about it a century earlier:

> *To gather the minds of men out of their brains as you encounter*
> *   them, to gather the love out of their hearts,*
> *To take your lovers on the road with you, for all that you leave*
> *   them behind you,*
> *To know the universe itself as a road, as many roads, as roads for*
> *   traveling souls.*

We were awake to this vision of the universe, and we traveled not alone, not in pairs, but as a unit, a shifting amoeba that gathered around the music and moved with it.

I was now aware also of darker motions, like the cold currents that move through a warm lagoon, chilling your legs and hinting at the vast indifferent depths just beyond the reefs. I lay on the wide hotel bed, glazing heavily, Whitman propped open in my lap to "Song of the Open Road," trying to reread it but sliding stickily off the page, unable to see clearly through the mucus in the air. Oprah babbled in the background, reminding me suddenly of a joke.

"Hey," I said, "did you hear about the cocaine bust that happened on the Oprah show, right backstage?"

"Really?" Melanie craned her neck around to look at me from her chair.

"Yeah, they found forty pounds of crack up her skirt."

Melanie rolled her eyes and laughed once, dismissively. "You're a regular riot."

I closed the book and lit a cigarette. We watched the show's conclusion, and as Oprah was looking into the camera and saying good-bye, Melanie giggled under her breath, muttering, "Forty pounds of crack." Then she was laughing, kicking her feet in the air, coming at me with a closed fist, "You asshole," punching my leg, and we were both laughing. "I'll give you forty pounds of crack," she said.

I reached around and grabbed her behind, "Feels like you've only got two or three pounds here, not nearly enough for a crackhead like me," and we were hysterical, melting together.

OUTSIDE THE U.I.C. PAVILION that afternoon I ran into Vince. He was talking to a trio of local girls, U.I.C. students probably, trying to convince one of them to ditch her friends and come see the show with him. He was waving two tickets like a magic wand.

"Well," the girl was saying, "we all came together, and we need to find tickets for all of us." She had on a baby T-shirt, exposing her tanning-salon midriff despite the slight April chill, and it was easy to see why Vince had homed in on her.

"Hey, I'm not saying we shouldn't find tickets for them," he said. "I'm just saying I have one for you if you'll accompany me." He used the phrase *accompany me* with a flare of his smile and a wave of the tickets, making it hip instead of courtly. The girl knew exactly what he wanted, and yet he managed not to seem obvious; he had a self-effacing mockery in his style that mitigated the bluntness of his come-ons, a blithe glimmer in his eye that said, No sweat, whatever happens happens, we're just having some fun. It really was something to see.

The girl pulled her friends to the side to confer with them—giggling, gleefully back in junior high again. They looked like sorority girls, out for their one Grateful Dead adventure. Any other tourhead would have stared at them passing but recognized instantly that they were in another league, prebetrothed to the MBAs and MDs of their parents' imaginings. Not Vince. No one was out of his league. I walked up behind him.

"How about a blow job for one of those tickets," I said.

He turned to me, laughing, saying so the girls couldn't hear, "All depends on whether you swallow." Then he saw it was me. "Shit, Jason, what's up?" He grabbed my arm.

"Not too much," I said.

"Girls," he said, "one second. I need to talk to my friend here." And he pulled me a few yards off. "Man, can you get me some cheap pages?"

"That's what I was hoping you'd ask."

"Cool. I just drove out here from Berkeley, so I don't know who's haps or anything."

"Well, I'm happening anytime. After the show if you want."

"Yeah, that'll give me time to get together."

I gave him my hotel and room number and told him to stop by.

"Okay, well I gotta go close this other deal here." He moved back toward the girls. I stood staring, wanting to see which way it would go. The tan beauty dipped her chin to the side demurely and cocked one hip, smiling up at him. Done deal.

I walked back to the car and pulled out of the lot. Melanie was back in the room waiting for me to pick her up before the show. It was about a ten-minute drive. I eased the car into the hotel's underground lot and parked near the entrance. I decided to go in through the front door and walked up the ramp to the street, along the edge of the building. Out front there was all the normal activity—cabs dropping fares and waiting for others, the greatcoated doorman ushering people in and out of cars, a bellboy unloading a brass luggage cart into the trunk of a limo. The hotel was far enough from the shows that there weren't too many heads staying there. The revolving door released me into the recycled air.

I went to the elevators and pressed the call button. When the door opened and I got in, a middle-aged guy in a white T-shirt and black jeans slid in after me. I pressed ten, then asked him, "What floor?"

He looked at the panel of buttons and said, "Oh, you've already got it."

We rode up together. I let him get off first, and he made a right in the direction of my room. I turned and followed him and he stopped. "Whoops," he said, and went the other way. Not taking any chances, I stopped at a door across the hall from my room and pretended to be looking for my key.

"Jason," the guy said from down the hall. Reflex brought my head up to face him. He was coming toward me.

"You talking to me?"

"Yeah. You're Jason, aren't you?"

"No, man. Not me." I had my key out, but just stood there.

"Bullshit," he said. He grabbed me by my collar and held me away from the door, then knocked on it.

"Who is it?" came a woman's voice from inside.

"Jason," he mumbled. I twisted against his grip, but it was solid. I decided against hitting him.

The door opened and a woman of about eighty was smiling at us. "Yes?" she said.

"Oh, sorry, ma'am," said the man.

"Satisfied?" I asked.

"Do you know this boy?"

The woman squinted at me carefully, making sure, then slowly shook her head. "No, I don't think so."

"Grandma, come on," I said. "You don't recognize me?"

She shut the door quickly.

4

ALL I COULD THINK OF was the acid in my room, directly across the hall. It was enough, I knew, to send me away for twenty years in some states, since the sentencing guidelines had been established for pure LSD, but not specifically worded, so prosecutors tended to count the weight of the blotter paper. A gram of pure LSD was enough to make tens of thousands of hits, and my hundred sheets would weight at least a few grams. I knew of people doing years for a few hits.

"That was good," the man said, smiling at me. "Grandma. Nice try, really. Now where's your room?" He shook me hard by the neck.

"Room?" I parroted.

"I'm gonna find it," he said. "So you might as well point it out."

"You have a warrant?" Something steeled in my backbone when I heard myself say those words. The criminal's talisman.

"Warrant?" He laughed. Then he grabbed the key from my

hand and held it up. The room number was on it, staring me in the face. "Here's my warrant, *dude*." He said "dude" with a smirking disdain that was more like friendly ribbing than antagonism.

He dragged me across the hall, and as he opened the door to the room I was praying there was no old warrant on me, so I could skate on an illegal search and seizure. I would need a decent lawyer. He shoved me inside and walked in after me. Melanie was on the bed, still in a T-shirt and her underwear. She looked up from the television, unconcerned. "Hi Melanie," the man said. "Sit there," he said to me, pointing at a chair near the window. I did.

"Melanie Milliner-Shreve?" he asked her. She looked at me. I shrugged.

"It's just Shreve," she said. She was calm, assured, looking him right in the eye. I loved her then, knew it.

"Okay, good," he said. His arms and neck were wiry, his thin face etched around his too-large mouth, but he had a paunch coming in over his belt. He sat down between me and the door. "I'm going to ask you a few questions right now, and you need to answer them honestly. Are you in good health?"

She smiled. "Fair, I guess. No major complaints. Except I could use a little more exercise, and I eat too much sugar." She looked down at her shoulder. "And I can't seem to find my right arm."

He smiled at her, nodded his head to show he got it. "Are you here of your own free will?"

"Yes."

"Is this man," he cocked his head at me, "a danger to you?"

"No."

"Okay, so far so good. Here's the deal. I am a private investigator. Your parents are my clients. I am going to take you to them—"

"Oh fuck that!" Melanie said.

"You don't have a choice here, being a minor. Also," he looked at me, "they want you prosecuted for statutory rape, but I don't see any reason to go that far. What are you, twenty?"

"Nineteen," I said.

"Right, nineteen and seventeen." He shook his head. "Parents always envision some middle-aged pervert drug pusher brainwashing their little girls. I think we can all agree, parents overreact, right?" He smiled amiably at us. "And you probably love each other, right?" He looked back and forth between us, and when neither of us spoke, he laughed. "Woops, hope I didn't step on a nerve. Come on, kids, don't be afraid. Someone's got to say it first. Take the chance."

"That's between us," I said.

His face turned serious and he nodded. "Fair enough, sport."

"Listen," said Melanie, "I'm not going. So you can just fuck off."

The man smiled again and held up his hands. "Whoa, now. There is really no need for this to be unfriendly. My name's Tim, hi how are you, and I'm doing you guys a favor by not bringing the cops into this. I'm just doing my job. Now I need to bring you back to your parents, and I will do that, I'm sorry. If you want trouble, I can call the cops and file statutory charges, and then poor Jason here will be unnecessarily inconvenienced. So how about it?"

"Bullshit," Melanie said. "Seventeen is consenting age."

"That depends on the state," said Tim. "And if you want to nitpick, I could snoop around for drugs, get you both on possession, and Jason on contributing to the delinquency of a minor. Which is no joke." He looked at me. It would have been tough for him to miss the fear in my eyes.

Melanie didn't answer. She looked down at her own feet and pouted. Tim continued to smile absurdly at both of us. He looked like some degenerate comedian.

"Mickey Spillane you ain't," I said, trying to sound unconcerned.

Tim laughed loudly, pointing at me and nodding, then turned back to Melanie. "Why don't you put some clothes on, sweetie?"

She looked at me, then back at him. "I'm not your fucking sweetie." She slid to the edge of the bed and started pulling on her jeans.

"Oh, yes," said Tim. "There is also the matter of some money you guys took. Eight thousand dollars, I think it was."

"That money's mine," Melanie said.

"Well, you can debate that with your parents, but I need to bring it back to them."

"We spent it all," she said.

Tim hung his head and sighed. "Okay, nobody's going to believe that, but we can work on a mutual solution." He furrowed his brow and scratched at a thin scar on his left temple. "A grand or so should keep the parents happy—say you guys were living the high life—and maybe another grand for me and my friendship, and the rest you guys hold on to however you want. Sound good?"

Melanie stayed silent. It occurred to me that he really was in charge, and all our best options were his to dictate. He was being fairly generous. "Sounds like a plan, Tim," I said.

"Good man, Jason. Excellent. Now we're getting somewhere."

Melanie was still getting dressed, and Tim checked out her ass in the mirror.

"Do you know how fucking useless this is?" Melanie said. "I'm going to be eighteen in a few months anyway. Then they'll have to let me go. All this for an extra few months at home."

"Well," said Tim, spreading his hands and showing the knotted muscles in his arms, "what can you do? Parents, right?" His smile covered a great expanse across his face, his yellow teeth like the rind of a jaundiced orange. I hated him.

I helped Melanie pack her few things and then we divvied up the money. She had me keep the balance, worried that her parents might find it on her and take it away. I gave Tim twelve hundred for her parents, a thousand for himself, and kept the last thousand. I also had the hundred sheets of acid in my pack. Tim stepped into the hall and gave us a minute alone to say good-bye.

I wrote Harry Waldron's number down and gave it to her. "Here, I'll keep this guy informed as to where to find me," I said. "You can leave messages there." Outside the window, the sky to the east was already dark, the lake glowing a little brighter in the flare from the west. The show would be starting soon.

"This sucks," she said.

"Yeah, it does." I put my arms around her. "He was right, you know."

"About what?"

"We do love each other."

Melanie pinched my ass hard, and I jumped back, startled. We both laughed. "Don't go getting all moony on me," she said. Then she stepped up, put her hand on the back of my neck, and kissed me.

Tim already had her bag outside the door, so she was unencumbered. "I'll see you in August," I said. Her birthday was the fifth.

"Yeah. Take care of the car."

She opened the door and I watched them walk down the hall. When the elevator came, Tim said over his shoulder, "So long, sport." And they were gone.

At the show that night I tried to find someone I knew who

needed a ticket, but the first set had started and I finally gave my extra away to a guy I didn't know but had seen around. No sign of Cole, Saul, or Don inside. I found a spot on the floor where there were some familiar faces, but didn't do much dancing. The second set opened with "Iko Iko," a song that seemed to pop up whenever I felt like shit.

But looking into the future, I managed to dredge up a good feeling: touring alone, no women, no partners, would be a first for me. I thought of Whitman, of the sacramental aspects of the Road that might reveal themselves more readily to the undistracted mind. I decided I'd do my best not to take on riders for the drive to Irvine. In the past when I'd traveled alone, I had always been hitch-hiking. This would be different; no dependence on others, just me, the road, music, cigarettes. Chicago-LA was a great run, beautiful and eventful by two or three different routes. I would probably take the straight run, through Nebraska, the springtime Colorado Rockies, the Utah Canyonlands, maybe a night in Las Vegas, then Dr. Gonzo's famous blast across the desert to LA. Maybe I'd even drop a hit of acid for that.

But it was weird that night, sleeping alone. I thought I should at least have offered up some floor space to somebody. The room's comfort seemed wasted on just one person. Vince came by and bought twenty sheets, but after he left, the TV wasn't enough company. I realized I'd never slept in a hotel room alone. I smoked some pot, ordered spaghetti from room service, watched HBO. I smoked more pot, and became too stoned to sleep. With the lights off and my eyes closed, my rhythmically expanding and contracting head kept me awake, along with the movies on my eyelids— amoebic red and green splotches resolving briefly into figures: vague dancing horses, angry faces, crowds of bodies whipping by as if passed on a motorcycle, their noises transmitted through the membrane of reality as hisses and meaningless whispers.

THE NEXT MORNING I woke up and watched a few minutes of *Good Morning America*. They were interviewing a man who had sailed around the world by himself and broken some record. He still bore the leathery tan, and looked uncomfortable in the very hippest, very latest casualwear. They asked him if he ever got lonely out there, and he laughed. "Sure," he said, "but the hardest thing was learning to put up with people again." They all laughed. I thought about a wake-and-bake, but decided it was early for pot. I called my mother instead.

"Where are you?" she asked.

"Chicago. Going to LA in a couple of days."

"I spoke to Harry. He's sick."

"I know. He asked me not to tell you."

"When was this?"

"Last year."

"Well, things are worse. You know Harry, if he'll admit things are bad, they must be very bad. I'm worried; he could barely speak. He sounded like he might die right there on the phone, but he refused to let me go out there."

"What did he say?"

"He said it was just a bad day. But I don't know."

I was wider awake now, and I lit a cigarette. "You didn't believe him."

"No. Will you go see him?"

"Sure. After the Irvine shows I'll be driving up the coast anyway, so I'll stop in."

She paused. "I mean sooner. Right away. You didn't hear him. He sounded awful. He'll never ask for help, but I think he might need it."

"How about I call him and see. Maybe it was just a bad day, like he said."

There was another pause. "This is something you can *do*." Her voice modulated quickly from anxiety to barely contained rage. "I'd think you would jump at the chance," and she hung up on me.

I called back. "Boy," I said when she answered, "this is getting nice and neurotic."

"Shall I hang up again?"

"No. I'll go see Harry, Mom. I didn't know you were so worked up about it. I'll leave here tomorrow and drive straight there."

She immediately softened. "Thank you. You can always see more Grateful Dead concerts, but think if Harry needed help and no one went."

"All right, I'm going. So no more lecturing, okay?"

We finished and I rolled out of bed and dressed.

5

I ARRIVED AT HARRY'S on a pristine Northern California spring day. Three small puffs of cloud drifted off to the east like an interrupted smoke signal; otherwise the sky was spotless. Firm directionless wind swirled and cooled my skin as I climbed out of the Toyota. I had decided not to call, so I could show up and see what the real situation was. Liam answered the door. His hair had gotten longer and now draped in silver ringlets past his shoulders. He smiled and shook my hand, then turned and led me toward the living room.

Harry was slumped in the center of the huge leather sofa watching *Star Wars* on the rear-projection big-screen embedded in the wall in front of him. In one hand he held a translucent pear-shaped blue plastic mask from which a thin tube coiled over to a slender gray oxygen tank by the arm of the sofa. In the other hand was a lit cigarette. Coming down the wide hallway behind Liam, before we entered the room, I saw Harry take a drag, exhale it, then clamp the mask over his face and pant.

"Look what the cat drug in," said Liam.

Harry looked up, smiled when he saw me. His face, already gaunt, had shrunken, leaving doughy folds at the corners of his mouth and along his jawline. The new paleness of his skin made his eyes into black plastic buttons. He was an old snowman, melting there on his California couch. "What the fuck," he said, pausing to breathe, "are you doing here?"

"Just passing through," I said. "Wanted to see how you were."

He didn't get up, so I went over and leaned down to hug him. He patted my back with the oxygen mask. "You need a fucking shower," he said.

I stood up. "Thanks for the heads-up. I've been on the road for three days, and the shower at the nineteen-dollar motel I stayed at last night just spat brown water and made the pipes knock like crazy."

Harry picked up a remote from the sofa near his thigh and paused the laser-disc player. "So what's up? You on your way to some Dead shows?"

"Yeah, they're playing right up the road in Monterey in a few weeks. I was wondering if I could stay here till then." I didn't tell him I was missing shows in Irvine and Palo Alto in between.

"Sure. You can have the little room. You alone?"

"Yeah, just me."

"That's a change. You've usually got company. What happened to that gorgeous thing you brought here last year?" He placed the mask over his nose and mouth for a few breaths.

"That didn't last." I fell into a recliner near Harry.

"Nothing going on now? No girlfriend?"

I smiled. "She was kidnapped by a private detective her parents hired, and taken back to New York."

Harry eyed me for a second. "No shit?"

"No shit," I said. I loved having extreme stories to tell Harry. He respected outrageousness. "The guy broke right into our hotel room in Chicago four days ago and took Melanie away. He even swindled us out of some money while he was at it."

"So, this girl has not quite cleared the age of consent, I assume." He smirked and looked healthier for a moment, a hint of blood in his cheeks.

I pointed a finger at him. "She's seventeen. She'll be eighteen in August, and then she's coming out here to meet me."

"Good for you," Harry said. He picked his cigarette out of the big glass ashtray, but it had burned down to the filter and gone out. He added it to the small mound of butts in the center.

IN HIS TINY BASEMENT, Harry had boxes and boxes of old photographs. After discovering them, I started making regular trips down the narrow concrete steps to browse through them, usually while Harry was napping. Most afternoons he'd get tired and drag the oxygen tank on its little cart into the bedroom, flick on some soft Mozart, and doze off for an hour or two. Harry couldn't handle silence. Even when someone was with him, having a conversation, lack of background noise made him jittery. There was always a TV, radio, or stereo on in any room he was in. He preferred crowded restaurants when we went out to eat. The only exception to this was when he soaked in the hot tub on the deck; out there, the rumble of the jets was sufficient to mask whatever it was that oppressed him.

Most of the photos were portraits—of old girlfriends, their children, of paying customers (these were kept in manila folders with names and phone numbers on them), of his wife and her family in Naples. One of Harry's old girlfriends had two incredibly beautiful twin sons, and there was a whole box of pictures of them, from age five or six to their late teens. They were identical, black-haired, with cold, chasmic blue eyes. I'd heard Harry talk about them. Both had been models, and one had gone on to front a rock band. Flipping through them, I was mesmerized, found myself drawn to their sharp features and smooth bodies as I would be to a woman's. I shut the box and wrote it off to Liam's phenomenal hybrid home-grown, making permeable the mental membrane between the sexes. All perception is just chemical.

At the top of the next box were two smaller boxes, the kind used for good eight-by-ten stationery. They were held shut with brittle yellowed strips of tape, and marked on top with time-browned black fountain pen. One read "Summer 1955" and the other "Summer 1960." I opened the 1955 box, cracking the old tape with my thumbnail. Right there on top, looking straight at me, was my father, age twenty-one, looking far too cool. His short sandy hair was growing out a little messy, and a wispy hint of beard darkened his chin. He wore a beaten brown leather jacket, cut thin and tight to his waist, the zipper halfway open. An unfiltered cigarette dangled from his lips. Just unbelievably cool.

The pictures were of a motorcycle trip my father and Harry took across Turkey one summer. I had a vague memory of my father having mentioned it. The black-and-white images were of tiny Anatolian villages, wizened old women selling bread, the two beautiful black BMW bikes parked outside a headman's hut, and along tiny empty roads with vast poppy fields on both sides; only one shot of Harry: thick-haired and smooth-faced, with his hands together and head tilted heavenward in an attitude of prayer or thankfulness outside an open toilet stall, the porcelain god looking haggard and badly cared for inside, squatting there on grime-streaked gray tiles. The last were some pictures taken in the streets and covered markets of Istanbul—my father (had he really been that thin?) holding up a small kilim next to a wooden table piled with them; another with his arm around a portly smiling woman in an overly opulent sitting room, younger, thinner women arranged on sofas in the background, all of them smiling and leaning to get into the shot.

The pictures brought waves of memories of Turkey from when we had lived there. The shady little street in Ankara where James and I had played soccer with the local toughs, kids twice our age, earning their respect because unlike the military brats we spoke Turkish; images from a trip to Istanbul: the cavernous indoor market, the merchants looking sternly out from behind their wares; leaving my yellow Keds by a pile of sandals and battered leather shoes outside the Blue Mosque. I remembered a fat grocer down the street from our house who used to exclaim happily whenever my brother and I came in; he would give us free bananas, holding them outstretched and peeling them for us ceremoniously. All these memories were just flashes, bright snatches of film burned on some inner retina, but another, deeper one rose up, slowly—chipped white paint on a door frame, the unpainted lip of the transom above, fear.

A moment I hadn't thought of since I was a child. Walking (being led?) through the door of a bedroom in a neighbor's house. The little girl, Ayşe, had used to run among us during our war games and heal us. If you were shot, you weren't allowed to get back up until she came and laid hands on you—it was a way of resolving disputes over coming back to life, but also of surreptitiously enjoying the touch of her tiny hot hands on your forehead, your stomach, your leg. I knew before I came through the door that she would be there under white sheets, taking up almost no room in the single bed, a tiny repository of great pain. She wanted visitors.

Her friends, she called us, though we barely knew her. My mother told me she had asked for me. Her mother had spilled a pot of boiling water on her (she got underfoot in the kitchen, we were told), and she was badly hurt. The worst burns were across her chest and were bandaged, but two-thirds of her face was deeply reddened, a curvy line separating the pale unharmed skin from the glowing pain. She didn't react when I approached, and didn't speak when I said hello—it hurt to move her mouth, her mother explained to me, but she knew I was there. Seeing her, imagining the horrible state of the skin on her chest which I couldn't see, I felt like a grown man. Only a grown man would be visiting a friend with ghastly injuries, trying to be of some comfort, it wasn't the kind of thing that happened to a child's friends. I pursed my lips the way my father did when something bad was beyond his control, and told her she would be okay. I thought of laying my hands on her the way she did to us when we played, but that would have been childish and useless. I was five years old, and bad things had begun to happen in my life the way they did in the lives of grown-ups (my father's father had died of cancer before I knew him, my mother's best friend had been rendered deaf by a virus), and I felt expanded, transformed by that fact into someone my parents could be proud of, a man who would take things in stride and be a comfort to those he loved. I don't remember ever seeing Ayşe again, though I must have.

I thought of Melanie. She still hadn't called, and I wondered when she would. I replaced the photos in the box and closed it. I knew what the 1960 box was, and I kept myself from opening it. I would talk to Harry first.

Upstairs, Harry was awake and back in the living room, watching a flyweight boxing match off the satellite dish. He was frowning and smoking when I walked in.

"Feeling okay?" I asked.

"Stop asking me that." He groaned involuntarily as he leaned forward and tapped one of the long white Carltons from the pack in front of him. "Look at that," he said, gesturing toward the TV. "Those little spics can sure take a beating."

"Jesus, Harry." I couldn't stop a small meaningless grunt of laughter from popping out of me—the automatic response to something meant to be funny. "That's an ugly thing to say."

Harry pulled hard on the cigarette, his thin rubbery cheeks caving deeply in. "Someday, you'll learn the pleasure of occasionally saying something ugly." He looked at me and grimaced, shook his head. "No, you don't see it yet. But believe me, it feels good sometimes, so don't fucking judge me with your hippie self-righteousness." He went back to staring at the fight.

I sat in the armchair and shut up, unable to come up with any response. Going back over what he had said in my mind, I became aware of fuzzy borders around his words, trailings-off in tone before phrases were done, erosions, softenings of fricatives that I couldn't solely attribute to his trouble breathing. A little afraid, I said, "I've been looking through your old photos downstairs."

"Find anything interesting?"

"Yeah, a lot of great stuff. Your portraits are so good."

He waved his cigarette at me dismissively.

"I found the box of pictures of your trip with my father in Turkey."

Harry smiled, "Yeah, pretty cool, huh?"

"Very cool. I was wondering, though. Last year, when I was here, you talked about your trip to Italy with my mom as being your time of freedom, of raw experience. How come you didn't mention the motorcycle trip? It seems like that would qualify if anything would."

"That trip? It was a fucking nightmare. Maybe your father was feeling carefree—he spoke the language a little from courses at Harvard, and had a steel-plated stomach—but I was miserable, had the runs the whole time, couldn't eat the food, spent most of my time squatting over holes in the ground and wiping my ass with leaves. I developed a killer fucking rash that made riding the bike a living hell, ended up buying clothing from villagers just to wipe myself without screaming."

I laughed. "That explains the shot of you praying to the toilet."

He smiled. "You laugh, but that filthy toilet was the first one we'd seen in a month, and it had toilet paper. I really was thanking God. It's the only time in my life that I've felt sincere about a prayer."

"What about the room full of women in Istanbul?"

"Again, no fun for me. I took a picture of your father going in, then scurried back to our hotel to puke and shit some more."

"It was a whorehouse?"

"Yeah, the best in Istanbul. Legendary. Used to cater to the sultans, the guide told us, when they got sick of all the women in their harems." Harry laughed. "Either that or the guide had cousins there and was throwing business their way."

I came up against the thought of my father in a whorehouse like running into the edge of a door: smiling and moving along one second, then thrown back, dazed and startled. But I reminded myself that he had been twenty-one and hadn't even met my mother yet.

"The other box I didn't open," I said. "The one marked 1960. It's of your trip to Italy, right?"

"Yeah. Go ahead and look if you want. There's nothing shocking in there." Harry stubbed out his cigarette and pressed the oxygen mask over his face. He breathed hard into it, then reached over and turned up the flow.

"Maybe I will. Later on."

HARRY'S COUGHING FITS, when they were bad, were epic. They could go on for ten, fifteen, even twenty minutes, and reach uncanny levels of nuance. I became a student of them. A fast, rhythmic bark meant he was just getting started, and if there was a pause during this section of the fit, it only meant he had found a moment when he could suck desperately at the oxygen tank before tumbling back in. There were other pauses that could seem more like endings, and continued to engender hope in me, but were followed by long, scraping intakes of breath and then even huger coughs, and eventually I learned to identify the slowly dying wheeze that meant his lungs had emptied completely of air and were struggling to reorient themselves to expand again: his own body was knocking the wind out of itself. Sometimes I heard these fits while I stood out on the deck smoking, and I'd crush out the butt and tell myself I was quitting. Once I managed twelve smoke-free hours.

Harry started taking Percodan, which he said his doctor prescribed, but which was delivered once a week by a guy named Mike who always stayed for a joint if there was one around. Mike brought over a box of whippets one day, and he and I spent the afternoon sucking nitrous oxide and listening to Laurie Anderson on the headphones. Harry soon stopped hiding the fact that he was drinking. We were out for dinner in Carmel, and he ordered a beer.

"Don't you look at me that way," he said when the waiter had withdrawn.

"Come on, Harry. Is this a good idea?" The drunken Harry was a person I'd never seen, but had heard enough about to be afraid of.

"It's just a fucking beer. I could be dying, I'm entitled to enjoy myself. Whose roof are you sleeping under, anyway? Who's paying for this meal?"

"Okay, whatever," I said.

"Not whatever. Fuck whatever. Whatever I want, that's what I'll do. I refuse to be caponized in my own house."

"Caponized?"

"Look it up." His beer arrived in a tall tapered glass, and he drained half of it and lit a cigarette. Usually he didn't smoke until we left a restaurant for fear it would set off a coughing fit, and he could see that thought in my eyes. "Don't worry, I'm not really smoking it. It just helps my disposition to pretend." He pulled in a small mouthful of smoke and expelled it without inhaling, flicked the head over the ashtray.

He switched to vodka tonics and was drunk by the time we got home. I had trouble helping him walk and dragging the oxygen tank at the same time, but I got him inside and onto his bed. He began coughing as I lay him down, and there was a new depth, a swampiness to the sound that came with the booze.

"Oh god, Harry," I said.

The fit subsided relatively quickly and Harry shook his head. "Jim, Jim, Jimmy," he said. "You mizzerble prick."

"What's that?" I asked.

He looked up at me, surprised. "Your father," he said. "Fuck I loved that mizzerble prick, you know that?"

"Yeah, I know."

"But he *was* a mizzerble fucking prick, you know that? I'm sorry, but yes."

"Okay, Harry. Okay."

"He was a wily muzzfucker. Oh-ho," Harry laughed wheezily and almost coughed. "Wily. Knew how to get over."

"All right, Harry, we'll talk tomorrow."

He closed his eyes and drifted for a second. "Jimmy! Fuck, I'm sorry, but maybe you had it coming. Fucked me first, you know."

"Okay."

Harry lay back, and I draped a blanket over him. "Gimme cigarette," he mumbled.

"No," I said. "Sleep now." I headed for the door.

"Fucked me and I still loved you," Harry mumbled. I shut off the light and left.

6

"NEVER LIVE IN A SMALL WORLD," my father used to say to us. "That's where people get to fearing and hating each other, because the world they live in is small and doesn't account for the full range of possibility the real world will always present. People think they're free of prejudice only until they're faced with something truly unexpected." When he gave my brother and me this speech for the first time, we were seven and eight years old. We were at Disney World and had just come off the "It's a Small World After All" ride. "It's not a small world," my father said, leading us to a bench near the ride's exit and sitting us down. "Remember that. No matter how fast planes get and how much everyone knows about each other, the world will still hold infinite differences and can always surprise you. You have to know that, and love it because of that! Don't believe the bullshit these idiots try to force-feed you," he gestured with his hand toward the ride. He was speaking vehemently, his voice climbing in volume, and some parents of smaller kids coming off the ride were veering away from us. "I'm sorry, guys, but it makes me mad. You start believing that stuff and you run around smiling stupidly and expecting everything to be beautiful and happy and not too different from you—oh yeah, maybe some wooden shoes here, a bonnet there, maybe a sombrero or a turban, but nothing disturbing, nothing surprising, nothing that can't be incorporated into the great Disney pantheon of pastel diversity! Nothing that can't be Americanized!"

We heard a lot over the following years about this line of thinking and got this speech in different forms a number of times. Thinking back, I suspect he had agreed on the trip to Disney World for the purpose of introducing us to this lesson. I'm pretty sure it was he who suggested the "It's a Small World" ride. My brother and I were more into the roller coasters.

In the back of my mind I had always known, though it was never discussed, that my father really was a spy. It was the only thing that made sense. If he wasn't, his death was horrible, useless, and worst of all, a misunderstanding. If he was, it was brave, honorable, reasonable even, in some sense. I hinted to friends at boarding school that he had been on some kind of mission when he died, more than just covering a story, but of course I was sworn to secrecy and could say no more about it. As I got older I sometimes thought of the contradiction between his liberal views and his being a spy, but that just deepened him for me. For what was a man without his contradictions, his dichotomies, his surprises. To pigeonhole him would be to place him in that small world he always scorned.

THE DEAD CAME for two shows at Laguna Seca, in Monterey, and Harry hooked me up with tickets through a friend of his. From the minute I got there, the shows were a throwback to my early days—the vibe was open and free: perfect California weather, people walking around just beaming. Out of the blue sometimes, after weeks of plodding along, Dead shows could form a utopian bubble around a venue, and even before the band took the stage it was understood we were somewhere special and had better savor it while it lasted.

I ran into a girl named Fern in the lot before the first show. She and I had shared a night together by the ocean two summers before, a night that in my mind had taken on almost magical significance: I understood that thinking of it over the course of my life would become a kind of touchstone as I got older, a reminder that I had really lived and experienced great things. I hadn't seen her since that summer, and because the memory had become so dreamlike for me I was taken aback when she walked up to me in the flesh.

"Jason," she said. "Hey Jason." She put her arms around me and held me soft and long, and it felt good to realize that she remembered that night the same way I did. That whole brilliant summer came flooding back to me: the deepening of my friendship with Randy as we crisscrossed the country, the beautiful sense of true belonging; though I'd been on tour for six months prior, that summer was my real initiation. After the last shows in Ventura, Regina had dumped me for a paunchy old hippie named Ara, and even that had not only lost its sting in the bright fog of memory, but come to seem necessary to the whole experience.

After Ventura, I had gone to Santa Cruz to kill the six-week hiatus between shows and hooked up with a group of Deadheads and drifters that fluctuated between five and thirty people. We stayed mostly at a place called Greyhound Rock, a beach just north of town where a huge rock, big as the fuselage of a 747, sat just off the shore. At low tide we could walk out to its backside without getting wet, and at high tide it became moated by water a few feet deep. The beach was backed by a tall cliff of stone and earth against which the light of our bonfires would ripple at night, liquefying it into a reddish tidal wave looming over us. From behind the cliff the moon would rise very late, making its appearance deep into our revelries, its cool light mellowing the wild nights at just the right time and sending small intrepid parties walking or wading out to the rock to climb it and watch the sky from there. Sitting on the rock, I sometimes imagined it buried underground, as it had been before the sea beat back the earth and uncovered it—gave it life under stars and sun and moon, made it a roost for seagulls and seals and dreaming hippies. Buried, it might have lasted forever, but the sea had spent centuries freeing it, and now embraced it like an old friend, lapping at its sides, and eventually would wear the rock itself away, carry it off in tiny particles as it had the sand around it.

Fern woke me late one night. The quarter moon was halfway to the sea from its zenith, which made it about three or four in the morning. I didn't know her well, but there was a familial vibe among the group.

"Jason, shooting stars," she said. "Wake up, shooting stars."

There were a few others awake, and they all sat with their heads tilted back, mouths and eyes wide open. Fern was a small blonde with a round face and great earthy brown eyes. She was usually too shy to have a comfortable conversation with, but that night acid had made her feel she clicked with everything, with the universe, as it sometimes could, and right then she could do no wrong.

"Come out to the rock," she said. "We'll watch from there." She brushed some hair out of my face with the easy gesture of a longtime lover.

I looked up and saw a meteor dart brightly across a piece of sky.

"Okay."

It was high tide, and I offered to carry her on my back to the rock.

"No, I want my feet in the sea."

We were both barefoot anyway, and we waded out, the sand soft and giving under our feet. The surface of the rock, until you got to the rounded crest, was pockmarked and rough and had to be climbed slowly without shoes. When we got up top there was a chilly breeze and our wet feet got cold. We found a position lying on our backs with our legs interlocked so we could hold each other's feet in our hands and warm them.

"Are you glad I woke you?" she asked.

"Yes, very glad," I said. Her feet were small and cold in my hands. The meteor shower was a big one, and the sky was streaked with fleeting luminous trails. One, brightest of all, came over the top of the cliff and bisected the entire sky to a point just inches above the horizon. We gasped, and heard the gasps of the others on the beach. When our feet were warmed and dry, I spun to her and lay with my head near hers. She rubbed my hand and tucked her head into the crook of my neck.

We kissed for a while. She stood up and took off her thick sweater and long skirt and laid them down as a bed, shivering lightly in only her T-shirt. She took that off, too. I stripped and lay down by her, lowering my face toward her huge eyes, feeling welcomed.

"You're not looking for a girlfriend, are you?" she asked.

"No," I said. "I don't think so."

"Good. Because I think you're great, but I can't have anyone trying to crawl inside me right now. I'm being an island."

"Hey, I'm just a passing ship, then."

She moved on to somewhere farther north a few days later.

There in the Laguna Seca parking lot she released me and we looked at each other. "Wow," she said. "It's so good to see you."

"Yeah," I said. "You look great." She kissed me on the lips slowly. The extreme fineness of her hair in my hand was familiar.

"You know," she said, "these are the first shows I've been to since that summer." Her look was piercing, expectant.

"No wonder I haven't seen you around." I was thinking about all the distance between me and Melanie. Distance had always been part of the equation of commitment for me. Surely with three thousand miles' separation there was no question of cheating. "Where have you been?" I asked.

She kept her intense look trained on me, and I started to feel uneasy. She nodded her head, as if in confirmation of something unspoken. "I can't believe after almost two years I finally come to a show, and I see you." She took my hand. "Come here. There's someone I want you to meet."

She led me through the dirt-and-grass lot. We bore right along the side of Chico Joe's brown school bus and stopped behind a pale blue VW van. "Wait here," she said, and walked around the side. The van had Oregon plates. I heard her talking, then she emerged with a tall, brown-bearded guy in woven Guatemalan pants and an oversized flannel shirt. The shirt looked way too warm for the day, but he seemed cool and comfortable.

"Jason," said Fern, "this is my husband, Indra. Indra, this is Jason."

He put his hands together, prayer-wise, and bowed to me. I thought of the picture of Harry praying to the toilet.

"Good to meet you," I said.

He smiled.

Fern looked at him. "Is he awake?"

Indra's look was doubtful, and he cast a glance my way. "No, he's sleeping. We should let him sleep."

Fern seemed to hesitate for a moment, her eyes still locked with his, then she said, "No, he can sleep anytime." She looked at me, "One second," and she went back around the side of the van. I felt a sudden need for a cigarette and reached for my pack.

"Smoke?" I asked Indra as I knocked one free.

He shook his head. "Nope." He smiled provisionally and turned away from me, began fiddling with the latch on the van's back door, which was loose. He was that type, I could tell, the fixer-upper, endlessly competent.

I lit the cigarette. I heard Fern cooing at the van's side door, and then she emerged carrying a child, a little boy who had one eye half open in the late sunlight, the other hidden behind a rotating little fist. His hair was starkly white, his skin pale but glowing with health.

"Jason," said Fern, "this—" she paused for dramatic effect . . . "is Jason."

"Wow," I said, light-headed. "Where'd you get such a great name?" I dropped the cigarette on the ground and approached the boy, smoothed his silky hair.

"He just turned one last month," Fern said. The corners of the boy's big, dark blue eyes were turned down in a squint, and he frowned, staring at me. "Say hi-hi," said Fern. The boy remained silent. I looked from him to Indra, who was standing off near the van observing, his thin eyes the color of heartwood. I smiled at little Jason, but his face was a blur now; in spite of me, my mind was doing the math, and the numbers kept adding up perfectly.

"Oh," I said, shaking the boy's hand between two fingers. I

laughed once, just to loosen my knotted voice. Fern was looking at me, smiling.

"Don't worry," she said. "Indra is his daddy. I just thought you should meet him." She bounced him lightly in her arms, then added, "That's all."

My throat was clogged, and I leaned down close to the boy's face, kissed his nose. I felt I should speak to him. "Hi there," I said. He frowned again, staring.

"When he gets old enough, I'll tell him how his spirit was a shooting star that fell from heaven right down to me one night."

I stepped back. Cracks were developing in my power to assimilate: this was real. "Yeah," I croaked. "Listen, thanks." I found myself starting away, then looked back. "Thanks," I said again, though thankful wasn't what I felt. If I'd been a dog, my tail would have been lodged firmly between my legs. My legs were yanking me away, and I stopped them for a second. I laughed again, stupidly, at myself, hoping they understood. "Jason Burke," I said, and spelled it. "That's my name, in case you need to know it." It was as much as I could manage before letting my legs have their way.

But as the evening wore on, the idea grew on me. Here in the Dead's resplendent bubble it seemed possible that my own responsibility could be satisfied by the act itself, the fact of authorship, and the occasional good thought. I began to feel pride, a sense of increase: having seen my existence outside myself, in the realm of others, I was, by extension, connected with others in a new way. I walked through the crowds glowing warmly, high on nothing but this fact: I was . . . What? I couldn't even let myself think the word, too scary, and really it wasn't true—I wasn't. But I wondered if my own father had felt this when he'd gotten the phone call. They had been living in Turkey, and my mother had come back to the States to have me. I'd emerged in the morning, so he would have heard in his afternoon, maybe at the office. I imagined him taking a walk through the hot streets of Ankara afterward, feeling just this way. I could see the crowded sidewalk scrolling past him, no one knowing why this big Westerner was smiling, I could hear the clamor, the honking *dolmuşes*. As I walked, a ghost of his face merged with mine, and I felt some kind of love rise up in me, the love he'd felt for me on that day, and I squeezed my eyes shut and tried to be rid of it. It didn't belong here. I lit a cigarette, and found I was shaking my head involuntarily. This was my place, my home, and he was invading it. Of course it wasn't the same, I told myself. He had already been a father. I was the second.

The sun set just as the show was about to start. Bruce Hornsby had opened, but I hadn't gone in to see his set, just heard it faintly tinkling in the distance. As I looked at the sudden red glow in half the sky, fading upward to scattered shards of pink cloud, tapering invisibly into darkening blue—the world's own uncommon glory—the bubble disappeared: there was no clear border between day and night, and no separation, I saw, between now and then, between this place and the others. This idea I had of my life on tour being self-contained, completely independent of all that had gone before—an idea I was only now identifying, just as it dissolved—was a falsehood, unnatural, the result of feeble barriers I had constructed. Those barriers had been leaking the whole time. The sun had set on every day of my life so far, and would set impartially on each one coming. Suddenly clear-eyed, I was ashamed of the way I'd run from Fern in the lot. I resolved to go back to them after the show.

The show was a great one, which didn't surprise anyone. The "Sugar Magnolia" opener, instead of seeming tame and saccharine, was perfect for the vibe, everyone just smiling and kicking up their feet. There would be time, later in the second set, to get introverted and way-out. That was what the "Space-Wheel-Other One" run was for, the Boys firing on all cylinders. During "The Other One," I saw Don dancing at the edge of a group of swirlers. His hands as he moved were alternately clenched into fists and flapping loosely at the ends of his slithering arms. His eyes were closed. Seeing him then, it was as if all other glimpses and looks at him had been impeded by inner eye scales, as if he had always been dancing there, on that piece of ground with his siblings all around. Dharma, the original self. It was why we came. I remembered a party that first summer in Santa Cruz, at a house in the hills. Everyone had been tripping heavily. There was a great band that played "Low Spark of High-Heeled Boys" for at least an hour, and a crazy guy in the kitchen with a twelve-gallon stew pot cooking buds into mush for brownies. It was that night that Don and I had become friends, had danced and smoked and tasted the sugary stew and been on exactly the same wavelength the whole trip. I watched him dance and didn't approach until Jerry wound the beat down into the opening riff of "Wharf Rat."

Don stood straight and opened his eyes. I called his name as I came up to him.

"Hey," he said. "My brother, my brother," and hugged me. I could tell from his eyes and the slinky feel of his body that he was high on Ecstasy. "I didn't see you at the Frost shows."

"I wasn't there. I'm staying with a friend near here."

"Cool." He stared into my eyes, that Ecstasy connection, the need for intimacy, oozing from him. "Jason, listen, we're cool, right? All that other bullshit, it's nothing. Right, brother?"

"Yeah," I said. And it was true. He hugged me again.

"You remember," he said, letting me go, "that summer we met? Just up the coast from here. Remember Greyhound Rock?"

"I remember. In fact, I just ran into Fern tonight. Remember her?"

"Fern." Don smiled. "Yeah, I remember. Quiet girl. A little hottie though. You did her, didn't you?"

It was like being smacked, hearing it put that way, but I said, "Yeah, I did."

"What an amazing time. Hey, you coming up to the Bay after these shows?"

"I'll probably stay around here for a while, with my friend."

Don strode quickly over to a pile of bags and clothes by a light pole and pulled a small knapsack from the top. He took out a pen, tore off a scrap of paper, and wrote on it. "Saul and I got an apartment in Berkeley. This is our number. Anytime you're around." He handed me the orange scrap.

"Thanks," I said. "I'll give you guys a call."

I wandered closer to the stage, and when the band went into "Around and Around," I let myself go, dancing hard to its crescendos, pushing everything else aside. But when they encored with "Iko Iko," once again I was preoccupied, unable to join the party. I just swayed my head to Garcia's lilting solos.

As soon as it ended I headed for the lot. I wound my way through the gauntlet of postshow beer, food, and T-shirt sellers back to where Fern and Indra's van was parked. Except it wasn't. I knew I had the right spot because there was the brown school bus, but their van was gone. I'll have to find them tomorrow night, I thought, but felt a faint suction in my chest that wouldn't listen to that bit of reason, and nudged me toward despair. Wandering through the lot, I met up with the Jersey crew at their turtle-top Dodge van and stopped to smoke a joint with them. As I hit on the soft, skunky fattie, I realized again that I had spent the whole show stone sober. I let the smoke expand in my lungs, sink into me, as natural as a drink of water.

GETTING BACK TO HARRY'S after the show was something like going straight from a circus to a funeral parlor. If anything the difference was greater. Liam was sitting in the small library off the front hall, reading an R. Crumb comic. We'd decided it was best not to leave Harry alone, and one of us was always there.

"Hey," I said. "How is he?"

Liam rolled his eyes and jerked his head toward the living room. "He's up."

"Is he drunk?"

"No, he's still in the twice-a-week stage. It won't be long now, though." He went back to his comic.

I walked down the hall to the semidark living room. The shifting light from the big-screen slid over chairs and sofa and Harry with his O-tank and blanket, as if he were sitting in front of a huge aquarium filled with electric eels. The sound was muted, and from the stereo came loud, distorted guitar and low, unintelligible singing.

"How was your show?" he asked.

"It was great." I looked back at the TV and saw he was watching a satellite porn channel. A man, stone-faced, businesslike, was inserting his dick into a woman's ass. It was the same size, shape, and color as the orange plastic flashlights we'd had at summer camp, missing only the sliding white switch on top. I decided to try for humor. "I didn't know you still went for this stuff, at your age."

"I don't," Harry said. He waved the remote at the screen and looked down at the crotch of his slacks. "I might as well be watching *Wheel of Fortune*."

"You mean that isn't Vanna White?"

"I don't know. They haven't showed her face yet."

We both laughed. I sat down in a chair and stared at the screen. Mr. Flashlight's thrusts were relentless, mechanical.

After a minute, I said, "I have a son."

"What?" Harry still didn't look at me.

"I saw a girl I slept with once a couple of years ago tonight, and she's got a little boy with my name. Looks like me, too."

Mr. Flashlight pulled out, and the woman spun and knelt and opened her mouth wide. It wasn't Vanna White.

"But what does that mean, really?" Harry asked. "Can you be sure?"

Mr. Flashlight spilled on the woman's face.

"She all but told me, and she's not looking for me to do anything, she's married and he's become the daddy. I feel she's telling the truth."

Harry hit a button on the remote and an Indonesian soccer game came on. He turned to me. "Well, join the club. Father but not Daddy."

"What do you mean join the club?"

He gave me a lowered look, through his own eyebrows. "Who do you think those Jost twins are?"

"Those boys? The models? They're your sons? Where'd they get their looks?"

Harry chuckled. "Thanks." He turned away from me, as if he'd heard something in the kitchen.

He turned back. "They don't even know it. Vanessa was seeing me and an investment banker. Guess who won out when she got pregnant?"

"Jesus, Harry." I shook my head. "The man of many mysteries."

Harry eased a cigarette from the long red pack and lit it, cranked up the flow on the oxygen tank. He breathed heavily into the mask before taking his first drag. "Well," he said, blowing smoke, "looks like you're shaping up that way, too."

THE NEXT DAY I went to the show early to try and unload the eighty sheets I was still sitting on. I found Vince and talked him into taking fifty at a discount. The other thirty I sold piecemeal to people I knew and familiar faces. No sign, through all this, of the pale blue VW van with Oregon plates. I asked around after them, and no one seemed to know who they were. Once again the weather was perfect, the vibe sunny, but I couldn't hook into it. I didn't know what I wanted or what I'd say when I saw Fern, but the previous day's meeting had left me deeply bothered, mostly with myself. I walked every inch of that parking area and didn't find them. The Boys cranked out another tremendous show, which pulled me out of my funk at its high points, but between songs and sets I continued to feel a weight on me. Then after a rousing second set that raised my spirits, the final encore of "Black Muddy River," with all its talk of walking alone, sent me away in a brooding mood. It had been exactly a month since the detective took Melanie away in Chicago, and not a word from her. I thought of trying her parents' number. I needed to talk to her, to know she was still thinking of me.

7

THE BUILDING THAT CONTAINED Saul and Don's two-room first-floor apartment wasn't strictly in Berkeley, as Don had said, but just off Telegraph Avenue, far enough south to be in Oakland. The watermarked wallpaper in the hall was the color of tobacco spit and swooned at the corners weighted by chunks of crumbled plaster. The carpet was faded red and didn't extend the full width of the hallway, covering only a strip in the center. There were holes in it. A flooded-basement smell filled the building. Inside the apartment, the baseboards and moldings were cracked and separated at intervals from the wall, the paint so old it barely existed. Two small windows looked onto an alley fenced off at both ends, making a perfect refuge and latrine for the bums who came and went through a thin gap where the chain-link was torn away from its post at one end. The building across the way was a cinder-block warehouse and had no windows or doors facing the alley. Beyond it was a porn theater.

Don shut the door quickly behind me. "Hey Jason," he said,

moving back toward the low thrift-store table in front of three plastic chairs. Obviously furniture hadn't been a priority. "Want a base hit?"

It had been over half a year since my last freebase binge had scared me into going back east to my mother, but I slipped back into it as if no time had elapsed. That sugary taste of the first hit, the sheer beauty of the rush—so good that it seemed this time would be different: there could be no crash from something so pure. Then just as quick the initial crash and the deep jones, all energy, all concentration, focused on that glass pipe.

"Saul's out scoring some downtown," Don said. "So don't worry about the comedown."

Two hours later, when Saul got back, Don and I were already cocaine puppets, moon-eyed and unsmiling, our tiniest actions—lighting cigarettes, peeping out the windows, sipping on cans of Pabst Blue Ribbon—connected by taut wires to the last hit and the next.

"Shit, you guys are deep in," Saul said.

"You score?" asked Don.

Saul looked at him sternly a moment, just fucking with him. "Look at you. Yeah, I fucking scored. I ever come back empty-handed?"

Saul sat in the third chair, but instead of reaching for the pipe, he dragged the bag of powdered coke toward himself. From a cardboard box under the table he took a rolled-up T-shirt, unrolled it, and laid out a syringe, some cotton balls, a spoon with its face bent backward, and a lighter. I watched him fix a speedball, cooking a chunk of black tar heroin into some water and sprinkling the coke last into the brown liquid. He dropped a tiny piece of cotton into the spoon and drew the solution through it into the needle. He held the needle up in front of his face and flicked it, pushed one tiny drop of liquid out the tip. "Oh, yeah," he said, speaking as if to some disembodied entity in the room. Don had loaded another hit of freebase and was smoking it. I went into the bathroom before Saul got the needle into his vein. I stood over the toilet pinching my shriveled dick and watched three or four drops eke out. When I returned to the room, Saul was leaning back in his chair and breathing heavily, making me think of Harry, except Saul's panting was more like sex than dying. His eyes were closed, one hand opening and closing involuntarily, his lips pushed into an O through which his breath came and went in perfect rhythm. His left arm was bent, and when he straightened it the crook had become a Rorschach blot of drying blood.

"Two bats fucking," I said.

"What?" said Don.

"Nothing." There was no place for humor in a serious binge.

I resisted doing the heroin, sticking with beer to try and level myself off. Mixing the two was a new line I wasn't ready to cross. Don was smoking it off tinfoil, chasing the rising smoke with a tube of paper. We ordered Chinese sometime in the middle of the night, but when it got there I couldn't eat so I did another base hit. Eventually, Saul and Don switched to straight dope and went into the other room to crash. Don left me with a half-gram rock of freebase, which I made last almost until morning.

My mind whipped itself into a state of tightly wound paranoia. The lack of a television only made it worse, leaving me alone with my thoughts and throbbing vision. I turned off the light and between hits listened to my own panting and the nighttime city sounds. My eyes adjusted, and the darkness seemed bright as daylight; I could see every crack in the plaster wall across the room and hear the bums pissing and shuffling around in the alley—they never talked to each other, and that made me nervous, as if they were trying to be stealthy. I'd suck in a hit, the bluish-white rush taking over for one glorious moment (shorter each time), and then on the crumbling peak of the high I'd perceive ugly, imminent dangers: first, and most reasonably, my own death of a heart attack, with no one around to dial 911; but as the night wore on it began to be cops outside the door; then finally, after even the bums had crashed out, malign gnomes haunted the shadows outside the windows, not exactly crunching grit and beer cans with tangible stubby feet, but threatening to round that final corner if I should lose control, to slip past the bars and stoop over me, to munch bloodily on my amped-up, stupid heart.

It was in this state of gnome-terror that Saul found me when he wandered out to piss in the late morning. He took one look at my face and said, "Fuck. Just sit there." He retrieved a chunk of the tar from a package in his pocket and gathered Don's tinfoil and tube. He dropped the chunk onto one end of the foil and handed me the tube. "Here, smoke this. Don't be stupid." He held the lighter under the foil for me as I sucked in the smoke, which was bitter and felt sticky in my mouth. When I had my hit, the chunk wasn't even halfway depleted. Saul gave me the lighter. "Take this. Chase that fucker around until there's none left." He got up and shuffled into the bathroom.

I did as I was told. Half an hour later, when the dope high had begun its first tapering off, I was capable of sleep. Don had an old sleeping bag in the closet. I unrolled it, struggling to keep my limbs in motion and my eyelids at half-mast, and lay down on top of it. As I was drifting it came to me again, for the first time in a day, that I was a father. The word was one I had avoided even thinking in relation to myself, but now it sounded in my head like the striking of a gong, and I whispered it involuntarily, and the hoarse sound of it echoed in my ears and slithered through my cells. A *father* who had spent the night on a freebase roller coaster, imagining cops and evil gnomes and coming god knows how close to death. But I was unable to feel the shame and remorse my thoughts were trying to conjure, which reflected off me like heat: I was a thermos full of chill liquid that would stay cold for hours, as advertised. The cold liquid, I found, was knowledge. Knowledge that as I fell asleep crept deep into me and was beyond question; such great comfort to know how little everything mattered.

FOR FOUR DAYS WE BINGED, then we all needed a break. I drove back to Carmel, where I had left Liam in charge of overseeing Harry. When I got there, Liam was gone and Harry was passed out in bed. The house was a wreck—dishes piled high, plates, glasses, liquor bottles, ashtrays everywhere. I decided not to wake Harry. That could wait. I called Liam.

"Listen," he said, "I'm his friend, his gardener even, but not his fucking baby-sitter or punching bag. He gets past a certain point and he can fend for himself, far as I'm concerned."

"You've seen him like this before?"

"Hell yes. It's twice a year or so. I got him into detox last time. This time I wash my hands."

Liam gave me the name of the fancy detox outside LA where Harry had been a year earlier. He wished me luck. "By the way," he said before we hung up, "your girlfriend called from back east. Harry took the call, but couldn't remember what she said. Just that her name was Mary."

"Her name's Melanie."

"Well, there you go."

While I waited for Harry to wake up, I cleaned the house. It felt strangely good, as if in clearing away the bottles (a couple of them half full, which I poured into the sink) and cigarette butts, scraping and scouring the dishes, I was clearing the grit and debris the binge had left inside me. I did a thorough job, mopping the sticky kitchen floor, wiping down the glass top of the coffee table, vacuuming the carpets. It was like scratching an itch. I called the rehab and the woman on the phone remembered Harry; I tried to decipher her attitude toward him, but her neutral tone gave nothing away. I gave her Harry's credit card number, and she reserved him a bed for the following day. I found a can of vegetable soup, which I put on the counter next to a clean saucepan, ready to heat for Harry when he came to. But he didn't. Every time I checked on him, he was still out, wheezing peacefully under the quilted bedspread, his feet in their gray socks poking from the end. Around eleven that night, I went to bed.

Sleep, however, didn't come quickly, tired as I was. The itch I had been scratching by cleaning was still there and had crept quietly into my bones. I felt dry inside, and uncomfortable. I kept drinking glasses of water, rolled around for two or three hours before finally dropping off. Something woke me a few hours later, and waking I knew why I was so restless, must have realized it in my sleep because there it was waiting for me: my body was coming off four days of heroin. The knowledge was like a paperweight in my skull, and I wanted it gone in the same way I would want a headache gone. But that wasn't what had woken me. I lifted my head from the pillow and listened, but I couldn't hear anything. I got up and climbed the stairs. At the top I made a left toward Harry's bedroom, but the door was standing open and he wasn't on the bed. I turned and went into the living room, where I now saw the light of the TV leaping whitely around.

"Hey there," said Harry, waving his open bottle of Bacardi at me as I walked in. "Thought I heard someone putzing around out here. Nice job." His voice sounded very old.

"I thought I cleared all that shit out," I said, pointing at the bottle.

Harry swigged on the rum, then touched the side of his nose.

"I reserved a bed for you at the Rakoff Center. There are commuter flights out of San Jose every couple of hours tomorrow."

Harry sneered and drank some more. "Eat shit," he said calmly.

"I figure we can leave the house around noonish. How's that for you?"

"You gonna make me?" he growled, then began to cough. He descended into a deep fit, and I ran for his oxygen tank, which he'd left in the bedroom. I dragged it to him and twisted open the valve. Between coughs he was able only to take single breaths from the tank. He doubled over violently, and it sounded as if his intestines might squeeze up his throat and flop out onto the table. Instead he just puked, thin brown bile gushing from him like the first spurt of water from a rusty hand pump, puddling on the glass table. For a moment after that he couldn't breathe at all, his eyes bulged gruesomely, and another small draught of liquid expelled itself as he tried to suck air, this one spilling over his chin onto his sweater; finally he was able to rake in a long breath and scream once, hoarsely, at the pain the bile caused in his raw throat. He continued to cough for a few minutes, groaning in pain during the tiny breaks, and I went to the kitchen for a glass of water. When the fit subsided, he took a small sip of water and curled up on the couch, his arms crossed and his knees pulled up. I got a blanket. He wouldn't speak to me, but nodded his head as I draped it over him. "You're fucking killing yourself," I said. The expression on his face was one of fathomless anger.

I went back to the kitchen for a rag. When I turned on the light and went to the table, I saw that the puddle across it was striped with sinuous red lines. "There's blood in your puke, Harry," I said. "Look at that." I showed him the rag. He didn't answer me.

THE NEXT DAY he continued drinking, mixing his booze now with Pepsi. He ignored any reference I made to the rehab, in fact avoided speaking to me almost completely. I acted as though it was a foregone conclusion that we were going, packed a bag for him and a small one for myself, and to my surprise, when I came to drag him out the door he resisted only verbally—telling me to fuck off, mind my own business, leave him be, all while getting up and coming with me. I loaded him into the passenger seat of his Mercedes and got behind the wheel.

"Notice anything different about me?" Harry asked.

"You mean besides being drunk and needing a shower?"

He nodded. "Yeah. Besides that."

"I give up." I was pulling out of the driveway. It was a dazzlingly bright day, and I flipped down the sun visor.

"I quit smoking."

I thought about it. I hadn't seen him smoking since I got back. "That's great, Harry."

"You make me quit drinking, and I'll have to start smoking again."

I shook my head. "I'm not making you do anything."

At San Jose airport, I bought us tickets on a commuter flight to LA with Harry's credit card (mine round-trip, his one-way). Harry insisted on first class. I led him toward the gate, gripping his arm from behind at the biceps. He veered rightward when we passed the bar.

"One drink 'fore the flight," he said.

"Harry, the plane's boarding," I said, which was true. I pulled on his arm and straightened him out. His gait was becoming more unsteady, and I found I needed to hold him up. Every thirty yards or so we stopped and I gave Harry the handheld traveling oxygen tank to huff from.

At the gate we were waved through onto the plane without pause and settled in a pair of expansive seats in the third row. There were only two other first-class passengers, sitting separately in front of us, and before the door was even closed a flight attendant began making the rounds, taking drink orders. I realized why Harry had insisted on first class. When she got to us she leaned down close to us solicitously and smiled. It was a universal flight-attendant smile, but contained a watered-down kind of genuine friendliness. She was blond, slightly plump, a cute woman of about twenty-five with red cheeks and a tiny nose.

"Can I get you gentlemen a drink before takeoff?" she chirped.

"No thanks," I said, but Harry cut me off.

"Vokka tonic!" he almost yelled. "Make it quick!"

She nodded and retreated toward the galley. She served the two men in front of us their drinks, then came back to us. Her expression had solidified into one of professional competence, but I could see she was worried. She didn't lean down this time. "Sir, I'm sorry, but we are not allowed to serve alcohol to intoxicated people." She was speaking to me.

Harry forced the slur out of his voice, but the effort seemed to take the lid off his anger: "Just give me a fucking drink," he said. "I am not drunk."

"I'm sorry, sir. Technically, we shouldn't allow you to fly at all."

"We're on our way to a detox," I said.

She nodded. "I'm not going to stop you. But I can't serve you." And she turned and walked away.

"Fucking bitch," Harry said.

She came back. "Excuse me? What did you call me?"

"Nothing," I said. "Please, I'm sorry."

"Yeah, sorry," said Harry. "I use' th'rong word."

She paused a moment, her tame little blue eyes, which were embedded a touch too deeply in her round face, flicking back and forth between us. She was not a decisive person. She started away again.

"I meant to say cunt."

She turned back. "That's it. You both need to get off the plane." She walked toward the front to get backup.

A few seconds later the captain and a male flight attendant were at our seats. "Sir," said the captain. "Airport security is on the way. You need to exit the plane."

"Come on, Harry," I said, getting up.

"Fuck you."

"Come on," I said. "I had to drag you on this plane to begin with. Now you got what you wanted. Let's go."

But the captain and the other man were on him first, picking him up and carrying him down the aisle. Harry had gone limp but was pleading his case with them, his tone softer. I took our bags and the little O-tank from the overhead and followed. What Harry was asking was for them to pause at the front so he could apologize to the stewardess. They did this, and she stepped out of the galley to face him.

"I'm sorry," he said, "that you're such a fucking tight-ass bitch."

"Okay," said the captain, and they whisked him out the door.

At the entrance to the gate area we were deposited into the custody of an airport cop. The captain explained the situation and the cop said, "Okay. You both just need to leave the airport. Come back when you're sober. Follow me."

"Thanks, officer," I said, but Harry resisted me, wouldn't budge.

The cop took Harry's other arm, and together we started dragging him. He didn't weigh a thing.

"Look at you," Harry said to the cop. "You little asshole." The cop was about six-three, two-fifty.

"Watch it, buddy, or I'll have to arrest you." The toes of Harry's rubber-soled shoes squeaked on the shiny floor, dragging behind him.

"Please," I said. "I'm trying to get him to a rehab."

"Okay," said the cop.

"Fucking pig," said Harry. "Pig. Jerk. Cock. Foreskin. Lumpa shit."

"Can you get him to shut up?"

"I don't know," I said. "I don't think so."

"Piss-stain," Harry said. "Stinking fuckwad."

The cop sighed loudly.

"Please," I said. "Just get us to the door."

When we reached the exit, the cop disengaged from Harry's arm and left him on my shoulder. "You get him out of here," he said. Then he looked at Harry. "You go with your son, get some help. You're lucky I'm not locking you up."

Harry's face became an expression of the purest, the most disdainful hatred, fell into it as if it were the one emotion his features had been created to express. Staring at the cop, he looked like a man confronted at the door of the courtroom with his daughter's rapist. He seemed suddenly sober and stood free of me. "Last night," he said, "I fucked your mother in the ass and came on her face." His voice became smooth and slow, dripping with hate, "And she *loved* it."

The cop moved forward and grabbed the front of Harry's shirt, cocking one fist back. I stepped away from Harry. This was his business now. Harry looked satisfied and stuck out his chin. There was a split-second pause, and then a few teeth came flying toward me. It seemed like a 3-D movie effect until one of the teeth bounced off my cheek—except in the movies the blow would have made a big sound. I couldn't believe how quietly it happened. I was three feet away, and I barely heard that big pink sandbag of a fist hit Harry's elegant jaw. I could see why Hollywood dubbed in fake sound effects, because the real thing is a surprisingly dull weak sound that probably wouldn't carry to the back row of a small theater. The cop was holding him up by the collar of his shirt. Harry's head drooled red saliva and bobbed wildly, like some grim dashboard ornament. The cop slapped him again, let him go, and Harry fell heavily on his tailbone. "Now get the fuck out of here," said the cop, and walked away.

"Puthy," Harry called after him. "I thoo yah fuckin' ath."

I leaned over and grabbed Harry around the rib cage to help him stand. "Shut the fuck up, Harry," I said. He let me help him to the car, and as we struggled through the lot his ribs felt like twigs under my hand. I wanted to squeeze him hard enough to break them.

"Hey," he said. "Eathy. Jeethuth."

When we got to the car, I put him in and handed him the tank. He clamped it over his face. The front of his mouth looked doughy and soft, flapping with his breathing where the teeth were missing. A bit of blood pooled in the bottom of the mask. I walked around the back, depositing the bags in the trunk, and climbed in. I had made a decision. I handed Harry a rag I'd found in the trunk, for the blood.

"Now we're going to drive to LA."

"Thake me home," Harry said. He was dabbing at his mouth gingerly.

"You want to go home? Fine. I'm going to find all your booze, pour it out, keep the car keys, and disconnect the phone. If you come quietly to LA, we can stop at a liquor store on the way. Your choice."

THE THIRD LIQUOR STORE we stopped at didn't card me, and I bought Harry a six-pack of raspberry wine coolers and a bottle of Tylenol.

"What th'fuck ith thith?" he said when I put the six-pack in his lap.

"That's your drink. I said I'd get you a drink."

"No, fuck. Go back in. Get thom vokka. Thith zhit ith a zhoke."

"Live with it."

I cut over to Highway 5 and headed south. I called the center from Harry's car phone and got directions. Harry drank his wine coolers fast, we stopped once for him to piss, then he mercifully passed out. I took the car up to a hundred, not really caring if I got pulled over. Harry was totally motionless, his chin against his chest, and I spread the rag in his lap to catch the still-pink drool. I didn't turn on the radio; we just flew along in that German silence. I was thinking that after I dropped him off, I'd get a motel room, then drive up the coast the next day.

It was night when we got there. The Rakoff Center was in an eastern suburb of LA. It was large, but all one level, spread out in wings across the burgeoning desert. Harry woke in pain and miserably hung over and was in no mood for confrontation. Checking him in went smoothly. They recommended no phone calls in the first two weeks unless it was an emergency. The two women who helped get him into his room were friendly and competent, and seemed unfazed by Harry's bloody mouth and puke-stained clothes. They said they could get someone to fix his teeth if he wanted.

"I'll call you in a couple of weeks, Harry," I said before leaving.

Harry didn't answer, but stared at me and set his misshapen mouth in anger.

"By the way," I said. "Do you remember what my friend Melanie said when she called?"

No answer.

"Liam told me you took the call."

He waited a second, then spoke, as if with great effort. "Zhe thaid forget her. Zhe's finizhed with you."

"Come on, Harry. For real."

Harry's eyes went blank, as if I were an apparition that had just disappeared. The nurse was inserting an IV, and he looked away from both of us out the scratched Plexiglas window, where in the darkness there was nothing to be seen.

I got my motel room near the highway and picked up a six-pack in case I had the same trouble sleeping. I watched cable and drank the beers and fell asleep easily. The next morning when I got under way, something hit me. I'd planned to make a leisurely and meditative drive up the coast to Harry's, clean the place up again, make myself comfortable there, chill out, read some books, watch satellite TV. But I popped in *Kind of Blue* and was seduced by the way the flitting sunshine played against the suave rhythms and the gray leather that covered the seats and the steering wheel, making me feel cut off from the world in the most desirable, luxurious sense: above it all. What hit me was that I was behind the wheel of a beautiful Mercedes and had a house in the Carmel hills, with a hot tub and big-screen TV, all to myself. These were things that just couldn't be squandered.

I made the call from the car phone and Saul picked up. I told him the situation and gave him directions to get to Harry's house.

"Can we bring anyone else?" he asked. "Like girls?"

"Yeah," I said. "Girls are fine. But if you're going to bring any other guys, just no one I don't know."

"You got it."

Saul and Don showed up in a blue '73 Cadillac Fleetwood they'd just bought, with Cole, two girls, and a guy I'd never seen before. One of the girls was Scar, and the other was a puffy-cheeked, black-haired girl named Blinka. It was short for something. The guy was skinny, about six-foot-six, with a jet black beard and shifty blue eyes. His voice was smooth and convincing from out of that long echo chamber, but his eyes ruined the effect.

"Jason, you know Tall Ted, right?" said Saul.

"I don't think so."

"Oh. Okay."

"Hey. Hi," said Tall Ted, pushing an elongated hand toward me, reining in his wandering eyes to look at me for a second.

"Hey there, sweetie," Scar said, and gave me a short hug.

We spent the first afternoon in Harry's living room watching laser-disc movies, drinking beer, and smoking pot. Scar was marginally linked to Don, sitting next to him and sharing cigarettes, but Blinka seemed to have just met everyone except Scar, who had brought her along. Blinka sat near me on the couch, kicked off her sandals, and tucked her feet up next to her thigh. The soles of her feet were dirty. Black hairs began at her ankles, stark against the pale skin. Her face was pretty—reminded me of girls I'd seen in Romania as a child, with red heart-shaped lips and round black eyes set into white, white skin—but had a few red blemishes, a thin gap separating her two front teeth, and a downy hint of mustache. Her bush would be thick and wiry, spilling onto her thighs.

Saul was making trips to the bathroom, and I knew he and Don had brought something heavier than pot. After the second movie *(The Empire Strikes Back)*, Saul broke out some coke, and we started doing lines. Saul didn't do any, but continued his trips to the bathroom. I was flipping lamely through the convoluted maze of channels, never having learned how to operate the satellite dish.

"This is some nice blow," Cole said after snorting a line.

Scar, sitting on the floor across the table from him, sneered. I was the only one who saw it. "Yeah, good thing you're here to enjoy it," she said. She was a little drunk, but the coke was sharpening her up. I realized at that moment that I had forgotten all about Dawn and what happened to her. I felt nauseous remembering the prison, our kiss, my subsequent silence.

"What?" said Cole, looking up.

Scar mugged at him, shrugging dramatically. "What?" she parroted.

Cole shook his head and looked away from her.

"You got any extra funds to invest?" Ted asked, and I realized he was talking to me.

"Funds?"

"Yeah, to invest."

"No," I said. I got up and went to the bathroom down the hall. When I came out of the bathroom, Scar was waiting for me.

"All yours," I said.

"I need to talk to you." She pushed me back into the bathroom and shut the door. "You going to let him just hang out and party like nothing happened?"

"Who, Cole?"

"Who do you think? Yeah, him. I didn't say anything to those other guys, but you know what he did. You should find some reason to kick him out."

I took a long breath. "Look, Cole is an old friend. I still haven't asked him about what happened. I don't know his side."

"His side? What do you think he's going to say? Of course he'll deny it. Why would Dawn lie?"

"Like I said, Cole's an old friend, and I can't just kick him out without seeing what he has to say."

Scar poked my chest with her finger. "You don't fucking even want to know. You'll believe anything he tells you, probably."

"No, I won't. I'll ask him when the time is right, okay? I'll do it soon. But I'm not kicking him out unless it turns out he did it."

"Prick," she said. "Get out of here so I can pee."

WHEN WE SETTLED BACK to watch *Scarface*, Saul took a spot by Blinka and draped an arm around her. She didn't seem to mind, but didn't respond either. "Hey Scar," Saul said, "is this guy your uncle or something?" Don and Scar lay together on the floor in front of the coffee table, she using his leg as a pillow. "Ha ha," she said. Scar had calmed down and was just avoiding talking to Cole at all. Night had conjured itself outside without us noticing, and the room was dark except for the light of the TV. We sat watching the movie, laughing when Pacino delivered his classic lines, occasionally snorting some coke. We stopped it halfway through to do something about food. After trying a few places, I finally found a pizza joint that knew where Harry's road was and agreed to deliver there for an extra ten bucks.

Don threw in a bootleg from his bag and we listened to "Estimated Prophet." During Bobby's vocal rap before the final jam,

Don said, "Check this out, coming up. There's a moment when Bobby sounds like someone stabbed him right in the gut." Bobby was working through his "No, no, no's" and then into descending screams. "Right here," Don said, and Bobby made a guttural sound, like a scream stifled by blood in the throat, a wet bark of pain. It did sound like a stabbing caught on tape, and we all laughed. Don rewound and we listened to it again, with Don miming the scene, tiptoeing across the carpet as if sneaking up on Bobby, then at the right moment reaching around and driving the knife in.

When the tape ended I put on a CD of *Blues for Allah*. Despite his professed disdain, Harry had a few Dead CDs; his music collection was nothing if not complete. I turned it up.

When the instrumental "Stronger than Dirt" came on, Don started a discussion about what the name might mean.

"Mean?" said Saul. "What does 'Milking the Turkey' mean? What does 'King Solomon's Marbles' mean? It doesn't mean shit. It's just some tripped-out psychedelic wildness. The kind of shit you think of on acid."

"So the shit you think of on acid is all meaningless?"

Saul laughed. "Most of it, yeah."

"Jason, what does it mean to you?"

Don had just done a line of coke, and I did one, too. "I don't know," I said.

"It's biblical," said Cole. "Ashes to ashes, dust to dust. God made man from the earth, and all that. Man is more than just electrified dust walking around till the charge wears out, then disappearing: stronger than dirt." He looked around at all of us who had fallen silent, staring at him. "None of this stuff is meaningless, otherwise why are we doing what we're doing?"

Don put both his hands on the table in a deliberate, showy gesture, widening his eyes at Cole. "Now *that* is some deep guano you're slinging there, Tex."

"Or," Cole went on, "it could mean something completely else. It could be the slogan for a fucking laundry detergent. Who knows? It's the music that matters, not what it's called, anyway."

"Wrong wrong wrong," said Ted. He stood up. "I'll show you what it means." And he started dancing, eyes squeezed shut, his feet planted firmly on the carpet, long sharp arms flying around him. He was biting his lower lip and exhaling through his teeth loudly on the downbeats, he was wobbling, flailing, awkward, but right in the groove, locked into the complex jam. I felt like laughing at his crazed motion, but at the same time it was somehow impressive.

He stopped abruptly. "Understand now?"

Don smirked and cut me a look.

We all listened to the music for a second, nodding our heads. Saul grabbed the remote off the table and shut down the stereo. "Enough, already," he said. "Save that crap for the Spinners and the God Squad." He picked up the other remote and unmuted the TV, started flipping channels and suddenly came upon the porn station. Two women were making love in a giant canopy bed.

"Holy shit," said Saul. "You didn't say you had porno on this thing."

"Well, I don't know how to work it," I said.

"Change the channel," Ted said.

"Fuck that," said Saul.

Ted shrugged and went downstairs.

We fell silent and watched the woman being serviced fake an orgasm. She sounded more like someone was giving her a spinal tap than oral sex. In the next scene a man entered a flower shop and asked for an arrangement for his wife's birthday. I recognized him as Mr. Flashlight. It wasn't long before the woman behind the counter was on her knees sucking on his flashlight, the fat head squeezing back and forth past her lips. She pushed forward until the entire shaft was in her mouth, her nose against his body.

"Now that's impressive," Saul said.

Scar snorted. "I could do that."

"Bullshit," said Saul. "On a cock that size?"

"Sure. I haven't met a cock I couldn't swallow. I don't think there is one."

"Oh, I beg to differ. I'd lay fifty bucks you couldn't do that with mine."

"Fifty bucks?" Scar sat up. "You're on."

Saul laughed. "Seriously?"

Scar looked at Don. "You mind?"

"What am I," Don said, "your husband? But you haven't seen what he's got. Be careful." He went back to watching the screen.

"Fifty bucks," said Scar. "You're on. If you can get it up, that is."

"Oh, I can get it up. You're serious about this?"

"Just lay your cash on the table."

"Okay, let's get it straight. All the way in, nothing left showing. That's what we're talking about." I could see him fearing the loss of his fifty dollars.

"Don't worry," Scar said. "Let's go down the hall."

"No," Saul said.

"What, you backing out?"

"No. We do it here. With witnesses. Or not at all. And you need to help me get it up."

Scar laughed. "You asshole. Trying to get out of it. Okay, we do it here, but you get it up yourself. This is a bet here, not a fucking orgy."

"Deal," said Saul. He went back to watching the movie, which had become the scene I had watched with Harry before; it was the same movie. Saul started rubbing himself through his pants.

"I'm out of here," said Blinka. She stood up, throwing Saul's arm off herself. "Tell me when it's over." She went out onto the deck with a pack of cigarettes.

Not wanting to stare at Saul, who was rubbing himself, or at Scar, who was drinking a glass of water, I stared at the screen. My own hard-on was going strong. After a minute Saul stood up and said, "Okay, I'm ready." He was smirking nervously as he unzipped. It really was quite magnificent, bigger than Mr. Flashlight's in all its dimensions.

"Jesus," Scar said.

"No backing out now," said Saul.

"Who's backing out?"

I thought of Blinka outside, disgusted with these proceedings, and it occurred to me that this was an opportunity to usurp Saul's claim on her. "I guess I can do without this," I said, and went outside.

Blinka was leaning on the rail, looking out at the night, which was dark, clouds hiding moon and stars. One bare foot was cocked up slightly behind her, only the toes flat on the wood. I remembered being out there with Jane, a year and a half earlier.

Blinka was smoking.

"Can I bum one?" I asked.

"Are they done?" she asked, handing me the pack.

"No. I decided I didn't want to see it. It's a little sick."

Through the open sliding door I heard Saul saying, "Come on, before I lose it."

Blinka laughed softly and so did I, but I felt the truth in what I had said. I lit the cigarette and leaned on the rail next to her, and we stared out together at nothing. After a moment there was the sound of clapping from inside, and Don whooped, "Oh, yeah! No question!"

We watched the rest of *Scarface* after the pizza arrived. Saul paid Scar and sulked about it. "You could have at least had the decency to finish me off," he said.

Scar laughed. "Finish yourself off. I'm not running a fucking charity here."

Blinka was now sitting with me, snuggled close, and Saul looked a little defeated, all those inches going to waste.

Things progressed the way those things do. Drugs can elongate time and annihilate it. More interminable movies on laser disc, soaks in the hot tub (a godsend on coke), occasionally a beer run in Harry's Mercedes, people slinking off at odd hours, singly or in pairs, to catch three or twelve hours of sleep. The second day, once we were all well immersed, Saul stopped going to the bathroom to shoot up. I kept avoiding being alone with Cole, considering over and over how I would confront him. I couldn't seem to find the moment. Scar was right, I didn't really want to know. Cole, for his part, was avoiding Scar, just doing his drugs and keeping a low profile.

For two days Blinka kept me at bay, snuggling with me on the couch, sleeping with me, but deftly deflecting my attempts at going further. In the hot tub I noticed that her breasts, though the nipples sprouted wavy dark hairs, were beautifully shaped and even paler than her legs. Don and Scar were scrumping like monkeys and had appropriated Harry's bedroom, running off every few hours, when they weren't too high, to slam the headboard against the Sheetrock.

For a while the third day it was just me, Ted, and Blinka in the living room, trying to kill the coke-jones with beer and hits of tar heroin off tinfoil.

"So you sure you don't have any funds to invest?" Ted asked me. "I mean, this is your place, isn't it?"

"What's it with you and funds?"

"If I can find some investors, we can get very rich, bro."

"Okay, you've got me curious."

Ted tilted his towering, mantis-like upper body forward and looked at me conspiratorially, his blue eyes shot through with veins of white like cracked ice. "I've figured out how to manipulate the stock market with my mind," he said.

I raised my eyebrows. "Really."

"Yeah, I just pick a stock and force it up by sending out good energy about it into the ether. Within a day or two it jumps, every time. It takes a lot of mental and telepathic power, but it works. All I need is someone with some money to invest, and we'll be set. What do you say?"

I felt like laughing, but the coke crash precluded that impulse. "I don't have any money to invest. And this isn't my place, I'm just taking care of it."

Blinka sniffed—as close to a laugh as she could get—and said, "Great job you're doing."

"I can prove it to you," Ted said. "Get a *Wall Street Journal* and I'll prove it."

"No need," I said.

"Hey dude, this is not a joke. I've spent some time perfecting this, saving up my inner energies. It's not easy. I haven't eaten meat or had an orgasm in six months."

This time Blinka laughed out loud. "But it's fine to snort coke and smoke heroin, I guess."

"Drugs flush out in a day or two; it takes weeks to recover the

242

energy spent on an orgasm." He turned back to me. "I've run tests—we could turn five grand into fifty in no time."

"Look," I said, "forget it. I still don't have any money." I thought of the four thousand stashed in my duffel downstairs and made a mental note to hide it better.

Ted looked dejected, and I realized that he'd been planning this pitch the whole time, that bringing me on board his scheme was possibly the main reason for his being there. It wasn't clear whether he believed what he was saying or was a scam artist, but I was leaning toward him believing it.

"I'd like to see you do it, though," I said, not wanting him to feel insulted.

He shook his head. "Nah. It's a waste of energy if you're not into it."

Blinka had just done a tar hit and was leaning back in the deep leather of the sofa, breathing like someone who's had a long day on her feet. "Let's crash," she said.

I did one more hit and we let our softened legs carry us down the stairs. Moving along behind Blinka, watching her legs lower her carefully from step to step, I felt a flash of that kinship that comes from being high with someone—from knowing you both occupy similar distorted spaces. I remembered flying down the stairs of the dorm at boarding school behind Benton—the white cinder-block walls bouncing past—after doing bong hits in his room; or spending a whole day with Dave Townsend, a big soccer-jock I didn't even like, after taking acid together. It was a kind of cool closeness that took no account of personality; it could accompany friendship, or slide right past aversion without dissolving it. In the guest room, Blinka stripped to her underwear and T-shirt, as she had the other times we'd crashed together, then, before climbing into the bed, she took off the shirt. We kissed a little, as we had before, then she reached into my boxers. After half an hour, our lazy lovemaking started to turn restless, then frantic. After forty-five minutes we were switching positions every three, as I strove to push myself over the top. Finally she tapped my shoulder like a wrestler giving in. "Hey, let's go to sleep. You've got dope dick."

"Dope dick?" I was relieved to be off the hook, and I rolled off her.

"Yeah. It's great for the girl, not so great for the guy if he can't finish." She lay back next to me. "Better than whiskey dick any day, though."

I put my head on her chest and closed my eyes, experiencing just before sleep the humid smell of her skin.

SOUND. A mosquito advancing, retreating, advancing again. The whine a splinter in my sleep, forcing me out of it. Warm flesh on my face, breeze on my feet. The little plastic phone in the hall was ringing, a high electronic burp, and wouldn't stop. It pulled my head away from Blinka's chest, my body out of bed and toward it. I've never been one of those who can easily let a phone ring. To me, the sound has always seemed imperative, like a crying baby. I stumbled naked across the room, through the draft from the sliding door that, partly shaded by the deck above, opened out onto a grassy, bright California afternoon. I opened the inner door and went into the hall.

"Hello." My throat felt filled with dead flies.

"Hello? Harry? Is that you?"

One of the flies buzzed to life, and I coughed. "No. Harry's not here." I already knew who it was. "Hi Mom."

"Jason? I didn't know you were still there. What's going on? You sound terrible." I pictured the sound of her voice as a swarm of tiny spheres being translated through the vast network of wires, released on my end as a tinny electronic ghost of itself.

"Nothing's going on. I have a little cold and I'm resting."

"How's Harry doing? Neither of you has called me in so long."

"Harry's fine, Mom. He's actually feeling a lot better. He went down to Santa Barbara to visit some friends for a little while, and I'm taking care of the place." The lie was instinctive. Partly because I was so used to lying to my mother about anything to do with drugs or alcohol, and partly because Harry had always kept my secrets from her. It was his business if he wanted to tell her.

"Do you have his number down there? I'd love to talk to him."

"He just left yesterday. He was going to call me with the number when he got there, but I haven't heard from him yet. I'll tell him to call you when I talk to him."

"Okay, sweetie. And what about you? You need to take care of that cold. Are you sure it's not the flu? Maybe you should see a doctor." This was the way she told me she knew I was lying about the cold.

"I don't need a doctor, Mom. I'll be fine."

"I worry about you, though. Would you go see a doctor anyway? For me? I'll pay for it. You can use my credit card."

"Look, if I don't get better soon, I'll think about it. Okay?"

"All right. Are you eating well?"

"Mom, I'm trying to rest. I'll call you in a day or two."

"I love you," she said.

"I love you, too."

I put down the phone, which was a small single unit that hung itself up when placed facedown. Scar walked out of the other guest room down the hall and headed for the bathroom between the two rooms. She was naked, too. She stopped and we looked at each other, two naked beasts. Her big breasts sat wonderfully high on her chest, and her wide hips gave her lower body the shape of a fig. The brown hair between her legs was shaved into a neat vee. She smirked sheepishly, then we both laughed, and she walked into the bathroom. It seemed she was making the rounds, because the other guest room was where Saul had set himself up. I hoped it wasn't something that would cause problems.

The phone rang again under my hand. It would be my mother, with more tiresome advice. I cleared my throat and made the decision to answer it.

"Hello."

There was a pause. "Jason?" Melanie's voice traversed the line much more intact than my mother's. It struck me deeply, as if she had just appeared in front of me, and created a pang of guilt.

"Yeah, hey." I turned my back to the bedroom doors. "How are you? Where are you?"

"I might not be able to talk for long. I'm in the basement of a church. My parents put me in a treatment center, and I'm not allowed to make phone calls. I got caught the last time I called. Did he give you the message? He seemed fucked up."

"Yeah, he was drunk. All I knew was that you called."

"Well, now they're taking us in a van to AA meetings twice a week. That's where I am. I found a phone in an unlocked office."

"Wow. Are you okay?"

"Yeah, but I can't wait to get out of here. It's a long-term program, but they can't hold me after I turn eighteen. Can you send me a plane ticket? A girl I know who got out said I could use her address and pick it up when I get out."

"Yeah, of course." The pesky thought of Blinka in bed in the next room flew out of my mind—I hadn't even finished, I reasoned—and I felt a surge of anticipation. "I wish you could come sooner," I said. "I wish you were here now."

She breathed deeply on the other end. "Me too. I better go. Make the plane ticket for the fifth. And make it out of Boston. It's easier to get there from where I am."

There was a pen on the hall table, and I wrote on my hand: *Aug 5. Boston.* "Okay. Got it." I pictured meeting her at the airport. It occurred to me that I hadn't been outside in three days, except to climb in the hot tub at night. Melanie gave me the address in Massachusetts, which I also copied onto my hand, and we hung up. Scar came out of the bathroom.

"Who was that?" She scratched her neck, her arm lightly jostling her breasts.

"My girlfriend," I said. I went back into the bedroom and started to get dressed. Blinka woke up and rubbed her eyes.

"Come on back in here," she said, throwing back the covers.

"Not now. I need to get outside. I'm going out to pick up some coffee and bagels for everyone. I'll be back." And I breezed out of the room, feeling starved for sunshine.

THE SUNSHINE DIDN'T HOLD UP ITS END. It didn't suffuse my mind with heedless optimism the way sunshine should. It didn't make the world seem a vast expression of goodwill, a reassurance from God or whomever that things could always go my way. It didn't even flush out the ugly, amorphous thoughts that always lurked in the shadows after a binge, threatening to become feelings, fears, weights on the heart. What it did was melt the mass of mucus lodged in my head and send it dribbling out my nose, and sting my eyes till they gushed. I steered Harry's car down the hill, wiping my nose on the shoulder of my shirt, rubbing my eyes with fingers that smelled of tobacco. The tall thin trees that arched overhead before the main road, three on each side, looked dragged down by their leaves, barely able to support themselves. Branches thicker than the trunks hung over the road. For the first time I noticed how unnatural these trees seemed, how top-heavy, close to collapsing under their own weight. I eased out the clutch and stepped on the gas, shooting out from under them.

I picked up a bag of bagels, some cream cheese, and a pound of fresh-ground coffee at the strip mall down the road, but on the way back my stomach became restless, bubbling softly with discomfort. I smoked a cigarette, and that settled me a bit. When I walked in, Saul, Don, and Scar were gathered in the living room. Saul was kicked back in the big armchair with the remote, and the porn station was on; I couldn't see the screen from my angle, but I could hear the shrill cries of the actors. Don was smoking a hit of tar off foil, and Scar was watching him.

"Breakfast," I said, holding up the bag.

"That's brunch," Don croaked, still holding the hit in. He let it out. "This," he held up the foil, "is breakfast."

"Well, somebody else can make the coffee and bagels," I said. I dropped the bag near the kitchen door. "I feel like shit. I'm going down for a shower." I sniffed and wiped my nose on my shirt, rubbed my eyes.

"Get over here," said Don. "Level yourself out."

"I don't think so."

"Fine." He loaded another hit onto the foil and handed it to Scar. "Go out on the deck and tell Ted it's his hit, will you?"

I walked out the sliding door and found Ted sitting on the wood planks and leaning against the hot tub. "Don says it's your hit if you want it."

His eyes were closed in the sunshine, but he tilted his head in my direction. "Are they still watching that porno?"

"Yeah, they are."

He cracked his eyes thinly at me. "I can't watch that stuff right now. It gets me too polluted, what with being celibate for six months and all."

"Well. Okay." I started back in.

"You know what my fantasy is? My ultimate fantasy?"

I stopped. I tried to think of some way to avoid hearing it, but finally said, "What?"

He opened his eyes all the way and smiled brightly, like he'd just gotten some good news. "It's to eat out a redheaded chick while she's on the rag, so the blood gets all over my face." He was still smiling. There was no sign he understood the deep strangeness of what he'd said. "I'll probably never get to do it though."

After a second, I started for the door. "Well, you can always dream," I said.

As I passed through the living room, Don held up the foil. "You sure now?"

"Yeah," I said.

I was halfway down the stairs when my mind flipped, turning my body around. It came upon me as a happy decision, filled with brightness, one that would do what the sunshine had failed to. As I climbed back up the steps, the dead-end day suddenly seemed rich with possibility.

"Okay," I said, striding into the living room. "Give me one."

"Coming right up." Don tore off a new piece of foil and loaded me a hit.

Exhaling what was left of the bitter smoke, what hadn't soaked into my lungs, I felt my tear ducts snap shut like tiny frightened clams. I had done the hit standing, but found myself kneeling before I blew it out. Then I lay back, fully reclined on the carpet, closed my eyes, and laughed.

"Look at you," Saul said. "What's so funny?"

I didn't answer him at first. I was laughing at Ted's fantasy. And at how easy it was to feel good. Lying on my back, I shrugged. "It's just incredible," I said.

In the shower I made the water very hot. I breathed the thick steam deeply, twisted the massaging showerhead until it was a rhythmic bombardment of water pellets on the back of my head, twisted it back and sat down in the tub, the water sprinkling over me from above as I nodded mildly. It felt good, and I stayed in for a long time. I washed my hair, I washed my feet. I made myself perfectly clean before turning off the water and stepping out into a beefy white towel. It seemed important to be perfectly clean, to add that pleasure to the ones I was already feeling. My first thought when I saw the blue smudge on the back of my left hand, as I ran the towel over my body, was dismay that I had missed a spot, that I wasn't completely clean. I brought it close to my face and examined it, racking my brain as to how it had gotten there. It was like thinking through gobs of pure raw cotton: comfy, but slow. It came clear as the layers of cotton pulled away, like an iron cannonball packed inside, its blackish mass unexpected under the softness. *Fuck*, I thought. "Fuck, fuck, fuck!" I said.

I tried to read what was there, tried to find some afterimage on the skin of the original letters, but it was just a faint blue smudge.

8

GLIDING IN THE MERCEDES on 17, just north of Santa Cruz, Saul and I saw an accident. The right lane was closed off with flares, and we had to slow down quickly. A cop was waving cars to the left. A red Mazda was pulled to the shoulder, dented on the left front quarter panel, the back bumper caved in. An ambulance was parked in front of it. In front of the ambulance was another car, an old Chevy with no visible damage, and ahead of that another ambulance and a cop car. A man was sitting in the driver's seat of the Mazda with the door open, his feet on the ground, and a paramedic was crouched near him tending to one of his legs. Two black men were standing by the trunk of the Chevy, being questioned by a cop. One of the men was gesturing with both hands at the road, and the cop was writing in a notebook, not looking at him. We passed the second ambulance, and in front of it was a small kidney-shaped heap covered in dark blue plastic. No one was near the heap. Sixty yards up from the heap was the mutilated wreck of a chopped-out Harley. The long custom forks were severed and the front wheel was nowhere in sight.

"Jesus," I said. "I guess that was the rider back there."

"Yeah," said Saul. "Fuck. Poor bastard."

The gruesome sight seemed improper on such a bright summery day. Things like that were supposed to happen at night, were supposed to pass by like dreams, lit only by flashing red and blue. But something about it fit with the way I felt, too. The incongruity of the scene with the bright day was in line with what I was doing.

Saul had started to run out of heroin and wanted to make a trip to the Bay to cop some more. Somewhere during the conversation in which he convinced me to go with him and take the Mercedes, I had stepped across a line in my head, and I felt the fear and excitement of being on new ground. The decision that occurred to me was to put off the discomfort the end of the binge would bring, but I realized the converse was true too, that when you move away from something, you must move toward something else, and I found myself accepting it. It was another new thing. *Let's try this thing*, said my mind. *Let's see what it's like to be strung out.* I even felt a twinge of pride for going into it with open eyes, and believed that would make it easier for me to know when enough was enough and quit.

"So what the fuck is Scar's problem with Cole, anyway?" Saul asked.

"What do you mean?"

"Don't tell me you haven't noticed. She hates him. I asked her what it was about, and she said nothing. I think she might be a racist. What do you think?"

"I don't think she's a racist."

"You say that like you know something."

"I do, but there's no need to be spreading it around."

"Come on. Now you have to tell me. I won't spread it around."

"Give me a cigarette," I said. He did, and I lit it with the dashboard lighter. "Okay, you know Big Dawn?"

"Yeah, I know who she is."

"You know what happened to her?"

"I heard something about it."

"Well she's a friend of Scar's, and Scar thinks Cole is the one who set her up."

"What makes her think that?"

"Dawn said Cole was the one who introduced her to the guy who turned out to be a cop. I think a few people went down because of that guy. I sold him some Ex myself, but was never arrested for some reason. Because they couldn't prove it, I think. The stuff I brought to the room was vitamin B, and me and the cop and the drugs were never in the same room together. Pure fucking luck."

Saul was nodding. He lit a cigarette. "You think Cole did it?"

"Fuck, I don't know. Maybe he did. I guess he probably did."

"You think you would have done it?"

I paused. "I hope not. I guess it's hard to say what you'd do faced with that kind of situation, though."

"You got that right." Saul tapped his window button, opening it an inch. "Cole didn't do it. He didn't set her up."

"How do you know?"

"I was one of those people, who went down. That guy Will had been running deals with people for weeks, but couldn't get near Dawn. They wanted Dawn. They popped me, and I was looking at serious time. I didn't know Dawn well enough to give her to them, but Cole did. I introduced Will to Cole as if I had grown up with him—hey, I had to make them promise not to touch Cole, and I had to beg Cole to just introduce them, not make a profit, told him I'd make it up to him. So he did it."

"And Cole never knew?" The calmness with which he was telling me this astonished me, but also put me more at ease with hearing it.

"Well, he figured it out after. He knows now. But at the time he didn't." Saul blew smoke at the open air outside. "Hey, you're not going to tell anyone this, right? This is all in confidence."

"Sure, man, no problem," I said before thinking. "But there are quite a few people who think Cole set Dawn up."

"Not too many, I don't think," Saul said. "Most people don't know what the fuck happened." There was a long pause. I noticed I'd slowed to below the speed limit, and sped back up. Saul's window hummed open, and he flicked the cigarette out. "I'd never do that to a friend, you know that. Right? That Dawn was an ugly bitch anyway. I heard she was always ripping people off."

I didn't answer. I had a headache. My nose suddenly ran, and I wiped it on my sleeve. I wanted a hit of heroin. "You got another hit of dope for me?" I asked.

"No, man. All out. That's why we've got to get there. Nothing illegal in the car, though, so you can step on it."

I put my cigarette out in the ashtray, and stepped on the gas, easing up to eighty-five. After a few minutes, Saul said, "Listen, if you were tight with her I'm sorry. She wasn't a friend of yours, was she?"

I thought about this, wiped my nose again. "Not really. I knew her, but not too well."

OUR FIRST STOP was an Oakland Western Union, where Saul picked up money that had been wired to him by some buyers back east. Then we drove to a Berkeley motel, where I waited in the car while he went in and picked up the Ecstasy they wanted.

"Okay," he said when he got back in, "let's head to my buddy Jim's place to package this up. He's always got boxes and tape and whatnot. Back down to Oakland."

"You mean Jim and Sasha?"

"Yeah, you know them?"

"Sure I do."

Sasha answered the door. She saw Saul and said, "Jim's not here."

Saul stepped aside so she could see me and said, "Hey, could we use your place real quick? Just to put together a package?"

Sasha smiled. "Hey Jason. Sure, come on in." She opened the door and gave me a hug as I walked in. She didn't hug Saul.

Saul made a right down the hall, toward Jim's office, my old room.

"Come here," said Sasha, and pulled me the other direction. "Check this out." She led me through the doorway into the living room, and there on the couch was Jane. She was perched at the edge of her seat, her hands clasped under her chin, looking right at me as I entered. She gave a small smile, not lifting her head off her hands—just a hint of the real thing, but it killed me anyway. I sniffled and didn't speak for a moment.

"Hi," she said.

"Hi."

She got up and walked over to me. She hugged me, and I wasn't ready for it. I realized the second she touched me that I should have withdrawn from my nerve endings and watched it from a small distance, the way you do with a good-looking cousin. But there I was, feeling the ridges of muscle on either side of her lower spine, the cushion of her breasts on my chest, her amazing tousle of hair in my face. She dropped her head forward and kissed my neck, and the kiss ran like a charge to my head and down to my toes. I stepped away from her before she could feel me getting hard.

"I thought you were back in Connecticut."

"I was. But U-Conn dropped my deferment and didn't accept me when I reapplied. I'm going to CCAC in the fall. I just moved back."

I nodded, then I finally broke through my surprise and smiled at her. "That's great. You living with Sasha and Jim?"

"Just till I find a place."

Saul walked in, saying, "You got any frigging packing tape around?" He saw Jane and his jaw dropped. "Hey, hey. What the fuck are you doing here?" He hugged her, then stepped back. "Look at you. You look great, babe."

"Thanks." Jane moved back to the couch and sat down.

No one spoke for a second, then Saul laughed. He looked from me to Jane. "Wow. Old home week, huh?" He turned and spoke to Sasha, "So where's the frigging packing tape?"

"I don't know. If it's not in there we might be out or something."

"Whatever. I'll just use Scotch tape."

"What is it?" Sasha asked. "Ex?"

"Yeah," said Saul.

"How about leaving us a couple of hits?"

"Sure, you got it." He went back down the hall.

I sat in a small wooden chair, and Sasha sat by Jane. "So," Sasha said, and we paused again. "You know we were just talking about you, before you got here, weren't we, Jane?"

Jane cut Sasha a sharp look, then said, "I guess we were."

"Nothing too awful, I hope."

"Far from it," said Sasha.

"How long has it been?" Jane asked quickly.

"It's been a while." I took a Camel from a pack on the table and lit it. "Last time you saw me I was getting my face busted, I think."

"Oh god. I can't believe Don did that. I feel so bad about it."

"It's okay. Don and I are cool now. In fact, he's staying with me down in Carmel at this place where I'm house-sitting."

"Wow," said Jane. "I'm glad to hear it." She didn't seem happy about it.

"You guys going down to Ventura next week?" Sasha asked.

"No," I said. "I don't think so. I'm just going to wait for the Greeks."

"Hey, you know Jim bought four tickets apiece for the Greeks, and right now it's just me him and Jane. You want to come with us?"

Sasha's blithe tone belied the magnitude of this offer. Greek tickets were always hard to come by. "Sure," I said. "That would be cool. You want money for them now?"

She waved her hand in front of her face. "No no. Just pay us then. We'll save them for you."

Before we left, I gave them the number at Harry's and said I'd call them before the Greek shows to hook up with them. Saul and I were on our way down the stairs when Jane opened the apartment door and called me back. "I'll meet you down there," I said, and ran up. She pulled me in and pushed the door shut.

"What are you doing hanging with him?" Jane whispered.

"What do you mean?"

"I mean Saul's kind of a heavy. I just never pictured you two to-gether."

I felt a fist close inside me. "I guess I could say the same to you, couldn't I?"

Without taking her eyes from mine, she took a slow breath and let it out. "Whatever," she said, and opened the door again. "See you later."

"Later."

I almost stumbled, rushing the stairs on the way down.

"NOW WE GO TO MAMA'S," Saul said in the car outside the post office after he'd mailed his package. He directed me through downtown Oakland and out the other side to a neighborhood I'd never been to. It was an area of run-down wooden houses, most in varying shades of brown. A lot of people were out, walking around, yelling to each other, kids riding bikes across lawns and popping wheelies. No one was white. We parked in the driveway of a two-story house whose fresh white paint shone as conspicuously among the dingy houses around it as we did getting out of that silver Mercedes. The lawn was just a rectangle of packed brown mud, and we traipsed across it to the front door.

Before he knocked, Saul said, "These people are cool, but never try coming back here on your own. I'm serious."

The guy who answered the door was our age, but stood about six-four and must have weighed two-eighty. "Hey, big Lee," said Saul.

"Who's this?" He sounded like a young James Earl Jones.

"This is my old old friend Jason. Don't worry, he's down."

The guy stood aside and let us in. The hallway inside was covered with peach-colored wall-to-wall carpet, which looked as if it extended into every room downstairs. It was very clean. "Take off your shoes," the guy said.

"New carpeting, huh?" said Saul.

"Yeah."

We left our shoes by the door and followed him down the hall.

From a room near the end came a woman's voice, "Who is it, baby?"

"It's King Saul, Mama."

"King! Hi, baby."

We entered the room and Saul said, "Hi Mama." The woman was short and thin, and had stood and approached the door to meet us. Saul gave her a hug. "This is my friend Jason, Mama."

She looked at me over his shoulder. "He knows the drill?"

"Yeah. No problem."

"Good. Hello, Jason." She walked over and hugged me, and her body felt like a balsa-wood model in my arms. I looked at the sofa across the room and wondered how the guy who had met us at the door had reached it so stealthily. But he was still standing next to me. The man on the sofa was identical to him in every way, except his shirt was white instead of blue and he seemed to be wearing an ascot. "You've met my son Leon," she said to me. "And this is his brother Lionel." Lionel nodded to me from the sofa. "Ain't they the most beautiful things you've ever seen?"

"Mama," said Leon. "Come on." He seemed genuinely embarrassed.

"You hush," she said. "I'm allowed to show off my babies."

Saul and I sat on another sofa along the inside wall. The room was spare and very clean. There were the two sofas, two cheap wooden coffee tables, and a plush blue recliner. On one side of the recliner was a small three-shelf unit that held framed pictures of Leon and Lionel in various stages of growth. All the pictures were interior and looked as though they had been taken in that house. Nothing hung on the walls. The legs of the small table in front of us sat on coasters to protect the carpeting. Leon went and sat across from us with his brother. They both stared at me.

"That your car?" Leon asked.

"No, it's borrowed."

"Your daddy's car?"

"No, a friend's."

"It's a nice car."

His gaze was consciously blank, and I imagined that in his mind he was weighing the value of the Mercedes against the risk of killing me and Saul. "Thanks," I said.

Saul sat back and draped an arm along the back of the sofa as if he were in his own living room. "How's every little thing, boys?" Mama had left the room.

Leon and Lionel looked at each other, then shrugged and looked back at Saul. "Can't complain," Lionel said. His voice was starkly different from Leon's, a raspy, almost cartoonish squeak. One of his hands came up and he ran a finger along the inside of his blue silk ascot, which was tucked into the white T-shirt.

Mama came back in carrying a small black nylon gym bag. Her face was thin and drooped around the edges, tugging downward at the corners of her eyes and her large mouth, and as she walked she seemed to be frowning in amusement. She was much lighter-skinned than her sons, and looking past her masklike features I realized she probably hadn't reached forty yet. She put the bag on the table in front of us. "You boys want to fix yourselves up?" And she left again.

"Sure, Mama," Saul said. He unzipped the bag and started rummaging inside. He came out with two orange-capped syringes, each sealed in its own plastic wrapping, a few cotton balls, and a lighter. Mama came in again and put in front of us a glass of water and a ceramic saucer that had a lump of tar heroin and a spoon on it. It had the look of some sweet delicacy offered at a tea party. Saul opened both the syringes.

"Um, usually I just smoke it," I said.

Mama was easing herself into the recliner that was obviously her throne. She looked at Saul. "I thought he knew the drill."

"Don't worry, Mama," said Saul. He turned to me. "This is the way it works here. You've got to get high before we do business."

I looked at Mama, feeling a little comforted by the benign expression on her face. "Is it okay if I just smoke it?"

She smiled, but I stopped feeling comforted. "No, baby. That ain't good enough."

"Come on," said Saul. He had dropped the chunk of tar into the spoon with some water and was starting to cook it. "Don't get all freaked out."

I looked from Saul to Mama, then across to Leon and Lionel. Everyone was staring at me. "Okay," I shrugged. "No problem."

When Saul had both needles ready, Mama got up and walked over to me. "Give me that one, baby," she said, and took one from him. "I want to do him up." She laughed high and soft. She sat by me and took my arm across her lap. Her birdlike hand caressed the crook of my elbow tenderly. "Look at that. So fresh you don't even need to tie off. I'd give my right arm for veins like that." She laughed again, maybe at the irony of her own statement, for it was my right arm she held, that I'd given her. Melanie flashed through my head. "Hold still now, Jason," Mama said, her voice dropping to a low whisper. "Just relax. Here comes your golden fleece."

I felt the prick of the needle and closed my eyes. I felt it come out, and pressure where it had been, and she folded my arm up on itself, and then warm, phantasmal molasses gushed through my brain, filled my body. The impact of my head hitting the wall behind the couch was a far-off little displaced orgasm. A sentence came into my head and as I thought it I realized I was whispering it aloud: *This is what I've been looking for.* There was a wisp of sensation at the edge of my throbbing euphoria, in a place I identified as my forehead, and a voice in my right ear, "Oh, yeah, baby. Oh, yeah. Baby baby baby." Then nothing at all but the goodness, too much to contain.

When I opened my eyes again, Mama was back in her recliner. The room was skewed. I was sunk deep in beautiful muck. She was talking softly with her sons, who still sat on the sofa near her. Her tiny husk of a body had produced those two mountainous things. It was hard to believe it hadn't killed her. I had an image of her body splitting open as they grew inside her, the two of them stepping full-grown from her demolished remnants. I thought the drug had created some kind of shiver in my equilibrium until I realized Saul was shaking me.

"Hey, where's the money you brought?"

I had agreed to go half-and-half with him on a thousand dollars' worth. I went to reach into my pocket, but my arm didn't move. The fact that I was telling it to move and it wasn't moving did not worry me. It was a mere fact. I wouldn't have worried right then if someone had placed my arm on a chopping block and raised an ax above it. The capacity for worry had been erased from me. As I kept trying to move my arm, I became oriented slowly to the fact that I was lying on it. I sat up, the room righted itself, and I dug in my jeans for the little roll bound by a rubber band. I dropped it in Saul's hand.

"Nice," he said.

I had my bearings now, and I felt a mild twinge of disappointment that nothing had actually changed, that the real world had soldiered on without me. But I was still gone, and the disappointment cruised away from me in the flow of the high, like a twig on floodwaters.

Mama took the money, counted it, then Leon left the room.

He was gone at least ten minutes, and no one spoke, except when I took out my pack of cigarettes and Lionel shook his head and squeaked, "No smoking, dude." The word "dude" sounded like an insult coming from him, like a white guy saying "homey" in the wrong way. When Leon got back, he placed a small package of wrapped newspaper in front of Saul. Saul looked at me. "You okay to drive?"

"I don't know," I said.

"Well, I can drive." He stood up and put the package in his pocket. "Thanks, Mama. Thanks, boys."

"You take care now, baby."

"I can drive," I said.

Leon showed us to the door and let us out.

There were four guys gathered around the car, looking at it. When we approached they lifted their heads. They were teenagers, fifteen or sixteen. One of them stood immediately in front of the driver's door. He was six feet tall and rangy, perfectly proportioned, an athlete. One of the other kids, across the car, carried a baseball bat and had an outfielder's glove tucked into the back of his jeans. The kid blocking my path gave me the serious look of someone with a serious question. "This your car?" he asked.

"Yeah," I said, reaching into my pocket for the keys, but not pulling them out. The world was still soft, and I realized that if I had to move fast I wouldn't be able to.

He looked back at the car. "This is a sweet ride, man."

"Thanks," I said. "Excuse me." I made a half-move to get around him. He didn't give.

The three other kids snorted as if restraining hysterical laughter. "Excuse me," one of them mimicked, attempting a British accent.

"Let me try it out," the kid in front of me said.

"What?" Saul had come back around the car and was standing next to me.

"Let me try driving it," the kid said. "Just around the block."

"No," said Saul.

"Man, it ain't your car, it's his. Come on, dude. What do you say?" Again, I had the same sense about the word "dude."

"Sorry, man. I can't do it," I said. "We need to go."

Again the other three guffawed, and the same one mimicked, "Sorry, man."

"Aw, shit, come on. If I had a Mercedes I'd let you drive it." This produced more laughter from his friends.

I stepped toward the car, and he leaned back against the door.

The other three came over to him and stood facing us. The one with the bat held it high on the shaft in both fists.

"Walter."

The tall kid looked past us to the house. Leon was in the doorway. "Yeah," said the kid.

"You lost your fuckin' mind?"

"Just trying to get a ride in this car, Leon."

"Get your ass off that car before I put my foot in it."

The kid stood straight but didn't move out of the way.

"Get the fuck out of here," said Leon. "Go on."

They started walking away. The kid with the bat did a stutter-step toward me as he passed, lifting the bat, but I was too high to flinch. I hoped they'd mistake it for courage. The kid Walter said over his shoulder, "Motherfuckin' junkies."

I backed out too fast and pressed my taillight into the sharp corner of an old Buick's bumper. I stopped and looked over my shoulder at the sound, which was like small breaking sticks.

"Just go," Saul said, and I found first gear, felt the rounded, inaudible thump in that smooth gearbox that promised velocity, released the clutch like slacking the reins of a spooked horse, and let that big engine pull us out of there.

THERE ARE TWO TIMES OF DAY ON HEROIN: dusk and night. Night feels more comfortable, because it is what it is, there's no real change in it. The daylight hours become an eerie protracted dusk, and for the strung out, true daylight ceases to exist. A thin, smoky filter has been drawn across the sky (or across the eyes—does it matter which?), and even the brightest light seems attenuated. I became aware of this only because when night did fall, halfway back to Carmel, I realized it had seemed to be about to fall for hours. This had the dual effect of an expected and an unexpected arrival; expected because it followed dusk, surprising because after so long a dusk it might not have been coming at all. But it came, like cool relief, while we had hills to our west, and I turned on the headlights.

Night was night, judgmentless, and moving through it made it easier to feel human. The reach of the headlights became my purview, and I concentrated my attention there, unburdened by all that might be happening outside it. Sure there were streetlights and strip malls and other cars, and glowing homes climbing the hills above the road once we got off the highway, but none of that concerned me. I didn't look up at those homes with their soft incandescence, as I might have, and imagine the lives within, the beautiful people and the promise that lay before them; didn't insert myself into those lives as a longhaired painter or screenwriter with svelte girlfriend draped across the couch inside while I took a drink on the deck and watched the perfect ellipse of a Mercedes's headlights slide past on the road below. I sat comfortably in the gray leather and was contained by the darkness in the car and the bubble of light flying out front.

The first thing I noticed when we pulled into Harry's driveway was that my Toyota (I had begun thinking of it as mine) was not there. Don's Fleetwood sat in front of the garage, and next to it was a little blue Ford Fiesta. Inside was a scene so unexpected that my first instinct was to walk out, drive away, then return after it had changed back to reality. Lined up on the sofa were Don, Scar, and Cole. In the armchair on one side sat a fortyish woman I'd never seen before, and in the other chair, to the left, sat Harry. They were all watching television. Don was packing pot into a bowl.

"Hey man," Don said, smiling.

"Come on in, Jason," said Harry. He waved at me with his arm high in the air, as if I might have trouble picking him out. I walked into the room. Saul stayed standing at the end of the hall behind me.

"Hi Harry," I said. "What are you doing back?"

"I get to ask the first questions here. Like where the fuck is my car?"

"It's in the driveway."

"Okay, where the fuck is my stereo?"

I looked at the corner behind him and saw that all his components were gone, as were the speakers and the wood-encased subwoofer, which had left four circular dents in the carpet. "Jesus," I said. "I don't know."

"It was Ted," Don said. "We crashed out earlier, and when we got up he was gone with the stereo and your car."

"Which brings me to my next question. What are all these fucking hippies doing in my house?"

Don laughed, and Harry looked at him and laughed for a sec-

266

ond too, but I could tell when he looked back at me that he wasn't joking.

"I'm sorry, Harry. I didn't expect you back so soon."

Now Harry really laughed, and I saw that his teeth were fixed. "I guess not."

"You want us to clear out?"

Harry flipped his hand at me. "No no. Stay. Spilt milk and all. You and I will have this out, but I'm not prepared to do it now. I'm in no shape for ugly scenes. I just walked out of treatment Against Medical Advice. But I brought my nurse with me, to keep me safe. You remember Sarah?"

The woman across the couch smiled at me, and I recognized her as the nurse who had helped get Harry settled and put in his IV when we got there. She was blond, just starting to go gray, with a puffy prettiness and a wide ass that made the leather armchair look as if it had been custom-made for her. She wore a brown cable-knit sweater, blue synthetic slacks, and white nurse's shoes. I said hi to her. Don passed her the bowl and a lighter, and she put it to her mouth and began taking a hit.

Cole's brow was furrowed as he watched Sarah take her hit. "Ted took my car?" I asked him.

He met my gaze. "Yeah. We just woke up and he was gone. I can't believe it. I guess he really wanted to try out that scheme of his."

"You knew about that?"

Cole gave a laugh. "Who didn't? He blabbed about it to every-one who would listen."

"That fucker," said Saul from behind me. "We're going to find him."

The thought of my money jumped into my head. "Shit. Hold on," I said. I ran downstairs and into my room. I dug into the bottom of my duffel for the pair of socks I'd rolled my cash up in. I unrolled it and counted the money, and it was all there. Over three grand. I put it in my pocket and went back up. On my way up the stairs, something occurred to me.

"Where's Blinka?" I asked back in the living room.

"She disappeared, too," Don said. "She must have gone with him."

This struck me as hilarious, and I started laughing. I pulled a straight chair out of the kitchen and sat on it. "Oh, Jesus. That is too much," I laughed. "Too fucking much."

"I can't believe she did it," said Scar. "I really can't. I wouldn't be surprised if he knocked her out and kidnapped her."

"Shit," laughed Don, "I hope his last name's not Bundy."

I looked over at Harry, who was taking all this in with a bemused expression. The glass in his hand was clear and fizzy, with a wedge of lemon, and contained no ice. I hoped it was just seltzer. "If you guys find him, I'll press charges," he said.

A FEW DAYS WENT BY and everyone stayed. Harry was taking it all a little too well, but I figured he was sheepish about the trouble I'd gone to getting him into detox. He wasn't drinking, and I wondered how long that would last. We all sat around smoking pot and drinking soda, since Sarah forbade alcohol in the house. Harry wasn't even smoking cigarettes, but took small hits of pot every so often. His cough hadn't improved. Saul went back to shooting up in the bathroom, and I did hits of my half of the heroin as seldom as I could manage, taking it down in my room with the window open. Sarah went grocery shopping, cleaned the house, cooked big pots of spaghetti for us, and monitored Harry's health. He was on a new series of medications that she picked up at the pharmacy. She would make sure he took them at the appointed times throughout the day, make sure there were always extra oxygen tanks, and help him move around the house and get in and out of bed. At night she slept in his bedroom, and while I didn't see a cot or evidence of another sleeping arrangement, I got the distinct feeling that they weren't having sex. She didn't speak much, but smiled at anyone who glanced at her and got stoned right along with the rest of us.

I gave strict instructions to everyone that if Melanie called they had to get the mailing address from her, but the phone almost never rang. Given time to think about it, Harry started liking the idea of us finding Ted and offering him some kind of comeuppance. By the third day he was set on it and wanted us to go down to the shows at Ventura and look for him. Don needed to be back in Oakland for some business and wouldn't go, so Harry offered his car if Saul and I wanted it. Taking the Mercedes on a road trip was incentive in itself, and Saul seemed gung-ho on the idea of kicking Ted's ass, so we decided to go.

VENTURA WASN'T CALLED THE DUST BOWL for nothing. The parking area was just an expanse of red dust that migrated upward into the air in thicker and thicker quantities as the day went on, kicked up by cars, people, dogs, and the wind. If you blew your nose into a tissue, it came out rust-colored. We cruised the lot in the Merc, just to be seen, and stayed high the whole time, Saul spiking and me doing foil hits in the backseat. We asked around after Ted, spreading the word that he was a scumbag and had stolen from us. As we traversed the lot, I couldn't help keeping my eyes peeled for that pale blue VW van with Oregon plates, but I never saw it. We got no leads the first night. The show that night was only half-decent. They encored with "Touch of Grey," and we scoffed and left as soon as we heard the jumpy opening riff. "I wouldn't mind that tune so much if it wasn't for all the bozos chanting along with it," Saul said.

"At least it's not 'Day Job,' " I said. A lot of people were screaming their heads off: this was about to become the Dead's first-ever top-ten single, and it was the song many in the crowd had come hoping to hear.

The second night was a better show. It opened with a tight "Mississippi Half-Step Uptown Toodeloo," which grabbed me and made me once again reproach myself for losing touch with why we were here. Jerry's lilting midsong solo cut through everything brightly, with a kind of wry humor, leaving cynicism crouching shamefaced in a rear corner of my mind; I was watching him in the middle of the solo and saw him pause between licks to bring his right hand up and push his glasses up his nose, like a venerable professor gathering his thoughts during a brilliant lecture. I couldn't help but smile. At the end of the tune, as they entered the sweet coda, his notes were at first uncertain, childlike, seeking the right scale and key, trying to find the deepest groove, like a confused supplicant puzzling out a Zen koan. Sometimes he never ascended from this tentative noodling, and the song would fizzle into the final chorus, but when he did it was like discovery, revelation. That night he found it and began proclaiming it more loudly, the guitar finally howling with pleasure and leading him unfailingly into the last lines: "Across the Rio Grandio; Across the lazy river."

After the show, Saul found Orange Man, a guy who knew Ted and had seen him in Berkeley two days earlier driving a Toyota.

"That's my fucking car," I said. "He stole it."

"No shit?" Orange Man had walked into a hotel room once wearing an orange shirt and orange pants, and someone had said,

found him. Saul and Don had grown up together in the same borderline neighborhood in west Philadelphia and become unlikely friends, Don the straight-A student gone bad, Saul the hoodlum-turned-hippie. They had pulled each other toward a center of sorts. But vestiges of their old selves remained, for Don in his penchant for reading modern philosophy and intellectualizing his career as a drug dealer, for Saul in his somewhat wistful fascination with violence. Every so often, those first two days at Ventura, Saul would tilt his head back as if in some mild reverie and say, "I am going to destroy that motherfucker," or "Oh, boy, I'd hate to be him."

Saul became dejected after we learned that Ted wasn't in Ventura. As we walked away from Orange Man, Saul hung his head and muttered something I didn't hear. Over the next few hours, his dejection transformed slowly into even greater hatred of Ted, as if by not coming to Ventura Ted had fucked us over again. "I knew something was shifty about that fucking guy," Saul said. I didn't remind him that he had told me not to worry, Ted was cool. Finally all this malice seemed to solidify into a solemn commitment to keep looking, to find him down the line. We sat in our motel room after the second show, getting high and watching crap on HBO, waiting for the nudity. Neither of us had said a word for about half an hour. Saul put a big shot into a vein in his leg, fell back on his bed, his eyes drifting shut, and mumbled, "I am really going to fuck him up good."

The next night, before the show, Saul got in an argument with some kid over whether or not Garcia did heroin. The kid, a local beach-head who had come up to us looking for some "fry," as they called acid down there, wouldn't see the truth. "Bullshit," he said finally. "Jerry's no fucking junkie!" And Saul stuck a fist in his gut. It was an almost gentle gesture, totally silent and unexpected, and as he executed it Saul smiled like a parent at a deluded child. The kid doubled over, unable to breathe. "Come on," said Saul as he walked away. I followed.

I SPENT FOUR DAYS AT HARRY'S after Ventura, kicking. It wasn't as tough as I expected it to be, with all the stories you hear. No one ever tells you the first time's the easiest, or that two weeks isn't long enough to get locked in at the beginning. No one ever tells you that everyone kicks once or twice, that you'll be back. There were chills and sweats, and loss of appetite. I tossed in bed for hours at a stretch and took long soaks in the hot tub. It was just me, Harry, and Sarah in the house. I told Sarah I had the flu, but she caught on, having been a treatment nurse. She brought me broth and water and sat with me for a few minutes each time. In her prematurely lined face I began to see a tremendous sadness, or a compilation of different sadnesses piled onto one another. With the sickness, my eyeballs felt sandblasted, and I could see through everything. She had been badly hurt by someone. Hers was a face, framed by wisps of dry sandy hair, that showed the ravages of love the way a desert shows the effects of water—arroyos, carried-off dunes, washboards—even in its complete absence.

The second night she gave me one of Harry's pills, which put me to sleep for ten hours, and I woke up drained but knowing the worst was over. In the morning I wandered up to Harry's room, where he was in bed watching TV, smoking a cigarette. Sarah was out.

"Smoking, Harry?" I said. "I thought you quit."

"I did." He took a small drag and inhaled it gingerly to keep from coughing. "Some things don't last."

It didn't seem right for me to chastise him, so I sat down in a straight chair near the bed. He had CNN on. He liked world news during the day. If anything, his face was even more gaunt than it had been before he left. Something was sucking at him from the inside.

"It doesn't fucking matter anyway," he said.

I took a cigarette from the pack of Marlboro Extra-Light 100s on the bedside table, tore off the filter, and lit it.

"It does if it kills you."

"That's the thing that matters least."

"How so?"

"No big mystery." He was still focused on the TV. "Just that when you're gone you're not around to know you're gone. What could matter less than an event you have no awareness of? In fact, without awareness, everything ceases to matter by definition. When I go, nothing will matter anymore."

"What if it matters to me? I'll still be here, I hope."

"It may matter to you. That's your business."

"Isn't that a selfish way to see it?" I was chastising him despite my decision.

Now he looked at me. "You're saying I should curtail my smoking for the sake of my loved ones? That's such a tired old fucking argument. Give me a break. Why don't you quit drugs and Dead tour for your mother?"

"Okay, point taken."

He turned back to the TV. On the screen was video of an American journalist lying facedown on a narrow paved road, about thirty yards from the camera. They'd been replaying the footage for forty-eight hours since it happened, and no matter how badly I wanted to shut my eyes, leave the room, I couldn't keep myself from watching it. Soldiers were standing over him. There was a gravity to the shaky, surreptitious camera work and the overcast gloom of the shot that would have made it obvious what was going to happen even if I hadn't seen it before. Harry turned the sound further up. One soldier stepped up casually with his automatic weapon and shot the man in the back of the head. His body jumped once and lay still, the camera spun crazily and the image was lost. The female anchor was saying the name of the journalist and the South American country where it had occurred.

"Motherfuckers," Harry said.

"I thought it didn't matter," I said, trying to sound clever to mask my own anger.

"Not to him it doesn't," he said, waving the remote at the screen. "Not anymore." Another moment passed, during which the newscast switched to coverage of another war. "I mean look at this. Human fucking beings. Pillar of evolution. God's beloved creation. All the things we tell ourselves to pump up our species-ego. But all we can do is kill each other, starve each other, divide the world into arbitrary tracts and build borders with weapons; shit, we might just get around to blowing the whole fucking thing to hell if we really hit our peak. How could it possibly matter? What could it possibly *mean*?" Harry said the last word with visible distaste. He sucked another small drag from his cigarette, then took a few breaths from the oxygen tank. "If it means anything," his voice darkened angrily, "it's that God or whatever is an evil, sadistic little fucker, and human nature is in his fucking image. Maybe that's it, maybe fighting it is unnatural, maybe the way to enlightenment is to live fully in our truly evil self-serving fucking nature! Ever think of that? Maybe Idi fucking Amin is the real Buddha." He paused here and panted into the mask, then spoke more quietly, shaking his head. "No. We're just a bunch of animals with big brains who've figured out better ways to tear each other up. Somewhere along the line there was a flicker of something in the ooze that became a cell, and BOOM! suddenly we've got masses of complex organisms shooting at each other with AK-47s." Harry smiled at the end of this, without looking at me, trying to catch his breath. I could see he was amused on top of being worked up.

"Tough to argue with that kind of reasoning," I said. I was halfway through the cigarette. I twirled the head clean on the edge of the ashtray.

"Hey," he said. He was staring at me. I looked back. "Seeing that guy gunned down probably made you think of your dad, didn't it?"

"Yeah, I guess." The way the journalist's body convulsed kept replaying behind my eyes. As if he'd been jolted with electricity.

"Me too. You know, he was a better man than I. Though that's not saying much I guess," he chuckled and then got serious again. "He was doing good work. He was the real thing, a true believer."

"What do you mean?"

"You and I never talk about him, do we?"

"No."

"Well," Harry looked away from me, "we know we both loved him." We sat there smoking. The TV was playing an advertisement for a magically impervious wood treatment; raindrops were stopping in midair a few inches above a deck and rolling off toward the lawn.

"What do you mean, true believer?"

"Oh, he was dedicated to what he did. Do you have any idea how much he loved your mother? And you." Harry's voice was deteriorating, and he tried to clear his throat.

"I guess I do."

"Good." He coughed once. Sports coverage came on. "Damn!" Harry rasped. "Fucking Mets."

I was glad for the change of subject. "Oh, now *there's* something that matters," I said.

"Closest I've found," Harry chuckled, watching the baseball

scores. "Listen, all that stuff before, I don't mean to force my jaded outlook on you, I'm just babbling. Everyone believes what they want. Why don't you give me a tirade about beauty and God and human sanctity and we'll call it even."

"Not sure I have it in me." I wondered if the journalist had died instantly.

Harry put his cigarette out. "Oh come on. I'm listening." That crooked grimace-smile crept onto his face. "I promise not to laugh when you tell me Jerry Garcia is God."

I smiled back. "Yeah, and Phil Lesh is Moses. I saw him turn his bass into a snake, I swear it wasn't just the acid."

"Yes," Harry snickered under his breath, tapping another cigarette from the pack. "Freeing the suburbanites from bondage."

I sucked a last drag and put mine out. I had the taste of damp ashes in my mouth. "Coffee?"

"Jesus, yes. And make it quick." Harry laughed aloud as I left the room, maybe at something on the TV. The sound was like a large bird with an obstruction in its throat.

MELANIE CALLED the night before I left for the Greeks. It felt good to hear her voice, as it had before, but I had made my plans to go with Jane and Sasha and Jim without really thinking of her. I had begun to accept my loss of the address the way you do a lost wallet. Hearing her voice brought it back, though, and flooded me with relief. I told her about the car being stolen and got the address from her again, this time writing it on a piece of paper.

"How are we going to get to shows?" she asked.

"Don't worry. We'll figure something out. There's always a way."

"You going to the Greeks tomorrow?"

"Yeah, I'm going."

"Lucky asshole."

That night, Harry let me buy the plane ticket by phone on his credit card, and I had the airline mail it to the address in Massachusetts.

THE NEXT DAY I drove the Mercedes north, with Harry's permission. He never left the house anymore, anyway, and his stationary existence was softening his character, if not his outlook. I drove along the coast on Route 1 the whole way after Santa Cruz, past the beach where I had lived that summer with Don, through Half Moon Bay, through the green light of the eucalyptus forest in the hills that opened onto Pacifica, high along the creamy cliffs that reminded me of a picture from a children's book of Greek mythology, then Daly City and into San Francisco. I was in motion, but not in the same way I was used to. Somehow the Mercedes, along with the knowledge that I wouldn't be following the tour to Wisconsin after the Greeks, made this feel more like a commute than a journey. Ground already covered. There were things pulling me forward on this trip, things that had me magnetized, but I didn't like the idea of naming them so I told myself it was still the music, the tribe. I met Cole at the downtown hotel where he was staying. He tended to get rooms a little removed from the action during Bay area shows.

In the small messy room with Cole was a couple, two scraggly West Coast heads I didn't know, and Cole told them he'd see them later. He introduced us as they were leaving, but their names didn't register.

"So," he said when they were gone. "You wanted to talk to me?"

"Yeah." I lit a cigarette. "Got any beers or anything?"

"No, nothing. There's a glass if you want some water."

"No. So listen. I got the story from Saul. I know what happened with the whole Dawn situation."

Cole nodded his head and pursed his lips, as if he'd been meaning to talk to me about this. "Yeah, that was a bad scene."

"You know Dawn thinks you set her up."

"I guess she was bound to."

"And you're okay with that?"

"What can I do?" He tapped a Camel straight from his pack and lit it with my lighter.

"She's probably told other people besides me."

"I know. Like Scar."

"So you're okay with what Saul did?"

"Look, Saul didn't know Dawn, and he did everything he could to protect me from going down. He was looking at serious time. He did a fucked-up thing, yeah, but in the end I couldn't help feeling like he'd gone out of his way for me. It sounds weird, but in a way he did. I'd already met that guy Will, and probably would have ended up selling something to him. I came out of it clean, and with a clean conscience, too. I was pissed at Saul for a while, but we patched it up, and I'm not going to go around telling everyone it was him. That's not me."

I thought about this. "Okay. I can respect that. It's your rep, I guess."

Cole dove across the gap between the beds and embraced me roughly, wrestling me into a headlock, laughing. "Forget that shit, will you. The fucking Greeks start today, and we better get going." He was rubbing the top of my head with his palm, then punched my arm. I laughed and struggled against him, but he was too strong. I was in his control. "This is no small thing," he said. "Make no mistake. This is the Grateful Dead at the Greek Theater!"

part three

WHEN MY FATHER DIED, we stayed in Cyprus three days, until his body arrived from Syria, then we flew to New York. When I think about those three days, I sometimes manage to remember them as grief-filled, agonized; that is how I encourage myself to remember them, how I imagine describing them to people (though I never actually talk about it with anyone). The truth, which I can't always avoid, is that I felt very little grief or agony during those three days, and have suspected myself, in years to come when I did feel those things, of mustering them for propriety.

What I felt, primarily, was the same sense of expansion I had experienced at the little girl Ayşe's bedside. The sense that I was growing, becoming human. It occurred to me that my father had lost his father, and later his mother—it was part of who he was. Now I was a kid who had lost his father. It didn't seem unfair, it seemed inevitable. I didn't feel forced into the role of fatherless boy, I felt in some way freed by it. It was who I was. I felt it most when I was outside the house, walking by myself, or seeing other kids, friends from outside the family. It was as though people had a new respect for me. I felt cooler. People were careful what they said around me, other kids were fascinated to find out what had happened (I could see it in their eyes, though none asked) and it felt good to get that kind of consideration.

I would take walks just to get out of the house. My mother would nod understandingly when I said I was going for a walk, thinking I needed to be alone to grapple with my grief. But I left to escape, not grapple with anything. In the house, with my mother and brother, I felt obligated to act stricken, the obligation like a lead blanket across my shoulders. But as soon as I walked out the door alone, the weight lifted. I wasn't happy. Far from it. But I was myself, I was the tough, smart kid who had lost his father and become deeper as a result, and I was free.

On my walks I climbed trees, sat in the branches watching the world. It meant something to me, to sit aloft supported by a living thing, embracing it, feeling its strength. Trees became friends, and through my hands I could understand them; sitting in their branches I could become acquainted with earth and sky. The tree's roots ran into the earth as deeply as its branches climbed the sky. It was there that I felt most at peace, because the trees understood me too, not judging my stolidity, which so resembled their own. I could look off into the distance, inhabiting the space between present and future, where there was no impatience, no action, nothing required. I could put my ear against the bark and listen for the silent inner life flowing from the whole planet into the tree and out into the air; I could feel the sun on my skin as leaves do.

Walking home, I looked into the eyes of people I passed, to show them I wasn't afraid. I thought my father would understand, wouldn't mind me not grieving. He was a big advocate of playing the hand life dealt you as best you could.

But I also knew others wouldn't understand. I knew what was expected of me. So I moped around the house when I was inside, staring at walls and doing nothing. My brother, the tough one, cried the whole time it seemed. He was always running to Mom's arms and bursting into tears, and she would hug him and shush him quietly and tell him it was okay, Dad was in a better place. Sometimes, just so as not to be left out, I would go over and hug her too, while he was bawling, and she'd rub my head and shush me too, though I wasn't making any noise.

The trip back was long. Mom wore a black turtleneck and black slacks, and I imagined her as one of the old Muslim widows in Turkey, swathed in black for the rest of her life. James and I wore sweatshirts and jeans, which felt strange. It seemed we should be wearing black suits. When our flight was called, we walked out of the gate onto the hot tarmac of Larnaca Airport. James and I flanked our mother, and warm gusts tried to push me backward, but I leaned into them. I've always remembered that moment so well because at the time I got a mental picture of myself that I liked: stepping through the door into the wind, hair twirling romantically on top of my head as I squinted toughly in the sunlight. The way Clint Eastwood might have walked out that door. The two people on my right faded into the background, and I fixed my eyes past the planes on the scrub-brush and wild-olive-tree horizon. People in general faded into the background. There was just me and the world, and we understood each other. I was expanding again, filling my own skin, which had begun to sweat in the heat. My mother pulled me toward the shuttle bus that would take us to the plane.

We had a long layover in Zurich, and after eating in the cafeteria, I asked if I could have ice cream for dessert.

"Of course you can," my mother said. "James, do you want some?"

He shook his head and looked at me, as if to say *How can you eat ice cream at a time like this?*

She gave me some money, and I went up and bought a dish of vanilla ice cream. I brought it back to the table and ate it while they watched me, saying nothing. I felt their watching as a pressure. It seemed that with each bite, they expected me to stop, to realize the futility of ice cream and back away from it. I finished the bowl.

"Can I have some more?" I asked.

"I guess so."

This time I bought chocolate. Again they watched me eat, as if it were a test. When I finished, I asked for more, and she kept saying yes. Looking back, I realize something strange must have been moving in her as well, not to stop me. Five dishes of ice cream later, I started to feel sick. Mom looked at my blanched face and said, "I think you've had enough."

"I want some more," I said. My stomach was turning over, and a pain was developing in its center that I knew would get worse.

"No. I don't know what I was thinking letting you eat so much."

I gripped my stomach for a second, then pulled my hands away from it. "Please!"

"No, honey. Look at you. You're getting sick."

"But I want more," I said. And I did. "Mom, please, just one more bowl."

"I said no. Let's go back to the gate."

I began to cry. It seemed so unfair. What was the difference between five bowls and six? "It's not fair!" I said, and cried louder. I was disgusted with myself—this crybaby was definitely not who I was. I leaned over and threw up on the floor next to my chair. A creamy light-brown lake. After everything, to be beaten by ice cream. My stomach was in real pain now.

"Oh no, sweetie." She came around to me and held me and wiped my mouth with a napkin. I couldn't stop crying from the pain in my stomach and the wanting more ice cream. "It's okay, Jason," she said, rubbing my back. "Don't worry, it's okay." I felt like a liar. I knew she thought I was crying for my father, but I let her comfort me. I was too much of a coward to tell her she was wrong. James just sat in his chair across the table, silent. I was looking at the floor, at the sweet puddle spreading on the black-flecked linoleum, so I didn't see his face, but I imagined he was disgusted with me. If the day in the tunnel before our father died was our last true experience together, I feel as though this was the point at which our lives diverged.

James and I began at different boarding schools the following fall and from then on saw each other mainly during vacations. Mine was an all-boys school. No one there thought it strange that I preferred to be alone. Word got around of my father's death, and people accepted me for what I was, untainted by any knowledge of what I had been. I was the fatherless boy, the tough kid moving on from tragedy. People respected that. I got good grades and didn't get teased by the upperclassmen the way most of my dormmates did. I took up football and became the youngest player on the J.V. team, though I sat on the bench most games. By all accounts I was adjusting beautifully. No one, including myself, knew how much I hated it. I didn't think to question any of it. I thought, this is what you do. You look at the place the world has created for you, you own that place as completely as possible and people respect you for it, and you succeed. Happiness wasn't part of the plan; it was a wild card and couldn't be the goal because it couldn't be counted on.

This philosophy was more nascent than articulate in my mind, but it was there.

The next year I applied for a single room, but didn't get it. I was put with a new kid, who had transferred from a pre-prep that stopped at seventh grade. His name was Thaddeus, and he introduced me to pot and sixties rock. He immediately fell in with a crowd of older stoners, and they were always hanging out doing bong-hits in our room, since our faculty dorm master was notoriously lax. I started smoking with them, and in this crew I found that I could be alone without being alone. That was the magic for me. When you got high, no one else could own your high or control it, but at the same time you all went there together. It was an instant community, one of people who wanted to create their own worlds, control them—and they were succeeding without being miserable. This changed everything. The relief I felt at not having to be stoically alone the rest of my life (which was how I had imagined it) took me by surprise. It overwhelmed me, and sometimes I had to put Thaddeus or one of the other guys in a headlock and wrestle him around, laughing, just to keep from choking up with happiness.

Drugs could be counted on. You knew what you were getting. You knew about the high, and it was a sure thing, but you also knew about the crash, the hangover, whatever the downside was, and its extent was predictable as well. Being high was an achievable goal. I grew very quickly to hate the school, the teachers, anyone who would try to control me and tell me what I could and couldn't do. I got "talked to" by innumerable teachers and counselors about the change in my personality, by which they meant the change in my performance, since having no imagination that's how they measured everything. Right before I got kicked out the first time, my mother drove up from the city and picked James up from his school on the way. We had a tense lunch in the nearby town and then she went to meet with some faculty and left James and me in my room. I put on some Doors and we kicked back. James, uncomfortable in the role of big brother, tried to talk to me.

"How do you like it here?" he asked.

"Not too much," I said. "I have some friends, I guess. It's all right."

"Listen," he leaned forward, but kept his eyes on the carpet, "it seems like you're getting into trouble you don't need."

I knew Mom had coached him in the car, told him maybe I would listen to him, and he was trying to do his duty. He hated it, but he would try anyway. I felt sorry for him, and loved him suddenly.

"Don't worry," I said. "I'm fine."

"I know you are. It's just that Mom is worried. And they might expel you."

"Yeah, well."

"Can't you just be mellow about partying and still get your work done? I mean I do bong-hits now and then, but I keep my shit together so people won't get on my case. It's not that hard."

"Yeah, you're probably right. I should try and do that."

He leaned back. "Anyway, whatever." I could see he was relieved at having said what he had to. "Don't worry about it, just don't freak Mom out."

"I'm not worried about it. You want a bong-hit?"

He looked at me and his eyes widened, then he laughed. "I don't think that's a good idea."

"Come on," I said. "You're going to miss out on some killer Alaskan Thunderfuck."

"You're quite the little stoner, aren't you?" He smiled and shook his head.

I pulled back the corner of the tapestry covering my overstuffed chair, reached into a hole in the arm, and extracted my green, two-foot U.S. Bong. There was a rolled-up pair of tube socks stuffed in its mouth to contain the odor. "Sure you won't have one with me?"

"No," James said. He was still smiling, but he didn't look relieved anymore. "Who are you again, and what the hell did you do with my little brother?"

But I didn't see myself as having changed in any fundamental sense. I had merely discovered a way to be true to my own rugged, individualistic vision of myself and still be happy. I had given myself permission to enjoy life.

1

OUTSIDE, THE HIGH DESERT WAS RED, its heat thundering in through the sunroof and overpowering the air-conditioning. Melanie's bare legs were white, pale from being sequestered in the Massachusetts treatment center. She had just opened the roof and was standing up into the sunlight, whooping along with "St. Stephen" off the *Live Dead* CD on Harry's great system. She'd gotten in from the East Coast two days earlier, a free woman, an adult. We were in Nevada, headed for Denver. In the rearview the Sierra Nevada was still discernible, blue silhouettes wavering through the heat, a cool distant memory; and in the far distance to the north were more bluish humps; but directly ahead the land lay sere and lifeless, the highway bisecting it straight as a scalpel cut. I only had enough tar to get me to Denver, but it would be okay. Saul had people there.

After the Greeks, everyone had cleared out of the Bay for summer tour, except me and Saul (and Jane). It hadn't taken long for me to get strung out again, and Saul had helped me turn some mail-order deals for stuff people back east wanted, so I wouldn't use all of Melanie's money. She didn't know yet. I'd been taking my hits in secret, carrying around folded tinfoil and the tube of a wide pen in my pockets. But I couldn't keep her in the dark about it for much longer, not while traveling together.

From the night she arrived it had been like before, only better. Sleeping together, I'd felt again that sense of skewed balance that somehow galvanized my desire. She'd gained a little weight and turned it into muscle in the treatment center's gym, and her body, with its deformity and its precise ways of moving, was a perfect extension of her strange, intelligent mind; it knew what to do and when: just when I thought the grip of her thighs on my hips was as good as it could get, driving me toward the edge that was so far off through the dope haze, she would push me up, throw one leg back, turn onto her side and bring me back in, putting one foot on my chest and using me for stability—and these goddess-like, clairvoyant movements, always at the right moment, lifted me into a frenzy of pleasure that surpassed the drug while they lasted.

She was singing along with the CD, twirling her hand in the hot eighty-mile-an-hour wind, her voice muffled, its substance whipped away into the emptiness behind us. Harry liked Melanie and had insisted that I take her to the Red Rocks shows in his car. So we were headed for a Colorado getaway—three shows at Red Rocks outside Denver and two shows down in Telluride. It was impossible not to share some of Melanie's excitement, Red Rocks being the single greatest concert venue in the country, but things were in a whole different light for me: once again that smoky-filtered light that kept anything from getting too bright. Once again that feeling of estrangement from sunshine. I pulled the car to the shoulder. The road was empty in both directions.

"What are you doing?" Melanie yelled down from above.

"Come back in here. It's getting hot."

She sat down and I hit the button to close the sunroof.

"Yeah, turn up the fucking AC," mumbled Saul from the back, where he'd been sleeping. "Any gas stations coming up? I have to use the bathroom."

"I don't think so," I said. "This is a pretty barren stretch. It's going to be a half hour or so."

"Why don't you just piss here?" said Melanie. "Since we're stopped. There's no one around."

"What if it's not piss I need to do?" asked Saul.

"Oh, okay."

"Well, that's what I need to do," I said, and got out. I went around the hood and out a few steps into the red hardpack. As I walked up to a dry but still-rooted tumbleweed, a desert hare bolted from inside it and raced at breakneck speed away from me, not slowing down until it cleared the cover of a small rise fifty yards away. I looked around. That tumbleweed was the only cover near the road for half a mile. I stepped to the side and peed next to it instead of into it, in case the hare wanted to come back to it. I thought of Hunter Thompson's theory of why rabbits jump into the road in front of cars, how they do it by mistake the first time, but then get addicted to the adrenaline rush and start doing it on purpose, waiting for the cars and needing to get closer and closer each time to achieve the rush, until finally one hits them. I stared toward the rise, but the hare didn't show itself again.

When I got back to the car and opened the door, Saul said, "I don't know if I can wait another half hour." He gave me a significant look from behind Melanie.

"You can," I said.

"But I don't want to. This is absurd."

Melanie was lighting a cigarette with the dashboard lighter, leaning forward with her eyes slitted.

"Look, man, I'll get us there as quick as I can," I said. "Just chill for a little while."

"Jesus," said Melanie. "What do you think I am, fucking stupid? Just do your drugs in the car, whatever it is. It's not like I haven't seen you guys going in and out of the bathroom the whole fucking time."

"Ha!" Saul laughed. "See? Can't get anything by this girl."

"Yeah, she's a frigging genius," I said, and climbed in.

"No need to insult her," Saul said.

"No, I'm serious. She really is a genius. Probably smarter than both of us put together." I was proud of this fact.

"The insult," said Melanie, "was trying to hide shit from me and thinking I wouldn't notice."

"Yeah, well. I was going to tell you soon."

"Wow, you don't fuck around," Melanie said, and I saw she was looking into the backseat. In the mirror I could see Saul pulling his works out of his knapsack. "Are you into this, too?" she asked me.

"Already with the questions." I put the car in gear. "I don't use needles."

This was true. But what I didn't say was that ever since the day at Mama's, I had clung involuntarily to the memory of the mainline rush. As time went past, the memory was fading, until I could barely remember what it had actually felt like, except to know it had been phenomenal. The more the memory faded, the more I obsessed about regaining it. It seemed too good a thing to forget, to allow to sink into the opaque past, and I had been toying off and on with the idea of doing it again, just as a reminder; if I could just do it once more and consciously commit it to memory, then I wouldn't have to worry about forgetting it. If there was one thing I believed in, it was the importance of experience—of not skimping on it in life, and not taking it for granted. I kept this noble thought in my head as much as possible when I found myself craving that high again.

We were out on the road, climbing smoothly to seventy-five miles an hour. The entire horizon was still devoid of any movement as far as the eye could see.

"Watch out for bumps," Saul said from in back.

IF YOU DIDN'T NOTICE the protruding jawbone, the marks like bee stings on the backs of his spavined hands, the creases in his face as if his skin were made of putty, it would have seemed impossible that Saul's friend Drew was a junkie. He was jovial and gregarious when we arrived at his apartment in Denver, flapping around and popping off one-liners like an emaciated, red-haired Robin Williams. The apartment was very messy but not grimy—no week-old dishes in the sink or embedded dirt in the furniture or hardened food lying around, just clothes and newspaper and junk, balls of dust and lint along the baseboards that swayed and shifted in the breezes caused by opening doors or moving people. There were cheap little novelty toys mixed into the mess everywhere: action figures, dolls, plastic soldiers, superballs, Weebles with mustaches drawn on them, jacks, Pez dispensers, toy cars, decoder rings.

"Do you have a child?" Melanie asked.

Drew smiled at this quizzically, his long mouth crooked across his drawn face, then he laughed abruptly, a loud bark. "No way. I just like little toys and stuff. I collect this shit, I guess you could say."

He told us we were welcome as long as we wanted to stay. He took money from Saul and me immediately and went out to cop some dope. "White dope," he said. "Good stuff. My connection for tar went south recently, but I found this guy who's hooked with the China white, and it's even better." He stepped out the door, then turned back. "Oh, by the way, don't answer the door. Nobody comes to see me here. No one knows where I live. So don't let anyone else in."

There was no TV, so while we waited for him to get back Saul and I played with the toys, tossing balls back and forth, messing with a fancy yo-yo we didn't really know how to use, putting the action figures in sexual positions. Melanie sneered at our antics and kicked back on the couch to flip through a book she'd found on the floor called *We Rule the World*. It was two hours before Drew returned. He seemed flustered, a little shaken, when he came in the door.

"Christ," he said. "It's a bad scene out there."

It was clear from the way he said it that "out there" meant the world at large. His eyes said he'd been doing coke.

"What happened?" asked Saul. "You get the dope?"

"Yeah, I got it. I had to park my car at a mall and catch a cab on the other side to drop my tail."

"Tail?" Saul laughed. "Come on. Who's following you? The cops?"

"I don't know. I don't think so. There's other people that want to fuck with me."

Drew went to the window and peeped out at the street, then shut the curtain. This was typical coke-fiend shit, and Saul said, "Do some fucking shmeez and calm down."

We gathered around the small table and Drew pulled out the dope, a sandwich baggie with white powder in it.

"It doesn't look like much," I said.

"It doesn't take much with this stuff," said Drew.

"Can I smoke it off foil like tar?"

Drew looked across the table at me through his bushy red eyebrows. "A beginner, huh?"

"Kind of."

"Yeah you can chase it like tar if you want. Or you can snort it." He was dipping the corner of a matchbook into the bag and dumping some into a spoon. "Though that's a fucking waste," he muttered.

After I'd done my hit, Melanie wanted one. I said, "No, baby. I don't want you getting into this stuff."

"Look who's talking. You're the one who's strung out, so don't project that shit on me. I just want to try a hit."

"I'm not strung out," I said.

"Oh, bullshit." She grabbed the foil from the table in front of me and put some of the powder on it. I made a feeble reach for it, not really trying, and she turned away to avoid me, picking up the lighter. "Hypocrite," she said.

Saul, getting ready to put in his hit, shook his head and chuckled from across the table. The dope was powerful, and I had to make my way to the bathroom to throw up. The hallway softened, became slightly gelatinous, as I moved through it, and squeezed me warmly, like an intestine. I was headed in the right direction, and it was helping me along. The bathroom door had a poster of Frank Zappa sitting on the toilet, looking like he'd just woken up. It occurred to me as I took it in what an icon the toilet is, how we refer not to individual toilets but to one proverbial throne: "the toilet"—something universal, unifying, about it. Zappa stared at me, and his blank, regal look of defecation was somehow comforting. Puking on dope is not the burning, painful affair it is normally. Your stomach just contracts, as if it were the most natural thing in the world, and its contents exit smoothly. The seat was up, and as the last of the microwaved bean burrito and Pepsi I'd had for lunch flowed out of me, I read the legend inscribed at the top of the porcelain bowl: *American Standard.* I nodded my head, feeling, as LSD had taught me sometimes to feel, that wisdom was being imparted to me in ways I was only occasionally aware of. Just as I finished, Melanie joined me and started puking while I washed my mouth out at the sink. "Not all it's cracked up to be, is it?" I said.

She swiveled her big light brown eyes toward me for a second, the pupils shrunken to specks; the way they moved reminded me of a lizard Benton had kept in his room at school, named Budu, whose conical eyes operated independently. Budu had slunk off to a corner of his terrarium one day and stopped eating the baby crickets we dropped in. It took him weeks to die. Near the end, desperate, we had blown pot smoke into the cage, thinking it might make him hungry. Melanie smiled with one corner of her mouth, as if she'd read my thoughts. She took some toilet paper and wiped her chin.

On my way back down the hall, I noticed there were two bedrooms, each furnished with a bed and dresser, decorated with posters and tapestries.

"You have roommates?" I asked Drew.

"No," he slurred. "This isn't my place, really. The two guys who live here went to Asia for the summer and let me stay here. They go to DU. The rent's paid. They've got serious money. They won't be back for another two months. I had a little room in a flop, but things got too hot and I had to vacate."

"They've got serious money but no TV?"

"Well, I hocked their TV." He smirked sheepishly. "I'll get it back, or I'll get them a new one."

———

IN THE MORNING I woke next to Melanie on the living room floor and thought of Jane. The bed of quilts we'd made was in disarray. The window faced east, and summer sunlight struggled with inner gloom at the edges of the curtain, lighting the wall on either side and throwing a triangular shape near my feet. Melanie was still asleep. I put my hands behind my head. Jane and I had slept together four times in the weeks between the Greeks and a late-July show in Oakland. I had told her about Melanie, how I didn't want to confuse anything, and we agreed to keep it casual. Now, even though there was no doubt in my mind that Melanie was the one for me, I was conflicted. Melanie's sharpness, her caustic intelligence, her quirky ways in bed, all electrified my desire. And more important, we clicked—in conversation and banter I felt so at ease with her; I figured I was in love with her. I couldn't see not being with her. Jane I forgot about for days at a time, but when she drifted into my thoughts, with her deadly smile, her freckled breasts, her long, perfectly tapering legs, I wanted her, badly. Wanting Jane felt different than any want I'd experienced before; maybe that's what made it so powerful, and personalized what was essentially lust—that quality of otherness. Was it just that she was the most physically beautiful woman I'd slept with? It seemed possible, but I felt there was something more there, something almost spiritual in my perception of her beauty, my communion with it, in her offering of it to me in particular; in sex we achieved an otherworldly union that began dissipating immediately afterward. We were unable to transpose it into everyday activities. In a way, this made sex with Jane even more desirable, since it was its own unique world, attainable through no other means.

"Penny for your thoughts," Melanie said. She had been staring at me.

"It'll cost you more than that," I said.

She rolled to me and rubbed my neck, then my chest. "Name your price."

"Believe me, you can't afford my thoughts."

"Oh no?" She kissed me.

I shook my head. "Mm-mm. Way beyond your means." I put my arm under her right side and lifted her on top of me. I lifted the hem of her T-shirt and she helped me pull it off. I ran my hand up her ribs to what would have been her right armpit if there had been an arm there to complete it. She smiled at me, and I felt it inside me as a blessing, a timid ecstasy that would flee any direct contact and so could never be pursued or spoken of. The blue curtain on the window glowed behind her in the head-on sunlight, framing her pale, pale face in a backlit sapphire. She dipped down out of the light and kissed me again, then lay flat on my body and reached behind her to move her underwear to the side. I slid a hand between us and guided myself in. Slowly, she began moving. When the speed reached a certain point, she sat up, pushing on my chest with her hand. In the sudden open space I caught a movement, and saw Drew standing at the mouth of the hallway, staring. His face, under that tuft of red hair, looked sallow, like produce past its time: an old, misshapen lemon.

"Oh," he said. "Sorry." But he didn't move.

Melanie looked over too, and lay flat again, laughing slightly. Drew entered the room and walked toward the kitchen. I pulled the covers up over us. As far as I was concerned, the spell was broken. I was getting soft. But Melanie said, "Hey Drew?" without turning toward him.

"Yeah."

"Could you give us five minutes?"

"What? Oh, yeah, sure. Sorry." He was in the archway leading to the kitchen. He turned and walked back down the hall.

"Thanks," Melanie called.

"No problem," he said.

I was fully soft by now, thinking it was futile. That beautiful moment was lost, mood destroyed, world altered back. "I don't know," I said when she reached down to touch me.

But, "Shhh," Melanie said, and buried her tongue in my ear, sliding down to my nipple and biting, hand on my balls. And so she created a new, raw animal mood, rolled me on top of her and kissed me wantonly, pulled at her underwear and said, "Rip these off me," which I did, putting enough force into the third try so they came fluttering away. This charged me up, and she provoked me until we were colliding hard, tipped me over the edge with her hand and her voice.

WHEN SAUL AND DREW started putting together their morning fixes, I decided to hold out for a while. Mostly this was a reaction to Melanie's disgusted look.

"Got any coffee?" Melanie asked Drew.

"No, but there's a deli a block and a half up with decent coffee." He was holding up his full syringe and flicking it, to get the bubbles to the top.

"Want to go?" she asked me.

"Yeah, sure. In a few."

Melanie went down the hall to the bathroom.

"You have a ticket to the show tonight?" I asked Drew.

"The show?" He snorted. "Fuck no. I'm not into that hippie bullshit. You wouldn't catch me at one of those concerts if my life depended on it."

"How'd you and Saul meet then?"

"We grew up together. Me, him, and Don. Then him and Don got into that shit and went off hippie-dipping around. I came out here to go to school." He spread his arms as if displaying the table in front of him. "You can see how that turned out."

When Melanie came back, I went down the hall. While brushing my teeth, I realized I had all the paraphernalia in my pockets. We'd divvied up the dope, and I had mine in a twisted ball of Saran wrap, inside a square of foil. I pulled it all out and dropped just a little hit onto the foil and smoked it. Then I decided on a shower.

RED ROCKS. What can be said about it? There is no finer place to see a concert. It's made up of stairs and benches and ramps built into the site of a natural amphitheater formed by wind and plate tectonics out of the rust-colored rocks, perched high on the eastern lip of the Front Range. The audience faces east, and all you have to do is raise your eyes above the stage and the wall of rock that backs it to be looking far out across the Great Plains, downtown Denver slightly off-center to the left.

I'd kept my dope intake to a minimum, but it still nagged at me as we traversed the crowds before the first set. There was always a slightly disconnected feeling about joining a tour in the middle anyway, especially a summer tour, and being on heroin only exacerbated it. People who had been there the whole time had formed friendships, alliances, partnerships, and had been soaking in that tour's particular aura all summer; it was a little like coming into a new school in the middle of a spring semester. That summer had been a mob scene, everyone said, with the Dead opening for and backing up Bob Dylan at many of the shows. After the Greeks and Alpine Valley and a show in Ontario, it had been a summer of football stadiums and crowds swelling with the sales of the new album and all the radio play "Touch of Grey" was getting. The tour got written up in *USA Today*. People were blissful to be back in a smaller venue, seeing the Dead as masters of the show rather than an opening act. Dylan was great, went the general consensus, but enough was enough. All this I gleaned indirectly from walking around and talking to folks before the show, but it was hard to lose that tangential feeling, at least until the music started.

A preshow rain shower prompted the Boys to open with "Cold Rain and Snow." Hearing the throaty opening riff, I knew I still belonged there, as much as I ever had, but I couldn't feel it in the same way. When the first set started I took Melanie and went wandering, looking for the deeper connection. I saw Anthony and his dreadhead crew in with a larger group of people dancing on Phil's side, down near the stage, and we joined them. People greeted me, hugs were given, and I pulled Melanie into the group to dance, to forget. That summer-tour feeling was cresting all around. And I got into it for a little while: the feel of the place was deep, the prehistoric heartbeat of the rocks complicating the music, the people bright, all different kinds of dancers, smilers, swayers, swirlers, smokers, beer-drinking boppers, tripsters, spinners. During the set-closing "Let it Grow," I looked back at the crowd and the mountains and the sky behind, and saw the show for a moment as a jewel, set in the amphitheater—and by extension the Rockies—like a gem in a bracelet: an ornament on the body of the country, glittering in the coming darkness.

Night became complete during the break. For the second set I sat on one of the retaining walls facing the stage and watched Melanie and the others dance. I looked out past the stage, the suburbs of Denver spread out like constellations, giving onto the velvet darkness of the plains beyond. To the south, two small lakes bordered the highway and reflected the stream of headlights passing outbound from town. Jerry sang "Crazy Fingers" sweetly. As strange as I felt about being strung out amidst all this, I was suddenly deeply comforted, reassured, by the thought of the dope folded up in my pocket. I looked for the brightness of downtown and couldn't find it. I knew I was looking in the right direction. Then, against the almost black sky, I saw it: the bare silhouettes of the buildings not lit up. The tall buildings were all dead, shut down, a small ashy core against the surrounding sprawl of lights. All life had moved from the center to the fringes, like a fire burning outward.

2

DEATH SNEAKS AROUND. I should have had some inkling of its nature and not been surprised, but it's so easy not to remember. It doesn't necessarily strike in threes, but this time it did.

The second night, we were talking to Anthony before the show, and he said, "You hear what happened to that guy Judah?"

"Judah the sadhu? What happened to him?"

"The story I heard was that he was tripping yesterday in some state park around here, and he lay down at the bottom of a stream. He was using his didjeridoo to breathe through, sticking it up out of the water. But I guess the space of air inside the thing was too big, and it filled up with his breath until he was just breathing stale air. Maybe since he was tripping he didn't notice it, but he passed out and drowned. Some folks he was camping with found him. His hand was still clamped on the didjeridoo."

"God," I said. "He's dead?"

"Yeah."

"I can't believe that." I remembered when I had last seen him at

Ventura, how he'd looked me off and ignored me. For some reason I felt guilty.

"Who was this guy?" Saul asked. "Did I know him?"

"I don't think so," I said.

"I remember him," said Melanie. "We met him in Hampton, right?"

"Yeah, that's him," I said.

"That's sad. He seemed so magical."

"Yeah," Anthony nodded. "Let's smoke one for him." He pulled a joint from his breast pocket.

An hour later, in the top parking lot nearest the entrance, we were looking for some good preshow food and came across a little huddle around the side door of a black Chevy van. Furtive glances were being thrown by a few heads gathered around a tall figure—who from the corner of my eye for a second looked like Judah. But it was Tall Ted, doing a deal of some kind. Saul saw him at the same time I did and said, "Holy shit."

"Wait here," I told Melanie. "That's the guy who stole all the stuff from us."

I could tell Ted was the seller in the transaction from the way the others were looking at what was in his hands, which as we got closer I saw was a small sheaf of blotter acid. We walked right up to the edge of the huddle without him looking up and seeing us. He was naming prices and detailing the wondrous strength of his product.

Saul must have been thinking of what he would say for a while, practicing it in his head, because it was perfect. And later on, when I thought back on it in light of what happened the next morning, it seemed an eerie premonition. It was too bad that I was the only one who got the joke. All of them, even Ted, stared blankly at him when he said, "Good morning, Mr. Benson."

It took Ted only a second to regain his composure, and he said, "Hey guys. Hang on a second while I do this thing. Then we can talk."

"We need to talk now," Saul said.

"Hold on."

"No." Saul stepped in and told the three guys buying from him to clear out.

"But this is our van," one of them said.

"Sorry." Saul took Ted's arm and walked around the back of the van. I followed.

"Why would you need to be selling sheets?" I asked Ted. "I thought you were going to become Ivan fucking Boesky on the stock market."

We stopped at the back and Ted said, "So how's it going, guys?" as if he hadn't heard anything we'd said.

"How's it going?" Saul pushed him against the van. "Where's Jason's car?"

"Whoa, whoa." Ted held up both hands. "I don't have it. I was going to pay you all back for everything when I got the money going."

"Well, you're going to pay us back now."

"Listen, if you wait a few weeks—"

Saul shoved him again. "Empty your pockets."

Ted's shifty eyes were flashing back and forth a mile a minute, and he was unconsciously wiping his palms across his chest. Adrenaline was taking him over.

"Try something, dickhead," said Saul. "Try something on me. I will be happy to fucking bury you."

I almost laughed at this, the crime-movie melodrama of it.

"Empty your fucking pockets into Jason's hands right now."

Ted's shoulders slumped, and he began doing it. Saul had to

prompt him at each new pocket. At the end I had five sheets of acid, something shy of three hundred dollars cash, mostly in twenties, a small wooden pipe, a corner bag of nice pot, and an expensive-looking black folding hunting knife.

"Where are the car keys?" I asked.

"I told you," he said, "I don't have the car anymore."

"How are you traveling?"

"With some friends."

"Uh-huh. Is Blinka still with you?"

"What?" Ted squinted in the direct sunlight on his face, raised a hand above his eyes.

"That pocket, too," Saul said, pointing to a pocket inside his jean jacket. "What's in there?"

Ted hit me with a glancing punch across my cheek and took off. It didn't hurt much, but was enough to make me drop the stuff in my hands onto the ground. Saul went after him for twenty yards, but Ted was flying faster than he could run.

Saul stopped and yelled, "Get off tour, you slimy fuck!"

I was picking up the money and sheets and stuffing them into my pockets as Saul came back over. Melanie was next to me. "Are you okay?" she asked.

"Yeah," I said, rubbing my cheek and working my jaw. "We got something out of him, anyway." I looked up at Saul and laughed. " 'Good morning, Mr. Benson.' That was good."

He smiled. "You caught that, huh?"

We kept our eyes open the rest of the night, but there was no sign of Ted at the show or afterward.

THE SOUND of the door splintering at 9 AM pierced my sleeping mind in a strange place. I shot awake in full déjà vu—I'd heard that sound in my sleep before, and I couldn't be sure if I was actually waking up or having a vivid memory of waking up from the vantage of some distant, half-asleep future. I'd lived this over and over again: coming awake to face a squat, burly man with black eyes set close together as if in deliberate imitation of the barrels of the sawed-off shotgun in his hands, which was raised to shoulder level and pointed at us. The first jolt of real fear that ran through me had the smooth, glaucous quality of memory also. All this worked to make me a little calmer than I might have been.

He said something in Spanish. Melanie looked up and screamed. The man yelled something and shook the gun. I put my hand over Melanie's mouth, but she'd already gotten the message and shut up. The man said something else, but I was frozen. I managed to say, "No habla. Please."

"Droo," he said, and I understood that. I stayed frozen. None of us moved for a long moment, like statues arranged around the grim centerpiece of the shotgun. Then he said something that I took to mean don't move and walked down the hall. There were no voices, no angry yells or screams of fear and protest. Just two muffled blasts, spaced calmly apart, the length of a musical rest. Then the man walked back into the room. At the front door he turned to us and mimed zipping his mouth closed, then raised his eyebrows. I nodded vigorously. He pointed the gun at us and made two firing noises from the back of his throat, like a boy in a war game. Then he left.

We didn't move. Melanie was breathing as if someone were sitting on her chest, and when I came back into myself I realized I was, too. I pulled her close to me. Then Saul came stumbling in. From the way he was walking, I expected to see blood streaming from his body somewhere. He was dazed, but as I looked him over he seemed uninjured.

"Let's get out of here," he said.

"What about Drew?"

Saul shook his head. "Let's just get out of here before the cops come."

I got up. Melanie was crying now, long low sobs straining at the back of her throat. "I'll be right back," I said. I went down the hall and through the door of Drew's room without really thinking about it. I've wished many times since that I'd thought about it, that I'd stopped myself. There he was. I didn't feel wise, or ennobled, as at Ayşe's bedside; I didn't feel any expansion of my world or distance from the incident as I had with my father's death. One shot had hit him in the side of his chest, the other in the face. There wasn't much of his head left. I leaned over and threw up, closed my eyes, and turned from the room, trying to shove the sight aside. But it was burned into me, and only became more vivid with time. Over the next few days I would try not to close my eyes, because all I could see in the darkness of my mind's eye was Drew's destroyed body.

We did as Saul said and got out quick. Gathered whatever we saw around that was ours and shoved it in bags. At the door, Saul said, "Either of you guys ever been arrested and fingerprinted?"

Melanie shook her head.

"No," I said.

"Good."

WE COULDN'T THINK of anywhere else to go, so we drove out to Red Rocks. There weren't many people there yet, only stragglers, homeless road-rats, and early birds getting the good spots to sell food or beer or clothing. Saul said we shouldn't tell anyone about what had happened, in case word got around. There was no need to be connected with it.

We had tickets, but somehow I couldn't see going to the show that night. Melanie and I walked around, looking for someone to buy our tickets. It was already getting warm in the spaces between the cool dry gusts off the mountains as we trudged back and forth on the switchbacked driveway leading up to the venue. Melanie was quiet. She looked puzzled. I took her hand and led her around like a child. It reminded me of Hampton and her bad trip. Everyone we encountered who needed tickets wanted them for free or offered us a few dollars. The people with money in their pockets hadn't shown up yet. I was about to give up trying to get face value for them when I looked up the road ahead of us and saw a familiar car—an old black BMW 2002—pulling into a parking space. It had a bright yellow license plate on it, and I thought it must be a different one, but as we neared it Randy climbed from the driver's door. Coming so suddenly upon his lanky figure, draped in a long black trench coat, on that morning felt like seeing an angel. I dropped Melanie's hand, and for a moment I even forgot about Drew and the scene in the apartment and just jogged toward him, smiling. A thin redheaded girl was getting out the other side of the car, and Randy's eyes were on her.

"Randy," I said.

When he looked at me his face remained blank for a second, then he said, "Jason."

We hugged. Sometimes a hug is real: long and tight but with no false injected energy, no sex, no trying, just the deep and powerful knowledge of friendship. We hadn't seen each other in over a year.

"How are you?" I said. My nose was running, and I wiped it on the shoulder of my shirt.

"I'm great. Things are good. Wow." He smiled and cuffed my head softly. "What about you?"

"I'm okay. Jesus, some shit has just gone down, though." I shook my head. Melanie was standing next to me now, and the redhead was standing next to Randy. "This is Melanie," I said. "Melanie, this is Randy."

"I remember Randy," she said.

We made introductions all around. Randy's girlfriend's name was Dana. They had met in Santa Fe, where they were in art school together. Both of them glowed with health, their faces burnished from days outdoors, their smiles easy and bright with love.

"You don't look so good," Randy said to me.

"Yeah, well, it's been a rough morning."

"What happened?"

"You don't want to know." I let my eyebrows drop and took on a grave expression. The idea of saying it out loud made me aware of a disjunction between what had happened and the reality I was moving through, a disjunction that was helping me function and might be broken by speaking the words. The thought came to me: *It really did happen.* Again the picture of Drew's body on the bed. It was probably still there. How long till someone found it?

"Why not? Was it something that bad?"

"Worse," I said.

"You're not talking about Judah, are you? I heard about that."

"Me too. No, something else."

The four of us sat on the ground by Randy's car, and I told him the story. It was hard. Telling it brought a wave of adrenaline on me, and I found it hard to maintain the grave expression that seemed necessary. My vision blurred a little, and I kept having to fight inappropriate smiles—which weren't smiles at all, but might have been misinterpreted.

"Was it a random break-in?" Randy asked when I was done.

"No, not at all. The guy even said Drew's name. I guess he

must have owed some serious money or ripped off the wrong people, or something."

"Jesus, Jason. Who are you hanging out with?"

It was these words that echoed in my head all the way back to California, along with the expression of concern and bafflement on Randy's face—an expression that was trying to reconcile the thought of a brutal murder with the idea of Dead tour. In my mind I was trying to keep the two separate instead of reconciling them: the murder had happened in Denver and had nothing to do with the tour. After Randy said that, a heavy gloom came over me, and I felt a great distance between us; I became afraid at the thought of all the mistakes I'd made, was making, would make. I imagined the progression of Drew's life: a succession of mistakes, errors in judgment, thoughtless acts, and weaknesses leading directly to that bloody, pointless end—and I felt a whole new fear, one that, in depth if not size or sharpness, dwarfed the fear I'd felt when faced with the barrels of the shotgun: the fear of change. It's one thing to consider change now and then, conceptually, but another completely to feel its urgency, its utter necessity, to realize at your core that it will have to be absolute. Nothing is more terrifying.

I knew Randy didn't see the distance between us the way I did. He urged me to go to the cops, and I just shook my head. I didn't try to defend the decision. "We need to get back to California," I said. We gave our tickets to him and Dana.

Randy gave me his number and said, "Anytime you want to get away, or whatever, come to Santa Fe. You're welcome anytime. Both of you."

Saul was supposed to meet Don in Telluride, so he found a ride and stayed on. Usually the way back from somewhere seems shorter, but this time it was interminable. Even at high speed, we seemed to crawl up over the Rockies, down onto the flat, across the

313

broad stretch of Utah and Nevada. I had enough dope to keep me comfortable for the trip, then I was going to kick. I swore it to myself, and to Melanie. This was not what I had signed up for. But I began to realize that I had never had any real notion of what I was signing up for; I was quick to sign when the first paragraph looked good, figuring I'd chalk the rest up to experience. Randy's words were still in my head: *Who are you hanging out with?* And the confusion in his eyes, as if he'd really been asking, *Who are you?*

WHEN WE GOT BACK, Harry had taken a turn for the worse. He stayed in the bedroom and kept the oxygen mask strapped constantly to his face, lifting it only to speak. When he did speak, it was clear he was still all there, but the effort was great and it hurt him, so he mostly lay still flipping channels with the remote. Sarah brought him soup, which he slurped from the bowl, his eyes keeping intense contact with the TV through the steam as if it were a beacon he was navigating by and at any moment might be lost in the fog.

I sat with him by his bed the afternoon we got back, watching a cable rebroadcast of a Senior PGA celebrity pro-am golf tournament. Harry managed a chuckle when a late-night talk show host shanked one into a lake. I offered to put on a CD for him if he wanted to listen to some music, take a break from the TV. He stayed silent for a moment, as if considering it, then dropped the remote and lifted a corner of the mask.

"No thanks," he rasped. "Music just ends up freaking me out." Through the hoarseness, I heard a quaver in his voice, and saw in his eyes when they flicked toward me an abyss that scared me back into silence. I had thought of telling him about Drew, but decided against it. We sat staring at the TV in silence, and I wanted to leave, but sensed Harry was glad I was there. I restrained myself from lighting a cigarette, and snorted when the celebrities made bad shots. Harry stopped making any sounds other than his shallow breathing, like an ailing Darth Vader, into the mask. When the tournament ended, I looked over and saw Harry had fallen asleep, so I tiptoed out.

My dope was gone, and I was resolved to kick. When the sickness started, I lay down, and Melanie came and sat with me.

"Is there anything I can bring you?" she asked. "Anything that might help?"

"Not really," I said.

She lay down with me and stroked my head. She brought me water and Coca-Cola. The sugar eased the discomfort a little at the beginning. By the time it got dark, things had started to get worse. "You should sleep in another room," I told her.

"You think?"

"Yeah, you don't want to deal with me all night." I didn't want to put her through a hellish night, but I was sort of hoping she would stay.

"Maybe you're right." She kissed my damp forehead and went down the hall to the other guest room. She wasn't the nursemaid type.

I was more strung out than I'd thought. I had moved beyond restlessness and chills. That night I sweated and shivered and puked—not the languid painless puke of the high, but bitter, stomach-wrenching heaves that continued even after there was nothing left to expel. In the middle of the night I dragged myself upstairs and went into Harry's bedroom, stepping through the door from silence into the slow hiss of the tank. Sarah was sleeping next to him on the king-size bed, but on top of the covers, with her own blanket. I went around the bed and shook her lightly.

"Sarah," I whispered, averting my rancid breath.

She opened her eyes smoothly, as if she'd been expecting me.

"Can I talk to you?"

She slipped from the bed and followed me into the hall. She closed Harry's door behind us.

"Are there any narcotics around?" I asked. "Just something to ease the transition, take the edge off, you know?" I was hugging myself and shivering.

"Narcotics aren't going to ease the pain, they'll only make it harder in the long run. You know that, right? Go downstairs and I'll bring you something, though."

I nodded, a little dejected. "Thanks."

She brought me two sleeping pills and a glass of water. I took them. She sat on the edge of my bed.

"You know Harry's real sick, right?"

I pulled the covers to my chin. "Yeah, I know."

"He won't go to the hospital. I'm not even sure a hospital would do any good right now. But you need to pull yourself through this. He loves you. I'm going to tell you straight, this could be it for him."

I didn't say anything.

"That doesn't mean he won't improve again. He could still last awhile. It's hard to tell."

I still didn't speak. I was struggling to keep the water I'd drunk down long enough to dissolve the pills, but Sarah misinterpreted my silence.

"I don't want to scare you or anything. I mean he'll probably be around for a good while, but you never know with these things is what I'm saying. Okay?"

I nodded and let out one syllable: "Mmm," and even that was

too much. I leaned over and retched into the bucket I'd put next to the bed. In the clear liquid I saw one of the pills, but not the other.

"Oh, no," Sarah said. She got up. "You'll be okay. Just get yourself through this." She went back upstairs. I felt a deep jealousy when I thought of the ease with which she would fall back asleep.

After what felt like an hour, I got up and took a towel out to the deck. I lifted the thermal cover on the hot tub and dipped my hand in. It was cool. Someone had turned it off. I went back inside, into the bathroom, and ran a very hot bath. It didn't put me to sleep, but at least in the hot water I felt I could relax a little. I kept running more hot to keep the temperature up, until I saw gray light through the small frosted window behind the toilet. I realized that the coming of day would bring no abatement of the sickness.

When it comes to addiction, decisions get made sometimes in a dim netherworld that has the advantage of admitting no emotion, no consideration, no reason. Those things may be just outside, pounding and screaming and carrying on, but the membrane is soundproof. A destination took shape in my head, and all else became pale and hollow, unimportant. I climbed out of the bath, dried off, dressed, and went out to the Mercedes.

BECAUSE OF THE COLOR OF THE LIGHT through the bathroom window, I had expected an overcast sky, but it was just that the sun hadn't crested yet, and the sky was blue-gray with its approach. By the time I reached the highway the sun was up. I'd forgotten my sunglasses, and my watery eyes stung at the brightness. The spectral tinting that distanced me from everything when I was high had been rudely pulled away, and now instead of being unable to connect with the sunlight, I felt stabbed by it. I had to shade my eyes with one hand as I drove, even though the sun wasn't shining directly at me. I switched hands on the wheel every minute or so, because my arms got shaky quickly, and I set the cruise control at the speed limit since it ached to keep my ankle steady on the gas.

I didn't really know where I was going, only the exit I needed to take. I figured I'd get there, find the place, then kill time until it was a decent hour. The trip spun by in a blur—the sleeping pill must have had some effect, because when I passed signs for Hayward, I didn't remember getting onto 880, and suddenly it was foggy. I was driving like a sleepwalker.

How I found it I don't know. I didn't even have a street name. I drove around the area for over an hour, my own haze compounded by the low fog which allowed only about two blocks' visibility. All I was looking for was that fresh white paint standing out amid all the peeling browns, fading whites, and rotting wood porches. It was a weekday and people were leaving for work, walking toward old cars in driveways, waiting at bus stops, plodding along sidewalks in sneakers with their work shoes in plastic bags swinging at their sides. I felt like something evil, corrupt, sliding quietly among them: my shirtsleeves were caked with mucus from wiping my running nose and watering eyes, and the side of the car was streaked with my crusted vomit and expectorations. People at the bus stops watched me pass, their heads swiveling slowly with me, their faces blank, vacant of the interest or disapproval that might have made me feel human. After a certain point, it stopped mattering how long it might take. I would have driven around that neighborhood all day, all week, eternally. It began to seem like my purgatory, as if maybe I needed to glide through that foggy ghetto with my stomach in knots for a few thousand years, to clear myself of sin before I could ascend.

I found it only when I thought I was starting to get too far from the highway and was thinking about working my way back. I turned a corner, thinking, This is it, I've gone too far, and there it was, in the middle of the block, shining like a pill dropped in the dirt. I pulled into the driveway behind a pale Oldsmobile. At the door I hesitated, making sure my face was clear of snot, running my hands through my matted hair, then rang the bell. Fifteen or twenty seconds went by. I was afraid to ring it again. Then I heard footsteps and the door opened.

"What the fuck?" was what Leon—I was pretty sure he was the one with the deep voice—said.

"Hey, remember me? I'm Jason, Saul's friend."

He looked at me flatly, as if trying to solve me.

"Remember? King Saul. Right?"

Another moment, then he hung his head and stepped aside to let me in. Two things happened as I passed through that doorway: first, anticipation of the drug kicked the withdrawal into high gear, and I gagged and started to sweat cold grease; and second, a dark flower of fear began to bloom at the back of my chest cavity, near my spine, its edges fizzing with electricity. Before he closed the door, I saw him crane his neck to see the car in the driveway.

He put a finger to his lips and walked in front of me. He led me not to the living room we'd been in before, but to a smaller room closer to the door, where there was a TV and the remnants of a late-night pizza. He pointed to a chair and shut the door behind us. I sat down.

"Mama's still sleeping," he said. "What you need?"

"I don't know," I said. "Just a little something."

He fixed me with a look of exasperation. "First you show up in the morning," he pointed a finger at me. "Don't tell me you came in here without enough money. You know we don't do nothing less than five hundred. You want less you can get it on the street. Tell me you have five hundred or walk, motherfucker."

I nodded. "I have it." I had that much in my pocket, and another five hidden under the seat in the car. "Five hundred then, okay."

"You ain't going to get it right away, 'cause we still got to re-up in a while. And it's going to be white dope this time, not tar. But I can get you a little tar now to get you straight, so you don't go puking all over the furniture."

The door handle turned and it opened. It was Lionel, looking in. "Who you talking to?" he squeaked. He was without his ascot, and I saw why he wore it, and probably why he spoke the way he did: an ugly, puffy scar all the way across the base of his neck like a malicious smile, where someone had once cut his throat. He saw me and said, "What the fuck?"

"Go get this boy something to get him straight," said Leon.

"What we running here, a fucking clinic? What the fuck is he doing in here?"

"We'll set him straight on the rules later. Right now he needs a hit or he's going to mess up the rug."

"He won't mess up the rug if he's not in the motherfucking house!"

Leon stepped close to his brother. "Well, he is in the house. Now shut up before you wake Mama." He put his mouth to Lionel's ear and whispered, "Just go get it." I saw his hand on Lionel's shoulder, squeezing slightly. Lionel nodded and closed the door.

Leon sat down and turned on the TV, a morning talk show. We sat watching it. I was having trouble focusing. Some asshole guest was ranting about how we could turn our lives completely around in a matter of seconds, just by having a positive outlook. His name was something that sounded like Platypus. He was getting all worked up about it, smiling and pointing his finger into the camera. "Be happy *now!*" he kept yelling. I wanted to climb through the screen and kick him in the face. I wanted to watch him spitting teeth and blood. Ten minutes later Lionel came back in carrying a capped syringe already filled with light brown liquid. "Got your fix for you, little boy," he said. He set it in front of me on the table. "All ready to go. Even threw in a little coke for you, as a early Christmas present."

I picked up the needle and uncapped it. I looked at it for a few seconds. "This is a clean needle, right?" I asked.

"What you think, we gone give you motherfucking AIDS?" Lionel laughed. "Go ahead, man."

"Well, I . . ." I looked at Leon, but he was watching the TV. I looked back at Lionel. "I've never really done this to myself before."

He shook his head. "You ain't even a good junkie. Well I ain't Mama, and I ain't gone do it for you. You have to figure it out. Just put it in the vein, pull back on the thing to see if blood comes in. If it does, you in, if not, pull out and get the air outta there and go again." He snorted, as if he were disgusted with himself for even giving me that much help, and left the room. Leon took some napkins from next to the pizza box and tossed them in my lap.

"Don't get blood on anything," he said.

I got it on the first try. Slid the needle horizontally into the vein of my left arm the way I'd seen nurses do it to me when they drew blood, pulled the plunger back a hair and in came a curling of dark blood like a red bean sprout. I pushed the plunger slowly in, pulled the needle out, and blood trickled down my arm. I barely got the napkins pressed to the spot before the whole world froze and fluttered and whitened, like stuck film just before it burns through. They had killed me, I realized distantly, with the last still-thinking cluster of cells in my brain. They'd given me a hot shot and soon I'd be meat in the trunk of that Oldsmobile. I was jetted upward, riding a muscular, godlike waterspout that seemed destined to force me right out of my body. But even the fear of dying was annihilated in the rush. Everything was annihilated. I threw myself open, laid myself bare to it. I was flesh, skeleton, pleasure, stretched veins and sinew, eyeball jelly, toenails, love, gristle, enzymes, electricity, purring atoms, and I was peeling away from all that, cell by cell becoming discarnate. Death was splendid.

When the coke rush subsided, instead of crashing to earth I was set down in the warm flow of the heroin high, which had been there all along, like groundwater bubbling from miles deep. I was probably not going to die. I felt no relief, since fear had already left me, but only a kind of detached interest at my ongoing existence and a mild, underlying disappointment. I tried to scratch my nose, but my hand came only halfway up before falling again to my side. Then I nodded out.

Leon was shaking me. How long had passed? Not more than a few seconds, it seemed.

"Let's go. We've got to leave." He shook me again. "Let's go. You got to come back a little later. You can't stay here."

I said, "Yeah, okay," but couldn't push myself up off the couch. My vision was impaired by my eyelids.

"Shit," he said. "Help me with this boy. He's coming along."

"Help you?" came Lionel's squeak. "What's he weigh, three or four pounds?"

Leon grabbed my arm and pulled me to my feet. His grip felt vague in my shoulder area, and it was like being under remote control. I knew if he let me go I would collapse. I hoped he knew it, too.

"Where are we going?" I asked. Leon just dragged me toward the front door. "Where are we going?" I asked again.

"What? You saying something?"

"Let me take his car," Lionel said.

He was going through my pockets roughly, and it felt like a rape.

"Hold still," said Lionel. "Look at this. Motherfucker's got a blade. What you gone do with this? Cut someone?" He was holding up Ted's knife. I'd forgotten I had it. He unfolded the blade. "Looks like maybe you already did. Didn't clean it off too good, did you?" He closed it and shoved it back in my pocket. "Man, Leon, the kind of people you let in here."

I heard the car keys jingle. Lionel walked out the door in front of us. I tried to check my pocket to see if he'd taken my money, but Leon had my right arm and my left wouldn't reach.

"I'd like to know where you're taking me," I said.

"Man, quit mumbling. You ain't saying nothing."

I repeated myself, this time concentrating on hearing my own words, but could make out only a kind of polysyllabic moan. I guessed it had to be my voice.

He loaded me into the backseat of the Oldsmobile. The vinyl felt cool and beautiful on my face. I managed to sit up and lean against the door. Leon got behind the wheel and started the engine. He turned to look at me.

"Listen, we are going to pick up some other guys and re-up from some people. You just stay in the car and keep your mouth shut. You got it?" My eyes had drifted away from him and closed on me, so I couldn't see his expression. "Yeah," he said. "You feelin' fine. Just chill."

We backed out of the driveway. The car was in motion for a few minutes, then the doors opened and men were talking. I opened my eyes. A tall thin guy with very dark, blue-black skin was sitting in the seat in front of me talking to Leon. "Who the fuck is this?" he asked.

"Just some baggage. Don't worry about him."

I heard breathing and realized someone else was sitting in the seat next to me. I looked over. It was a white guy, small and muscled and unshaven, brown hair buzzed to within a millimeter of his skull. He turned toward me and nodded once. His eyes were like gray pebbles.

The car was moving again. "You guys make it home all right last night?" Leon asked.

"Yeah," said the guy in front. "We was good boys and took a cab. That was some funny shit."

They had all been out drinking the night before. Leon and the guy in front started laughing about various things they remembered. They talked about a barmaid they'd liked.

"Man, that chick was all about my shit," said the guy.

Leon laughed. "Oh you poor trippin' motherfucker. The sad thing is you really believe that shit."

"Damn right I do."

Leon laughed again. "She was one beautiful thing."

"Oh, man! The things I would do with that. I spend so long up that ass you'd have to forward my mail. I wanted to put her in the trunk and take her home." The guy started banging on the roof of the car and screaming through a cupped hand, simulating the sounds the woman would make trapped in the trunk. He kept doing it over and over, and each time he and Leon laughed harder and harder.

"I bet she takes mammoth shits." It was the white guy. His voice was a little nasal and had a precise, college-educated kind of enunciation. He had a demented grin on his whiskery face. He was looking back and forth between Leon and the other guy. They stopped laughing.

"What?" said the other black guy.

Leon went back to staring silently at the road.

"What kind of shit is that?" said the black guy, looking at the white guy. "That ain't right, man. You need some help. What the fuck did you say?"

The white guy shook his head, still grinning. "Nothing."

The black guy turned back around, saying, "Man, you just ruined my appetite."

I nodded out again.

They were dragging me out of the car, and I hit my head on the door frame. I barely felt it, but the sound was like a block of wood being hit with a rock. Someone said, "Woops" and laughed. Then I was being loaded into the backseat of the Mercedes. I had enough motor control to go along with them, but not to fight them.

"This his car?"

"Yeah, I guess so."

"Shit."

"You wait here. We'll be back."

"Why you cartin' this guy around?"

"Yeah, why are we?"

"Shut up."

The door closed. I heard the motor of the Olds as it pulled away. I sat up, was mostly awake now. I looked out the windows; the neighborhood had noticeably improved. It was suburban. We could have been on the outskirts of Daly City or Hayward. The houses were all small and well kept and close together. I checked my pocket and my money was still there. Suddenly I didn't feel like waiting for them. I got out, went around, and climbed into the driver's seat. But no keys. I checked my pockets again. Looked around on the floor, in the glove box, under the visor. No keys.

I sat back and tried to think. It was slow going. Each thought stretched out like an ocean. Why would they take the keys? A mistake? Maybe Lionel just shoved them in his pocket without thinking. Or some other reason, something I wasn't thinking of. Wild thoughts started forming, more quickly than the others. I considered abandoning the car and walking away. But that would be the end of Harry's car. If they wanted to kill me, wouldn't they have done it already? Maybe they were debating that issue right now, what to do with me, how to get my money and the car and get rid of me. They wouldn't have to kill me to get it. But this was my life. I tried to use the car phone, but it wouldn't work without the key. In the end the fear gathered force and took over. It got to where the only thing keeping me there was the value of the Mercedes, and I wasn't going to die for a car. I pulled the rest of the money from under the seat, then got out and started to walk. I didn't know where I was headed, just moving in the direction opposite from where I thought they'd gone.

Hands jammed in my pockets, sneakers thumping pavement, hair blowing across my face, I moved forward. I was keeping an eye out for a pay phone so I could call Harry's, maybe get Melanie to bring me an extra key for the Mercedes in Sarah's car. But the streets were residential. I made a few turns, when it was obvious there were no businesses ahead of me, and kept passing white and beige little houses. A guy working on a black GTO, the hood up, looked at me as I passed.

"Nice car," I said.

He nodded, then after a second said, "Thanks."

I stopped. "Any chance I could use your phone?"

He stood up straight and put his hands on his hips. In one of them was a big crescent wrench. "I don't think so."

"Can you tell me where we are?"

He just looked at me. "You better move on, buddy."

I continued walking. I wondered if he'd call the cops. It seemed unlikely. At the next intersection I tried to remember which direction the sun had been in when I started walking. When in doubt, make a left, I told myself. I made a left. More of the same, houses, little yards, driveways. Once again I was lost in a residential purgatory. Maybe I had just moved up a notch to a slightly higher level of purgatory from the one I had been in earleir in the day: in this one the houses were nicer, the streets cleaner, the visibility better, and I wasn't sick. But I was on foot. I turned over in my mind what these differences might mean—it all meant something at times like this. A small white dog crossed the street thirty yards in front of me, its presence highlighting the lack of people. I watched it, and when it saw me it stopped for a second, then came trotting up to me. It seemed like a good sign. It stood about eight inches high, with curly white hair that was caked with damp mud around its mouth and throat. Its tongue fell out and it began to pant, reminding me of Harry trying to catch his breath. I leaned down and petted it, ruffling its ears. The dog liked that, and pressed against my hand, licking me. Then I smelled it. What was caked on its fur was not mud, but shit. I pulled my hand away and stood up, sniffing it. It smelled bad enough to be human shit. The dog retreated a few feet as if it sensed the idea of kicking it crossing my mind. "Oh, very funny," I said, and kept walking, wiping my hand on my shirt. The dog didn't follow me.

Most of the parked cars around were sitting in driveways, not on the street, so I noticed the Mercedes right away when I saw it up the block. The Olds was idling next to it, brake lights glowing. I stopped walking. The reverse lights on the Olds came on, and the car whined toward me. It rocked to a halt next to me and Lionel rolled down the passenger-side window. He had on a purple ascot tucked into a yellow silk shirt.

"What the fuck are you doing?"

I had forgotten about his voice, and the nasal squeak took me by surprise.

"Um, nothing," I said.

"Nothing?"

"Looking for a phone."

There was a woman watching two small children playing on a lawn down the block, and that made me feel safer.

"Yeah well we got your shit, so get in here."

"You have my keys?"

"Yeah I got your keys. Get the fuck in here."

"Look, I just want to leave. Okay?"

"What?" The expression on his face—one eye squinted, mouth set straight—reminded me suddenly of my father when he was trying to work out a problem in his head.

I decided on a bold front. "Just give me the keys, man."

"We didn't get you straight and cart you around as a motherfucking charity venture. Now get the fuck in here and buy this shit." He turned to Leon, who was driving. "I thought you said this faggot had money."

"Leave it," said Leon. "Just give him his keys and let's go."

"Fuck if I do!" He looked back at me. "You ain't getting no fucking keys till you get in this motherfucking car and show me that motherfucking money."

I peered through the back window and saw the white guy looking at me coldly, and the other guy looking forward, up the block, at the woman and her kids. I didn't want to die.

"Fine," I said, and started walking away from them toward the Mercedes. "I'll get another key."

I heard the car door open behind me, and then I was pulled backward by my hair. It felt as if the earth jumped out from under me. "Too fucking much," he said. His voice sounded like some crazy dwarf in a movie. Except he was twice my size. I landed on my tailbone and was slapped across the face almost immediately. The white guy was holding my arms down, and Lionel was going through my pockets. He pulled the thousand dollars out. "Well here it is. Looks like more than five bills. Tell you what," he slapped me again and it hurt, even through the heroin. "I'm going to keep the rest for your bullshit. A little fee for my trouble."

"Hey," said the white guy. "He smells like shit."

"Lionel," Leon was saying from in the car, "get back in here. Get your ass back in here."

Lionel stood up and got in—from ground level I saw one solid, fat thigh in blue slacks lift itself in, and one black Reebok sneaker, before the door slammed. The white guy let go of my arms and climbed in back. "I mean not just bad," he was saying, "but like actual shit."

"Do not come back to see us, asshole," squeaked Lionel.

Something landed on my chest and they screeched away. The pain in my left hand was sudden and I confused it with emotion for a second—thought I was having a pang of guilt and fear and depression, which maybe I was—but I pulled my arm over in front of my face and saw that my hand was bleeding. I flexed it, and the fingers moved strangely, stiff and misaligned. It had gotten caught under the tire when they peeled out. The longer I looked at it, the worse it looked. *Mangled*, was the word that popped into my head. The backs of the knuckles were laid bare, bone showing through on the middle one, and the fingers were skewed, the pinkie actually turned ninety degrees to the inside, its nail missing altogether.

"Are you all right?"

It was the woman from the yard. She had one child in her arms, and the other, older one by the hand.

"Yeah," I said. "No problem." I rolled to my side and pushed into a sitting position. As she took in my appearance, I saw her realize that she had brought her children into a crime scene. She squeezed the child in her arm tighter and took a step back.

"You're hurt."

"Yes, I am." I was looking around me on the ground, and I saw the key to the Mercedes a couple of feet off.

"I'll call 911," she said, backing away.

"No, my car's right here. I'll drive myself to the hospital." As I was crawling over to the key, I noticed the bag of white powder to its left. I sat back on my heels and picked both up with my right hand. My left hand I kept cradled near my stomach. It was shaking violently, and the shakes were threatening to spread into my body. I stood up, listed to the left, and almost fell, but got straightened out and turned to face her, saying, "Don't worry. I'm going to be fine," but she was already running back to her house, carrying both children now.

I NEEDED A HOSPITAL, but I didn't even know where I was. In a haze of pain and heroin I made my way east. My hand wouldn't stop shaking. I rested it in my lap, but there was no comfortable way to hold it. I felt hot and turned on the air-conditioning. Once I found the highway, I drove past the southbound entrance and made a left to go north. I didn't think about it—was just suddenly headed north. I was still quite high. I pressed the buttons on the CD changer until Steely Dan came on, the cheery-sad strains of "Black Cow." I listened to the whole *Aja* album, and it fit my world so well—raising my outlook up a notch ("Chiii-nese music always sets me free")—that I started to feel better. Life was complex, dark, significant, gorgeous, rhythmic, and one needed to experience it, all of it, with passion, dive deep into all its crevices. I sailed north, the music loud. "Home at Last," with its Homeric allusions, started blazing from the speakers ("Well the danger on the rocks is surely past / Still I remain tied to the mast / Could it be that I have found my home at last?"), and as I moved north, fog materialized again; in its bright ambience, as if the sun had melted and whitened and taken over the whole atmosphere, I could see everything that was happening to me as beautiful, necessary.

I drifted past the other cars on the road as if they were standing still, the people in them locked only in an illusion of motion. None of them had mangled hands, or hard drugs pumping in their veins. They all had plans, places to be, things to attend to. None of them lived life as the spontaneous odyssey it was meant to be. I looked at them as they slid slowly backward past me, their bored faces. None of them allowed danger into their lives. In fact their lives were devoted almost completely to minimizing danger in one form or another, I could see that. I thought of Odysseus having himself tied to the mast so he could listen to the sirens. I felt a kinship with him. There were those who would plug their ears, and those who couldn't resist the opportunity of hearing something so beautiful, no matter how painful or dangerous it might be. I sped up, weaving smoothly across lanes, between trucks, owning the road at ninety-five, invincible. I opened the bag of dope, steadying the wheel with my bad hand, dipped the corner of a matchbook in, and snorted a bump.

101 took me into the city. Soon, in front of me, the Bay Bridge rose up like a monster out of the fog, its far side invisible. I headed for it. It wasn't until I passed the Treasure Island exit, in the middle of the bridge, that I knew where I was going.

THE HOUSE WAS LIGHT GREEN, an almost translucent color that blended into the misty air. I felt I ought to have been able to see right through it. I sat in the car, pulled to the grassy curb, idling. It wasn't morning anymore. Rare for the fog to stick around so late into the day in Berkeley. I picked up the car phone, turned it on, and flipped through my address book.

"Hello." Her voice was a little rough, as if she'd just woken up.

"Did I wake you?"

"No. Who is this?"

"It's Jason."

"Jason? Your voice sounds weird."

"I'm on a car phone."

"No, that's not it. It's lower or something. You just sound different."

"I want to come visit you."

A pause. "When?"

"Right now."

"Where are you?"

"Close."

"Um, okay. How close?"

"Look out your window," I said.

Jane's moonlike face appeared in the upstairs window of the house, from behind a thin flowered drape.

"See the Mercedes?"

"Yeah. Jesus. Hi there."

"So can I come up?"

"Come on up." She broke the connection.

I snorted more heroin before getting out of the car. As I walked to the door my hand throbbed, but the pain was receding—not

332

away from me, but deeper into me. There was the unsettling awareness that it wasn't shrinking. It was like a piece of wood, pulled deep underwater by some rope, but still straining toward the surface. Maybe if I kept it under long enough it would get waterlogged.

"Oh my god!" Jane said when I came through the door to her apartment at the top of the steps. She ran to me, and one of her beautiful arms went around my waist, as if she thought I might fall.

"I'm okay. I'm fine," I said, but leaned into her a little because it felt good. Her hand was on the back of my neck, and I realized my hair was still damp from all the sweating I'd done. I went to her plaid thrift-store love seat and sat down carefully. Then she saw my hand.

"Oh my god!" she said again.

"You're going to have to stop saying that." I held my hand palm up close to me, to hide the worst of it.

"What happened? Oh god, it looks bad."

"Someone ran over my hand in a car."

"You need a hospital."

"What I need right now is a bath."

"You do kind of smell like shit," she said.

"So I've been told."

"Worse than shit, actually. Like shit combined with other bad things."

"Okay," I waved my good hand. "We've established that."

"Are you drunk? You sound drunk. Jason, let me drive you to the emergency room."

"Please," I said. "Please just run me a bath."

She looked at me for a second the way my mother used to when I was a child and I'd done something particularly upsetting and unexplainable, for which there was no excuse. Then she went into the bathroom.

"Jane," I called after her. "You are really . . ." I heard the water start running, and after a moment she came back out. I said, "The most beautiful woman I've ever been with."

"Yeah, yeah."

"Come over here. Sit with me."

She shook her head and smiled. "Maybe after you've had your bath. Right now you smell like shit."

"It's not mine, you know."

"What?"

"The shit. There was this little dog. I petted it, and it was covered with shit."

"What about the puke on your shirtfront, and the stuff around your mouth?"

"Oh. That's mine."

Jane nodded sagely from her chair across the room. "And then someone ran over your hand."

"Right. The funny thing is, I'm pretty sure it was a mistake."

Her eyes widened. "Pretty sure? You mean someone was trying to hurt you?"

"Well, kind of. But the hand thing I don't think they meant."

"Why were they trying to hurt you?"

I got up and walked toward the bathroom. "You know, that's an interesting question. They did steal five hundred dollars from me. But they could have stolen a thousand and didn't. I'm pretty sure it was my fault, in a way, now that I think about it. I was kind of freaking out. Help me get my shirt off."

She got me undressed and helped me into the bath. Then she sat on the toilet and looked into my eyes. Her look turned a little sideways and she nodded as if she'd just gotten something. "You're high on dope. Look at you."

I was slowly submerging my bad hand in the hot water, and I winced as it brought slivers of pain to the surface.

"Are you deep in?"

"Fairly deep."

"Let me see that hand." She took my forearm and lifted it out of the water, taking her first close look. "God, Jason," she turned away, "I can't even look at it." She looked at it again. "It's really bad. No joke. You need a doctor."

When I was clean she gave me a T-shirt with a picture of Donald Duck on it and a clean rag to wrap my hand in and helped me back into my jeans. But when she tried to get me out the door I wandered into her bedroom and lay down on the bed. She pleaded with me, shook me, pulled at me.

"Just lie down with me for a few minutes," I said. "Please. I need that."

"Five minutes," she said. "And then we go?"

"Yes, yes, yes."

She stretched out next to me. I put my head on her shoulder. It felt so good. "Oh, god, you're so beautiful," I said. She draped a long cool hand across my face.

"You know," I said, feeling everything should be understood, "I don't love you."

She pushed some hair off my face. "I know."

A minute went by.

"You did, though, didn't you? Before?"

"Yeah, I guess I did. At the beginning."

"I messed it up with you," she said. "It could have gone differently if I'd just known what I was looking for from the start."

Another minute.

"Remember Judah?" I asked.

"Yeah, with the turtle shell."

"He died at Red Rocks."

"Oh no." She was still stroking me, but sounded genuinely upset. "How?"

"That's the worst part of it. It's too stupid. I can't even say it. He drowned, that's all."

"That's awful."

"And this guy we were staying with in Denver died, too. He was murdered."

"Jesus. Who are you hanging out with?"

"Good question." I was having trouble telling the difference between her body and the dope high cushioning me. I ran my good hand along her side, felt the swell of her hip, that holy place, under her baggy silk pants (I remembered her dancing in them at the Kaiser), slid up along her stomach and pinched a nipple.

"Don't do that."

The nipple was hard, but I stopped.

"I have a son, you know. I'm a *father*."

She didn't speak.

"It's true. His name is Jason. Little Jason. Isn't that nice?"

"Come on. Time to go."

I kept my head on her, and she didn't move. "Isn't that nice?" I asked again.

"Who's the mother?"

"Oh, just some girl. Her name is Fern. She lives in Oregon with a Hindu god, that's all I know." I put my hand between her legs, and she crossed them. I propped myself on the elbow of my bad hand and rolled on top of her. I kissed her neck, swooned over the freckles there, licked them. A hint of patchouli lingered, creating innumerable concert halls in my mind—more holy places— and I was almost there, I dug my face into her neck, inhaled her kinky hair, tunneling into the beautiful past. Her breast fit perfectly in my hand. "I love you," I whispered to her skin.

"What are you doing?"

I pulled back and looked at her. I kissed her lips, and she responded, then pushed my face away.

I sat up, still on top of her.

Something came across her face. I tried to read it. Then she punched me in the gut. As I doubled over I fell onto the bad hand and screamed, though the pain was distant.

"I'm sorry," she said, sliding out from under my leg and standing up. "Oh god, I'm sorry."

I rolled onto my back, cradling the wrapped hand to my chest and breathing hard.

"Come on," she said. "I'll take you to the hospital."

I stood up, detaching myself from both pains. They were like great ships moving away from the dock, steam horns blasting. I waved to them, inwardly. "I can get myself there."

I went into the living room and sat on the love seat. Jane followed me. I pulled the dope out and dumped some onto the table, pushed it into a line with the edge of a magazine. I tore a strip off the cover of the magazine and rolled it up, then snorted the line. It was maybe a little too much.

"You're going to drive after that?" Jane asked as I went to the door.

"Yes. Yes I am."

She tried to talk me out of it, but I didn't feel like being in a hospital right then, so I didn't give in.

"Fine," she said. "But don't come crying to me if you die in a wreck."

After a second, we both laughed at that. I looked at her and smiled, but had the feeling the smile looked somewhat gruesome.

"I won't." I patted my pocket to make sure the key was there. "See you," and I went out the door.

As I descended the stairs to the vestibule, sliding along the wall with my good shoulder, a black canvas Chinese shoe hit the back of my head. I turned around. She was standing there with one shoe on.

"What's with all the domestic abuse?"

She gave a difficult little laugh, then took off the other shoe and threw it at me. It curved in the air and missed. "I hate you," she said.

"Don't hate me because I'm beautiful," I said.

She laughed, then started crying.

I said, "I'll call you," and walked out the door.

3

I GOT BACK, through dreams and delusions, windows rolled down and music blasting to keep me from nodding out, drifting in and out of reality, going thirty miles an hour when the road became curvy. At one point I imagined I was in the passenger seat and Harry was driving me to the airport; I was flying home to help my mother through some unnamed difficulty, and to enroll in college—the delusion was quite complete; Harry said something to me, which sounded like "You never know with squanderers," and it felt important that I understand what he meant. It was hard to know whether this delusion, and others, happened in real time, or whether they were retrospective dreams, false memories of delusions created by my wandering brain.

But I got back, and Harry was gone. Sarah was in the living room, fielding phone calls. She just looked at me, said something into the phone, and hung up. "Jason," she said. "Harry's gone."

"Gone?"

"He died this morning."

Melanie was yelling at me. Where the hell had I been? I started apologizing, over and over, and could think of nothing else to say. I stumbled back into Harry's bedroom. The bed was made, perfectly, stretched smooth and tight as a blank canvas. They were both following me. It took a few minutes for them to notice my hand, wrapped in the white rag, blood showing through on the back like the map of some new continent. I had been watching the stain grow the whole way down.

WHEN WE GOT TO THE HOSPITAL, I was looked at by an Indian doctor. "We will get you stitched right up, good as new," he said as he unwrapped the rag. His accent was very light, barely there at all. When he saw the hand, he said, "Oh my. This is serious. You might need surgery." He looked at it closely. "How long ago did this happen?"

"I don't know. Eight hours. Or maybe four." The heroin was wearing off, and the hand hurt badly now.

"You should have come sooner."

Melanie was sitting in the corner of the room, not saying anything.

"Is this where they brought Harry?" I asked her.

She shrugged. "I'm not sure."

"Do they bring bodies here?" I asked the doctor.

"Bodies? What do you mean?"

"Like when someone dies. Do they bring them here?"

"Sometimes, yes. Why?"

"I have a friend, Harry Waldron, who died today. I was wondering if he might be here."

"He died in the accident that caused this?"

"No. Completely unrelated."

"Well, I could check for you." He put my hand on the metal tray in front of me, which was covered with white paper. "Leave this here. Don't move it. I'll get a nurse to clean it up, then we'll need some X rays. I'll ask about your friend. What was the name again?"

I told him.

"All right." He shook his head. "You've had a hell of a day, haven't you."

He walked out. A minute later he stuck his head in and said, "I'm sorry, your friend was not brought here," then popped back out, like a bad-news cuckoo clock. Melanie came over and sat next to me on the bed. She put her arm around me, rubbing my shoulder. It was the first touch she'd given me since I got back. I started crying, which took me by surprise. The tears were happening in another place, and the grief was like a newborn pterodactyl inside me, straining at its amniotic sac, trying to stretch out its bony wet wings and crack its still-soft beak to make its first squawk, after which there would be no silencing it. I clamped my teeth shut and spoke through them, "Please stop."

"It's okay," she said, still rubbing.

I shook my head. "Please." Tears were flowing more freely now. I had to do something.

"Don't worry," she said, touching my neck.

I lifted my hand up and smashed the back of it down onto the tray. I think I screamed before I passed out.

THEY CLEANED ME UP and sent me home that night. My surgery was scheduled for the next morning. My mother would also arrive the following day, to make Harry's arrangements. No one took my dope from me, and I was still doing it. In fact, the doctor gave me some pain pills that I stashed away for a rainy day. Melanie left me alone in front of the TV, going into the bedroom to watch with Sarah. I stared at Harry's big screen for a while, then went downstairs to do a line, and after that continued down into the basement. I dug around among the boxes until I found the one marked "Summer 1960," which I still hadn't looked at. I slit the old tape on the box with my fingernail.

The photo on top, if I'd found it in the street, I would not have recognized as my mother. She was leaning back against a low, ornate stone parapet, sunlight bright behind her but her smiling features still clear. Wind was making a wild pennant of her hair. I'd seen pictures of her as a young woman before, and of my parents' wedding, but this seemed to be a different person. She was glowing with happiness and had an untamed mischief in her eyes. It wasn't just a picture of my mother as a young woman, it was a picture of a girl I would have loved to meet, someone I could have had fun with, fallen in love with, and it surprised me—as with the top picture in the other box, where my father looked so unbelievably cool. It occurred to me that both of them had had their freest, most golden times with Harry, that they had each gotten something from him they couldn't get from each other.

I flipped through the photos. Only a few were of places I recognized: the Spanish Steps, the Colosseum. One outside a church made me think of a story my mother loved to tell, of she and James and I being turned away from St. Peter's Cathedral by a nun because her dress was too short, and how humiliated she'd been, then on the way down the steps realizing I wasn't beside her, and turning around to see me (age five) back at the top, my fists raised to the nun, trying to box her.

Most of the pictures were taken on little cobbled side streets or inside small bars and restaurants. There were quite a few in the same bar, with the same regulars, all lifting drinks toward the camera, mouths open in song or toast. All of them had my mother in them, but there were none of Harry, who was behind the camera. In one, she was reclined luxuriously on a tiny bed in a clean white room that must have been their room in the pensione; she was wearing a simple short-sleeved blouse and loose canvas pants, her feet bare, and a cigarette hung languorously from her lips, her eyes looking away from the camera and glowing in the light from a window outside the frame. I stared at the photo for a long time, until it seemed I had been in the room when it was taken, as if it were a little motel somewhere on Dead tour instead of a pensione in Rome.

At the bottom, finally, there was a picture of them together, taken outside the bar they had frequented. Harry was in a soft dark blazer and my mother in a flowered summer dress. She was smiling, and he was maintaining the stoic seriousness of a young artist. His face struck me as familiar. Something in the wide high cheekbones and the eyes. All at once, it hit me. I'd known Harry all my life and I'd never seen it. Maybe it was seeing him so young, and standing next to her, the two of them together (I realized I had seen them in the same room only a handful of times). But now, looking back and forth between their faces, it was clear. Harry's face was James's. Or James's was Harry's, with minor softenings around the edges—his cheekbones wider and a little less sharp, his eyes rounder but, now that I thought of it, the same hazel color. The thing that shocked me most was that I had never noticed it before.

I closed the box and put it back on the stack. The basement had an exterior door, which let out at the side of the house, and I unlocked it and went out. I turned right and walked out onto the lawn. I crossed the expanse of dark grass to the other side, where knotty trees bordered the property. The sky was clear, but the moon was not up yet, or had already gone down. I stopped be-

"Jason," she called from down the hall. "Is that you?"

"In here, Mom."

She walked in smiling, but bearing appropriate levels of gravity in her face and gait. "Oh, sweetie, look at you," she said as she hugged me. My hand was encased in a more elaborate splint, which held each finger in a specific position and immobilized my wrist, and I kept it elevated, embracing her with my right arm.

"Mom, this is Melanie."

"I'm so glad to meet you, Melanie." She noticed and assimilated Melanie's missing arm in one quick, uneasy flick of her eyes. She held out her right hand and Melanie took it in her left.

"Same here, Mrs. Burke."

"Call me Elizabeth. Let's have some lunch."

I said, "I'm not hungry."

"I'm starved," said Melanie.

"Are you too tired to sit with us, Jason?" my mother asked.

"Not at all." I didn't quite like the thought of my mother having Melanie alone.

Sarah came in, and we sat together quietly, a little stiffly, while the three of them ate sandwiches and I drank a glass of lemonade from a powdered mix. It was strange to see my mother sitting on that sofa, right in Harry's old spot.

"So, Melanie, where is your family?"

"In New York."

"Same as me. And how do they feel about what you're doing?"

"Here we go," I said.

"It's a perfectly reasonable question." She looked back at Melanie, smiling.

"They don't exactly approve."

"No. Well that's too bad."

"How do you feel about it, Mom?"

She had her answer ready. "I just wish you had some perspective on it. It's one thing to be carefree for a while, but at a certain point you need to start building a life. This Grateful Dead thing can't go on forever. There are compromises that can be made. Just because you go to college or get a job doesn't mean you can never see another concert, or take a vacation and see a few. But this constant obsession, it just baffles me."

"I can see how it would."

"There's no need to be rude."

"I wasn't. I was being understanding."

"You were being patronizing."

"You get what you pay for."

She speared a mayonnaise-smeared chunk of potato and raised it to her mouth. "I refuse to escalate this," she said, and ate it.

I WAS STILL OUT OF IT from the medication they'd given me and the heroin I'd snorted before leaving for the hospital, and after lunch I went downstairs for a nap. I woke to a distantly familiar sensation, a gentle pull toward the edge of the bed. I opened my eyes and looked at my mother, sitting on the bed near me. Outside the windows, behind her head, it was last light. She reached out and laid her hand on my forehead. Its coolness, the same bygone concern in her face, the sudden invasion of this childhood scene as if I'd been granted another chance and this time things would be different, almost set me crying. I turned on my side, resting the bad hand gingerly along my body. The pain was starting to seep through.

"Hi," I said.

"How are you feeling?" she asked.

"I'm okay."

She placed her hand on my arm, just above the splint. "How did this happen?"

"It was an accident."

"What kind of accident?"

"I was looking for something under a car, and the guy behind the wheel didn't know it and hit the gas. The tire spun out on my hand."

She nodded. "Ouch."

I smiled at her. "You got that right."

She had on a soft white cable-knit cardigan, and she took her hand away from me and pulled the sweater tighter around herself. "Jason, we need to talk. Maybe when you wake up a little, we could sit down and talk about some things."

"Sure, Mom."

"I'll be upstairs." She stood and walked out, closing the door behind her.

I let a few minutes go by, my eyes open but unseeing, then rolled from the bed and pulled a pair of shorts on. I picked up the bottle of prescription painkillers from the dresser and looked at it, shook it, heard the rattle of pills inside, put it down. I dug into the pocket of my jeans and found my packet of heroin. I dumped a small line onto the dresser and snorted it. My hand was throbbing, so I snorted a little more.

I went upstairs and found my mother sitting out on the deck. Night was encroaching, she had a drink in her hand. She faced in, toward the house, which seemed unnatural with the dusky valley stretched out behind her. "What are you drinking?" I asked.

"Gin and tonic."

"Think I'll have one, too." I went back to the bar by the kitchen and made myself a weak gin and tonic. Both were recently purchased, since the bar had been barren for weeks.

347

"Should you be drinking that on top of your pain pills?" she asked when I went back out.

I sat down. "If there's one thing I've become an authority on . . ." I stopped. "Believe me, this is tame."

"I suppose so."

We sat for a moment, drinking. I fished a cigarette out and lit it. I felt strangely at ease with her right then. "So," I said, "what is it?"

She leaned back. "First, Jason, I'm sorry about Harry. I know how much he meant to you, to all of us. I know it's hard."

I nodded.

"Why didn't you call me, though?"

"When he died?"

"To tell me he was so sick. I wouldn't have minded knowing."

"Maybe you should be asking yourself why *he* didn't call you."

"I know why he didn't. But I thought you would."

I turned away from her to look out at the valley, darker now. "Sorry."

"But that's not what's important. I don't want you to feel bad."

"Too late."

"Jason, I want to get you help."

I shifted my eyes to her. "What?"

"I know what's going on with you. Sarah told me. You need help, the sooner the better."

"She told you what?"

"That you're on heroin."

I hung my head and shook it, "Oh, Jesus," laughed under my breath, pulled on the cigarette. The rush was just blooming in my chest.

"Is it true?"

I didn't answer, but looked away again. I snorted disdainfully.

"I guess that means it is."

"Yeah, yeah, *okay*. It's true. Okay? So there it is." I flicked my cigarette hard out into the lawn.

"I don't want to fight you about it, Jason. I just want you to get better, to get you some help."

"What if I don't want help?"

Her face hardened, as it could so quickly. "You want to be Harry?" she asked in a tightly wound monotone. "You've made a good start. Your friend is dying and you go off to buy drugs, in his car. You leave your poor girlfriend to witness it, not knowing where you are. You keep going like this and someday you'll hate yourself as much as he did."

"He didn't hate himself," I said, but I knew it wasn't true.

Her voice calmed a tiny bit. "Let's not fight about Harry. This isn't the time. This is about you, sweetie. I've called a center in the city, and they can take you. You can stay with me when you get out."

I remembered having the same conversation with Harry, and what he'd said to me. I imagined saying "Eat shit" to her, intoning it in Harry's dismal low drinking voice, and laughed.

"Is this funny?"

"No," I said. I knew what my next move had to be. I looked into her eyes as directly as I could, though the high and the darkness were fuzzing my vision. "He was James's father, wasn't he?"

The expression on her face froze, but in thought, not surprise, as if she were trying to remember the answer. She spoke quietly. "Probably." Then, "Yes, he was."

I nodded. "James doesn't know, does he?"

She shook her head. "I don't think so. Did Harry tell you?"

"No. I figured it out, looking at some pictures of you and him in Italy, seeing your faces together at that age."

She looked at her drink, forgotten in her hand, the ice become fragile shards, and took a sip. "I'd like to see those pictures again."

"I'll show you where they are."

"You've turned the tables on me. Changed the subject. Nicely done."

"So, were you with Dad at the time? Did you cheat on him?"

She looked me straight in the eyes for a moment, all pretense gone, her expression incredulous that I was asking these questions, but open, making it clear she would answer in spite of my indiscretion. "If you want to put it that way. Your father and I had cheated on Harry before that, and I left Harry for him." I could hear tears welling in her voice, along with an edge of self-righteousness. Her face fell. "That's all, really," she waved a hand to shut me up, "I was young. We were kids, like you," she gestured at me to emphasize my situation, my lack of judgment.

I put my elbows on my knees and hung my head. My body was sinking in on itself, and I felt beautiful. Breathing was a form of sex, and I did it through my nose slowly and deeply. Thinking of Harry I lit another cigarette. I poked my consciousness down through the high (it was safe now, I was covered) and saw fear, guilt, fatherhood, grief, all mulched and piled down there like a compost heap in my gut, steaming inside. "I'm not going to rehab, Mom," I said.

Just then, Melanie stuck her head out the door from the living room. "Hey, what are you guys up to?"

Both of us just stared at her.

"Oh. You're talking. Okay." And she went back in.

My mother waited a second. "I wasn't going to tell you this yet, but I guess I might as well. Harry left his estate to be split evenly among you, James, and the Jost twins. The catch for you is that I have control over your part. I can decide when to give it to you, or not to give it to you."

I raised my head. Breathed more beautiful air. "I never expected any of Harry's money," I said.

"I know. But if you can get yourself clean, get your life together, you'll have it."

I looked at her. "This was your idea, wasn't it? You talked Harry into giving you control."

"No. Harry was the one who brought it up when he first told me about his will. It was his idea from the start."

Through the glass door I saw Melanie walk across the living room into the kitchen, where Sarah was cooking something. "So, you want me to go to rehab for the money."

"I just want you to go. I'll be honest, if it's money that gets you there, that's okay with me. As long as you get clean."

I felt, through heroin's cushion, the fear of change I'd had a few days earlier, as if this moment was what the fear had been presaging. I saw Drew's body, the red softness of it impossible not to associate somehow with food, and gagged gently. I inhaled smoke. How many turning points had Drew missed? How many wrong turns had led him there? I tried to imagine Harry's body, as if I hadn't driven away, had been there with him when he'd passed and seen him lying in his bed the previous morning, but it appeared as a mirror of Drew's, blown to bits, and I blinked it quickly away. There could be no hesitation, or I'd turn back.

"If I go, will you take five thousand of that money and give it to Melanie?"

"Why?"

"I was kind of responsible for her car getting stolen, and I spent a bunch of her money."

"Yes. If you promise me you're not tricking me into giving it to you indirectly."

"I promise, Mom." I hefted the decision in my mind then, surprised at its finality, its ponderous mass, and wondered how far I could carry it.

My mother slid her chair over and hugged me, and I let her. "Since we're getting stuff out in the open," I said into her hair, "I have one more question."

"All right." She pulled back slowly.

"Dad really was a spy wasn't he? He was CIA or something, right? That's why they killed him."

She shook her head. "No, sweetie. He wasn't. But I'm sure they believed he was."

"Come on, don't bullshit me. I can keep a secret."

"There's no secret. He was a journalist, nothing else. I thought you knew that."

"But I always kind of thought— And Harry hinted . . ."

"I'm not lying to you. He was not a spy."

Somehow, that was the cruelest news of all.

THE NEXT MORNING I sat in Oakland airport, the address of the rehab center tucked in my jacket pocket next to the last of my heroin, the fight with Melanie still ringing in my head. The night before we'd talked about the situation calmly and seriously, but in the morning, as we were getting dressed, she said, "Are you coming back?"

I finished buttoning my jeans. "Like I said, I promised my Mom I'd stay around afterward, try and get my shit together."

"So you don't care too much about being with me."

I hung my head. "I care, Mel. I don't know what to say. Maybe you should come back to New York when I get out of rehab. Just for a little while, so I can satisfy my mom."

"No way." She was pulling a black T-shirt down over her head. "I'm done with that place. I'm not going back there."

I shrugged, "Okay." I sniffled and dragged the back of my hand across my nose. I went into the bathroom and peed, blew my nose, then did two small lines off the counter by the sink. I sat down on the edge of the tub and waited for the high to start kicking in. The fact of where I was headed made me feel good for a second, like a free pass on my last day of being high, then the fear returned.

"You asshole," Melanie said when I walked back in. "You fucking used me, spent my money partying, got my car stolen, now you just skip out without a second thought."

"First off, I told you I was getting some money from my mom to make up for your car and your money, didn't I?"

"Yeah, that's convenient." She turned away from me and sat on the bed. "You know that's not what I'm talking about anyway."

I went around the bed and sat by her. "What then?"

She gave me a disgusted look. "*What* then? What do you think? What am I supposed to do? How do you expect me to fucking feel about this, Jason? You're leaving today for God knows how long and you didn't even try to make love with me last night, or this morning."

"Is that what it is, really?"

She stomped on my foot and got up. "No! That's not what it is! It's . . . I don't know." She kicked the closet door with the sole of her foot, and it rattled on its hinges. "It's a fucking Gordian knot is what it is."

"So, just cut it."

She pointed her hand at me, drew her fingers into a shaking fist, holding it in front of her face and staring at it like a lovelorn Elvis. "Don't fucking play clever," she said to her hand.

I stayed seated. "Listen, maybe I won't stay out there." I was whispering, in case my mother was nearby. "Maybe I'll come back in a month or so when I get out, okay. But I just don't know."

She stared at me, made her face an angry mask. I saw something take hold in her expression, some resignation gaining a foothold. I turned away and started shoving clothes into my duffel with my good hand.

She asked for Saul and Don's phone number and I gave it to her. They were still on tour, but they'd be back in a week or so. They were the only people she really knew. I told her to have them hook her up with Cole. I trusted him to take care of her; he was good with newcomers. I realized as we were going through this that if I hadn't been high, I wouldn't have been able to leave her, to sit and listen to her yelling and crying and still walk out the door. It was the dope that was getting me to rehab, in more ways than one. She refused to come to the airport with us, so we said good-bye in front of the house with a long, forced hug.

Before boarding, I snorted more dope in the airport bathroom. The walk down the tunnel into the plane felt like a retreat. A businessman in a cheap blue suit slumped along in front of me, his soft vinyl briefcase bristling with messily stuffed papers, as if they didn't matter anymore, the account having been lost. The plane was almost empty. I sat by the window, strapped myself in, felt the rearward press as the plane accelerated, and watched California fall away below—thinking of Whitman's "flashing and golden pageant of California"—tall wistful dusty trees becoming radiant shrubbery as I rose, shrinking office buildings becoming temples of noble ambition, each house a miniature Xanadu. Distance beautifies. Had I just gotten too close? The flight attendant leaned in and said, "That doesn't look like any fun." She was looking at my splinted hand. "Can I get you something to drink?"

I faced her. She was dark-haired, about fifty. "Vodka tonic," I said. But she carded me and I settled for orange juice.

A while later the Sierras bunched up underneath us, shining Lake Tahoe marking the Nevada border, the desert shimmering in the distance. All this, I knew, a little dimmer in my tinted vision than it actually was. I sucked bits of pulp off an ice cube and spit it back into the clear plastic cup. Route 80 dropped through the mountains below, then snaked out into the desert from Reno, a gray cable carrying slow-moving blips of cellular information: parents, children, friends, outlaws, cops, truckers, hitchhikers: lives. The horizon was lost in blue-brown August haze.

part **four**

I HAD MET HARRY ONLY ONCE before my father died. We were on a month's vacation in the States the summer I was eight, part of which we spent in a hotel in New York, seeing the city and visiting my father's mother, who died the following year. Though I had been to New York before, my earlier memories are mostly of the inside of my grandmother's apartment, small and dark except for the living room, which had windows on two sides, where she used to serve James and me the purple cookies we loved her for; we had dubbed her Granny-Purple-Cookie some years earlier. But this trip supplied my earliest concrete memories of the city itself.

We were living in Beirut then, and every morning James and I walked three blocks to the American school past tanks and machine-gun-toting soldiers. The civil war was still in the hills, but we could hear the guns at night sometimes. At school, instead of fire drills we had air-raid drills. We scoffed at the miniature New York rats we saw in the subway—in Beirut they looked more like cats, and drivers would swerve wildly trying to hit them. But the buildings in New York were giants compared to what we knew from Ankara and Bucharest and Beirut, and I liked to walk up to them and put a hand on them and look up. Touching something so massive, I felt drawn somehow up to its great height. Their ranks went on forever, there was no end of this city; even when you reached the end of the island, it continued across the river. The four of us stood on the observation deck of the Empire State Building, taking turns looking through my father's huge high-powered binoculars, feeling a little superior to the people dropping coins into the lame old pay telescopes. We plodded through the Metropolitan Museum, tired and cranky, then went outside and ate hot dogs in the park. I remember seeing a man missing a leg sitting on the sidewalk next to his crutch, holding a cup and a sign that read "Vietnam Vet." I asked my father if I could give the man some money, and he gave me a dollar. The man flashed a whiskered yellow smile when I put the dollar in his cup, and I felt proud not to be frightened of him.

My father went out on his own our last night there, to have dinner with an old friend. There were quite a few hushed conversations between him and my mother about this dinner beforehand. When he left, I asked my mother who Dad's friend was, and she told me an old friend from school, they'd had a falling out, but were reconnecting. Late that night I woke up and heard them get back. The friend's voice was deep and jovial through the wall, and they were laughing. The door between the two adjoining hotel rooms opened, and my father came in. He went to James's bed first and leaned over it. I heard him say, "Hey buddy. Sorry to wake you. You want to come in the other room for a second? Just to say hi?"

James groaned and sat up. "What?"

"Come on, put your robe on."

I sat up too, and said, "Hi Dad."

"Jason, you're up too?" He came over to my bed and sat down. He ruffled my hair gently. "How are you, buddy?"

"I'm fine," I said. His breath carried the smell of bourbon, which at that age I knew only as the smell of Dad's nighttime party breath. He had on a thin cashmere sweater, which I loved, and I rested my cheek against his chest and hugged him.

He rubbed my back. "Come on, you put your robe on, too. My friend Harry wants to meet you guys, and we're leaving tomorrow."

I was eager. Coming out to join the grown-ups in the middle of the night seemed immensely interesting. The thing is that I remember being woken up so much better than the actual time in the next room with Harry and my parents. After being introduced, James and I kept calling him Mr. Waldron, but he insisted on Harry each time, saying we were making him feel old. I sat on the couch in my bathrobe and had trouble staying awake while they talked. James was awake, but true to form he didn't say much. My father and Harry smoked cigarettes and talked mostly to each other, sometimes saying something out the sides of their mouths that would make the other laugh. My mother sat in an armchair and seemed a little unhappy. I thought she was angry with my father for waking us up. As I kept dozing off, the light in the room became fuzzy, and my eyelids seemed connected to a system of pulleys attached to the heavy sinking weight of my brain inside my head, and the voices faded intermittently into the storybook my mother had read to us when we went to bed, a story about a magical seal that turned into a boy and was adopted by a fisherman and his wife. I was the boy in my half-sleep, diving into a stormy sea to save my drowning father, knowing I would become a seal again and never return. The two-panel illustration of that moment—the boy diving powerfully off a jutting rock, then surfacing as a seal—was engraved on my mind's eye.

I remember this snatch of conversation:

Harry: "What ever happened to The Urn?"

Dad: "As far as I know, The Urn is still ensconced at the Travellers Club, or wherever, still preying on old ladies."

Harry: "Or old men, as the case may be." Laughter.

And one moment remains vivid for me: the hug my father gave Harry before he left. My mother was leading James and me off into our room, so I was awake. I had seen my father hug men before, and kiss their cheeks Middle Eastern–style, but always in brief, perfunctory embraces. This was something else, two men squeezing each other tightly and exhaling simultaneously, not rushing it. "Good to see you, Harry," my father said softly as I walked past, staring at them hugging. I think it was the first time I realized that my father had a life outside what I knew about him, things outside of family and work that were his own. That was the real beginning of my interest in Harry. I wish I had known how important that night was. I wish I remembered all of it perfectly. It was the only time the whole family was ever together in one room.

August 1991

DEPARTURE, ONCE AGAIN, filled me with hope and sadness and exhilaration. The plane entered low cloud cover soon after leaving Minneapolis in a light rain, the drops on the window steadily accelerating and finally disappearing. No one on the planet knew where I was or where I was going. Outside, the darkness was broken only by the red light flashing into wisps split by the wing, until the vapor thinned and we rose into the clear night above. Looking out the window, I could see the tops of the clouds, silvered by the moon, now and then the glow of a city like an alternate moon underneath. Somewhere over the Rockies, the clouds broke and the country stretched out like a blanket of intermittently scattered diamonds. I felt all alone in the sky, and connected to the lights below, the people who had kept them on for me. An old song came into my head:

"Keep your lamps trimmed and burning, for this old world is almost done."

The preceding few years came in and out of focus in my mind, my memories sometimes filled with details, but usually just blurry sequences gathered around a single crystal moment. Often thinking back, I lost track of chronology, trying to place things in relation to the few milestones: the first two rehab centers; my arrest and thirty hours in a holding cell for possession; stealing a taxi at Christmastime to try to run fares for money, then getting freaked out and dumping it in the middle of the first fare, leaving the passenger in the backseat. The things I did remember tended to surface in random, disconnected ways, like possessions in a flooded house:

—Sitting in a bar, high, somewhere in lower Manhattan, waiting for someone, listening to Nina Simone over the speakers. Her voice, the sound of it, usurped my consciousness. It crawled right inside my body and curled up and squeezed my heart softly, I retreated into the background while that mournful, imperfect voice led me through an entire lifetime like leading a child across the street. I saw my own death, but forgot what I'd seen.

—The sound of a nightstick clanging on the quarter panel of my old Toyota to wake me up and get me moving. Hot grit embedded in my cheek from the backseat.

—A guy I met trying to cop dope on a sweep night, when everything was closed on the Lower East Side. He was my age, we even looked a little alike. Seeing each other at the third closed dope spot, we shook hands and traded names like two salesmen on a train. We drove to Brooklyn, where he said he knew a spot. The spot had only coke, which he bought, shot up in my car, then tried to steal the car after we ate a slice of pizza. He had no weapon, and tried to use threats of violence, death, to get me just to give it to him. A lame scuffle ensued—two weak, skinny junkies pushing

—A very pretty, emaciated Italian girl, a junkie, who worked the street outside a place I stayed in for a few weeks; we went to see Walt Whitman's house together. She used to ask me for dates whenever I walked past, and I always refused her, but we smiled and developed a certain junkie rapport. After a while she stopped soliciting me and just smiled and said hello. One day I did a big mail-order deal to some acquaintances in Colorado and I had in my pocket the profits: two hundred dollars and thirty bags of heroin. I felt like celebrating, doing something worthwhile. As I passed her she said hi and I stopped to talk. It was raining hard and we stood under the eaves of an old brick building. She had a beautiful accent, greasy black hair, big blue eyes. Her face was sunken below her towering cheekbones, and she didn't bother with lipstick. "Want to take a ride to New Jersey?" I asked her. "I'm going to see Walt Whitman's house." She said she didn't know any Walt, and was reluctant to leave the city. A great poet, I told her, long dead. "Come on," I said, "I have three bundles." That did it. I got directions over the phone from the Jersey tourism board and we got high and took the Holland Tunnel, then the turnpike through the rain to Camden. My sense of direction gave way when we exited the highway, though, and we drove around and got lost. I stopped to ask a trench-coated man with a red umbrella, and he said, "Who? Never heard of him, sorry." A gas station attendant said pretty much the same thing. After driving for a while longer through the gray back streets, breathing the dismal effluvium of sopped leaves and earth thrown airborne by the pounding rain, swerving to avoid huge lakes and rivers swelling from the gutters, we pulled over to get high again. She tried to give me head, but through the dope and the condom I couldn't get there and told her not to worry about it. I dropped the condom out the window and said, "Nothing's coming to fruition today." We drove back to the gas station and asked about the highway. "That I can help you with," said the attendant.

—My mother's voice (her face isn't part of this memory), saying "Paperbacks only," over my shoulder when I came by to get books and she had caught on to the fact that I was selling my father's first editions. In its sternness, an accusation. In its sadness, just like Nina Simone's.

—Slouching in jeans and a hospital gown in the smoking room of the Minneapolis treatment center with a sixty-year-old compulsive gambler/alcoholic named Ivor, picking raindrops on the window and betting cigarettes on which would reach the bottom first.

On the plane, I slid into sleep. I dreamed Fern was in the seat next to me, and that she was my wife. I woke up startled when the wheels slammed into the runway.

I TOOK THE BAY BRIDGE because I wanted to go through the city, but stayed on the freeway. I cruised south with the windows all down, late-night summer air swirling through the rental car. I didn't really have a destination that night. There were two days before the shows—three shows at the Shoreline Amphitheater south of Palo Alto, which I thought would be a good place to seek out all the old faces, maybe find Melanie. Once again, California, streaming past me at eighty miles an hour. There were more billboards along the freeway than I remembered. "If you lived here, you'd be home already," one of them declared, next to a pastel rendering of a condominium complex with a blue pool in its center. "Cool!" another trumpeted, with a picture of a black trumpeter wearing sunglasses—this one reminded me I was a smoker, and I pulled out a cigarette and lit it. I ran my hand through my hair, and down the back of my head to my neck, where the feel of bare skin was still new to me. I'd had my hair cut a week earlier, on an impulse, and it was very short.

A year earlier I'd gone to Minneapolis for my third rehab and had stayed clean since, working as a pizza boy and a cabdriver. Over that year in Minnesota, I had felt more and more strongly my connection with Melanie, even as I knew that it was probably just loneliness and depression looking for an outlet. In my unrestrained reveries, while delivering pizzas or driving my cab over hard-frozen streets, my semicrippled hand became a sign that we were meant to be together, and every time it ached or I fumbled with a shoelace I thought of her. The thumb worked pretty well, and the index finger too, but each successive finger was worse, with the pinkie just a flapping little twig whose tip would never again touch my palm. I couldn't play the guitar anymore, though I did start listening to Django Reinhart. The hand stiffened up in the cold and hurt in the morning if I slept on it wrong.

I got tired around Pacifica, but it was so late that getting a room seemed like a waste, so I pulled off the highway and turned west to the shore. There was a public beach there, with a parking lot, and I stopped and lay my seat back. It was nice to know I was safe from the cops, with nothing illegal in the car or in my system. This was the same beach where, six years earlier, Don and I had spent a morning swimming. It was the first summer we'd met, we'd been hitching back to Santa Cruz from the Bay after some Garcia Band shows, and we'd gotten stranded and spent the night under a bush by the entrance ramp.

I remembered waking at sunrise, and instead of hitting the road walking down to the public beach and swimming in the cold ocean. We appropriated a canvas chair that had been left overnight, and spent the morning in our boxer shorts watching the beach fill up with schoolkids and mothers and beach bums and surfers. We struck out into the light summer surf, and I remember feeling strong enough to swim all the way back to Santa Cruz. The sea was pulling us away, and we swam out until it thrilled me to look back and see the distance to the shore. Like dancing at a Dead show, it was a feeling of becoming part of something elemental and far out, a freedom unavailable on the prosaic land.

WHEN I WOKE UP, I drove to Mountain View, where the shows were starting the following night. I had been to one show in Chicago earlier that summer with another sober head from Minneapolis, but before that it had been years. The third motel I stopped at had a room available, but it wasn't cheap.

"What, do you raise your prices when the Dead come around?" I asked the guy at the desk. He was fat, with a Pirates cap perched on his massive bald head, and he just shrugged. I drove around back to where my room was, and as I was parking I noticed, down at the end of the row, a light blue Dodge van with a turtle-top. I got my stuff into the room, which was very basic and needed repainting, then walked down there. I looked through the windows of the van. I could tell it was owned by heads. The Jersey crew had never gone in for bumper stickers, but there couldn't be too many vans that looked like that.

I knocked on the door in front of it, and after a second it was answered by a burly guy with short dark hair and a T-shirt with a picture of Tony the Tiger popping out of a Steal-Your-Face symbol, one finger raised, saying "They're Grrroovy!" Tony had a joint hanging from one corner of his mouth.

"Yeah?" said the guy. He was eyeing me in a way that seemed suspicious of my plain black T-shirt.

"Nice shirt," I said.

He didn't answer me.

"Hey, is this your van out here?"

"No, I think those guys are next door." He jerked his thumb to the right.

I said, "Thanks," and went to the next room down.

Vince answered the door. His look was blank for a second, then his eyes widened. "Holy shit! Look who it is." He threw an arm around my neck, pulled me close for a second, and I felt his whiskers scrape my cheek.

Inside, Earl, Evans, and Frankie were kicked back on the two beds.

"What's up, man?" said Earl. He lifted his chin in greeting, then went back to watching the TV, as if it hadn't been four years since we'd seen each other.

Evans reached up and shook my hand. Frankie was rolling a joint, and there was a cooler of Becks between the beds.

"Where you been?" Evans asked.

"I was back in New York for a couple of years, off tour. Things got pretty ugly. I ended up in rehab last year in Minnesota, and I'm still living there."

"Still clean and serene?"

"Yeah," I said, "pretty much."

"Good for you. Congratulations." He sounded a little annoyed, but not insincere.

I walked in and sat in a chair by the far bed. Frankie lit the joint and passed it to me.

"Don't give that to him," Evans said. "Didn't you hear what he just said?"

Frankie shook his head. "No."

I passed the joint to Evans, who hit on it and passed it to Earl. I caught the obtusely ripe smell of the *indica* bud, which transposed itself in my mind into streams of random images—from shows, the road, other motel rooms—and I had to lean back and turn my head toward the wall to get a clean breath and clear my head.

"You guys know anything about my old girlfriend, Melanie? I hear she's still out here."

"Melanie. You mean One-Arm Melanie?" Evans asked. He was pulling his very long, straight blond hair into a ponytail.

"Yes," I said. "You know her?"

"Sure. She was your girlfriend?"

"Yeah."

"Why didn't I know that?"

"I knew that," said Vince.

"Well she's with Don now," said Evans. "They're all big-time and shit, practically live at the fucking Claremont. But it's a bad scene up there. Being clean, you might want to stay away."

I nodded and raised my eyebrows, letting this sink in, wondering why it made me so strangely excited that they had found each other. It was too much to think about so suddenly. "What about Cole? He around?"

"You didn't hear about Cole?" asked Vince.

"What about him?"

"Oh shit. Cole died, man."

"Jesus," I said. "How?"

"AIDS. He was fucking clean as a whistle when he found out about it. Talk about sledgehammers. He was in the hospital for a while. We all went to see him."

"God."

"Yeah, it was fucking depressing. It sucked him dry. He's okay now though. No more troubles for him."

Frankie reached forward to the boom box and turned up the music, clearly a vote for changing the subject. It was an old bootleg. "Viola Lee Blues," great early stuff. I looked instinctively around for the joint, but Earl had just put it out.

THE CLAREMONT, a sprawling, multiwinged edifice, sat at the base of the Berkeley hills. Its drive wound around islands of manicured bushes, grasses, and palms. It was a grand resort in the turn-of-the-century style, white from top to bottom—the color of genteel recreation. Pulling up to it in the van with the Jersey crew, I thought of the hundreds of workmen who had thrown their backs, their sweat, their days, into raising this structure, which looked as if it would last forever. I imagined that many of them would have been just back from some war, happy to be working and sweating safely in the California sun. I wondered if any of them, old men now, ever saved enough money to bring their wives there for a weekend, or just drove by to look at it, to contrast the permanence of their work with the disintegration of their bodies, and whether they took comfort in it. I wondered what it felt like to have built something like that. On the stereo in the van, "The Eleven" was decaying into ethereal electric ravings.

As we pulled in, Earl gave the joint to Evans. Evans hit on it and reached across me with it to pass it back up front.

"Let me see that," I said, and took the joint.

"Hey, you sure?"

I looked at him. "Not at all."

I hit on the joint, and the damp smoke expanded in my lungs. Frankie turned around in the passenger seat, smiling.

I exhaled and took another hit. The sky didn't crack open.

"How's that taste?" Frankie asked, off and on backlit by the streetlights coming through the windshield. The edges of his mane strobed golden. I blew a flashing white cloud.

"So fine," I said. The words dropped out smoothly, but stayed attached to the back of my throat by strands of sound. "What about Saul?" I asked. "I heard something bad happened to him."

"Yeah, Saul's in the slammer," said Vince. "He got popped big-time, right in the fucking Oakland airport. Supposedly it was a random thing, they had a drug-sniffing dog or something."

"Shit," I said. The joint came my way again, and I hit on it.

As the five of us entered the lobby, the red and gold carpeting stretched out around us, big as a playing field. Lush potted trees towered in the distant corners, and two more flanked a group of tan sofas and armchairs. Vince walked in front of me, and I stared at the frayed cuffs of his brown suede blazer. Frankie and Evans and Earl were in front of him, their long greasy hair swinging as they moved. It was hard to imagine making it all the way across that vast red expanse without being questioned as to our business there, and probably turned away. I felt, momentarily, a return to tour, an arrival home, in the tension of crossing that lobby. I was part of that bead of quicksilver once again. All of us were suddenly serious in the quiet, trying to act like paying customers but looking more like a troupe of desert castaways stumbled into a palace. Three other tourheads rounded the corner from the elevators, moving toward us, and nodded solemnly as they passed, caught in the same spell of restraint. But just before they reached the door-way, one of them, unable to resist the backdrop of staid silence, let out a quick, high-pitched whoop, a ball of jubilance that rico-cheted wildly off the walls and ceiling and sank deep into my body. The heads of the desk clerks whirled back and forth as if following the echoes—their eyes poked at us, feeling for cracks in our resolve, but we focused on the far side and pressed on.

"Well, Chinese bejeezus. Oh, man, look at you with the short hair. Look at *you*," said Don when I walked in behind the others.

He got up off the couch and embraced me. His breastbone stabbed my chest.

"Where the fuck have you been, my man? I heard you were in New York, having a hard time. I heard things were bad for you. But you look fine." He pulled back and looked at me. "In fact, you look so good I might just have to fuck you. How'd you get so fucking healthy?" He laughed and sat back down. I sat next to him. His exuberance was tainted with tinges of mania, eyebrows pinned to the middle of his wrinkled forehead, eyes restless. Coke had always been his thing when he binged. He took a lit cigarette from the ashtray and sucked on it.

"I got clean," I said. "Went to rehab."

"Sweet, dude. How long you been clean?"

"About a year. Not counting the joint I smoked just now."

"Yeah! That's the spirit." He reached out and pinched my cheek. His expression suddenly changed. "God, she's going to be surprised to see you." He grinned again, but was forcing it this time. He called into the other room of the suite, "Baby! Come out here!"

After a moment, there was a muffled voice from the other room.

"Hang on, I'll get her."

Don got up and went through the door into the bedroom. I stood up. When he came back in, Melanie was in front of him, and he had his hand over her eyes.

"You ready?" he asked.

"Yeah," she said. She sounded annoyed, but she was smiling.

Don pulled his hand away, and when she saw me her smile vanished instantly. Her cheekbones poked out too sharply, her eyes bulged a little, her mouth stretched too far across her face, lips cracked with chapping. But she was still beautiful. A clot rose in my throat.

"Hi," I said.

"Oh my god," she said. She covered her mouth with her hand. "How are you?"

"Okay." She made no move to approach me. "It's good to see you."

"Yeah," I smiled lamely.

She sighed, and no one spoke for a second. They were all looking at us.

"Want to go get some coffee or something?" she asked.

"Yeah, sure."

"Hold on." She stepped back into the bedroom and shut the door.

Don came over to me. He put an arm around my shoulder. "You know I love you, right, bud?"

"Yeah," I said, and put my arm around him. "I know."

"Good. But you're not going to do what you did to me before, are you?"

It took me a second to think of an answer, and finally I just said, "No. Don't worry."

He slapped my back and went to the couch.

Melanie came in wearing a long-sleeved black shirt with the right sleeve removed and sewn up, and sandals on her feet. "Baby, give me the car keys," she said.

"But you can't drive it," said Don.

She rolled her eyes. "Jason can. We'll bring you back a snack if you want."

Don looked at me. "You have a car?"

"I left it back at the motel."

He dug into his pocket and pitched the keys to me. "Be careful."

In the elevator, Melanie said, "Bastard refuses to trade in his truck for an automatic. I think he likes keeping me cooped up."

We didn't go for coffee. At my suggestion, we took Don's green Toyota four-by-four down to the marina. We drove listening to a Black Flag tape, which she turned up, and didn't speak, except when she noticed my left hand propped awkwardly on the wheel and said, "Looks like you're a little gimpy now, too." One of her knees stuck partially out through a hole in her jeans; the skin was so pale and the knee so thin that in the dim light inside the cab it looked like a bone, the knee of a skeleton. Without meaning to, I remembered our first show together, her bad trip. I remembered bringing the heroin into the room and putting it in front of her.

We parked and strolled along the water. Frankie's powerful pot still rippled inside me. Moored boats sloshed and clinked gently. We did some of the small talk that old lovers are supposed to—how've you been, seeing anyone, remember the last time—but then fell silent. It was a conversation full of silences.

"So I've got to ask you," she said. "Has your mother given you Harry's money yet?"

"No. I'm not pushing her. She said two years clean and we can talk about it." I kicked an empty juice box lying in the path with its little straw protruding from one end. It skittered along and then flipped into the grass.

"Vince told me about Saul," I said. "Actually I heard something about it back east last year."

"Yeah, poor Saul. I guess the lawyer got him a pretty good deal, though. Eighteen months and he'll get parole."

"Jesus. Vince said it was a random drug check at the airport."

"Fuck no. That's what we told people. It wasn't random. He

was working for Don. They'd been on him for weeks. Don's too careful, so they nabbed Saul. Tried to make him give Don up, but he wouldn't. He could have walked clean away, probably."

"Hm."

More silence.

Then, "You look like you're on junk," I said.

She stopped and glared at me. "What the fuck would you care?"

"Look, I've spent the past few years dealing with being strung out, so it's not like I'm clueless."

"I never thought you were clueless."

"How long have you been on?"

"Only a few months," she said. "For real."

I nodded. "Are you still angry at me? About the way I left?"

She shook her head and sniffed, started walking again. She took out a pack of cigarettes and offered me one. We both lit up.

"I guess I shouldn't be, right?" she said, with a hint of bitterness. "I should be over it."

"I didn't say that."

"Yeah."

We walked to a low retaining wall by some grass and sat on it. The night air seemed to gather and press softly at us, keeping the cigarette smoke bubbled around us until every so often it found a seam and rushed toward town. There were trees whispering behind us unseen, empty boats out on the water, and the bay lapping at the shore seemed trapped, its outlet to the ocean—the Golden Gate—too far away to be felt here. I was suddenly deeply sorry that I had smoked the joint. They said it over and over in my meetings, and I guessed they were right: you can go back, but it's not the same.

"Listen," I said, "I'm the last person to want to preach to anyone. But I care about you too much. You know junk leads nowhere, don't you? I've at least learned that. The farther you take it, the longer you go on, the more shit you just have to slog through on your way back. If you make it back at all. That's the reality."

I expected a dose of bile from her, what I would have given anyone saying those stupidly obvious things to me at the wrong time, and I was ready to let it go, to have said my thing and let the subject drop. But she just drew calmly on her cigarette and nodded, without looking at me.

Then she said, " 'The soul has that measureless pride which revolts from every lesson but its own.' "

I thought for a moment. "Okay, I give up."

Melanie smiled at me, her drawn face producing more dimples than I remembered. "Gotcha. I've been reading your man, Walt."

I tilted my head back, laughing. "A junkie quoting Whitman. Oh god, it's all too familiar." I looked at her. "That was a good one, though."

"I have to admit I've taken that quote out of context, seeing as what comes right before it goes, 'Prudence entirely satisfies the craving and glut of souls, Itself only finally satisfies the soul.' "

"That's big of you to admit."

We laughed together, and I thought it might kill me. I took a drag of my cigarette and blew smoke rings, watched them collapse. "In a way, I feel responsible, like it was me who got you into all this."

She snorted and shook her head. "Yeah, poor innocent little girl corrupted by evil druggie boyfriend." She looked at me. "Why'd you do this to me? If it wasn't for you I'd be pledging Kappa Kappa Gamma at Yale right now."

"I'm serious, though."

"Oh, shut the fuck up."

After a while she said, "You fucking bastard," but not angrily. "You were thousands of miles away all that time and I hated you for it, now you show up and we're still miles apart. Seems like we can never just be in the same place."

"Not yet, anyway," I said.

There was another pause.

"Don's all right, you know," she said. "He really is."

"I know he is. I know."

"Half of everything he makes now he puts aside for Saul when he gets out."

I nodded.

She looked away from me to the dark bay, her gaze floating far out over the water. I knew the look—not high, not sick, the space in between, lucid enough to assess your situation, to want to float away and leave your body and its troubles behind. "Do you think you might wait for me?" she almost whispered.

"I don't know," I said. "I might." I sucked on my cigarette, thinking of Harry, Cole, my father. "I'm tempted to turn back and join you."

"Don't do that."

Real silence came over us. She leaned into me and I put my arm around her. She flicked her cigarette into the water. It arced high spinning end over end, just as she'd done it in the parking garage on our first meeting, and dropped out of sight over the water wall.

I SLEPT IN THE NEXT DAY, then took the freeway south to Santa Cruz. Many of the larger downtown buildings had been rebuilt after an earthquake a couple of years earlier, and the town looked newer, less real. I stopped in a deli and had a sandwich for lunch. My memory of the town's layout was sketchy, and I had to ask the woman at the counter in the deli how to get to the coast road headed north. I had in my head the figure seventeen miles, which was how far I remembered Greyhound Rock, where we had ended up living that first summer, being outside of town. I kept looking at the odometer and checking the left side of the road for dirt pull-offs, but it turned out not to be as hard to find as I'd thought. The place was marked with a sign now, and a parking lot, and the old dirt path through the cut in the cliffs had been paved. There was even a bench placed halfway from the bottom, for resting. I walked down the path, which became dirt again before it reached the beach.

Along the back of the beach, near the cliffs, bulrushes swayed in the dunes, their rustling laying an undercurrent beneath the surging waves. Up near where they began growing was where most of us would bed down when it got late, sprinkled along the crescent in little groups. There was no evidence of the big fire pit we'd built.

I had the feeling of walking hallowed ground as I climbed one of the dunes and looked out toward the cove. So much had happened there, more than I could have known at the time. I think we'd all somehow felt it. Many of us were different people after that summer. It was what bonded Don and me, despite our differences and run-ins, what made it impossible that we could ever completely alienate one another. There are those friends you know you'll never really grow apart from. They may not be your closest or oldest friends, you may not even trust them completely, but you share something changeless with them: an important time.

The size of the group had varied, with drifters and small bands of heads arriving and passing on. Once we even had an Indian, a minister of the Peyote Religion, pass through. He said he had heard of the gathering on his way north and wanted to see if anyone would go with him to a ceremony he was putting together up in Washington. He showed us his bag of peyote buttons, but would not dispense any, saying he needed them, and besides, they were not to be taken just for fun. We asked him if he'd ever taken acid. He said he hadn't, and never would. A few guys left with him the next day when he moved on.

Standing there in the wind and staring out at the empty beach, I remembered a homeless drunk from Arizona who had spent a week with us. His name was Minowah, which was Indian, he said, though he was not. He had a total of five or six teeth in his head, and his voice sounded like a stripped gearbox. His first night there he was drunk and asked to try out my guitar. I reluctantly handed it over and was surprised when he lowered his head and gently put it in perfect tune. He disdained my offer of a pick and played with his thumb and forefinger. His chord voicings were all simple but precise. His ultrarough voice was right on key. He sang Don McLean's "American Pie," but not in the dopey fashion that would have invited a sing-along. There was real pain in each verse, and in his hands the song became the ballad of great loss it seemed it was meant to be, harshly rendered and rhythmically quirky. He got so worked up toward the end that he broke the B-string, but that didn't faze him. I felt the man was dredging up every ounce of pain and humiliation and sorrow he had gathered in his life, and it filled me with a solemn respect.

"That was great," I said when he was done.

He gave a little snort and a smile that seemed to say he knew it, but wished it wasn't so, for he would trade away his life for another in a second if all he lost was his ability to sing.

He bummed a cigarette from me. "You think you're something like me?" he asked.

"I don't know," I said.

"Well, maybe so, but there's one big difference. Know what that is?"

"No."

"Don't take this wrong, 'cause I don't hold it against you, but I can take one look at you and tell: you got people somewhere. Always have and always will. Something goes wrong, you can pick up the phone any day of the week and call mommy and daddy and they got your back. Am I right?"

"You're right about the mommy part."

"Earn it," Minowah said.

"What do you mean?" I smiled at him and cocked my head, trying to be friendly.

"Aaah!" He dumped the guitar at my feet and got up angrily. "You heard me," he said walking away down the beach. "Earn your fucking life."

The tide was either midway in or out, and the rock was separated from dry sand by only a thin, shallow strip of water, which disappeared during lulls in the waves. There was another much smaller rounded rock up on the beach, about five feet high, which I guessed had been uncovered in a storm. A man, whom I hadn't noticed before, was standing near it. He must have come down the path or out of the rushes when I was looking out to sea. As I got closer, I saw it was not a rock, but the body of a giant elephant seal that had washed ashore. The dead seal broke my nostalgic reverie. I walked around it, giving the man a look. He nodded to me. He was dark-skinned, Indian or Pakistani, balding, with a thick dark-gray beard. He reminded me of pictures I'd seen of the Bagwan Rajneesh—looked so much like a holy man that I thought of giving him the prayer-hands greeting of India. But from his clothes I realized he was more likely a scientist of some kind. He wore pleated khakis and a short-sleeved plaid button-down with three pens in the breast pocket. He carried leather boat shoes in his hand. I said hello to him, and he nodded again. I continued walking around the seal. It was on its side and still as high as my chin. It could have weighed a thousand pounds. I was suddenly sad at the loss of such a huge life. I wished I hadn't come across it here; this trip was meant to be about remembrance and new beginnings. It was not a favorable sign.

Though I knew the seal was meant to be that size, it was hard not to see such a mass of blubber as unhealthy, and to consider the possibility that its heart had failed trying to support it. It was old, that was obvious from the network of healed scars covering its neck like bark. This giant warrior had lived an eventful life. I stepped closer to its head to see the scars, and it reared halfway up and roared tiredly at me. Its black eyes both opened. I jumped back, my arms flailing.

"Be careful," said the man. "Don't get too close. They can be dangerous."

"I thought it was dead," I said.

"So did I at first."

"Is it sick?" I asked.

"I think so. I don't think it would be letting us get so close if it wasn't."

The seal raised its head again and looked at us. A deep groan came from its throat and then it flopped back to the sand.

"Maybe we should try to get it some help," I said.

"Yes," said the man, doubtfully. "I guess so. But sometimes an animal knows it's time to die. Maybe we should just leave him in peace."

We both stood there for a moment, pondering the great thing. Thinking it was dying was worse than it being dead. I wanted to go over and touch it, stroke its head, but I knew it would probably take my hand off.

I had planned to sit on the beach for a while, contemplating, remembering. Maybe climb the rock and stand where Fern and I had lain. None of my plans were working out. "I'm going to see about getting help," I said. "There might be something someone can do."

"Yes," he said. "Maybe you are right. If you go north, there is the Nature Center."

"Thanks." I looked back at him and raised my hand as I walked away.

He smiled at me, it seemed a little mischievously. "Be careful," he said.

"Okay."

As I drove, I became more and more depressed by the dying seal. I was not hopeful that anything I did would help it. A couple of miles north I saw the sign for the Nature Center. A schedule posted on it said it was closed that day. A dirt drive led into the trees east of the road and up to a wooden building with picnic tables on one side and a large vegetable garden on the other. A brown Chevy Suburban was parked in back of it, and I drove around and parked next to it. The door marked "Visitors" was locked, and a rack of brochures had a clear plastic cover padlocked over it. I walked out onto the deck that circled the front and sides and looked in a window. I was looking into a living room, a sofa covered with a dark tapestry and other mismatched furniture, and I heard a woman's voice. I continued to a door farther down and knocked. After a minute, it opened and a pretty blond woman stood there, a little boy of about five at her feet. The boy wore only a pair of white underpants.

"Hi," I said.

"Hello," she said. "We're closed today."

The boy stepped out next to me and pointed to the side of the house, where next to the garden was a fenced pen with two goats in it. One was black, the other spotty white. "See Gus and Shorty?" he said.

"Yeah, I see," I said. "Those are some nice goats."

"Know why we can't let them inside?" He was staring at me seriously.

"No I don't."

"Because they'll eat everything, even the curtains and tin cans, and if they run out of other things to eat they might eat my shorts."

I smiled at him. "Well, you wouldn't want that."

"And do you think if they finished my shorts they might start eating my little butt?"

"I hope not."

"Well, they would."

"What can I do for you?" asked the woman.

I told her about the seal on the beach.

She shook her head. "No, he's probably fine. They like to come up to rest when they're traveling, and warm their blubber in the sun. He was probably just tired."

"But he was letting us get so close, and not moving."

"First of all, you should never get close to them. They seem so fat, but they can move fast when they want to. They're quick animals, and smart. Believe me, I've seen enough of them. They're not afraid of you, which is why they let you get close, but if they feel threatened they can do serious damage."

"So you think he was okay?"

She nodded. "I'm sure of it. But thank you for being so nice, and concerned."

"Thank you," I said. "I'm glad to find this out. I hated thinking he was dying."

She smiled. The boy had walked over to the railing nearest the goat pen, and started yelling, "Gus, Shorty! Hi! It's me over here!"

We both looked at him.

"Samuel," she said. "Come in here."

The boy ran to her and I waved good-bye to him, but he just skipped through the door and into the house. She shut the door.

The little Japanese car bounced in the ruts, and my heart bounced with it. Pulling out the drive to the road, the sun had dropped closer to the horizon and was glaring fiercely off the molten gold ocean. I imagined diving in and becoming part of it, a long, superhuman leap from the cliffs, saw it clearly—the running start, the unreal arc of the dive—like something in a dream. I made a right and headed north.